BAD ACTORS

BAD
ACTORS

Mick Herron

SOHO
CRIME

Copyright © 2022 by Mick Herron

Published by Soho Press, Inc.
227 W 17th Street
New York, NY 10011

Library of Congress Cataloging-in-Publication Data

Names: Herron, Mick, author.
Title: Bad actors / Mick Herron.
Description: New York, NY : Soho Crime, [2022] |
Series: The slough house novels ; 8
Identifiers: LCCN 2021049127

ISBN 978-1-64129-337-2
eISBN 978-1-64129-338-9

Subjects: GSAFD: Suspense fiction. | Mystery fiction.
Classification: LCC PR6108.E77 B33 2022 | DDC 823'.92—dc23
LC record available at https://lccn.loc.gov/2021049127

Interior design by Janine Agro, Soho Press, Inc.

Printed in the United States of America

10 9 8 7 6 5 4 3 2 1

For Paul.
And for Emily, Thomas and Matthew.

People deceived by bad actors do wicked things for good reasons.
　　　　　　　　　　　　　　　　　　　—Bryan Appleyard

BAD ACTORS

The woods were lovely, dark, and deep, and full of noisy bastards. From his foxhole Sparrow could hear the grunting and thrashing of combat, of bodies crashing through foliage. Some things breaking were branches, and others might be bones. Sound travelled more cleanly in the countryside. This might not be true but it was interesting, which mattered more. Sound travelled more cleanly, so what he was hearing could include the fracturing of legs and fingers as well as splintering twigs. His foxhole wasn't constructed; was simply a ditch in which he'd secreted himself while the opening sallies played out. The initial clash of armies was where you lost your cannon fodder. Once the dumb meat had been carted from the field, war passed into the hands of the thinkers.

Something clattered overhead, in a tree's topmost branches. Only a bird. Meanwhile, battle continued: two forces of roughly equal size, blatant weaponry outlawed but anything that came to hand regarded as fair use. Sticks and stones for instance—and any experienced foot soldier had a favourite stick, a favourite stone, within easy reach when the starting whistle blew. Time, date, place, courtesy of social media. The old days, when you just rocked up to a car park near the stadium a few hours before kick-off, all of that was buried in history books and Channel 5 documentaries. Sparrow himself had been a toddler. Interesting, though: people thought, because they didn't see football fans rucking in public anymore, that it didn't happen. Just knowing that much about human nature was like having a big shiny key.

It was an education in itself, exploring the depths of other people's ignorance and gullibility.

Some shouting in the near distance now. Nothing as coherent as words: just the familiar Esperanto of grunt and injury, the outward expression of a hatred that was absolutely pure and totally impersonal. Amateur violence signalled national character. Just as the French variety, with its short jabs and rabbit punches, seemed as crabbed and hunched as French handwriting, so English violence had the hallmarks of a ransom note: capital-lettered and often misspelt, but getting the message across. As for Italians—today's opponents—they rucked the way they sang, their brawling round and bold and big-voiced, and if not for a relatively small turnout, they'd wind up kings of the woods today. Benito—the new Benito, whose predecessor had interestingly withdrawn from public view—would have led his troops away rejoicing. But that didn't, from what Sparrow had seen so far, look likely.

For his own part, his interest was clinical. Untethered to any football team, he was nevertheless fascinated by the loyalties they inspired, regardless of history, abilities and triumphs, or lack thereof. By the *Till I Die* tattoos supporters sported. This was a self-fulfilling promise, one that couldn't be reneged on without expensive laser treatment, and demonstrated the kind of drive that pre-empted second thoughts. And once you got a handle on it, you could steer it in any direction you chose. Aim it at a rival set of fans or . . . elsewhere.

From deep among the trees Sparrow could feel an approaching beat, not as stealthy as it thought it was, and underneath that a more primal rhythm, one close to Sparrow's heart. In the breast pocket of his camo-gilet, in fact: the thrumming of his mobile phone.

With the unhurried ease of a gunslinger he slipped it free of his pocket. "You pick your moments."

The crashing came nearer; the sound of a large, urban type imagining it was possible to be silent in a wood.

"Oh, you know. Day off. I like to get close to nature."

Excuse him a moment, he thought but did not say, and instead of listening to whatever his caller said next, fastened the phone into a Velcro-secured sheath at shoulder level, so he could speak and be heard and mostly hear, a long-established set of priorities. That done, he settled into a crouch and wrapped both hands round the stubby branch from which he had stripped all unnecessary twigs and leaves.

"Okay, this is the usual daily bullshit, nothing to worry about. Just because there's a problem doesn't mean we need a solution. We simply reframe the narrative. Hang on a sec."

A figure crashed into Sparrow's clearing and halted, scanning the terrain. Being of average height he was easily four inches taller than Sparrow, an advantage in most hostile situations except those where both parties have testicles but only one is wielding a club. Sparrow's caught the newcomer sweetly in the crutch. He made a noise like a baby seal and collapsed in a heap.

"Yes, or dispense with the narrative altogether. This time tomorrow it's yesterday's news ... No, I'm fine. Just doing some stretches."

While his caller launched into a soliloquy, Sparrow focused on his immediate situation: weapon in hand, fallen warrior at his feet, trees everywhere ...

Planet of the Apes.

He prodded his would-be attacker with a foot, eliciting a groan, then noticed the silence on the line.

"... Yeah, still here. And I have ideas, don't worry. You know me. Ideas is what I do."

Which was as well, because Anthony Sparrow had some work-related issues of his own that he'd rather his caller didn't know about. Some, though, might be alleviated by discussion with Benito once the more aggressive aspects of the afternoon's agenda had been settled. The fact that you were mortal enemies didn't mean you couldn't do business. If that were the case, you'd never get anything done. Besides, Benito was a fellow alpha. Sparrow mostly worked among malleable idiots, so it was something of a pleasure to negotiate on his own level.

Speaking of malleable idiots . . .

On closer inspection, he noticed that his victim wasn't one of Benito's crew at all, but on Sparrow's own side. Still, there he was, prone and useless, and Sparrow holding a club.

His caller was still talking, so he tapped a finger against his phone three times, a signal both knew meant the conversation had passed all useful purpose. Then waited a moment.

"Not at all. What I'm here for."

He waited some more. And then:

"Yes, prime minister. See you in the morning."

And, call over, Sparrow raised his club and brought it down as hard as he could, and then again, and again, until this anonymous creature was where all his opponents ended, dumb and dusted at his feet.

ACT II
CHIMP POLITICS

The wind, with its hands in its pockets, whistles a tune as it wanders down the road—a jaunty melody, at odds with the surroundings—and the theme is picked up by everything it passes, until all of Aldersgate Street, in the London borough of Finsbury, has joined in. The result tends towards the percussive. A bottle in the gutter rocks back and forth, *cha-chink cha-chunk*, while a pair of polystyrene cartons, one nestled in the other's embrace, whisper like a brush on a snare drum way up on the pedestrian bridge. A more strident beat is provided by the tin sign fixed to the nearest lamppost, which warns dogs not to foul the pavement, a message it reinforces with a rhythmic rattle, while in the Barbican flowerbeds—which are largely bricked-in collections of dried-up earth—pebbles rock and stones roll. By the entrance to the tube there's a parcel of newspapers bound by plastic strips, whose pages gasp and sigh in choral contentment. Dustbins and drainpipes, litter and leaves: the wind's conviction that everything is its instrument is justified tonight.

And yet halfway down the road it pauses for breath, and the music stops. The wind has reached a black door, wedged between a dirty-windowed newsagent's, visibly suffering from lack of public interest, and a Chinese restaurant offering the impression that it's still in lockdown, and plans to remain so. This door, irredeemably grimy from the exhalations of passing traffic, is a sturdy enough construction, the only gap in its armour a long-healed wound of a letterbox, impervious to junk mail and red-lettered bills, but a door is only a door for all that, and the wind has blown down bigger. Perhaps it considers rendering this supposed obstruction into dust and matchsticks, but if so, the moment passes; the wind moves on, and its orchestra goes with it. The shake and rattle and roll starts to fade, the theme toyed with one last time, then dropped. The wind is going places, and this grubby stage isn't big enough to hold it. It's heading for the brighter lights; for the stardom that waits, somewhere over the rainbow.

So the black door is left unshaken and unstirred. But just as it never opens, never closes during daylight hours, nor is it about to yield now, and anyone intent on entry must take the stagedoor johnny route, down the adjacent alley, past the overflowing wheelie-bins and the near-solid stench from the drains, through the door that sticks in all seasons, and then, once inside, climb stairs whose carpet has worn thin as an actor's ego, and whose walls boast mildew stains, and lightbulbs that are naked and/or spent. It's dark in here, a bumpy kind of dark, with sound effects provided by rising damp and falling plaster, and the offstage antics of vermin. The stairs grow narrower the higher they go, and the paired offices that lurk on each landing are furnished with shabby props, scratched on every surface and torn in all the ways they can tear—nothing capable of being damaged twice has been damaged only once, because history repeats itself, first as tragedy then as farce, and here in Slough House the daily grind is of such unending repetition that the performers can barely tell one from the other. More to the point they're not sure it matters, for the role of a slow horse, as this troupe are known, is to embrace unfulfilment and boredom; to look back in disappointment, stare round in dismay, and understand that life is not an audition, except for the parts that are, and those are the parts they've failed. Because Slough House is the end of the pier, the fleapit to which Regent's Park consigns failures, and these would-be stars of the British security service are living out the aftermath of their professional errors. Where once they'd dreamed of headline roles in their nation's secret defences, they've instead found themselves in non-speaking parts, carrying spears for Jackson Lamb. And given his oft-stated advice as to where they might put these spears, none of them should anticipate a return to the bright lights any time soon.

Which doesn't stop them hoping, of course.

The wind's tune has faded, and Slough House is as quiet as a mouse—it twitches and rustles, scratches and squeaks. Come morning its scattered cast will reassemble, and as in any office, familiar scenarios will play themselves out once more: the passive-aggressive feuding, the mind-crushing boredom, the ill-disguised hostility, the arguments over the fridge. None of this will ever change much. But as in any office most of those involved expect it to, as if some larger drama is about to begin, one that will erase their previous errors—missed cues, mangled lines, early exits—allowing the spotlight to fall on them at last. It's a reason for turning up, anyway; the possibility that their attendance today will mean they won't have to be here tomorrow, and that their future, instead of this endless tedium played out against broken furniture, will be one of shining triumph, in which everything comes out right. Even those who no longer believe this act as if they do, because otherwise, what would be the point? It's a small enough world without accepting that it'll never get larger. Better to go along with the fantasy that any moment now the curtain will rise and the lights dim.

That any moment now, there'll be some action.

Louisa Guy rolled her shoulder, swung from the hip, and punched Roddy Ho in the face.

That felt good.

Let's do it again.

Louisa Guy rolled her shoulder, swung from the hip, and punched Roddy Ho in the face.

This time, Ho's head went flying backwards into the gloom, landing on the grass with a damp thud, before rolling twice then coming to a stop, eyes down.

Which was satisfying, but also annoying. Once you'd knocked a head clean off, you could never get it to stay on again.

Louisa looked up at the early morning sky, its long clouds seemingly motionless overhead. She was on the back lawn of her apartment block, where one or two lights were coming on, her fellow-dwellers showering, breakfasting, getting ready for the off. Some would save the shower for the gym, get their workouts over before dressing for the day, but Louisa didn't belong to a gym. Gyms were expensive. Louisa ran instead, though this morning had opted to take Roddy Ho—or his stand-in; a department store dummy she'd boosted from a skip the previous weekend—and give him an education. It was only the second time she'd indulged herself this way, and it was disappointing to think it might be the last, but fair's fair, there was an argument that Roddy's stunt double was taking the method approach. She was pretty sure if she punched the actual Roddy Ho repeatedly, his head would go flying from his shoulders before long.

And when you thought about it, it was really Lech Wicinski who ought to be pounding Roddy to dirt this week. Then again, Lech was still too sore to be handing out punishment beatings.

She collected the broken parts and took them upstairs; showered, dressed, etc; and was soon behind the wheel, a piece of toast clamped between her teeth, heading for work. She'd used a gym regularly back in the by; the Service gym not far from Regent's Park. It occupied hidden levels below a local authority swimming baths, and on its mats, free of charge, agents in good standing could have the shit beaten out of them by experts. This wasn't as much fun as it sounded, but did have an upside: after you'd spent an hour being thrown around like a bag of wrenches, the expert explained what moves you might make to improve your situation. Louisa had generally come away feeling more capable than when she'd gone in.

But the key phrase in all of that was "in good standing," and slow horses were so far from standing well they had trouble lying down. Following her transfer to Slough House, the first time Louisa had tried to access the facility her card tripped the scanner, causing visible tension to the guard on duty, tension that relaxed to amusement once he'd clocked her ID. "Seriously?" he'd said. "You'd have more chance with a Starbucks card." Nobody had been around to explain what move she might make to improve her situation, though shooting him in the head suggested itself. Unfortunately the nearest guns were on the level she'd just been refused entry to, so she'd had to walk away unconsoled.

What made this bad story worse was, it had happened what felt like a lifetime ago, and things hadn't changed much since. And things kept on not changing, with unvarying regularity. Even when events occurred that shook the windows—like the Russian hoodlums' toxic rampage six months back, or the Wimbledon outing, just three days ago—they folded up so small, they might as well not have happened. When you asked *What next?*, the answer was always: *The same.* So you woke up next morning and were back in the office; there were extra stains on the carpet, occasionally a missing colleague, but you got used to that. Slough House absorbed differences, leeched them of flavour, and spat them out again; sometimes you were driving to work, sometimes you were driving home, but the space between was so dispiriting, you hardly cared which. On your way there, on your way back, you were still denied entrance to the gym.

Some had this lesson waiting—Slough House had a new recruit. One who fell into that rapidly increasing demographic, the too-bloody-young. Ashley Khan might have been in primary school when Louisa joined the Service, and acted like she still was. No one likes being here, Louisa felt like saying. It's not necessary to remind us you're unhappy. But Khan sulked as if there were prizes involved, and what had never been the most clement working environment had a new storm cloud in its skies. True, none of them were exactly rays of sunshine—Jackson Lamb was extreme weather on his best day—but having a new colleague was a challenge, a reminder of how bad things had felt at the start, and how bad they still were. Nothing you could do changed this. Because that was the deal with Slough House: you had all the self-determination of a clockwork fundamentalist.

Her own view, Louisa thought Ashley Khan would quit. Soon. She'd invested too little of her life in the Service to throw good time away after it; there was a whole world of stuff waiting once she'd got over her rage. Though her rage, it was true, did seem to have put its foot down. Not without cause, either: on Khan's introduction to Jackson Lamb, he'd broken her arm. This was the sort of first impression that made second impressions superfluous, and even for a millennial, raised by the internet, didn't fall within the range of expected behaviours. No, Ashley Khan's anger was going to have to find an outlet soon, or the woman would explode.

Now there was a thought.

Maybe she'd just short-circuit the whole process and bring a bomb into work.

And as the morning traffic thickened and her day began to crawl, Louisa wondered if that wouldn't be the most efficient way to deal with Ashley's anger and all the other issues bottled up in Slough House; simply to detonate them all together, in one final crowd-pleasing moment.

It had arrived through the post, like a bomb in the olden days, and she'd been tempted to hold it to her ear and listen for its tick. But it was important to maintain the cover of innocence, even with no one watching, so Ashley had simply collected the package from the doormat and carried it into her room, which was on the ground floor. One small window with a smudged view of nothing much, and a single bed that occupied most of the floorspace. There she'd sat and dismantled the parcel, revealing, in reverse order, a stapled cellophane bag inside a small cardboard box inside a jiffy bag. Her name misspelt on the label: Kane instead of Khan.

She'd torn this off for shredding. Put the box in the bin. Studied the cellophane bag and its ripe red content, which might almost have been a souvenir from an anatomy class: the muscle of some unlucky subject, a rabbit or a fox ... In keeping with such imagined butchery, there were rumours it could stop your heart. Not that its intended recipient had one.

Not much later than that, she was heading for work: a dreary destination at the far end of a dull commute. In an odd, be-careful-what-you-wish-for, or at least, be-careful-what-lie-you-tell kind of way, Ashley Khan's real job was now as miserable as the one she'd invented for her parents. *This company you work for, it has little online presence*, her father informed her. *Very little.* He was a man who cast a shadow himself. You did not, as his regular broadcasts throughout her teenage years underlined, you did not become senior partner in a leading dental practice without exhibiting drive. Without displaying gumption. *And what is it they do again, is it burglar alarms?* Ashley had thought she was being clever when she'd told her parents she'd found a job with a security firm. But all this conjured up for them was decoy boxes screwed onto walls, and signs reading GUARD DOGS ON PREMISES. BEWARE. A high second from St. Andrews had promised a glittering future, so how come she was stuck in an office job, the lowest rung on a shaky ladder? The ladder wasn't the only thing shaking. Her parents' heads had swivelled in unison: Ode to Disappointment. The household anthem.

On the other hand, had she told them she'd been recruited by the intelligence service, this information would have been dispensed to her father's patients one after the other, as they sat before him in open-mouthed astonishment. *Ashley, the eldest, she's working for MI5 now. Very important, very top secret. And rinse.* Worse still, any catch-up she offered would have had to include the bitter information that, far from flying high in her chosen career, she'd been derailed almost before it had begun.

You see, I was on a covert surveillance exercise, tracing this guy across London, only I was spotted by his boss . . .

We all make mistakes.

Who broke my arm.

As it was, she'd had to invent a workout accident.

"A collision, was it? On one of those stationary bicycles?" Her father's amusement alternated with a litigious glint. "Your uncle Sanjeev, did you forget he is a solicitor? This accident, there should be compensation."

Compensation, no, thought Ashley.

Payback, though. That was something else.

And if a certain type of onlooker could have seen Ashley Khan's smile through her face-mask, they'd have made sure to socially distance themselves the length of a carriage or two, and possibly adopted the brace position while doing so.

An incoming text roused Lech and he surfaced abruptly, every inch of him feeling like he'd Sumo-wrestled a walrus. This wasn't quite normal service. The post-Sumo effect was recent—a souvenir from Wimbledon—and sleeping through the night was rare too. Insomnia was one of the few traits he still had in common with the Lech Wicinski of old, who had been on an upward trajectory: a good job—analyst at Regent's Park—a nice flat he shared with his fiancée; walks by the river on Sunday; meals out with friends once a week. Insomnia, yes, but he'd learned to accept it, treating it as extra space, a quiet time when he had nothing but his own thoughts to attend to. Often he walked it off, striding through the city after dark, paying attention to details that were invisible by day, as if haunting a cinema after the audience had gone: here were the empty seats, the abandoned popcorn containers and takeaway cups; all the signs indicating that life went on here, just not at the moment.

And while this still happened—one night out of three he'd be roaming the streets; blowing this way and that, like litter— the rest was change. He no longer had a job at the Park, or a nice flat, and Sara had emailed yesterday to let him know—she wouldn't want him to find out any other way—that she was seeing someone else. So was Lech, but only in the mirror. The scarred face there was a whole new chapter in a different story; most of the damage self-inflicted, to conceal the original message carved by a bad actor. PAEDO. A lie, but what difference did that make? Had it been true, he'd have obliterated it just the same.

The scars he'd made to hide that lie had hardened to a mask. Something he could hide behind, and others shy away from.

And his days were no longer spent at Regent's Park but at Slough House, where the Park's cast-offs laboured. Their tasks were of the boulder-rolling kind: they never came to an end, they just felt like they might, right up to the moment when they began all over again. To be assigned to Slough House meant you'd committed some egregious error; had endangered lives, or caused embarrassment, or invited the wrong sort of attention, all of which were among the seven deadlies on Spook Street. Lech's own mistake had been to do someone a favour, and the only consolation he'd devised for himself since had been the promise that he'd never do that again; that from here on in, he was his only trusted friend. Being at Slough House actually helped in that regard. It was a place that encouraged you to remain behind your mask, and focus on rolling that boulder. Either you'd get it to the top of the hill despite yourself, or you'd come to your senses and give up.

But the resumption of normal service wasn't something you could guarantee against, and nor did a mask protect you from yourself. Or perhaps all this meant was, you couldn't hide from history; it would always roll round again and perform its favourite damage. He should know that by now. His Polish blood should have sung him the song. But that same blood had the tendency to remind him that he was involved in humanity, like it or not, which in turn meant he'd repeated the same stupid error and done somebody a favour. The same somebody, in fact, that he'd done a favour for first time round. Which was why, lying in bed, he had the not-unfamiliar sense of having kick-started something he'd regret.

To cheer himself up, he read the text that had woken him. It was from his landlord: the rent hadn't been paid. Which meant his bank had screwed up again—the second direct debit to have gone awry this week.

His alarm clock chirruped. Limbs and body bruised and stiff, Lech showered and dressed, drank a cup of black tea, and set off for work.

Normal service, being resumed.

Talk about not learning from your mistakes.

Spend enough time shadow-boxing and your shadow starts to hit back. Shirley should offer that at the morning session as a "learning." They were big on learnings, here in the San, especially when they came wrapped in metaphor. So, yeah: shadow-boxing. But when you're off the ground, she could add, your shadow can't lay a finger on you. Very good reason for getting high.

This was easy. Second day in, and Shirley Dander was on top of their shit already.

But going along with it would mean pretending she was okay with being here, and that might be a stretch for them to accept, given the forthright assessment she'd made of the place, its facilities and its staff within an hour of her arrival, and then again sometime during the second hour, and maybe a couple more times after that, before everyone agreed it might be best to call it a night. They'd think, in fact, that she was faking it to speed up the whole process of recovery and release. So no, best plan would be to stick with the dignified silence she'd mostly maintained since the previous morning. Dignity was definitely looking like being one of her better things, which, come to think of it, probably counted as a learning too. But there was nothing to say she couldn't leave here wiser than she'd arrived. It didn't mean she'd be removing this place from her shit-list any time soon.

Of course, putting its name on any kind of list would be easier if it had a fucking name in the first place. Instead, it was just known as the San, an abbreviation redolent of the Chalet School books her mother had forced on her when she was ten; books she had refused to read as a matter of principle, and then had refused to admit to reading as a matter of survival, because to back down from a principle was just baring your throat for the bite. There was no battle as fiercely fought as a girl's with her mother. Mind you, the battles fought by a grown woman with her mother could get pretty heated too, which was a good reason for making sure her mother never got to find out about Shirley's current whereabouts. She'd almost certainly blame it on Shirley's recreational drug use, and Shirley was sick of being hit with that particular stick. *If it's doing me harm, how come I'm fine?* A clincher, but it went sailing over her mother's head like, Shirley didn't know, an albatross.

Which was exactly the sort of crap they'd want to hear about: battles with her mother. Yawn.

They also wanted to hear about all the dead people, but they could go fuck themselves.

Light was sneaking through the blind, which meant they'd

be knocking on the door soon; a soft, polite knock, as if they didn't want to disturb her. And then there'd be hours of hanging around waiting for something to happen, which, when it did, would consist of Shirley sitting first in a big circle with a bunch of time-ruined losers, and then in a private pair with one of the happy-clappy therapists, in either instance refusing to join in because of the whole maintaining-a-dignified-silence thing. In between these sessions there'd be time to wander round the grounds, or do a jigsaw, or run amok with an axe—there was a workshop near the stables; there might be an axe going begging. She made a mental note to check. Then there'd be lunch, and then another group session . . . Christ. She'd never thought she'd miss Slough House.

Of which there were ghostly reminders here. Catherine Standish, for instance, haunted its corridors, having been one of the San's success stories. Because as all the slow horses knew—Jackson Lamb made sure they did—Catherine was a drunk; her history a sordid, vomit-flecked montage of emptied bottles and broken glass, which made it almost comic to see her now, like she'd had a broom handle surgically inserted. Ms. Uptight, in her Victorian spinster costume. Like butter wouldn't melt, when time was she'd melted more butter than Shirley had had hot toast. So yeah, she was currently top of Shirley's shit-list, above Louisa Guy and Lech Wicinski, who'd lured Shirl to Wimbledon in the first place; above Roderick Ho, because the whole bus thing was his fault; above Ashley Khan, who would turn out as annoying as everyone else; and even above Jackson Lamb, without whose say-so nothing happened round Slough House—ahead of them all was Catherine, because Catherine had made out that this was for Shirley's own good, as if Shirley should thank her for the opportunity.

People keep getting hurt, she'd said. *People keep dying. We have to look out for one another.*

Yeah, right. Shirley would be looking out for Catherine, that was for sure.

Meanwhile, it was about keeping her head down and waiting for everyone to realise that all she needed was for people to stop getting on her case. A few days, tops. And she could manage that, but she'd be happier if she'd had time to pack properly—all the sermonising about self-control and clean living would be easier to take with a bump of coke to help it down, not to mention it would increase their chances of getting her to open up. She'd be first to admit she was more voluble after a line or two. This whole place, now she thought about it, would benefit from a more lax attitude, and a bar wouldn't hurt either. She wondered if there was a suggestion box, and whether it would infringe her code of dignified silence to make a contribution.

Somewhere in the corridor she could hear footsteps, and a soft knocking on a door as some poor bastard was roused to face the day. Her turn next. Delaying the moment, she rolled and buried her face in the pillow. When you're up in the air your shadow can't lay a finger on you, but no one stays high forever. And once you hit the ground, your shadow's waiting.

I haven't hit the ground yet, she said out loud, but her voice was unconvincing in the bare little room, and then her door was softly knocked, and the day was starting too early.

Sheesh.

Or, to put it another way: . . .

Nah. He couldn't think of another way. Sheesh would have to do.

But seriously, the number of times Roderick Ho had to clean up other people's messes, you might as well go the distance: give him a uniform, cut his pay in half, and call him a key worker.

Also, this had been a perfectly good keyboard before Shirley Dander had decided to see how many pieces she could smash it into. Answer being: about as many as she'd smashed the other one into first. Stood to reason she was currently in a padded cell, though if anyone had a right to be mad it was the RodMeister. Whose car, let's not forget—Ford Kia: modern classic, you don't see them often—once again needed kinks ironed out, thanks to Dander. Wicinski too, come to that. And meanwhile, the office floor was covered in plastic, and when he'd asked Catherine Standish when she planned to get around to sweeping up—he was a patient man but it had been a couple of days, and that stuff got stuck in your trainers—anyway, yeah, when he'd asked her that, she about blew the bloody doors off. *Very* touchy. As for Wicinski himself, he was refusing to set foot in the room, preferring to squat in Dander's vacant office on account of—Roddy had heard him telling Louisa—if he had to spend time in Roddy's company, he was liable to stuff him inside the wastepaper basket and drop-kick him through the window.

Yeah, right. Come and try it, hopscotch-face.

Caught, for the moment, in a vision of Lech Wicinski doing just that, Roddy did what Roddy did best, which right now was a bit of improvised martial artsing using the broom he was sweeping the floor with. Watch carefully. You might learn something. Subtle as a cobra, Roddy held his broom at eye-level, two-handed. See not the stick. See the space between where the stick is, and where it will be. Fill that space using no sudden movements; capture, rather, the flow of the stick's desire to be elsewhere. Now blink.

He blinked.

He was still holding the broom, but it was pointing the other way.

No significant amount of time had passed.

Like to see Mr. Lightning try *that*.

And would like to see Wicinski try to stuff him into the wastepaper basket too. The RodBod would have him impaled

on a broom handle and rotating like a chicken on a spit before
you could say, well, *Sheesh*. Or *kebab*.

Whistling a tune of his own composition, itself a remix of
one of his own previous compositions, Roddy more or less
finished sweeping up bits of plastic and tipped them into the
bin—which was way too small to hold him—then looked
round to see what else needed doing. He had a phone call to
make, but wasn't quite ready yet. This, despite having been up
half the night thinking about it. Not that he had to do
anything more than be his own cool self, but still: sometimes,
being Roddy Ho took practice. Even when you were already
Roddy Ho to begin with.

But if the movies had taught him anything, it was that
inner steel and outer cool saw you through. And if they'd
taught him anything else, it was this: listen to the whackjobs,
because something they say will turn out important.

Like: *Any woman desperate enough to dress up as a cartoon
character is looking to get laid.*

Remembering Shirley's words, Roddy twirled the broom
in his hands again in another demonstration of self-taught
mastery. *Move not the stick. Let the stick move through you.* Roddy
and stick were one, and when the force flowed through
Roddy it flowed through the stick too, resulting in an almost
mystical marriage of whirling wood and implacable will. The
broom a blur in his magical hands: see him parry, see him
block, see him jab.

He jabbed.

The broom sailed from Roddy's grip and flew through the
closed window, bouncing off Aldersgate Street below in a
shower of shattered glass.

This was greeted by the squonk of an outraged car horn
and a shriek from a passing pedestrian.

Roddy blinked six times in quick succession.

This time, even he could tell, *sheesh* wasn't going to be
enough.

Windows, as it happened, were already on Catherine Standish's mind. If the eyes are the windows of the soul, she was thinking, what does that make windows? Not that she was given to whimsical speculation—it was frowned upon in recovery circles; she'd heard the phrase "slippery slope"—but this one was hard to avoid as she wiped away condensation to reveal a little of her office to the world, and vice versa. Of all Slough House's windows only hers were ever cleaned, and then only on the inside. If you only clean one side of the glass, you might as well clean neither. To the casual glance her windows were blotched and stained, and if that said anything about the state of her soul, Catherine didn't want to know.

And with the other offices' windowpanes unbothered by cloth or cleaning fluid, to inhabitants of the Barbican opposite, the building must seem like it housed vampires, a suspicion perhaps not dispelled by the faded gilt-lettering across the windows of the floor below, spelling out WW HENDERSON, SOLICITOR AND COMMISSIONER FOR OATHS in such ornate, seriffed flamboyance that it couldn't help but seem a fiction; an over-elaborate cover for dark deeds. Oaths and blood went together. But whatever business had once been carried on in the office she still thought of as River Cartwright's, it had ceased long before the building passed into the hands of Jackson Lamb, who would allow the building to fall around his ears sooner than suffer the intrusions required to keep it clean. His own window, anyway, was rarely open to view. His blind was mostly down. He preferred lamps with switches, light he could kill. The new recruit, Ashley Khan, had asked Catherine if Lamb were paranoid, a question to which the obvious answer—of course he is—didn't do justice. Lamb's history demanded paranoia: it was the role he'd been assigned. In a tragedy he'd be the last man standing, drenched in blood. In a comedy, about the same.

She sighed, finished wiping, and assessed her work: the slightly less filthy windows. A certain amount of effort, and almost no result. She might have been miming daily life in Slough House.

Floors were another story. Even failed spies should know one end of a broom from the other, and Catherine tried to make sure the offices were swept once a quarter by their own occupants, which in effect meant almost never. But the previous week, taking advantage of Lamb's absence on some mission doubtless involving food or cigarettes, she'd swept his room, releasing almost visible odours, and when she'd finished, there in the dustpan—among the rat's-nest tangles of hair and dust, and desiccated lumps of food, and thirteen disposable cigarette lighters—there'd lain a tooth, a molar, unmistakably human, its root darkened with blood. Nothing suggested it hadn't lain there for years. She remembered, ages back, finding a handkerchief on Lamb's desk clotted with blood, and thinking it a sign of life's impending retribution: you could not live the way Lamb did without inviting comeback. His lungs, his liver, his lights: some part of him waiting to be switched off. It had seemed freighted with foreboding, that handkerchief, the way handkerchiefs in plays can be, and she had tried to put it out of her mind since, only to find herself wondering now if it had been another of Lamb's cruel jokes, allowing his poor dental health to masquerade as something potentially fatal, for her benefit. This, after all, was what their relationship was like; lies were told with no words exchanged, and knowledge falsified in the absence of information. If she taxed him with that, he'd ask her what she expected? They were spooks. This was how they lived.

But she wouldn't ask him, because there were some things she didn't want to know, answers she'd rather remained in the dark and dust.

It was time to stop woolgathering and face the day ahead: weekly reports to assemble for Lamb, who never read them, and job-output stats to compile for Regent's Park, which didn't care. All that mattered to both was that the work of Slough

House continue uninterrupted, whether by something major like whatever had happened in Wimbledon the other evening, or by something comparatively trivial, involving, say, the sound of a window breaking two floors below, which Catherine would now have to investigate.

The condition of her soul notwithstanding, she allowed herself a brief, uncharacteristic curse word before heading downstairs, wishing she'd chosen a different day for an early start.

But some never had that choice to make.

Some will never wake again.

A few streets off the Westway, where the city makes its bid for freedom with one last flourish of bookmakers and bed shops, bridal boutiques and barbers, in a single-roomed annexe occupying what was once the back garden of what was once a family home and now houses thirteen individuals leading thirteen separate lives, a figure lies on a bed, fully clothed, eyes shut, still breathing. How much of his current state can be put down to natural sleep, how much to alcohol-induced coma can be gauged by the empty bottle by his side: the label reads *The Balvenie*, a brand way too classy for this venue. The figure's breathing is regular but laboured, as if heavy work were being done in that unconscious state, and the air it's processing is thick with cigarette smoke—there's an ashtray on the floor which needed emptying last Tuesday. One stub still smoulders, suggesting a recent companion, as it seems unlikely that the prone figure has been active these past few minutes. An unkinder view would be that it's unlikely he's been active this past month, but a bottle of scotch can have that effect, as indeed can two—a second bottle, equally drained, has rolled to rest under the room's only table: a battered, tin-topped thing with foldable leaves.

Nothing else in sight gives cheer. Against the wall is a sink unit, on one side of which unwashed crockery mounts up on a stainless steel draining board, while on the other, a two-ring electric stove plugged into an already overworked socket offers just enough of a nod in the direction of domesticity to allow a landlord to describe the room as self-catering. One of the two rings is dormant, and on top of it has been placed a plastic bag of frozen chips, torn open at the wrong end. A little diagram explains how to prepare them: they can be cooked in an oven or on top of a stove, supposing a chip pan is available. A chip pan, as it happens, is available, and in fact is close at hand: it sits atop the second of the two rings, which is glowing orange in the dusky light, and the viscous liquid with which it is filled is beginning to bubble and pop, causing the pan's wire basket to rattle against its sides. Spread out on the floor below is a newspaper, one of the capital's giveaways, its pages unfurled and unfolded as if someone has been trying to read all of it in one go.

It's a familiar scenario, this: a tabloid newspaper waiting to add fuel to whatever comes its way. Already a splash of oil has escaped the pan and landed on the ring with a big-snake hiss; not loud enough to penetrate a whisky fog, but a sign of more to come. The minutes will pass, shuffling their way towards the quarter hour, and before that milestone is reached the oil will have bubbled its way to freedom, at which point the minutes will give up, and the seconds come into their element. Things that were happening separately will start happening at once, and when the boiling oil spits onto the waiting paper, the paper will respond as it would to any good story and spread the news far and wide; across the threadbare carpet, over the shabby furnishings, and onto the figure on the bed itself, which might twitch of its own accord in its first few flaming moments, but will soon lose any such self-motivation and become the fire's puppet, twisting and baking into a flaky black museum piece, while the annexe burns to a shell around it. All of this will happen soon, and some of it's happening already. The oil burps in the pan, hungry. The cigarette stub smoulders its last, and a faint grey coil of smoke drifts towards the ceiling.

A few streets off, on the Westway, traffic roars into and out of London, embarking on an ordinary day.

But here in this cramped, shabby room, that day will never happen.

Meanwhile, back on Aldersgate Street, the shards of glass have been swept from the pavement, which is to say that Catherine Standish has marched Roderick Ho out and watched him sweep said shards into a pile—after watching him rescue the broom from the road—and then brush them into a cardboard box. There's an audience of sorts for this sideshow, but it's a desultory morning crowd made up of London's early pedestrians, and no one lingers long. These groundlings have other dramas to pursue, and this particular moment is merely a respite from their various starring roles, in which they answer phones and do battle with spreadsheets, serve customers and mend computers, police the streets and mark exams, sell cigarettes and ask for spare change, heal the sick and empty the bins, launder clothes and broker deals, write songs and typeset books, love and lose and sing badly in the shower, commit fraud and assault, drink themselves stupid, and are kind to strangers. With all this ahead of them, there's little time to linger. They move out of shot, and Roddy hoists the cardboard box, which rattles like a kaleidoscope, and carries it round the alleyway to the back of Slough House, where he dumps it in a wheelie-bin. Then he sulks his way upstairs, to spend the rest of the morning covering the broken window with a cardboard shield fashioned from taped-together pizza boxes, whose company logos smile onto the road below like unexpected adverts.

On Aldersgate Street a council lorry wheezes past tugging a series of trailers, each freighted with pipes and sinks and indeterminable items of metalware; travelling junkyards that look as if all the shiny bits have been extracted from some huge and cumbersome invention. And in the offices of Slough House the slow horses have settled themselves at their desks for another day, one which already seems askew from reality, as if things that happened in one order are about to be told in another.

But as long as they start happening soon, this doesn't really matter.

Oliver Nash had chosen a patisserie in which to meet Claude Whelan, because it was handy for both of them, and because you had to support small businesses, and because it was a patisserie. Nash's battle with his weight was an unfair contest. He had good intentions on his side, and a whole stack of diet books, not to mention words of advice bordering on warning from his GP, but his weight had a secret weapon: his appetite. In the face of which indomitable force, the massed artillery of inner determination, bookshelves and medical wisdom didn't have a prayer.

None of which went through Whelan's mind as they shook hands. They hadn't seen each other in years, but neither had changed much, and if Whelan wouldn't have gone so far as to say Nash was the shape he'd chosen for himself he was certainly the shape he was, and that was as much thought as Whelan had ever given the matter.

"How are you, Claude?"

He was fine.

"And can I tempt you to an almond croissant?"

No. He was a fallible man, and wouldn't claim otherwise, but he'd never had a sweet tooth.

Nash didn't pretend to regret having already ordered two. Coffee, likewise, was on its way: "Americano without, yes?" He had a memory for such things, heaven knew how. To the best of Whelan's recall—they had been colleagues, of a sort, once—Nash spent half his life taking meetings, drinking coffee with others. He surely couldn't recall everyone's taste in beverage.

They chatted until their drinks came. Though not one of life's small talkers, Whelan found this undemanding: Nash could provide both halves of a conversation if it proved necessary, and sometimes when it didn't. The patisserie wasn't crowded, and anyway held only half the tables it once had. On the nearest one, an abandoned newspaper revealed that the PM had just shared his vision of post-Brexit Britain as a scientific powerhouse, its trillion-pound tech industry the envy of the world. They chuckled over this, and drank coffee, and Nash put away a croissant without apparently noticing doing so, and at last said, "You're a busy man," which was the correct formula: nobody likes to be told they have nothing much to do. "But I have a favour to ask."

Whelan nodded, hoping this wouldn't be misinterpreted as a willingness to carry out the favour, but knowing it probably would. Hard to deny it: he was a soft touch. Not a busy man, either. He had things to do, but not enough to keep him occupied.

Besides, stopping Nash from continuing would have taken heavy machinery. This was odd, or ought to have been—Nash's role in the Service wasn't operational, but it was senior: he was chair of the Limitations Committee, which among other things imposed fiscal restraint on the Service, and might thus be assumed to warrant discretion, if not downright secrecy, an assumption for which you could probably find legal backing if you waded through the paperwork. But Nash seemed blithely unaware of the fact. To be in his company for more than two minutes was to learn three things about four other people, as someone had once remarked, and it hadn't been meant as a criticism.

Whelan raised his coffee cup, noticed it was empty, and put it down again.

Nash said, "I shouldn't say this. But you were requested by name."

Whelan supposed that was better than being hailed like a passing taxi. Nash, meanwhile, was waggling his eyebrows in a way that indicated the request came from above. He presumably hadn't been receiving messages from God, so Whelan settled on the next rung down. "Diana Taverner?"

He found it impossible to keep the disbelief from his voice.

Nash found it equally difficult. "Good heavens, no. Ha! No no no."

"So, then—"

"I doubt you've entered her mind since she saw you off the premises, to be honest." There was something innocent about Nash's lack of tact. It was as if he'd learned it from watching talent shows. "No, I was referring to Number Ten."

"The PM?"

"Well, I say Number Ten. But the PM isn't exactly hands on, is he? Got enough to do with all his . . ." Nash tailed off, as if the task in view, that of explaining what it was that the PM spent most of his time doing, was too daunting to wrestle with. "No, I meant Sparrow. You know. The PM's, ah . . ."

"His special adviser."

"Quite."

As the PM's enforcer, Sparrow wasn't as high profile as his predecessor had been—it would have been challenging to maintain that level of unpopularity without barbecuing an infant on live television—but those in the know recognised him as a homegrown Napoleon: nasty, British and short. Whelan had never met him, but that Sparrow was aware of him was only mildly surprising. A spad would be expected to know who was who, and as one-time First Desk at Regent's Park, Whelan had been a who in his time.

"And what exactly is it that Mr. Sparrow thinks I might be suited for?"

"He's concerned for the whereabouts of an associate of his."

"An associate?"

"That was the word he used. A woman called Sophie de Greer. Doctor. Of the academic variety. She was a member of this think tank Sparrow runs, an advisory body. Something to do with policy initiatives? He was vague on the details."

"And she's gone missing."

"Apparently. And he rather suspects . . ."

"Foul play?" suggested Whelan, hating the moment even as it was happening.

"Yes. Well, no. He rather suspects your old Service has something to do with it, actually."

Whelan said, "He thinks the Service has abducted a colleague of his? Our Service? That's absurd."

"Isn't it? Doesn't, couldn't, wouldn't happen. Exactly what I told him."

"Then why are you coming to me with it?"

Nash noticed the second croissant on his plate. It was clearly a discovery of some moment; he glanced around, as if making sure it hadn't been left there by accident, then indicated its presence to Whelan, as if he were the body to whom reports of such finds should be made. Whelan, unwilling to take part in this pantomime, waited. Nash sighed, sliced an inch off one end of the pastry and transported it to his mouth, his expression suggesting that the whole endeavour was an unfortunate necessity. Then glanced around once more. There was nobody near enough to hear his next word, even if he'd spoken out loud rather than simply mouthed the syllables. "Waterproof."

". . . I beg your pardon?" Then Whelan shook his head: he'd heard. "I mean, what, no, seriously? He said that?"

Nash nodded.

"And he meant . . . You're saying he thinks that's what happened? That someone triggered the Waterproof protocol?"

Nash said, "Well, he didn't come out and say it directly. But that's clearly what he was hinting at."

He picked up the knife once more, and sliced what was left of the croissant in half.

Whelan said, "That's ridiculous. There was an inquiry, I set it up myself. Waterproof, well . . . Okay, there was a certain amount of grey area. But the official line, the actual finding, was that the protocol was never used."

"Yes, I'm aware what the official finding was, and I'm equally aware that the report will remain sealed for years to come. Even a virgin like me can draw the line between those dots."

"That's as may be. But leaving aside any . . . discretion involved in the conclusions reached, how is a newcomer like Sparrow even aware of Waterproof's existence?"

"Because such is the role of special advisers, blessed be their name, that there is no document passes a portal anywhere on Downing Street that they can't lay their eyes on at will. And don't ask me how or why that started, because believe me I've no idea." No idea, but an evident distaste. The manner in which Nash tore into the last piece of croissant made this clear. "And now that this particular bee has entered this particular bonnet, it apparently behooves me to catch it and pin it to a board, or whatever it is one does with bees. I'm not an expert."

"But why me? I mean . . . You're in daily contact with Diana, surely. Can't you just ask her about it?"

"Well, I could and I can't. You know how political things get. And I rather have to stay on Diana's good side, if you know what I mean. Like I say, it wasn't my idea. It was Sparrow's."

"Well, what does he think I can do about it? I'm not a police officer."

"No, quite. Though I'm not sure that would carry weight at the Park, the way things are. Diana does rather seem to have pulled the drawbridge up."

"What makes you think she'll lower it for me? I've no authority there. You know that."

Arguably less than none. Because while there were many things about Diana that Whelan had failed to recognise while she was nominally his subordinate, this much had become clear since: that she practised a scorched-earth policy towards anyone not entirely committed to her advancement. In this, he realised, she was in keeping with the political zeitgeist, and he was self-aware enough to know that, had he recognised this at the time, it wouldn't have significantly altered the outcome. Even Nash, technically one of Regent's Park string-pullers, knew to tread carefully around Diana. String-pullers carry weight, but Diana carried scissors.

"Besides," he went on, "an official inquiry is a shallow grave. Anyone approaching it with a shovel is likely to find bones. That's how Diana will see it. That I'm trying to resurrect an old scandal, and hang it round her neck."

"Diana's not going to worry about bones that were buried by one or other of her predecessors." Nash's face was a bland mask. "More coffee?"

"'One or other'?"

"A turn of phrase." He wiped crumbs from his tie. "There's no need to look at me like that. I'm not telling you anything you don't already know."

"That if you need something done ask a scapegoat?"

"You're being melodramatic. If Diana needs to paint a target anywhere—which she won't—it's not your back she'll be looking at. It's Ingrid Tearney's." He lowered his voice. "There was a whisper at the time that Tearney, ah, waterproofed someone entirely for her own benefit while First Desk." He shook his head saying this: the evil that women do. "And then there's *her* predecessor, Charles Partner, who's been safely dead these many years. With that pair to choose from, Diana won't feel unduly paranoid if questions are asked about an ancient protocol that officially never existed in the first place." He paused. "Unless, of course, she *is* responsible for Dr. de Greer's disappearance. But that doesn't strike me as especially likely."

Even Whelan could hear the weariness in his tone when he said, "The whole reason I was appointed First Desk was that I wasn't tainted by anything Ingrid Tearney got up to. A clean pair of hands. Remember?"

"Of course. Anyway, we're losing sight of the wood for the trees. All Sparrow's interested in is the whereabouts of Dr. de Greer, and all you have to do is confirm that wherever she is, the Service didn't put her there." He still wasn't happy with his tie. It was possible, thought Whelan, he was trying to brush away some of its pattern. "A few questions, a few answers, and it's done with."

"It doesn't seem as if that'll get Sparrow any closer to finding out what's happened to his associate."

"But it'll close down a line of enquiry. Besides . . . Between us, I'm not entirely sure that's what he's really after. No, chances are, he's using the situation to let the Park know who's top dog. It's no secret he'd prefer the set-up there was less . . . independent." Nash had taken his phone out while saying this, and was playing with its buttons like a jazz pianist looking for a tune. Whelan's own phone pinged: incoming. "There. Now you know what I know." He slipped the phone back into his pocket. "A few questions, Claude. A plausible denial from the Park. Just so I can let Mr. Sparrow know there's nothing to his suspicions."

"In my day, which wasn't that long ago, it was the prime minister called the tune. Not his poodle."

"The poodles are running the bloody show, that's the problem. I expect to see the PM in a collar and leash any day now."

For a moment Nash looked old and tired, which rather shook Whelan. He'd always thought of Nash as one of Westminster's groupies, living for the gossip and the lunches, and generally unbothered by the moral dimension. It was possible he'd been wrong about that.

The waitress came and collected their crockery. Whelan found his gaze drifting in her direction, admiring the way her uniform adhered to her shape, and slapped his own mental wrist.

"I don't know, Oliver," he said, which was a lie. He did know. This shouldn't be touched with a hazmat suit on. It had politics scribbled all over it, and there was no way you could wander into that kind of firefight without getting bits of you shot off: your reputation, your career, your pension. It was politics that had proved his undoing at the Park. Well, and also the connection between a working-paper he'd written years ago, a massacre in Derbyshire and a bloodbath involving penguins, but that could have happened to anyone; it was politics had sharpened the knife. So yes, he knew: shake an apologetic head and walk away.

On the other hand . . .

Reputation, career and pension. He was probably overstating the risk. His pension was secure, and his career largely over; had dwindled to committee work and charitable enterprise, the rubble that remained after a failure to launch. As for his reputation, the circumstances demanding his departure from office had never been made public, so rumour and gossip had rushed to fill the gap. An unexpected rise to prominence; a sudden crashing to earth—whispers suggested a #MeToo moment, and men his own age offered sympathetic headshakes. No, his reputation was already shot. So perhaps what was on offer here was the opportunity to settle a score. With that thought, another name from the past popped up unprompted: Taverner's sparring partner, Jackson Lamb. He'd rather enjoy tilting his lance at that bad actor. And yet one more consideration: having a mission would get him out of the house. That could only be a good thing, surely?

He said, "Your face, Oliver." He gestured to the corresponding section of his own. "You have some . . ."

Then, while Nash was wiping icing sugar away with a napkin, said, "All right, then. All right. I'll give it a shot."

Okay, a soft touch. But he wasn't a busy man.

Catherine was busy that morning, not least of her tasks being an attempt to negotiate her way towards a mended window, which involved an extended conversation with Regent's Park's facilities manager. But the recent hiatus during which Slough House had been wiped from the Park's map—its location removed from internal records, and the slow horses themselves rendered formless and floating—had served to make an already thankless process a migraine-inducing ordeal, and it became clear that the functionary on the other end of the call wasn't happy about admitting the building's official status, let alone despatching a Security-approved operative to perform maintenance work there.

Perhaps, Catherine suggested, she should just go ahead and Google the nearest available glazier?

Which would be a breach of Service regulations: admittance of non-vetted civilian personnel onto premises deemed classified.

"Except you've just told me we're not deemed classified. We're barely deemed existent."

But Catherine's insistence on seeking the necessary permissions indicated her own belief that the premises were indeed a Service satellite, rendering any initiation of such non-approved admittance a breach of her oath of service, itself a regulatory offence.

"So if I hadn't sought clearance, I wouldn't have needed it?"

He seemed pleased she'd grasped the basic idea.

This wasn't a conversation to be relayed to Jackson Lamb, though he was also on the morning's agenda—whether or not Lamb liked things, in the normal human sense, was a matter for philosophers or possibly zoologists, but what was certain was that there were things he insisted happen, among them team meetings. Not that he went out of his way to prepare. When she crossed the landing to his room five minutes before today's gathering was due to start, carrying a small wooden stool and a bottle of hand sanitiser, he was slumped in his chair like a bean bag on top of a clothes horse; a cigarette burning in one fist, the other inside his trousers. Both his eyes were closed. The smell of tobacco almost overpowered a recent bout of flatulence.

She put the stool by the door; placed the sanitiser on top of it.

Lamb opened one eye. "Lubricant? Pretty optimistic for a staff meeting." He closed it again. "But I suppose it'll be a chance to swap these gender fluids I keep hearing about."

"As I believe I've mentioned already," she said, "it might be an idea to curb your boyish humour in front of Ashley. Give her half the chance, she'll bring a harassment charge."

Lamb adopted a wounded pout. "What did I ever do to her?"

"Broke her arm?"

"She's still on about that? Bloody snowflake."

This too was familiar territory. When Ashley Khan—a fledgling spook—had been despatched by Diana Taverner to tail a slow horse, and Lamb had sent her back to the Park bent out of shape, Taverner's response had been: You broke her, she's yours. Which, as far as Lamb was concerned, was tantamount to being made to suffer consequences for his actions, precisely the kind of moralistic bullshit he'd joined the Service to avoid. What was this, the Church?

A recitation he spared her today, perhaps because he was too busy scratching his crotch.

He was wearing a new shirt, she noticed; or a shirt new to her. It was only actually new if they came pre-frayed. Outside of a sixth-form college staffroom, Lamb was always going to come off worst when fashion statements were being made, but this was particularly ill-judged: a pale shade of lilac, it had the effect of making his skin look waxier than usual. On the other hand, it was of a piece with the rest of his ensemble: the grey woollen trousers, shiny at the knees; the lumpy, shapeless jacket, which just might, on second thoughts, have been made-to-measure. This had originally been either light blue and was now more-or-less evenly soiled, or dark blue and had faded. A yellowing stain she didn't want to think about adorned the left shoulder.

Still by the door, she said, "Are you going to tell me what happened in Wimbledon the other night?"

"Doesn't seem likely."

"Because Shirley's in the San. And Lech's lucky not to be in hospital."

"Which one's Lech again?"

"You've barely enough staff left to run an ice cream van."

"Getting through them nicely, aren't we?" said Lamb. "If the bloody Park didn't keep sending replacements, we'd have this place to ourselves by now."

"And if I hadn't twisted Taverner's arm, Shirley would be out on her ear. I know the phrase 'duty of care' means nothing to you, but casualties and rehab-placements go down on the end-of-year audit. Sooner or later, someone's going to ask what you're doing to your agents."

Lamb had adopted a glazed expression, unless she just had glaziers on her mind. "I'd have paid money to see you twisting Diana's arm. Did you oil up beforehand or just get sweaty in the act?"

"Would you mind removing your hand from your trousers?"

He did so, sniffed it, and wiped it on his jacket.

"It's like a chimps' tea party round here," she said.

"If you're offering."

"We're out of milk."

"I'll take it black," Lamb said. "As a concession to your miserable failures of housekeeping."

"This place is falling apart," she said. "And I don't just mean the plasterwork. If you expect me to keep on holding the fort for you, I deserve to know what's happening."

"If landing me in the shit with Taverner's what you call holding my fort, then don't start bashing my bishop. Or the plasterwork's not the only thing'll be falling apart."

"... How did I land you in it with Taverner?"

"Because anything you can twist her arm with pretty obviously came from me. And she's not one to shy away from getting her own back. In fact she usually does that first, to save time."

"Oh," said Catherine. Then: "I may have mentioned her entanglement with Peter Judd."

"Yeah, that would do it." This entanglement, involving Diana's accepting funding for Service ops from a cabal led by a notorious power-seeker, was not something she wanted public light shed on. Lamb looked at the cigarette he was holding, then stubbed it out in a tinfoil container squatting among the papers on his desk. "I'd be careful crossing roads if I were you. In fact, I'd be careful sitting quietly in your room. She's got a long reach."

"I think she's got more to worry about right now."

"If she can't protect the Service from a Number Ten land grab, she doesn't deserve to be in the job."

It had been Judd Catherine was thinking about, not Downing Street. "You think the PM's got an eye on the Park?"

"I think the PM keeps both eyes on the nearest pair of tits," said Lamb. "But that garden gnome that makes his decisions for him seems pretty keen on taking back control. And that would involve sidelining Taverner, yeah."

"I didn't realise you kept track of the Westminster bubble."

He put a hand down his trousers again. When it reappeared, it was holding another cigarette. "Only in case it causes me grief. Like that butterfly effect. Some arsehole flaps his wings in SW1, next thing you know there's a storm in my teacup. Speaking of which." He reached for the mug on his desk, and tossed it at her. About half an ounce of cold tea containing at least two cigarette ends scattered around the room, much of it spattering Catherine's dress.

"For heaven's sake!"

"That's for lying about the milk."

"Are you ever going to—oh, forget it!" She left the mug where it had landed and returned to her own room, where she did damage limitation with a box of tissues. While she was there, she heard the others coming up the stairs: Louisa, Lech, Roderick, Ashley.

It hadn't escaped her that he'd said nothing about what happened in Wimbledon. That had been the point of throwing the mug, she realised. He was always one for creating a distraction messier than whatever he was covering up. Which was either a very good attribute for a spook, or a very bad one. So he either did it deliberately, to give the wrong impression, or it came as naturally to him as smoking and farting, always supposing he wasn't faking them too.

She spent far too much time trying to understand him. She should just accept that he was what he was, and get on with life.

When she returned to his office, the others were filing in, Louisa, Lech and Roddy helping themselves to hand sanitiser as they passed. Ashley didn't. Catherine raised an eyebrow.

"I'll use it on the way out," Ashley said.

"Are they all here?" Lamb asked Catherine. "I lose count."

"It's not like it's a huge number," Louisa said.

"And why are two of them wearing masks?"

"Only one of them's wearing a mask," Catherine said. "And that's her right."

Lech made jazz hands. "Same face as yesterday," he said. "But I appreciate being noticed."

"Yeah, enjoy it. With your looks, it's the closest you'll get to consensual sex." Lamb looked at Ashley. "That's a funny hijab. What's it decorated with, germs?"

"It's not a hijab. And they would be emojis."

"Well, smiley face, ironic wink, you'd better get used to communicating that way. On account of I can't hear a word you're saying with that thing on."

"If you didn't hear me, how come you know what I said?"

"Best not to encourage him," Catherine said quietly.

Lamb gave his injured martyr look. "Eye roll. Pay no attention to Jane Eyre. She's been in a snit since I friend-zoned her."

"Could we get on with things, please?"

"Unless anyone else has something to contribute?" He stared at Roddy Ho. "Hmm?"

"Well—"

"Shut up." He gazed round at the rest of them. "Now, it won't have escaped your attention that there's fewer of you than there used to be. Which means there's more work to go round, because that's just plain maths. So you two," meaning Lech and Louisa, "can split whatever Dander was doing. And you," meaning Roddy, "find out what Cartwright was up to and finish it."

"What about me?" asked Ashley.

"You carry on doing what you're doing. Only do twice as much of it."

"I'm doing nothing."

"Yeah, so you could probably get away with only doing half as much again." He squashed the side of his nose with his finger and winked horribly. "Just make sure I don't find out."

"There's probably an emoji for that," muttered Louisa.

"Thank you, smartarse. Since you're crammed full of general knowledge this morning, tell the ship's monkey here where the Russian embassy is."

He gestured with his unlit cigarette at Roddy Ho.

"It's on Bayswater Road," Louisa said. "Why?"

"Because he pretty certainly doesn't know."

"I meant why—"

"Because one of us gets to give instructions, and the rest of us get to carry them out. See if you can work out who's who. My door's always open."

Lech said, "The stuff you've got us on already, the social media dropouts and the library lists and the rest, they'll pretty much take us forever to finish. So how do you expect us to do Shirley and River's jobs as well?"

"Well, that's something for you to brood on next time you're planning a jolly of your own, isn't it?" He opened the three left-hand drawers of his desk, and slammed them shut in quick succession. Then fumbled through his jacket pockets before producing a lighter. "If I wanted you to display anything, I'd choose something you can spell. Initiative's not the first thing that'd come to mind." He lit his cigarette and tossed the lighter over his shoulder. It landed with a plastic bump. "Your arse'd be the first thing that comes to mind. I appreciate that's a novel experience for you, but imagine how it makes me feel."

"I already knew where the Russian Embassy is," said Roddy.

"Amazing. Skillset like yours, you could work for Deliveroo, once you've learned to ride a bike."

"I can already—"

"Yeah, shut up. There's enough CCTV round there to stage an Olympic opening ceremony, right? Usual traffic stuff, plus local security, plus whatever the Park's set up to keep the Ivans in the spotlight. So you do whatever it is you do when you're not playing *Star Trek*, and hijack or lojack or just plain jack off one or other or all of these, and let me know when you're done." He exhaled smoke without apparently having inhaled any yet. "Because today's the day the teddy bear's having a picnic. And I want to know who's invited."

Which didn't so much cast light on the assembled company as push them a little further into the dark.

Catherine said, "Perhaps, when you're giving instructions, you could aim for more clarity?"

"Christ. I should use flashcards." He leaned forward, and all present, bar Ashley, braced. Sudden changes of position often signalled an oncoming fart. "The Russian Embassy— Russian, bear, get it?—the Russian Embassy's hosting a shindig this evening. And I'd like Kung Fu Panda here to provide a list of those turning up for caviar and chips. Is that clear enough? Why are you all retreating?"

"Eager to get on with the job," said Louisa.

"Nice to see some enthusiasm for a change. I'm pretty sure I'm due a tea break myself. Oh, wait. One more thing." He paused. They waited. He farted. "No, sorry. Forgot what I was about to say."

Lech and Louisa stopped off in the kitchen before heading to their offices: she put the kettle on; he leaned against the fridge and groaned.

"Take more painkillers," she suggested. "Has Bachelor been in touch?"

"Thanks for the sympathy. He called, yes."

"Everything okay?"

"I'd have said if it wasn't. Catherine doesn't know about any of this, does she?"

"Doesn't appear so."

"And he normally tells her stuff. You think this Russian Embassy do is connected?"

"I think Lamb wasn't kidding when he told us to keep quiet about it."

Or I'll do for both your careers what he's already done to his face, had been Lamb's codicil.

The kettle boiled as Ashley came in, still wearing her mask, and carrying a Tupperware box with a sticker attached. HANDS OFF, it read. "It smells like wet dog in his office," she said.

"I've stopped noticing," Louisa said.

"You do realise that's not a good thing? Can I get in there?" The fridge, she meant. Lech moved aside, and she bent to deposit the box, apparently trying to conceal it behind a tub of margarine.

"Is that your lunch?" Louisa asked.

"Uh-huh."

"Because the chances of Lamb not stealing it are up there with the chances of him going on a diet."

Ashley shrugged and shut the fridge door, then shut it again when it swung open. "Did he really make you all come in during lockdown?"

Lech said, "His point was, we're in the security service. If it got out that we're not remotely key workers, it might be bad for public morale."

"Because that's a priority with him," said Ashley.

"You have to understand," Louisa told her, "most of what he says and most of what he does is just to wind us up. That's what being at Slough House is all about."

"If the boredom of the work doesn't see you off," Lech said, "the stress of his constant goading might do the trick."

"Well when I'm back at the Park," Ashley said, "he's going to face the stress of some serious grievance procedures. Lots of them. He smokes in here. That's not even legal."

Louisa and Lech shared a glance.

"What? It isn't. There's a law."

"You do realise this isn't a temporary posting?"

"That's only when you've messed up. And I didn't. That bastard broke my arm. He's the one should be reassigned."

"That should matter," Lech said, "but it doesn't. Once you're here, you're here."

"It's like the Hotel California," Louisa elaborated. "Only for demoted spooks instead of cokehead clubbers."

"Well, Shirley," Lech said.

"Yeah, okay, Shirley. But my point stands. You don't get passage back to where you were before."

"I have no idea what you're talking about. What's California got to do with it?"

"Never mind. But forget about the Park. If you hate it here, quit. That's your only option."

"Well you both obviously hate it," said Ashley. "So why do you stay?"

The kettle turned itself off, bubbling steam into the air.

"In case we're wrong," Louisa said at last.

The file on Dr. Sophie de Greer was slender, and an hour spent on Google hadn't fleshed it out much. De Greer was an academic, attached to the University of Berne but on sabbatical these past six months, working in London with a group chaired by Anthony Sparrow, codenamed—or possibly just named—Rethink#1. Her discipline was political history, but her attraction for Sparrow was her status as a superforecaster; someone with a knack for accurate predictions, particularly, in her case, regarding electoral responses to policy initiatives. Such talents were assessed, Whelan knew, in clinical conditions: in de Greer's instance, in a string of tests carried out in Switzerland and France. One result gave her ninety-two per cent accuracy in forecasting voting swings in a series of local elections across four European states, an achievement, the file suggested, on a par with scoring a hat trick in a World Cup final. It would have impressed Whelan no end, if he'd admired conjuring tricks.

But superforecasting was, to his mind, flavour-of-the-month stuff. Every administration brought its own stage dressing, from Blair's "pretty straight guys," who had briefly imagined themselves the living embodiment of some TV liberal fantasy, to the current crew, a homogenous bunch—because those with independent outlooks had been culled in the first weeks—under the sway of a wave of Svengalis with that fetish for disruption that had rolled tsunami-like across the globe this past decade. Weirdos and misfits they proudly asserted, as if the groundstaff of any political movement had ever comprised anything else. Sociopathy had long been recognised as a handy attribute in politics. Only recently had it been considered worth boasting about. This was the context in which those with de Greer's peculiar talents were enrolled like jesters at a medieval court, which was better than being rounded up as witches, Whelan supposed. Better for them, anyway. How it would work out for everybody else had yet to be determined.

And lately, prized or not, Sophie de Greer—blonde, thirty-seven, five five; suit and tie in the accompanying photo, though presumably not always—had dropped off, if not necessarily the map, at least some pages of the A–Z; those covering Whitehall and the offices occupied by Rethink#1 on the South Bank, a short walk from Waterloo. Scheduled to attend a meeting chaired by Sparrow three days previously, she had neither turned up nor sent apologies; phone calls went unanswered, emails ignored. Later that day, one of Number Ten's security team was despatched to her apartment to determine that she hadn't fallen ill, died or ODed in bed, and reported back in the negative. Nor were there signs of abduction. It was hard to determine whether she had packed for departure, given the few belongings she'd brought to London, but it seemed that, wherever she was, she had a walking-round kit: wallet, phone, iPad, passport. There was no record of her having left the country, no apparent reason for her to want to vanish. Her flat, a six-month let, had weeks to run. Her position on Rethink#1 was "secure": Sparrow's word.

None of this amounted to much. And three days wasn't a long time to be invisible, in Whelan's opinion. Evidence of a more protracted disappearance lay all around him. In the furnace of government, of course, other metrics applied: Sparrow clearly expected hourly contact with—or from—his team, making a lapse like de Greer's an aberration. But was it mystifying? From all Whelan had heard, Anthony Sparrow was best kept at a distance; the PM's string-puller according to some, his headbutter-in-chief to others, he was nobody's idea of a good time either way. Perhaps de Greer had simply decided she'd had enough, and gone to seek more agreeable company: a bunch of drunk golfers, or a basket of rats. But there would always be those who saw, or professed to see, conspiracy, just as there would always be those who engineered it. Few were more aware of this than Whelan.

Because, prior to his elevation to First Desk, Claude Whelan had worked over the river. Scenes & Ways had been his department—Schemes and Wheezes, in the jargon; a typically schoolboy designation for what had begun, literally, as a cut-throat division, its original brief having been to plot assassinations. This had been during wartime, its current operatives would reassure newcomers, sometimes remembering to add "obviously." In Whelan's early years, destabilisation scenarios were the hot-button issue; leverage applied by major players to keep the ragamuffin nations to heel. Then the internet levelled the playing field, and the old rule-book was trampled underfoot. Once, you had to appear big to play the bully. Now minnows could be rogue nations too. Keyboards were weaponised, trolls emerged from under bridges, and somewhere along the way free elections turned into free-for-alls, as if democracy were a shaggy dog story to which a joke president was the punchline. All those decades of the arms race, and it turned out there was no greater damage you could inflict on a state than ensure it was led by an idiot. Somewhere, someone, probably, was laughing.

These thoughts required Whelan to shake himself like a dog waking up. The world's problems weren't his doing. His own problems, even: not all were his fault either. And yet. And yet. He had worked in a dirty business, which had helped produce a dirty world. Small surprise that when he'd been in a position to make a difference he'd been brought low by dirty tricks; a ruination engineered not by anonymous disruptors, but by the current First Desk herself, Diana Taverner, aided and abetted by the loathsome Jackson Lamb. And here he was, gifted an opportunity to poke around in Taverner's cupboards . . .

It was possible he was being used. Sparrow's ambition to open his umbrella over every aspect of the state machinery was well known, and de Greer's disappearance could be a ruse to allow him access to the Park. Letting Whelan run the investigation was a slap in the face to Taverner—having her predecessor investigate her actions presupposed a guilty finding. If that were all true, where did Whelan's loyalties lie? Not with either side. Not with any bad actor, whether in the Service he'd led or the government he'd served. So why not with himself, this once? It still rankled, his fall from grace, and why shouldn't he take some measure of revenge? It wasn't really him, he knew that. He was nobody's idea of an avenging knight. But wasn't it time for a change, and Christ, he was havering like bloody Hamlet. Enough. He had said he would do it. So enough.

Whelan read through the file once more, but learned nothing new. That done, he rang the Park and informed Diana Taverner that he was on his way to see her.

With her office door ajar, an inch-wide view of the landing was available to Ashley. If anyone entered the kitchen, she'd know. No matter how quiet they were, they'd darken her door.

A slim thing to concentrate on, but she had nothing else to do. Literally: nothing. It was like being an extra in a crowd scene—she was dressed the part, she took up space, she had no lines to deliver.

A week ago, she'd followed Lamb home, or that had been her plan—she'd wanted to see where he lived, *how* he lived. A mental picture was easy: a pigsty with a car on bricks out front. The possibility that he shared this dwelling she briefly entertained, but when she tried to bring a cohabitee into focus, the image seared and melted. Who would share their life with Lamb? Apart from the slow horses, obviously. Slow horses don't count. She'd learned that much.

But in the end, her plan fell apart. For two hours she'd waited on the Barbican terrace, roosting on a flowerbed's brick border. Her healed arm ached, a dull reminder of why she sought revenge, as—hood up, mask on—she stared across a meagre flow of traffic at Slough House. By this time in her career, her training completed, her hand-in assessed—and she'd done a good job on that—she should have been assigned to a Park department. She'd been hoping for Ops. Instead she'd had six months of administrative nightmare, fighting her reassignment to Slough House, which happened anyway. So here she was, and the evening had grown smeary and grey long before Lamb appeared, an unkempt figure spilling out of the alleyway. He paused to light a cigarette then stepped off down Aldersgate Street, weaving slightly as if drunk. Unpeeling herself from her perch, she flitted over the footbridge to follow him, maintaining that safe distance drummed into her at the Park: *far enough away that you can fade; near enough that there's no gap he can slip through.* Hood up, mask on. Everything was disguise.

The Old Street junction was busy, queues of traffic bidding for dominance, and the cold made Ashley's eyes water, adding lens-flare to the reds and greens and ambers, the yellows and whites. Lamb was a blurry solid amidst this flashing circus, crossing the road with no apparent regard for moving vehicles. A bus blocked her view but he was still there once it had passed, on the opposite pavement, hobbling north. There was a pub on that corner whose curved windows suggested a bygone era; behind it lay a patch of wasteground enclosed by hoardings. There'd been shops or houses there, but it was now a barely curated absence, a temporary space where you could park all day for twenty pounds. She was crossing the road when Lamb slipped past the horizontal pole guarding its single point of entrance. Did Lamb have a car? One not propped up on bricks? It seemed too normal. But if he did, and this was where he parked it, that was it. He'd soon be gone.

Her heart sinking—already sunk—she picked a shop doorway in which to huddle, waiting for the telltale glow of headlights, but none came, and no car hauled into view. Five minutes. Ten. She'd approached the pole at last and stood peering into the dark. There were only half a dozen vehicles on the cracked, sloping ground, which looked like a sinkhole waiting to happen, its only redeeming feature the absence of Lamb, and even this a drawback in the circumstances. The sheet-metal hoarding reached around three sides of the rough square; the fourth was a four-storey wall from which the vanished building had been sheared off, the ghostly outline of a stairwell visible on its battered surface. She'd been monitoring the only exit, which Lamb hadn't used. At the same time, she couldn't lose the feeling that he remained close by, watching her.

At length she'd turned and walked away, back up Aldersgate Street, past Slough House, down into the tube. She felt wrung out by the time she got home to her cramped room in her noisy house; wrung out but simultaneously seething. An hour later, cross-legged on her bed with her laptop, she'd found and ordered the Dorset Naga, and like a spy had tweaked her name when providing an address.

Her view of the landing broke and mended itself. She held her breath: in the kitchen, the fridge door creaked open, then closed. There was a moment's silence, an unusual blessing in Slough House, whose floorboards sigh when they're not in use and groan when they are, and then the figure moved past her doorway again, heading upstairs.

With no sign of glee on her face, in her eyes, Ashley carried on doing nothing, but in her heart there swelled the knowledge that her shark had taken the bait.

"You're looking tired, Claude. All well at home?"

Fifteen love, thought Whelan. And he'd not sat down yet.

"Fine, thanks, Diana. And you?"

"Oh, you know this job. Turn your back five minutes, there's another dagger sticking out of it."

"Don't remind me." The memory of Diana's own dagger still itched between Claude's shoulder blades. Long-term effects included the fact that he needed a visitor's badge to be here in the Park.

Where little had changed. The hub was still the hub, that hive of activity where the boys and girls—as they continued to be known—fiddled about on the margins of the right to privacy, and the air was still one degree too cold, and the season-specific lighting flickered now and then, as it always had done. Though elevated to First Desk status, Diana Taverner still occupied the same office: the one with the glass wall that frosted to opacity at the touch of a button, an effect, he'd once daydreamed, that replicated what you'd get if a bullet passed through it. Back then, he'd imagined a bullet might do Diana harm. These days, he doubted a stake in the heart would dismay her.

She invited him to sit; he sat. They discussed coffee, but briefly: she was busy, and he clearly wasn't worth the time. He made a comment about her recent appearance on *Question Time*; she took it as a compliment. They got down to business.

"Oliver tells me he's reactivated you."

She sounded amused.

"Hardly. I'm simply doing a favour."

"I would have thought all those committees kept you busy enough."

The committees—Whelan sat on several, notably the Pandemic Response body, also known as the Stable Doormen—were largely decorative; inquiries whose findings had been determined before their instigation, but whose existence had been deemed necessary to deflect attention from the issues they considered. The row over the lack of disabled BAME women on the panel examining the suicide rate among those denied Universal Credit, for example, had been raging for six months. But none of that was on his agenda right now, so he simply said, "Be that as it may. Oliver asked, I answered."

"He points, you march. Always the good soldier."

"I'm not sure duty is to be scoffed at. Or that this is the place to do that."

She inclined her head ever so slightly. "As you say. I don't mean to make light of your sense of responsibility. I'm just wondering why it's brought you to me. As I understand it, you're investigating a non-occurrence."

"If nothing's occurred, it shouldn't take long to clear up," said Whelan. "Is your confidence based on knowledge or magical thinking?"

"It's based on, I don't actually know where everybody is at any given time. But that doesn't mean everybody's missing. It just means they're somewhere else."

"Very neat, Diana. Shall we call in one of the philosophy graduates you have out there?" He gestured through the glass wall. "See how long it takes them to demolish your position?"

She sighed. "All right, all right. Sophie de Greer. You mentioned magical thinking, that seems to be her speciality. Lady Macbeth to Number Ten's would-be king hereafter. I get it that Sparrow doesn't want her wandering free as a cloud, but she's only been out of sight a few days. I really don't see what the fuss is about."

"But you've given it some thought."

She dismissed that notion without so much as a gesture. "Obviously, after your call, I had someone do background. You'll remember Josie? I think she was one of your favourites."

"I tried not to have favourites. It didn't make for a comfortable working environment." He shifted in his seat. "As for fuss, well. De Greer's involved in discussions, in policy talks, with very senior—"

"Unelected."

"—advisers to HMG. It's hardly surprising her disappearance has caused alarm bells to ring."

"She might simply have gone on holiday."

"She doesn't appear to have left the country."

"So? She's a Swiss citizen. Being here's a holiday. Has her visa expired?"

"No."

"Well, then. As far as I'm aware, and that's quite some distance, here in the UK we're not currently required to inform the authorities of our whereabouts on a daily basis. Since she's not subject to a self-isolation order, Dr. de Greer could be tramping round the Lake District, halfway up Snowdonia or being eaten alive by Highland midges. It's not actually any of our business."

"No, not until I was asked by Oliver Nash to investigate her whereabouts. At which point, it became our business."

"Not to pull rank, Claude, but there's a gap between 'your' and 'our.' You haven't been behind a desk in this building for some while."

"And yet Nash has the authority to, what was your word? Reactivate me."

"Don't get carried away. That's a visitor's badge, not a sheriff's star. Look, whatever's going on, it'll turn out to be dirty politics. That's how these people operate. De Greer's a troublemaker. I don't know what it says on her website, but that's what she specialises in. Making trouble."

"Superforecaster is the technical term."

"Does that sound like a job title to you? Last time we had one of those in Number Ten, they turned out to be even weirder than the advert asked for. Some Nazi-leaning incel pipsqueak. You'd think their vetting procedures would have tightened up."

Whelan could see this conversation getting away from him, and decided to reel it in. He said, "The word waterproof has been mentioned."

"... Waterproof?"

"I'm sure you recall the protocol."

Diana affected to pretend to remember. So many protocols, so long behind the wheel. "That's ancient history."

"A lot of things are fairly old, but that doesn't mean they're not still in use. Clocks? Kettles?"

"Retirement has made you skittish. Who on earth raised that rabbit? You're not telling me it was Oliver?"

Whelan gave her his best poker face.

"No, you're not telling me it was anyone. But we both know Oliver has loose lips, whether he's stuffing things past them or blurting things out. So it all comes down to whoever he's been talking to recently, doesn't it?"

He thought: He could just sit here without saying another word. There was every chance the conversation would continue without him.

The first time he'd heard of the protocol had been in this room, several years ago. Diana had been his guide to the underworld in those days, his first as First Desk. His ascent to the role had taken an unconventional route, and he was almost as much a stranger to the Park as any of those gentle souls who took the visitors' trip round the upstairs regions, where they were shown the acceptable side of the Service: its hallways and hatracks; the discreet busts in their nooks; the display cases of Cold War knick-knackery—radio transmitters in bootheels and the like. Oohs and Aahs were the appropriate response. A thin-lipped nod was the best Claude could muster as Diana had revealed the darker aspects to the role he'd been assigned; if not actually handing him the chalice—that had been a decision taken over her head—at least pointing out how battered and stained it was; how he should take care drinking from it if he didn't want a cut lip. His induction into the dangerous edge of things. His teacher among the dangers awaiting him, though he hadn't known that then.

Waterproof, he learned, had been briefly in use years earlier, in the wake of various events whose anniversaries were still marked by minutes of public silence. During that period, the Service had acquired a broad remit for dealing with those suspected of involvement in terrorist attacks. Public trials— "You won't need me to tell you," she'd told him—were preferred for those likely to be found guilty, while the more circumstantially involved received more circumspect treatment. Waterproof, in a word. A form of anonymised rendition. This wasn't about returning bad actors to the wings; it was about removing them from the cast list altogether. Records were sealed. Names erased. And the subjects never saw daylight again. Even today they'd be alive somewhere, some of them, living out what was left of their span in unwindowed cells in black prisons in eastern Europe. Cells the size of phone booths.

"A gateway drug to capitalism," Diana had told him. "All those former Soviet states leasing out their gulags to the west. A handy dumping ground for our undesirables."

And this wasn't still in use—not something he'd be expected to implement? Or defend, god help him?

No, the protocol had been consigned to the NH file. *Never Happened.* The most Whelan had to do was launch an inquiry that would ensure that no current Upper Desk need fear this particular chicken coming to roost in any of their drawers.

This much at least Whelan had recognised. London Rules. *Cover your arse.*

All of which was long in the past, but he had no doubt Diana's recollection was as sharp as his own, an intuition she now confirmed. "Well, whoever he's been talking to, he's barking at the wrong dog. There was a commission, remember? Your doing. 'No evidence that such protocol was ever utilised.' Not a finding likely to be overturned, not while the report itself is still in heavy wrappers."

Meaning, Whelan knew, that it was subject to the thirty-year rule.

He said, and was self-consciously mild of tone in doing so: "But we both know that Waterproof was used."

"Not during my tenure. But are you about to make a confession? Josie's somewhere about, if we need a witness."

The idea that he might have implemented something like Waterproof without Diana having been aware of it was almost amusing.

His poker face clearly wasn't doing its job. Diana shook her head. "Claude, whatever Oliver's playing at, or whatever he's been instructed to look like he's playing at, it's mischief-making, that's all. Waterproof's history, it's less than history. Remember the NH file? And before that, before it never happened, it was Charles Partner's brainchild, and only Dame Ingrid ever made full use of it. Charles, of course, is unavailable for comment. Ingrid's in North Carolina. Rumour has it she's taken up quilting. So if you're planning on hauling her before a truth and reconciliation committee, you'd better get a wiggle on, because I assume she's at death's door. No one would take up quilting if they expected to be doing it for long."

"I'm not sure the budget will sustain a long-distance trip."

"Welcome to my world. I have to go on bended knee if I want the shredder serviced." She mock-grimaced. "You should be thankful you didn't need coffee. We're buying a supermarket-brand, in bulk."

Whelan said, "None of which gets us nearer the point at issue, which is the whereabouts of Dr. de Greer. I'm operating on goodwill, obviously, but bear in mind it's a goodwill requested by Oliver. And one of the suggestions he's made is that I verify there's been no contact between the Service and Dr. de Greer during the time she's been stationed in London."

"Of course. Perhaps we could find you an office? You could hold court while I have my staff wade through half a year's worth of comms data on the off-chance we'll turn up something that helps. It might get in the way of any actual work, but listen, what's national security compared to your convenience?"

"Diana—"

"Or I could simply reiterate what I've already said. Wherever the woman's got to, it has nothing to do with us. Think about it. Why would the Service be involved? She's a Swiss citizen, haven't they got their own way of dealing with their misshapes? Dip her in chocolate and wrap her in foil or whatever. Because all this, this favour Oliver's got you doing, it's pretty clear he's having his leash tugged by Number Ten, by which I mean

Anthony Sparrow. Who presumably has de Greer hidden in his basement while he sets the dogs on us. Waterproof's his way in, that's all. The leverage he hopes to bring the walls down with, so he can walk in and take charge. But not while I'm First Desk, Claude. Maybe you could let Oliver know? And I think that brings this meeting to a close."

She could, he knew, breathe fire, and there was a moment there when she came pretty close. *But not while I'm First Desk, Claude.* There was a reason she'd always considered herself right for this job, and watching her seethe in her office, it was hard to deny she made a convincing argument. But Whelan, even while marking this, was noticing something else: that he didn't much care. He had his own problems. While watching Diana Taverner work her way towards fury might once have had him checking the exits, right now, he felt little more than an interested detachment. And the continuing resolve to do what he'd come here to do.

He said, "Glad you've got that off your chest. Could we get down to practicalities? I think phone records to start with. Let's assume she had actual numbers to ring rather than just the switchboard. So we'll begin on the hub and move out from there." He smiled. "Just official lines for now, but I'm not ruling out checking personal mobiles."

Diana studied him for a long moment, an unfamiliar glint in her eye. She looked like her lunch had just moved. But that went, and she spoke again. "All right. We'll do it your way. But you're not getting an office. You can wait in Briefing Two, I think that's free. I'll have someone bring you the paperwork once we've run a search."

"On a disk, if you don't mind." Whelan was maintaining that smile: it was beginning to feel painted on. "More searchable."

He wasn't so detached he didn't wonder if he'd gone a little far there, but Diana didn't even twitch. "As you say."

Whelan remembered full well where Briefing Two was, but

even so he remained seated while Diana sent for someone to escort him. He spent the interval running the scoring in his head, and was pretty sure Diana had been out in front for most of the conversation. But was equally confident he'd won the only point that counted: the one that finished the match.

There was a game you could play, if you were into childish shit. Roddy wasn't—a surefire way to tell a busy dude from a lightweight: no time for pissing about—but he'd heard the others at it, and what you did was, you saw a yellow car, and you mentioned it. End of. It beggared belief, what entertained the hard of thought.

Went without saying, though, that if Roddy cared, he'd be world-beating—it never happened that he saw a car without noticing what colour it was. No wonder the others never asked him to play.

Anyway, the reason that came to mind was, he'd spent half the day staring at images of cars; video footage of the front of the Russian Embassy—Bayswater Road, as if he'd needed telling. There'd been a steady stream of arrivals: catering for the reception, plus taxis and limos delivering early guests, shuttled from airports with cases and suit carriers. He captured screenshots, and sent them to Louisa to run through face-recog. His own program was faster and better, but she didn't know that, and it would give her an excuse to come and hang out with him.

"Black car," he murmured, as another visitor arrived.

The footage was black and white, but with cabs you could just tell.

The new arrival didn't pause to admire the place before going in, which maybe meant he knew it already. He had no luggage; just a small carrier bag from Harrods. And something about the way he got out of the cab suggested he was also familiar with the cameras trained on the entrance: the Service coverage—which Roddy was piggybacking; technically not a feature he had access to, but the word "technically" applied only to those for whom tech itself was a barrier—had its blind spots, and this guy was occupying them like a dancer working the limelight. The best screengrab Roddy could manage was a straight-on back-of-the-head. He popped it down to Louisa anyway, so nobody could say he wasn't covering all the angles.

A thing about all this work, though; he still hadn't made that call yet. *Any woman desperate enough to dress up as a cartoon character* . . . Anyone else, it would look like avoidance, but here was the Rodster's code: Chicks can wait. This stuff—he was basically spying on the Russians, dude—this stuff took priority.

Another taxi went past. "Black car," he said again. Man, this game was beyond average.

A draught snaked through a gap in the cardboard mosaic over the window, and he sat back in his chair. Sheesh—that thing with the window. Catherine Standish had not been pleased. But that was improv for you: you relied on the tools at hand. A broom wasn't combat-quality—you needed your actual staff to pull off the trickier moves. So when you were caught up in the moment and just grabbed what was nearest, well, windows were going to get broken. What was he supposed to do about it? Until they installed a dojo on the premises he was basically making do, and didn't see why he should take a bollocking simply for keeping himself battle-fit.

Speaking of which, a man needs to eat. He lunched off half a tube of barbecue-flavoured Pringles and a chunky KitKat, and was licking the wrapper when Louisa came in clutching a stack of printouts.

"Thanks for the extra work. Really, I've not enough to do without having a couple of dozen faces to run through a clapped-out recognition program. Can't you do it yourself?"

"I'm doing the actual surveillance."

"Oh, yeah, forgot. Men don't multitask." She glanced at her notes. "Okay, so. Eleven no matches of any kind. Seven around eighty per cent sure, all the possibles being middle-ranking business types with no security flags. Three tripped warning bells, they're probably FSB. That foursome who turned up in a van? They're a string quartet from Bath. The woman with the squint is a quite well-regarded poet, and you should let Lamb know that, because I suspect Lamb's really interested in poetry. As for the mystery man, and he's my favourite, the one you only got the back of the head of? I've got slightly more than twenty-three hundred possible matches." She slapped the notes down on his desk. "See, the thing is, you need a recognisable characteristic or two before the program does its stuff. Just having a head does not count."

"He was avoiding the cameras."

"You think?"

"It's pretty obv—"

"Don't send any more. It's boring, and the program keeps freezing."

Lech wandered in. "This the Russian Embassy gig?"

"Yeah, wonderboy here had me putting names to faces."

"I'd have told wonderboy to get stuffed." He noted the Pringles tube and the crumpled chocolate wrapper. "Which he seems to have done anyway."

"Sod off, hashtag features."

"That was my plan," said Louisa. "But Lamb wanted a list."

"He always wants lists. I think he's smoking them." Lech glanced at the cardboard shroud around the window by his desk, and said to Roddy, "I see you've installed air-con."

"Yeah, well, I see you've installed . . ."

They waited.

". . . Stupid marks on your face."

"I can't work out," said Louisa, "whether he's better at repartee or driving."

Recalling Roddy's driving talents, Lech rubbed a bruise or two before picking up the topmost of Louisa's printouts. "They have these three or four times a year," he said. "They bring in some lecturer from the homeland, who bores the locals rigid for a couple of hours, then everyone gets pissed. Taverner has half the hub watching the footage in case any celebrities show."

"Does that ever happen?"

"Molly Doran got excited once. Some living waxwork turned up, she said he'd debriefed Philby back in the day."

"She's collecting the set. One hundred spooks you must see before you die."

"Before they die, more like."

Roddy said, "You think that's Lamb's plan?"

They looked at him.

He said, "All these old spooks." He raised one eyebrow, or thought he did. He was actually raising both. "You think Lamb's bumping them off?"

Louisa approached Roddy's desk, leaned across it and stage-whispered into his ear. "You're not supposed to know about that."

". . . Okay."

"Best to pretend you never said it. You with me, Rodster?"

". . . I'm with you."

She patted his cheek softly. "Smart boy."

". . . Uh, Louisa?"

"What?"

He nodded at the nearest monitor. "Black car."

Louisa looked at the screen, looked at Roddy, looked back at the screen, and then looked at Roddy again. "Keep up the good work," she told him, and left the office, followed by Lech.

Home again, Whelan found the landline handset winking at him, but when he checked it was a cold caller, concerned about his financial arrangements. It was nice that someone cared. He pressed delete anyway.

After a protracted vigil in Briefing Two—an antiseptic chamber whose chief feature was the number of available sockets: they studded the walls, and lurked beneath little trapdoors in the floor—he'd been startled by the almost noiseless appearance of, inevitably, Josie-from-the-hub. *I tried not to have favourites. It didn't make for a comfortable working environment.* He knew all the horror stories about male bosses and their PAs but it hadn't been like that; he'd been aware Josie had a soft spot for him, but he'd never acted upon it. He was old enough to be her . . . Not that that mattered. He'd been, still was, married.

"Lord, Josie, my dear, how are you—"

And then that excruciating moment when he'd leaned for a hug, and she'd pulled back to the same degree.

"Of course, no, sorry sorry sorry—"

It would have been better without the apology. That way, they could both have pretended the moment had never happened.

Recovery was achieved in a politely brittle manner: It was good to see him, how had he been, how was retirement? He'd attempted refutation—not *retirement*, he wasn't *that* old, thanks, Josie, not quite yet—but was merely compounding his error. She smiled efficiently and handed him a love token. No she didn't: she handed him an oddly fun-coloured thing, bright pink. A thumb drive.

"The phone records? A bit raw, I'm afraid, but Diana said you were in a hurry?"

"Oh yes, very much, thanks. I'm sure I'll make sense of them."

Whether he would or wouldn't being beside the point by then. All he wanted was to get out of the building.

He signed for the thumb drive while Josie recited some boilerplate about not copying or transferring the enclosed material, and swore on his neverborn children that it would be returned upon completion of his investigation: a "standard security measure," though he wondered whether it wasn't also budget-driven. His visitor's lanyard, too, she needed back. She walked him up the stairs, and he felt like an inconvenient neighbour, or barely tolerated uncle. One you'd not seat next to your daughter, if you all ended up in the same taxi.

Old, yes, god. Replacing the receiver he said, aloud, "I'm sorry, Claire," and his wife's name made itself at home; busied itself in plumping up cushions and straightening the magazines on the coffee table before disappearing into the airy stillness of the house.

He made a pot of tea and a butterless sandwich—he'd forgotten to take a new packet from the fridge. One of a hundred small hurdles to trip over, daily. But the tea was fine. Semi-refreshed, he reached for his laptop and plugged the new drive in to discover that it contained two hundred and seventeen files, a number of them very large. It was impossible not to sigh. Had he really promised Nash he would see this through? Or had he simply agreed to poke around a little, and see if anything stirred?

Nothing was stirring on his laptop, that was for sure. When he opened the largest file, it unrolled a huge column of numbers, dates, times: the length of calls made to separate numbers at the Park, and the numbers from which they had originated. Did he really think studying this was going to provide any solutions? He felt like a patsy in a fairy tale, one who's just been tasked with matching up a cellarful of odd buttons, and closed the file before the numbers sucked him in. Then poured more tea, and leaned back and closed his eyes.

He thought: Diana thinks, or wants me to think she thinks, that I'm really looking into Waterproof and not de Greer. Which means she either wants me to do that, because she doesn't want me looking into de Greer, or she doesn't want me to do that and is only letting me think she thinks that's what I'm doing in order to make me think she doesn't care if it is. So she either wants me not to look into Waterproof, or wants me not to look into de Greer.

It was good to have clarity.

He pondered for some moments, and then checked the material Nash had forwarded. The details included Dr. Sophie de Greer's mobile number; the phone she hadn't used since she'd disappeared, and from which she'd removed the battery, or otherwise rendered untraceable. This he keyed into a search box he then applied to the fun-coloured memory stick. It took little more than two seconds.

One result.

Whelan hadn't been expecting this. Taverner's lack of resistance to his having these records had strongly suggested they would contain nothing of interest; did that mean she had a particular desire that he see the one hit they contained? She must know it was there; she'd never have approved handover of the files without first ascertaining what they'd tell him. Unless—and here was a novel idea—unless she'd been telling the truth, and had no interest in de Greer and no involvement in her disappearance. Whelan could feel his skull tightening. This was what Spook Street did to you. You stepped onto its pavements and the world instantly became unsure of itself; its depths an illusion, its shallows treacherous. All of it set dressing, apart from the bits that weren't, designed to make you think yourself in circles and never stand straight again.

The files had come with no key attached; no explanation of which number dialled sat on which desk. All he had was the number de Greer had called: a landline, out of sequence with most others on the list. More significant was the timing. The call had been placed on the afternoon of the day de Greer disappeared, which meant that any possibility that the two events were unconnected faded like a forgotten flavour, because the Park was the Park, and coincidence was outlawed within its precincts. The Park was where plots were hatched and nurtured and set loose from their cages, and no one knew this better than him.

He had the sense of standing by a long-grassed meadow, aware that some of the rippling on its surface was made by the wind; the rest by small creatures scurrying about out of sight.

The clock's ticking had grown louder, as good an indication as any of time passing. He attempted to put an end to this by arriving at a decision: the best way of finding whose phone de Greer had rung was calling it, so he called it. It took an unconscionable time to be answered, but when it was Whelan found himself holding his breath, and once he'd disconnected without speaking, he remained motionless for some while. It was as if he had just stepped into that long-grassed meadow. It was as if the rippling were heading in his direction, and he would soon feel either a soft breeze whispering past him, or some sharp-toothed rodents sawing at his legs.

In this last brief heatwave of the year, which faded every evening with the dimming of the day, London had dragged itself back to normal, setting the memory of two miserable years aside, and letting its age-old hallmarks reappear. So the river slowed to a crawl as the day departed, just as it always had, and the skies purpled in the distance, soothing the edges of office buildings. Sounds seemed softer: the sighs and exhalations of weary cars, and the buzzing of swarms of bicycles steered by skintight black-and-yellow riders, mere whispers compared to the frantic careering of rush hour, though the helicopters shredding the air overhead, ferrying important people to important places, were as angry as ever. Lower down, in the green spaces, trees soughed and whistled, and runners tapped to the pavements' beat in brutally expensive footwear; prams trundled on boardwalks by the lakes, wheelchairs rattled over paving stones, and music was everywhere, like mist; leaking from doorways, broadcast from speakers strapped to couriers' handlebars, and performed with huge sincerity and varying degrees of talent by buskers: someone, somewhere, was playing a cello while coins splashed into its case. Underneath this music, the liquid *lub-dub* that was London's heartbeat could be heard once more: the pouring of pints and glasses of wine; the sloshing of water in the bottles everyone carried; the streaming of piss into toilets and urinals, followed by the flushings of cisterns that sent it cascading into sewers, their pipes laid along the beds of forgotten rivers, which once lapped to the same tidal pull that amplifies the Thames. And most constant of all, visible everywhere if you knew where to look—in the building sites, in the long black cars, in the designer suits and jewelled throats, in wristwatches and cuf-flinks, tattoo parlours and nailbars, in a million glittering windows and a billion slot machines—the tumbling wet slap of money being laundered, over and over again.

Funny how her thoughts dragged her that way, as she was driven to the Russian embassy on Bayswater Road.

Diana had a nine o'clock appointment with the PM; their weekly meeting was a fixture but its timing varied, principally—she suspected—to provide him with a ready-made alibi should his domestic circumstances demand. Even without that clouding her evening, the embassy reception was one she'd regretfully declined some weeks previously, on the unstated ground that no one in their right mind wanted to spend a late September evening in the company of gangster-state diplomats, no matter how high-end the catering. But that afternoon's catch-up in the hub's screening room had turned, if not the world, at least the day upside down.

It had started ordinarily enough, the format the usual: Diana at the head of the long table, facing the video wall; her theme, as ever, *Impress me*. By her side, Josie—just back from delivering to Claude Whelan the data he'd wanted; she wasn't quite Oscar material, Josie, but she had her moments—and lining the table two rows of boys and girls, some of them hub, others from Ops; the former somewhat tense, as if the occasion kindled memories of seminars with a particularly tetchy tutor; the latter more pleased with themselves, a satisfaction evident in the amount of space they took up: elbows well apart when leaning forward, legs the same when they pushed their chairs back. Ops, their stances read, was rock and roll. Those on the hub might fancy themselves the brains of the outfit, but the streets were where doors were kicked down. The boys and girls from Ops didn't do the kicking themselves (you had Ops and then you had Muscle, a department which didn't actually go by that name but probably should), but if it turned out in the course of the meeting that any doors needed opening suddenly, the Ops guys were confident nobody would be looking at the hub sissies to take first go.

It wasn't always this combative. Well, it was, but it wasn't always so blatant. Meetings, though, brought out the worst.

The first half hour took a little less than twice that long, which was par for the course. There was a presentation (hub) on the importance of changing passwords at least once a month, a theme which rolled round with the regularity of a Take That farewell tour, and generated as much interest; and a head-cam recording (Ops) of a takedown of a suspected sleeper cell operating out of a two-bed flat in Brighton. This had proved a false lead—the "cell" was in fact a bridge school made up of off-duty bus drivers—but the process involved in storming the premises and scaring the shit out of everyone was textbook, and the subsequent night out worth a twenty-second rehash before Taverner cleared her throat and silence prevailed.

Then Josie wiped the video, and projected onto the wall images of those attending the reception at the Russian embassy that evening.

This too was run-of-the-mill, but had involved legwork, as there were attendees from Mother R rolling up to sample the canapés, so those from Ops responsible for babysitting the incomers looked suitably important, while the boys and girls from the hub prepared to chip in with background detail, the kind of small-print clarifications often overlooked by those wearing reinforced boots. Diana watched and listened while the guest list was toothcombed for anomalies, none of which arose from among the usual liberally inclined scientists, left-leaning playwrights and anything-for-a-sausage-roll poets;

while minor staff changes at the embassy were noted, and local firms catering the evening given a onceover; and while those appointed to monitor real-time coverage of proceedings were namechecked and offered the ritual handclap of relief by those not so appointed, and so on and so very much forth until about forty minutes in, when what had been a by-the-numbers recital went—a breathless Josie later related to non-attenders—from snore-fest to shitstorm in nothing flat, Gregory Ronovitch being the culprit.

Gregory Ronovitch, not previously sighted in this parish, was a visiting academic, Moscow-gowned, come to deliver a lecture entitled "*Battleship Potemkin*: An iconography re-examined." The photo accompanying his bare-boned CV—an action shot of Gregory alighting from a car on the embassy's drive, his welcoming committee limited to one bored security guard—revealed a middle-aged nobody with neat beard and centre parting. He wore sunglasses, true, but so did everyone else, so the detail wasn't cast-iron proof of mafia connections. Which meant that wasn't the reason Diana Taverner got to her feet, causing all ambient noise in the room—the taking of notes and wrangling of phones—to cease immediately. When Taverner got to her feet, a meeting was over. Either that or it had just become urgent, without anyone else noticing.

When she spoke, her voice was icy calm. It was said of Diana that she'd been known to frost the glass wall in her office without recourse to the button, a quip popular among those who hadn't been anywhere near when she was demonstrating its accuracy.

"Why the different angle?"

Nobody understood the question.

"It's straightforward enough. The other arrivals were shot from whatever direction it was, was it east? Which means this was taken from the west. Why so?"

There was a shuffling of paper, and somebody said, "Ah, this subject, Gregory Ronovitch? He wasn't caught full-face by the Service hardware. This was harvested from local security coverage."

"He wasn't caught full-face by the Service hardware," Diana repeated. "Almost as if he knew how to avoid that." Her eyes were fixed on the image on the wall. "Well, then. Someone. Anyone. Care to fill in the blanks on Mr. Ronovitch?"

Someone, anyone, but definitely from Ops, said, "Er, *Battleship Potemkin* . . . He's some kind of film critic, right?"

Josie, who'd attended more of these meetings than anyone else present, Diana excepted, sent up a decoy balloon. "He was a late addition, but I'll have a profile worked up before—"

But it was too little, too late. "No, really, don't. Let's just workshop it, shall we? Who's been babysitting, let's call him Greg?"

A young man at the back of the room raised an unhappy hand.

"And you're . . . ?"

The young man said, "Dean. Pete Dean."

"Well, Pete Dean, run us through Greg's movements since he hit town."

"Ah, he first arrived at the embassy yesterday morning—"

"From where?"

". . . The airport?"

"You're asking?"

"From the airport, ma'am. That would be Heathrow."

"You're sure about that."

"That's where the Moscow flight comes in—"

"And you had eyes on him as he waltzed through Arrivals."

"Ah . . . No, ma'am."

"And why's that?"

"Because there's only one of me? And I was assigned to three attendees?"

The clock on the wall was silent: it swallowed seconds, minutes, hours without chewing. But everyone present could hear a crocodile *tick tock* while waiting for Diana's response.

Which was slow in coming, but at least was fair. "All right," she said. "So you *assume* a Heathrow arrival. And I assume I'll have the CCTV footage of that waiting in my office before I get back there. And I further assume that the timings will indicate that he went from airport to embassy gate with no intervening outings. When did he arrive?"

"Ah, 11:45?"

"Mr. Dean, you seem to think you're the one asking questions. I promise you, you're not."

"11:45."

"Movements the rest of yesterday?"

A brief, panicky look at inadequate notes. "He remained in the embassy all afternoon, then was driven to his hotel, alone, just before seven."

"I'll make up the background detail, shall I?"

"Ah, the Grosvenor, ma'am. He ate in the dining room, again alone, then retired to his room. This morning he ate breakfast at the hotel, then made a shopping trip. West End. I, ah, have a list . . ."

"Highlights?"

"He spent two hours in Harrods."

"No prizes for originality. There's footage?"

"Yes."

"Josie?"

"Cueing it now," said Josie, and the viewing wall changed as she dabbed at her keyboard, now showing Gregory Ronovitch in the men's department at Harrods, holding two ties, visibly deciding between the two. If he'd chosen to pose for Pete Dean's study, he couldn't have adopted a more useful stance; a neutral observer would have assumed Dean was being asked his opinion.

"Here's another question," said Diana to the luckless Op. "Do you think there's a chance Gregory was aware of your presence in Harrods?"

"Ah . . ."

"In your own time."

"I didn't think so then."

"And now?"

"Now, yes. It looks like he clocked me."

"And following his shopping trip?"

"That first picture was him arriving at the embassy ninety minutes ago. Which was when I handed over to—"

"It doesn't matter."

Still on her feet, Diana approached the image on the wall so that it shimmered across her own head and shoulders. She looked out at the room as if she too had just been transported to Harrods, and was choosing a tie. Gregory Ronovitch's head was next to her own, almost touching, and much larger. The two of them stared out at Pete Dean taking the picture then, and at everyone else looking at it now, as if no time had passed between the two moments. Nobody spoke. The silence held for a quarter of a minute.

She said, "Someone. Please. Put me out of my misery."

It was Josie who got there first. "Oh my god."

"Yes, indeed," said Diana. "Anyone else?" She scanned the room. "Imagine it's important. Imagine you work for the intelligence service."

When realisation swept round the table it did so by morphic resonance, alighting on all present one after the other. Two heartbeats earlier, no one bar Josie had known what had triggered Lady Di. Now everyone did; the more foolish among them with mounting excitement, the rest with a sense of dread. Ops looked at hub and hub looked at Ops, and both wondered what might lie on the other side of the door Diana had just kicked down.

Someone, anyone, spoke. "He's grown a beard."

"He's grown a beard," Diana repeated flatly. "He's grown. A. Beard. Well. If I'd known we'd be dealing with Dick Emery, I'd have thrown in the towel long ago."

"But . . ."

"But yes, what?"

The speaker couldn't follow through. "He looks different. That's all."

He did, but not enough that it should have taken them this long. Diana Taverner herself had never set eyes on the man, but she'd studied the same footage they all had, had grown familiar with the way he moved, with the hand gestures, with the rubbing of the—admittedly clean-shaven—chin. There'd even been, for a while, a photo pinned up in the hub's breakout area; a rather self-conscious elevation of the man to celebrity status. The picture had shown him receiving a medal from the Gay Hussar himself, and wearing the expression most serving officers wore when posing alongside Putin, one adopted following instructions not to make eye contact, or sudden movements.

The silence in the room, now knowledgeable rather than ignorant, wasn't any more comfortable than it had been.

"So," said Diana at last. "How worried should we be, do you think?"

No one dared answer.

"Let me put it another way," she said. "Vassily Rasnokov, First Desk of the Russian secret service, has been in town since yesterday morning, and it's only just come to our attention. Gosh, do you think he's been up to anything we should know about?"

Mostly, Catherine Standish viewed her history as scenes from a flickery, black-and-white world, and knew that her current sober colours were the real thing: a little muted, several rinses short of dazzling, but true nonetheless. She moved among washed-out reds and faded blues, the greys and browns of city streets, but this was better than the monochrome existence of the drunk, who is always only one thing or the other. But there were moments, still, when she suspected that she had this the wrong way round, and that her alcoholic years were brighter, more Technicolor, than anything she knew today. Once, her daily palette had included deep dark reds and crystal whites, smokey ambers and velvety golds, each the colour of a curtain waiting to be drawn. Together, they made today's rainbows watery and thin. Made the noises from bars and public houses, the lights of off-licence windows, a welcome mat.

When she had such thoughts, she was careful not to chase them away too quickly—that would be to underline their attraction—but subject them to a quietly rigorous examination. These were the colours of blood and vomit, of false friendship and foul laughter. Blackouts were called blackouts for a reason. White nights were mental blizzards in which travellers got lost. Catherine might not be in Kansas anymore—or perhaps she was not in Oz—but wherever it was she wasn't, she was at least home. And when she wasn't home she was in Slough House, or, as now, moving from one to the other, picking her way past the noises from bars and public houses, between the lights of off-licence windows. There were other premises too, innocent ones, but they never called out to her as she passed.

Though someone did.

"Ms. Standish?"

She turned.

It was a middle-aged man, a little shorter than Catherine, with receding hair and glasses; pleasant looking—mild was the word that came to mind—wearing a fawn-coloured raincoat. There was an odd disconnect: she knew him, she did not know him. Then the name arrived. This was Claude Whelan, one-time First Desk at Regent's Park. She had once watched him descend a flight of stairs. But they'd never stood face-to-face, had never exchanged words. If he was interrupting her journey home, accosting her on a pavement, it wasn't because she was an old acquaintance glimpsed in passing.

He confirmed his name. Then said, "I didn't mean to startle you."

"But you did mean to follow me."

"I'm sorry. No harm was intended. But I need to talk to you, outside your office."

"Is this a work issue, Mr. Whelan?"

"It's connected."

"Because I've finished for the day. And unless I missed something, you've finished for your career."

He acknowledged this with a nod. "It's something I've been asked to look into. Unofficial, but . . ."

"But official all the same."

"Yes."

"And you don't want to encounter Jackson Lamb while pursuing it."

He paused, and then said, "Not quite yet, no."

She wondered if this were where it began, the inevitable unravelling. Not her own, but Lamb's—sooner or later, it was bound to happen; there'd be a panel of inquiry, or a lynch mob. But it didn't seem likely that Claude Whelan would be first in line with a pitchfork. It had been said of him, she remembered, that he was too meek to hang onto First Desk long; that the alligators were circling before his feet were on the floor.

"I'm on my way home," she told him.

"It won't take long."

"And it's turning cold."

"There's a place up ahead. Please. It won't take long, and it is important."

"And if I'd rather not?"

But he simply smiled, and said again, "Please."

The place up ahead, which she'd already known about, was a bar. Big glass windows; socially distanced tables. The sign on the door declared a thirty-patron maximum, but that was wishful thinking; the room was all but empty. Whelan held the door, and she walked in. How long since she had been in a bar? If she put her mind to it, she could perform the mathematics. All those years and months, all those days. They stretched a huge distance in one direction; in the other, they might crash into a wall any moment.

A waitress, wearing a visor, was hovering before they were seated.

"I don't know about you, but I'm ready for a G&T," Whelan said.

If I ever drink again, it will be like this. No special reason, no special occasion. Someone will offer me a drink, and I will ask for a glass of wine. When I drink again, it will be like this.

Not right now, though.

"Just water."

"Still or sparkling?" The waitress asked.

"Sparkling. Thank you."

"Ice and a—"

"Yes."

Whelan gave the waitress his full attention while placing his order, and Catherine remembered what else had been said about him: that while he had made much of his happy marriage, he'd had a roving eye. Something of a wandering car, too. A close encounter with an anti-kerb crawling initiative might have derailed him before those alligators had their boots on if he hadn't managed to quash the police report, or mostly quash it. Lamb had scraped what was left together and used the information to ensure that, whatever else he did while First Desk, Whelan never messed with Slough House.

At least some of that was presumably on Whelan's mind as they waited for their drinks, but he kept a tight lid on it, and in place of any more obvious conversational gambit recited a phone number.

When it became clear that he expected a response, she said, "That's Lamb's phone."

"I know. On his own desk?"

"Where else?" she said, though it was a reasonable question. Had the phone annoyed Lamb, which it could easily have done by, say, ringing, there was no telling where it might have ended up.

"What I mean is," he said, "if that phone rings, he'll be the one who answers it, yes? Not you."

"In general."

"Why only in general?"

"It's not complicated. The phone is on his desk. Sometimes it rings. He'll either answer it or not, depending on what mood he's in, and whether he's even there. If he's out and it rings and I hear it, I'll answer it. If I get there in time." It felt a little like explaining how stairs work. "I think that covers everything."

"There was a call on Monday afternoon," Whelan said. "To that number. At five forty-six. Did Lamb answer it himself?"

Catherine's mind fed off static for a moment, as anyone's would. "I imagine so," she said. "I didn't, if that's what you're asking."

"The call was from a Dr. Sophie de Greer."

"Am I supposed to recognise the name?"

"She's a government adviser, a Downing Street, ah . . ."

"Flunkey?"

Whelan blinked. He said, "That's the last phone call she's known to have made. Dr. de Greer hasn't been seen since."

Catherine lifted her glass to her mouth, felt the slice of lemon brush her upper lip. The sensation didn't take her back, exactly, but it suggested that the door was always open. She looked around. Bars had not changed since they'd been her daily backdrop; or, more likely, they had changed and changed back again. The theme of this particular establishment was industrial chic, or possibly warehouse glamour. The furniture was solid and blocky, bulbs hung from the ceiling in metal bowls, and the visible pipework followed a schematic no sane plumber would have devised. The walls these pipes hung on were distressed, or that was the word whoever was responsible no doubt used. Call that distressed? she wanted to ask. I work between walls that make these look ecstatic. The glass in her hand felt heavy, but held only water. If she was ever going to fall, when the day came that she fell, it wouldn't be with a Claude Whelan. Nor even with the Claude Whelan.

"I'm wondering if there's any light you can cast on this for me."

"You'd have to speak to Lamb."

"I intend to. But not before I've done a little background."

"I'm afraid I can't offer any. I didn't answer her call, and I've no idea what it was about." She put the glass down. "Sorry not to be of more help. But if we're finished . . ."

"Not quite." He also placed his glass on the table, and spent a moment adjusting its position according to some quiet whimsy of his own. He'd started his career over the river, she reminded herself, among the weasels, who dealt in data rather than human intelligence, and as a result were considered tricky when it came to social interaction. Whelan had been an exception: on his first day at the Park he'd set the Queens of the Database all atizzy by wearing open-necked shirt and chinos. But it was as well to remember that you could deck a weasel out in tennis whites, he'd still be a weasel.

He said, "You were Charles Partner's PA before transferring to Slough House, am I right?"

People didn't ask if they were right without knowing they were. She gave a single nod, and he went on:

"While Partner was in office he instigated a protocol. An illegal one."

"I wasn't privy to all that went on behind Charles's door."

"I thought you were close."

"So did I."

He waited, but Catherine had nothing to add.

"The protocol was called Waterproof. Does that ring bells?"

"Well, it's not an unfamiliar word. But I don't recall encountering it professionally."

"It involved disappearances."

That made sense. Much of her Service career had involved disappearances of one sort or another.

"There's been a suggestion that the protocol is still in use," said Whelan.

"I see," Catherine said. "So you think this—de Greer?"

"De Greer."

"You think this de Greer woman has been the subject of an historic, not to mention illegal, Service protocol? Based on a phone call she apparently made to Slough House?"

"It's a line of enquiry."

"For her sake, I hope you have others. Because anything on the scale you're suggesting requires organisation and resources. We have a fridge whose door won't close properly. Does that sound like we fit the bill?"

"It sounds like that's the way someone wants you to look. Slough House may be a damp and draughty teardown, but it's outlasted sturdier institutions. Not to mention my career, as you're well aware." He rested a finger on the rim of his glass. "Lamb and Taverner saw to that between them. In fact, any time Taverner wants a dirty deed done, it seems to me it's Lamb she turns to. And you know what they say about old spooks like Lamb. The past's their playbook. Partner was his mentor, don't forget. So yes, adapting one of his historical— illegal—schemes, that sounds right up his alley."

Or his passage even, was Catherine's involuntary thought, as a street sign not far from here came to mind. That "Lamb's Passage" seemed a vulgarity was an occupational hazard, one she wondered if the other slow horses suffered from: a Lamb-style Tourette's, brought on by proximity. Face masks no protection.

She said, "I won't pretend to have full knowledge of everything he's up to at any given time, but I can tell you Lamb wouldn't implement anything Charles Partner ever dreamed up. Or cooperate with Taverner, unless there was something in it for him."

"Taverner controls a large budget."

"He's not interested in money."

"Really?"

"Well, I wouldn't leave the petty cash where he could find it. But if I had a Swiss bank account, I wouldn't need to hide the number from him."

Whelan nodded, as if this confirmed something he suspected. Which irritated Catherine, who was pretty sure it was an act. She said, "Does that give you enough background? Because when you're ready to talk to Lamb, please let me know. I might bring popcorn."

"The call was Monday afternoon. Has anything out of the ordinary happened since?"

Well, this could go either way. What was ordinary for Slough House was everything but in most places. So it was tempting to tell him no, that the even tenor of slow-horse life had continued uninterrupted for months, but there was a point of principle here, one Lamb himself would endorse. Don't try to hide something from someone who might already know about it.

Catherine wasn't the world's best liar, anyway.

She said, "We've had an employee issue."

"What do you mean?"

"One of my colleagues had an . . . episode." Catherine reached for her glass, and took a sip. Water tasted wrong. "A rather violent one. She was arrested."

"When did this happen?"

"Monday evening."

"So it might have been related to the phone call."

"I don't see how."

"It's a matter of patterns, though, isn't it?" As if to underline the thought, he mirrored Catherine's recent action: reaching for his drink, tasting it. "What was the nature of this, ah, episode?"

She gave him the bullet points: the iron, the bus, the traffic jam of witnesses.

"Were the Dogs called in?"

The Dogs being the Park's internal police force, generally first on the scene when Service-related shit was hitting taxpayers' fans.

"And she's now, what? On bail? In a cell? Unemployed?"

"She's receiving treatment."

"So I'd imagine. Whereabouts?"

"In the San."

Whelan raised an eyebrow. "The place in Dorset?"

She nodded.

"That's a pretty exclusive, not to say expensive, form of rehab."

"She's a valued employee."

"No, she isn't. She's Slough House. Any public meltdown involving the police, she'd be cut adrift, you know that. So what happened?"

Catherine said, "I asked Diana Taverner for a favour."

Whelan stared.

"She owed me one. I gave her my lasagne recipe, she'd been pestering me about it for ages."

Without taking his eyes off her, Whelan finished his drink. Then asked, "How long have you worked for Lamb?"

"I try not to think about it."

"No, I can see why. Because he's rubbing off on you."

"If that were the case," she said, "I'd definitely make hay with that delightful image. Now, to the best of my recollection, Shirley's episode apart, nothing out of the ordinary happened on Monday or since. That being so, I think we've finished, don't you?"

"For the time being." The waitress approached and he shook his head, warning her off. Then said, "But not for good. Because I'm going to need to find out more about this phone call."

"I'm sure you'll do whatever you think best."

"Even if that means annoying Lamb."

"I'm not sure he'll notice, to be honest. But if I might offer advice?" Catherine stood, buttoning her coat. "Don't take him at face value. There's a reason Lamb acts the way he does."

"And why is that?"

"He's a joe. Always has been. Always will be."

"And you admire that."

"Admiration would be beside the point."

"But you're on his side."

"As opposed to whose?" Catherine wondered, but not until later; not until she was out on the street again, noticing how, even to her sober view, the colours had deepened with the hour's darkening, the washed-out reds and faded blues looking richer than before, the greys and browns an earthier, muddier soup.

Security at the embassy was of the fuck-you variety: suits, shades and visible earpieces, as if someone had rung Heavies-'R'-Us. Diana Taverner's invitation to enter was a hip-height hand-waggle, and once through the front door she had to surrender her phone to a woman who scanned the barcode on her e-mailed invite with an expression suggesting that a better time awaited her elsewhere. The only bright note was offered by the youngster who subsequently waved a wand over her, still fresh-faced enough to look like he might be channelling Harry Potter rather than checking her for tech. She nodded pleasantly, offering a smile that would pass for the real thing, and was swooped on by a functionary who ushered her through to a well-clad drawing room, all the while maintaining a polite distance. "Our apologies for the security, Ms. Taverner. But you know how it is."

"Of course. There are always chickens out there, looking to come home to roost."

"Forgive me. I'm told my English is good, but some idioms remain opaque."

The room was large enough not to appear crowded but

there must have been fifty people present, not including those bearing trays. These were, as usual, far younger and more beautiful than the guests, and on this occasion too, since the guest list leaned heavily towards the arts, better dressed. Diana had a glass in her hand before she'd taken three steps.

"Thank you."

"We're very glad you could make it this evening, Ms. Taverner." Not the server, but her welcoming functionary. "You have an admirer among us."

"Oh really?"

"Indeed. One of our guest speakers is most eager to meet you."

"How intriguing."

This dance, she thought, was as formalised as anything Jane Austen might have imagined; the polite lies offered; the half-truths exchanged, hoping to pass unnoticed. The spook world was its own quadrille. In recognition of this the company had arranged itself in small groupings, each distinct from the other, as if there were circles painted on the floor. But then, this had become the norm at formal gatherings, before the drinks had taken hold; everyone conscious of the clouds others walked in; of the area round a warm, working body that's full of sweat and spittle, and leaving traces in its wake. Diana remembered being told, when young, that the way to apply perfume was to spritz a dash into the air and walk through the mist. Not an image today's advertisers would reach for, the lingering nature of airborne particles being a tough sell.

Already, her functionary was yielding her to an approaching male. "Enjoy your evening, Ms. Taverner."

The newcomer was in late middle age; his head hair dark, his neatly crafted beard shot with silver. Five ten, she estimated. In good shape for his age and profession: like her, he spent his working days underground, surrounded by screens and well-trained staff; so like her, his apparent good health was testimony to early hours working out, or pounding round a park. His suit—new tie—bore no traces of recent international flight, and the smile with which he greeted her was in his eyes too, which had a greenish tinge. Diana had never met him in the flesh: MFD, as he was abbreviated on the hub. Moscow's First Desk. Her opposite number. She was no mathematician, but found herself wondering: Would such a meeting produce a zero? And then dismissed the frivolity in much the way Vassily Rasnokov dismissed the functionary: both departed without a murmur.

"Diana Taverner. I saw your name on the guest list, and was disappointed to hear that you'd declined. But this afternoon I was told that you'd become available, and it gladdened my heart. It would have been a disappointment not to meet, after all this time."

In the current manner, he clasped his hands and gave a little bow.

She said, "A previous engagement was cancelled. I was glad of it too. This is a rare opportunity."

"Rare indeed. I don't know about you, but there are people back home who will be furious we're in the same room unaccompanied."

"Same here."

"And others who would want me to bring back your autograph."

"I'm ahead of you there, Vassily. I have any number of people who can do me your autograph."

He laughed, without overdoing it, and raised a hand for the nearest waitress. When she arrived, he took a glass of mineral water from her tray.

Diana went on: "This is a surprise, though. I didn't see your name on the visitors' list."

He shrugged so hugely he might have been French. "I was a last-minute substitution. There was an illness, and a lecture had to be cancelled. Which would have been a shame, as the staff here were looking forward to it. It just so happened that the topic—"

"*Battleship Potemkin*," Diana contributed.

"Yes. Happens to be an interest of mine. So I thought, well, why not come over to London and give the lecture myself? And enjoy your beautiful city in the autumn sunshine."

"Which happened so swiftly that we have no documented entry for you."

Rasnokov shook his head, sympathy in his eyes. "Ah, paperwork. How many things fall between the cracks? But let's not look a gift horse in the teeth. It's very satisfying to meet you face-to-face. For you, maybe not such the pleasure, eh?"

She gave this a moment's thought. "Oh, I don't know. The beard rather suits you."

He seemed in a relaxed mood, but then, he'd had a reasonably laid-back few days. The hastily assembled itinerary Diana had received just hours ago had verified his arrival at Heathrow on Tuesday morning, though the passport he'd shown had been in the name of Gregory Ronovitch, which was also the name he'd used when checking in at the Grosvenor. He'd eaten there Tuesday evening, and had gone to bed asking for an 8 A.M. alarm call. Wednesday morning he'd breakfasted at the hotel, enjoyed a well-detailed shopping excursion which had taken in every second emporium along Regent Street, though had resulted in no purchases that wouldn't fit in a single bag, and then returned to the embassy for— presumably—meetings, after which the Grosvenor again, dinner and bed. This afternoon, following the catch-up meeting at the Park when his presence had dropped like a bagful of pennies, the luckless Pete Dean had picked him up leaving the embassy once more, this time with a seven-strong team counting his footsteps: they were treated to a crawl along the South Bank, culminating in a full hour and twenty-eight minutes during which Vassily sat on a bench with that morning's *Guardian*, gazed across the river, and made no contact whatsoever of any kind with anyone. That, anyway, was their claim, and even now that same team was back in the Park's viewing room, studying the footage at quarter speed like a bunch of poloneckers at an Andy Warhol retrospective. Rasnokov, meanwhile, had cabbed back to the Grosvenor, from which he'd reappeared fifty-four minutes later, freshly-suited, to head on back to the embassy.

And here he was.

She said, "The tie was a good choice. The one with spots was a little much, I thought."

"It's a question of what you can carry off, isn't it? I prefer the low-key look."

"Along with an off-the-cuff approach."

"I'm sorry?"

"I'm still wondering about the suddenness of your visit. You're sure it wasn't prompted by circumstances back home?"

"I'm not sure what you mean."

"I had the feeling, not long ago, that you were less than satisfied with some of the more, ah, provocative actions sanctioned by your boss."

"You're succumbing to wishful thinking, Diana. It's always satisfying to imagine, what shall we say, an opposition team falling prey to rifts and squabbles."

"It can be even more alarming to see a united front despite the criminal nature of the party line."

"We might have to disagree on issues of legality."

"Murder's a black-and-white matter, I'd have thought." She took a sip of champagne. There were other trays circling too: caviar, blinis. "Do you ever worry you're headed back to the bad old days?"

"The Cold War was a two-way street."

"I was thinking of older days than those. There were Tsars who wielded less power."

"If you're looking for flaws in public figures," Rasnokov suggested, "maybe you should direct your gaze nearer home. Your own Prime Minister, perhaps. A man who'd rather people remember the promises he's made than count the ones he's kept." He looked thoughtfully at the glass in his hand, but didn't drink from it. "Though of course, to call him your country's leader might not be entirely accurate. Say what you will about our president, but he is not a glove puppet."

"Well, I'm sure that's brought comfort to his victims."

"Are we going to discuss politics? There are flaws in every system, Diana. I prefer to leave reform to those who know what they're doing. Your own Anthony Sparrow, for instance. An interesting man, don't you find?"

"Don't believe all you read in the press."

"I wouldn't dream of it. But I meant in person. We had a most enjoyable conversation over dinner."

Diana nodded, because all the words made sense, and had appeared in intelligible order: enjoyable, conversation, dinner. Her apparent lack of concern failed to impress Rasnokov.

"You look, I'm not quite sure what the word I'm reaching for is. Unsettled?"

"The champagne," she said. "Poor quality brands have that effect."

"You're running through my itinerary in your head, yes? And you're wondering how I managed to squeeze in dinner with Mr. Sparrow without your being aware of it."

She couldn't tell whether he was toying with her; whether he knew Regent's Park had dropped the ball, and he'd been free to wander at will before this afternoon. "Really," she said. "You make it sound like you're newly arrived in a police state."

"Oh, no. Police states are famous for their efficiency." He drank some of his water at last. "But you can relax. I'm sure your people were doing their job. No need to dispatch them to, what's the name of this department? Slough House?"

He mispronounced the word; deliberately, she was sure. But she made no attempt to correct him.

"Your dining companions are your business, Vassily. I'm just surprised you found time to arrange such an outing. What with your unplanned arrival."

"It would have been a hasty occasion, yes. But I was referring to an encounter last month, back in Moscow."

"I see."

"Nothing official, Diana. A social gathering. The world has become such a small place, don't you find? Connections that could never have been made a decade ago are commonplace now. And anything that brings us together is surely better than the many things that drive us apart."

The thought of Anthony Sparrow, special adviser to the PM, having made a connection of any kind with Moscow's First Desk was going to bear closer examination. Especially if it had happened in Moscow itself. But for the moment all Diana did was smile, as if Rasnokov were confirming details she'd long since logged in her workbook. She sipped her champagne, mentally begged its pardon for her slur, and glanced towards a nearby couple, poets by the look, who had hijacked a waitress and were making short work of her canapés. Anthony Sparrow, Diana thought. Not technically a member of Her Majesty's Government. But a figure, nonetheless, who should definitely have filed a report of spook contact made when on a jaunt abroad. Or anywhere else.

Perhaps this train of thought made its way past her expression, because Rasnokov suggested again that she relax. "It's the curse of our profession, to be always thinking around corners. But this is a party. There is good food, good drink. Life is returning to normal. You should learn to enjoy yourself. London is full of opportunities, as so many of my countrymen have discovered."

"Largely because they're frightened to go back home."

"And still you cannot help yourself. I understand your hostility towards my government. But is this an appropriate occasion on which to indulge it?"

She nodded. "Perhaps you're right. I'm simply concerned

for you, Vassily. All pretence aside, we both know you work for a psychopath. The closer he gets to the end of his reign, the more blood there'll be in the gutters. I'd hate to think yours might run with it."

"Thank you. When you come to approach your own retirement, I'm sure you'll make necessary arrangements for your comfort and prosperity. Why think less of others?" He made a sudden bow. "And now, if you'll forgive me, I have to, what's that expression? Make some rounds. But I hope we chat again before the evening's over. It's been most charming to meet you. A human face, after all this time."

"It's been good to meet you too."

"And do relay to your Mr. Sparrow that I trust his association with Dr. de Greer is working out to his satisfaction. It was most interesting, our discussion about her work. I can see that, in the right hands, her talents would pay dividends."

She had to hand it to him: his timing was immaculate. He'd made his bow again, was off across the room greeting others before she could make a reply.

The poets had finished with the caviar tray and had moved on to a young man bearing a salver of smoked salmon. Diana was reminded of seagulls she'd seen, ripping sandwiches from the hands of tourists. She deposited her glass on a passing tray, and didn't look back to see if Rasnokov noticed her leaving, but would have put money on it.

Champagne and salmon, caviar and blinis, canapés stuffed with olives.

Or the last slice of pizza fished from a grease-drenched box, and garnished with extra cheese and onion, or at any rate, accompanied by crisps of that flavour.

Even with his face a scarred mask, it was possible to read Lech's disgust as he watched Roddy Ho shovel this delicacy into his mouth. "I think you've just invented the Unhappy Meal."

"All part of my five-a-day."

Lech stared. "You're aware that's not just counting how many things you eat?"

Ashley said, "Lamb stole my lunch."

"Yeah, if Slough House had a coat of arms, that'd be its motto."

"Does anyone know if he ate it?"

"That would be his usual approach," said Louisa. "Why? What was in it?"

". . . Nothing."

They were in Roddy's office, and on Roddy's screens was the continuing coverage of the reception at the embassy, this consisting largely of the drivers of various limos moodily smoking. Moodily was how the slow horses read it, anyway, though it was possible this was a nuance bestowed by black-and-white footage. On Bayswater Avenue evening had fallen, as it had on Aldersgate Street. One of the office's overhead bulbs had blown so the room was dimly lit, and a draught penetrated the cardboard shield covering the broken window. This stirred the dominant odours: the pizza Roddy was eating, the black tea in Lech's mug, the whispers of long-smoked cigarettes that pervaded Slough House, a constant reminder of their onlie begetter, Jackson Lamb.

Who had had left ages ago. He might come back, of course—Louisa half-believed he slept in his office—but for the moment he was off the premises, having departed in Catherine's wake. Louisa would have been home herself by now if not for the ever-recurrent fear-of-missing-out that all slow horses were prey to; well, all bar Roddy Ho, who was constantly at the centre of events, if only in his head. And it was possible, she told herself, that among these visitors to the Russian embassy—the liggers and lackeys, hungry for party food and propaganda—she might just spot one Alexa Chaikovskaya, absurd as that might sound. But was it? She'd be old now, seventies at least, but that was hardly a stretch for these former KGB types, some of whom seemed to undergo living mummification, still wheeled out on parades when slippers and a nice cup of cocoa would have been a kinder fate. Chaikovskaya had been a colonel in the eighties, and might have gone on to greater heights. Not that Louisa was up to speed on ranks in the Russian machine. River Cartwright would have known.

Someone was leaving, appearing as a shadow on one of Roddy's screens, silhouetted in the embassy's doorway. A woman, not the one on Louisa's mind, but recognisable nevertheless. Lech said it first:

"Lady Di."

"Why'd you call her that?" Ashley said.

Louisa and Lech shared a look. "Because everyone does?"

"No, they don't. Why would they?"

"... Because her name's Diana?"

Their mutual incomprehension would have made everyone present uncomfortable, if that number hadn't included Roddy Ho.

Onscreen, Taverner stepped inside a cab.

"Black car," Roddy murmured under his breath.

"Why would she be there?" Louisa asked.

"It's an official function," Lech said. "Why wouldn't she be?"

"I thought she hated that kind of thing."

"Gotta fly the flag, I suppose."

"Why did Lamb want us watching this anyway?" Ashley said.

"Did he say he did?" Lech said.

"Well, no, but . . ."

"But he knew we would, once he'd asked Roddy to hijack the coverage."

"Yeah," said Louisa. "You think it's Taverner he wanted us to clock?"

"What, because he reckons she's up to something dodgy?"

"To be fair, she usually is. Though I'm having trouble imagining it having anything to do with the Russians."

"On the other hand, there she is," said Lech. "Strolling out of their embassy."

"Yeah, right," said Roddy, rolling his eyes. "Because the best time for a secret meeting is when the place is full of people. Duh."

"Well, yeah, actually. Duh."

"I thought Taverner sent an underling along to functions," Ashley said. "When she wanted her RSVP to be 'fuck you.'"

"That's what the word in the Park is, huh?" said Louisa.

"Well, it was recently. Why, when was the last time you were there?"

"Touchy," said Roddy.

"It's pronounced *touché*," said Lech.

"What is?"

"So okay, for some reason Lamb wanted us to watch this,"

said Louisa. "And apart from a bunch of freeloaders turning up for gangster grub and gangster wine, all we've seen is First Desk leaving early. Do we feel wiser yet? Because I'm ready to go home."

"Lightweight," said Lech. "Can you give me a lift?"

"Which direction?"

"Chelsea."

Louisa held his gaze a moment, then sighed. "Yeah, okay. Come on."

"I wouldn't have guessed Lech lived in Chelsea," Ashley said when they were gone.

"He doesn't," said Roddy.

"I wonder what he's up to then?"

Roddy shrugged. "Do you do much social media?"

"Normal amount. Why?"

"Do you ever . . . dress up?"

"Not sure where this is going," said Ashley. "But I'm not following it." She went to find her coat, and on her way back down put her head round the door again. "Did you see Lamb after lunch, by the way?"

"Don't remember. Why?"

"No reason."

But she was scowling as she made her way down the stairs, and kicked the back door harder than necessary before stepping into Slough House's yard, its walls damply patterned with city mildew, and quietly reeking of loss in the late-summer evening.

Anyone watching Oliver Nash approach La Spezia that evening would have thought he'd been hanging around the Park too long. His every move betrayed an excess of caution. For a start, he made three passes—walking straight by the first time; pausing to study the menu the second; the third, hovering in place, making a play of indecision—which was one too many for a man casing a brothel, let alone a small Italian restaurant off Wardour Street. Before he at last braved the front door he paused to turn his overcoat collar up, and for all the street dazzle of Soho—the neon lights and mirrored windows; the pavements shiny with party-poppered sequins—you'd have thought Nash was stepping into noir, dimming everything to a monochrome rainbow: black and white and grey and white and black.

Once inside, he asked for a table for one, and was taken downstairs and placed in a corner booth. Two others were occupied, both by elderly couples audibly engaged in eating pasta, and by the time Nash was seated—after waiting in vain to be relieved of his coat; he settled for draping it on the banquette opposite—a laminated menu had been slapped in front of him, illustrated with photographs of the dishes on offer. All of this, too, would have puzzled any watcher. Nash's regular haunts required reservations and appropriate footwear. La Spezia's kitchen seemed more likely to be graced by a Pirelli calendar than a Michelin star. Besides, Nash was on his own, and dining solo was not his habit. A possible, if unkind, explanation might be that Nash had found somewhere he might indulge himself without witnesses; an arena in which he could not only let his appetite off the leash, but sit back and admire its turn of speed. But the cannier observer would be aware that Nash was studying his surroundings, and making notes on his phone. Oliver Nash was on the job.

> *scruffy but clean*
> *photo of pope*
> *framed football shirt (signed by?)*

He paused, unable to either make out the name scrawled in Sharpie on the shirt, or recognise the team colours.

> *floor tiled in red and white squares*
> *ditto tablecloths*

It wasn't evident that any of this information mattered, but he was here, and would follow his instincts.

staff young Italians, badly needing shaves

One such approached Nash's booth now and asked if he'd made his choice, or at least, so Nash interpreted his monosyllabic enquiry.

"What do you recommend?"

This earned a blank stare.

"What's the chef's speci—"

"Fettucini's good."

With prawns, though their provenance wasn't mentioned. The travails of the joe in the field. "Very well. And the bruschetta to start. And a glass of the Amarone." He squinted at the wine list. "That's number . . . seventeen. A large glass."

The young man disappeared through the swing doors into the kitchen, and Nash added *brusque service* to his list.

But the wine arrived swiftly, as did his starter, and the odours filling the room were promising. There was no piped music, which was a plus—*no muzak*—though a radio played in the kitchen, a football match. He checked his messages as he ate. Nothing of interest bar a note from Claude Whelan, seeking retrospective confirmation that he, Nash, had approved his, Whelan's, request to examine phone records pertaining to the hub . . . That wouldn't have gone down well with Diana. It was possible Whelan was less diffident than Nash had thought. He replied, then scanned the headlines: the PM had just shared his vision of post-Brexit Britain as a cultural powerhouse, its film industry the envy of the world—there was more on the Home Office reshuffle, which some were calling a bloodbath; and there'd been a house fire off the Westway. One fatality, as yet unidentified. He laid his phone aside, and thought back to yesterday's meeting.

It had been his first summons to Sparrow's presence, but

he was aware of precedents. Some had involved civil servants of forty years' standing, the resulting interviews curtailing their careers in the time it would take to drink a cup of tea, had such courtesy been offered. Others had learned that their departments were coming under new admin structures more directly controlled by Number Ten; "reforms"—a bastardised word if ever there was one—that were in reality a show of strength from a government whose weaknesses had been on national display over the previous eighteen months. This performance was largely due to the prime minister himself, whose sole qualification for the job had been the widespread expectation that he'd achieve it. Having done so, he was clearly dumbstruck by the demands of office: the pay-cut, the long hours, the pandemic, and the shocking degree of accountability involved. For a man who'd made a vocation out of avoidance of responsibility, this last was an ugly blow. Nash didn't much care about any of that—the man's character had been evident for decades, and people still voted for him—but it mattered that, as a consequence, the PM had come to rely on a series of advisers whom no one had voted for. And "rely on" was putting it mildly. While the PM still racked up soundbites on a regular basis, they mostly came out as "gottle o' geer." His lips might move, but it was Sparrow writing his script.

Sparrow's script-writing ambitions stretched beyond the odd political broadcast.

"How do you find Diana Taverner?" he had asked Nash the previous afternoon, before the topic of Sophie de Greer had been broached.

"Diana? She's an effective First Desk."

In other circumstances, the prospect of a no-holds-barred discussion of Diana's ups and downs would have been a thrill, but Sparrow was no gossip. Sparrow was the weasel under the cabinet table, his teeth bared and dripping.

"It's said she's close to Peter Judd."

"Judd was Home Secretary while Diana was Second Desk," Nash said. "Naturally they worked together."

"And have continued to . . . associate since. Though Judd has some dubious acquaintances."

Judd had set himself up as an old-school *eminence grise*, and was currently stage-managing the mayoral ambitions of one Desmond Flint, who might fairly be described as dubious, Nash thought, but was at least prepared to put himself before the electorate. As for the degree to which Diana was involved with Judd, Nash had wondered about that himself, but was wary of airing doubts in front of Sparrow.

He said, "That's the nature of the Westminster village. We all bump elbows with some we'd sooner avoid."

Sparrow received this with his customary lack of expression. "The Westminster village. Curious to take pride in its parochial nature, don't you think?" He didn't wait for an answer. "Her associations aside, Taverner's support for Number Ten has been underwhelming. I'd prefer First Desk to display a little more enthusiasm for the government she serves."

It did not escape Nash that it was a first-person preference Sparrow was stating.

He said, "If this is to sound me out about a possible, ah, move towards a replacement, I'd remind you that Number Ten has traditionally relied on the guidance of the Limitations Committee in such matters. And as its chair, I have to say Diana commands the Committee's respect. She can be abrasive, yes, but there's no reason to question her commitment to the government of the day."

"Very loyal. But as you say, Number Ten's reliance on the Committee's judgement is a matter of tradition. And tradition doesn't rank highly with myself or the PM. It's a drag on progress."

"Some might say—"

"Any such removal would be part of a larger reorganisation. First Desk has a ring to it, but overstates the case. His or her role is simply to carry out policy and instructions delivered by Number Ten. As for the Committee, I see that as being streamlined, but with more responsibility accruing. The PM himself, or one of his advisers, would attend meetings designed to formulate overall policies. The chair would then inform First Desk of instructions arising. Which would lessen the possibility of the Service involving itself in adventures detrimental to the government's larger aims."

"Such a structure might overlook—"

"And there'd be no debate about removing Taverner from office, since she'd resign sooner than suffer what she'd see as a demotion. So you don't need worry about a conflict of loyalties."

"... Conflict?"

"You'll be required to stay on as chair for the foreseeable future. I assume that's what you want?"

Phrased, thought Nash, as if he had been plotting his own advancement.

Sparrow was observing him, head tilted to one side as if in homage to his avian namesake, so he nodded. "When do you plan to announce these changes?"

"I'm sure the moment will present itself. Meanwhile, there's another matter. As it happens, not entirely unconnected." He had gone on to lay out the problem of his missing superforecaster, and the role Nash might play in resolving this.

When his main course arrived, it was soundtracked by a roar of approval from the kitchen: a goal, Nash assumed. Certainly his waiter seemed less morose. He paused long enough to assure himself that Nash had noticed the plate in front of him, and then went back through the swing doors, which flapped in his wake, a diminishing series of farewell gestures. Nash speared a garlicky prawn, delivered it to his mouth, and for a moment all other concerns disappeared. Food was a form of magic. But his meal diminished with every mouthful, and before he had finished, the spectre of Sparrow was rematerialising: Deeply out of place here, as much so as Nash himself, and that was the question, wasn't it? What on earth had drawn Anthony Sparrow to this obscure eatery?

It had been a little over a week ago that Nash had seen him on Wardour Street, mid-evening; satchel on his back and walking with purpose. Nash had been browsing in Foyle's before heading for a club on Shaftesbury Avenue, but spurred by mischief and the possibility of intrigue had changed direction. The adventure lasted less than a minute, Sparrow turning off the main drag almost as soon as Nash had spotted him, and heading for this restaurant. But instead of the front door he had used the entrance marked for deliveries, which Nash now assumed led into the kitchen. At the time, he had walked on past, abuzz. The notion that he'd stumbled on a secret dining hole, frequented by a Downing Street elite, was a rare prize, a morsel he could dine off for weeks. But care would be needed. Sparrow wanted to be feared, and didn't mind being hated. He wouldn't take kindly to having his secrets unearthed.

What was already widely known about him was bad enough. That he was a "disruptor," a self-described architect of the new future. That it was his habit to call fake news on anything showing himself or the government in a bad light. That it was also his habit to proclaim fake news a good thing, since it forced people to question what they heard. That such contradictions allowed him to claim victory in every argument. That he appeared to be running the country, with half the cabinet terrified of him, and the rest scared stiff. That when Number Ten boasted of approaching glories, it was Sparrow's pipe dreams the prime minister was passively smoking. That it wouldn't end well.

Given all that, it had been no surprise that Sparrow in person had proved a charmless bully. But—and here Nash forced himself not to look away from a grim truth—a charmless bully armed with the promise of advancement. This couldn't be ignored. The last few years had scraped the rosy glow off his investment portfolio, and the knowledge that this was true for many did little to alleviate the matter. There was an opportunity here to ensure that his future continued to feature the right kind of restaurant, and appropriate shoes. And he had never sworn fealty to Diana Taverner. There could be no treachery in witnessing her eclipse.

The doors to the kitchen swung open as another meal was carried to a table, and the volume of the football match grew louder, as did the attention of the kitchen staff. Nash could make out coathooks on the other side of the doors, on which hung several football jerseys, the same design as the trophy shirt on the wall. The doors strobed to a standstill, obscuring the view. He rather liked this place, he decided, and on impulse added to his list *surprisingly enjoyable atmosphere*. Again, not something he'd expect Sparrow to be susceptible to. Nash pondered that for a moment, wondering what he might be missing.

Then he caught the waiter's eye, and ordered more wine and a chocolate delice.

The second gin and tonic is the key. In this instance what it unlocked was a disinclination to go home, a disinclination that left Whelan poised, empty glass aloft, imagining that the picture he presented to the approaching waitress was one of attractive dishevelment. Another drink wouldn't hurt. Nor would a dish of smoked almonds. Behind her visor the waitress smiled, thinking about something else, and he smiled too, thinking about her. A large figure slid out of nowhere and occupied the chair Catherine Standish had vacated with the grace of a nesting hippo. "And a large scotch."

"Yes, sir."

"Very large."

"Yes, sir. We have—"

"Whatever's most expensive."

Which caused some confusion, but Whelan gave a reassuring nod, and she left to fill the order.

Jackson Lamb glared round benignly, like a momentarily appeased tyrant, settling into a kingdom that hadn't yet realised was his.

Whelan said, "Do you make a habit of following your staff?"

"It's more of a hobby, really." His gaze settled on Whelan. "But dodgy looking geezers hanging round bus stops, who wander off after my joes, well. Them, I keep an eye on." He arched a raggy eyebrow. "You never know who's got form when it comes to harassing a working girl."

So intent had he been on following Standish, on not alarming her by his presence, it hadn't occurred to Whelan that he should have been checking his own wake.

The almonds arrived. Lamb scooped a grubby handful almost before they were placed on the table, and poured most into his mouth. His gaze remained on Whelan throughout.

Who said, "Well, you're here. I was planning on speaking to you anyway. So this saves us both time."

"Good to know. When I've saved enough, I'll put the clocks back."

"You took a call on Monday afternoon."

"'Took a call?'"

"Answered your office phone."

"Doesn't sound like me."

"The call lasted two minutes thirty-seven seconds."

"Can't have been a dirty one," said Lamb. "My stamina's shot to pieces these days. I've had sneezes last longer."

"I see you haven't changed."

The waitress brought their drinks. Lamb kept his gaze on Whelan, but Whelan gave her an appreciative look.

"Seems like I'm not the only one," Lamb said.

Wherever he was going with that, Whelan wanted none of it. He said, "Sophie de Greer." Lamb's expression didn't alter. "The name of the woman who called you."

"I'd say you were well informed," Lamb said. "If you weren't full of shit."

"This won't help."

"I'm not trying to help. I'm hoping you'll fuck off and injure yourself."

"Help you I mean." Whelan reached for his glass. He'd rather be reaching for a weapon, he thought, ridiculously: When had he ever held a weapon? But there was something about Lamb: even facing him across a table felt like facing him across a trench. "All I'm doing is establishing the facts. And if you carry on being obstructive, my report will reflect that."

"And I'll get my wrists slapped."

"Treat it like a game, that's fine. But this is coming from all the way upstairs. If you don't cooperate, things will get uncomfortable."

Lamb lifted his glass and examined it for a moment. He'd asked for very large, which was what he'd been given, in bar terms. But if he'd poured this amount for himself, anyone watching would assume he was on the wagon. Without drinking, he said, "So tell me about this Soapy Gruyere."

"Congratulations, you're half right. She's Swiss."

"Someone has to be."

"And a political appointee. As you well know."

"I may have come across the name," Lamb conceded. "Isn't she Number Ten's new weather girl?"

"The term you're reaching for is 'superforecaster.'"

"'Superforecaster.'" Lamb shook his head in an exaggerated lament. "Still, I suppose the Swiss had to diversify from their more traditional pursuits. Chocolate, cuckoo clocks. Gay porn."

". . . Gay porn?"

"Well what did you imagine a hard-on collider was?"

He was going to have to take charge of this conversation before Lamb turned it into a lads' night out. "She's disappeared."

"Wonder if she saw that coming?"

"And you're the last person she called before it happened."

Lamb shrugged, and used his free hand to help himself to more almonds. The ones that didn't reach his mouth scattered, some falling into Whelan's lap.

Whelan said, "You were in your office all afternoon?"

"Usually am."

"And Ms. Standish takes your calls when you're not there."

"Does she? I've often wondered what she gets up to when I'm out."

"How did you come to know Dr. de Greer?"

"I didn't."

"Because there's some suspicion that the Service is involved in her disappearance. And the fact that she called you rather lends weight to that notion."

Lamb balanced a nut on a thumbnail and flicked it into the air. Whelan expected it to drop into his mouth, but Lamb apparently didn't: the almond disappeared somewhere behind him. "So your main item of evidence is something that didn't happen. Dream this one up in your mother's basement, did you? Because it has all the hallmarks of a conspiracy theory. And the sad bastards who fall for conspiracy theories always see more than what's really there." He leaned forward. "It's like that fable about the blind men who think they've found an elephant. When what they've really got is a length of rope, a wall and an old umbrella stand."

"I think we've heard different versions of that."

"And what you've got, Claude, is several handfuls of crap you imagine adds up to an elephant."

"You haven't asked how I know about the phone call."

"I don't need to." He smiled, unless it was a leer. "The Park's always had an unlimited supply of elephant shit. Comes from being so close to the zoo."

All of this, and the drink still untasted in his hand.

Whelan took a sip from his G&T. "Whatever's going on, I plan to get to the bottom of it."

"Save your strength for getting into that waitress's knickers. I mean, you've no chance of that either, but at least you won't get too badly hurt." Lamb paused. "On the other hand, hassle my joes and I'll take it as a declaration of war."

A spurt of anger cascaded through him, as hot and wet as a stomach bug. "Joes? Your 'joes' are a bunch of wrecks. That Wicinski character should be behind bars if what I've heard's true. As for what's her name—Dander?—it's not treatment she needs, it's a padded cell. Slough House isn't a department. It's a psychiatric ward."

If his outburst shook Lamb, he didn't show it. "As ever, you're missing the big picture. It's my psychiatric ward. And it's off-limits. Whatever you think your jurisdiction is, it runs out well before it reaches mine."

"Is that a threat?"

"Only arseholes and idiots make threats. And I'm not an idiot." Lamb got to his feet with a suddenness belying the weight he carried. Not to mention the glass in his hand: the surface of his whisky trembled, but no liquid sloshed over the sides. "Dander's treatment's none of your business. But thanks for the drink." It barely resembled a drink, the way he put it away; it might have been a thimbleful. And then he was gone.

As it turned out, it was the fourth gin and tonic that was actually the key. Because by the time Whelan had drunk it, by the time the frightening bill arrived, he had replayed the encounter several times over in his head, and come to the firm conclusion that Lamb had been lying about the phone call.

And while he wasn't entirely certain that Lamb had also caused Sophie de Greer to vanish, he had an inkling of where he might have put her if he had.

If the regularity of Diana Taverner's meetings with the PM suggested a stable relationship between Number Ten and the Service, such stability was of the kind a folded-up beermat beneath a wonky table offers—it would do at a pinch, but sooner or later you're going to need tools or a new piece of furniture. If this crisis point had lately seemed closer at hand, that, Diana suspected, was due to Anthony Sparrow, whose own position seemed secure enough. *The prime minister makes me look like Greyfriars Bobby*, Peter Judd had once told Diana, and it was true that the PM's sense of loyalty was most observable in its application to his own interests, but it was also the case that he had, in the past, defended Sparrow against the slings and arrows of an outraged media. Loyalty, then, was not beyond him, even if most observers reckoned this had more to do with his belief that *The Godfather* was a guidebook than adherence to a principle. Whatever the cause, Sparrow seemed a fixture, his untouchability reinforced by the fact that, unlike cabinet ministers, he didn't rely on the electorate's approval, so the PM could be reasonably sure that irrelevancies like public opinion and the national good weren't unduly skewing his advice.

On the other hand, what Sparrow had been doing cosying up to Vassily Rasnokov on a mini-break in Moscow would bear investigation. At the very least, a direct question or two.

She'd had time to call back at the Park before heading to Number Ten, and there had verified that no report had been filed by Sparrow regarding an encounter with Rasnokov the previous month. He had, though, been in Moscow: the occasion had been a "fact-finding mission," its duration three days, and the official calendar indicating twenty-seven meetings, their subject—and presumably their object—trade. But what rattled her more than the possibility of a covert encounter being buried between appointments was that Rasnokov had let her know about it. That he was making mischief was evident, but whether the plaything was herself or Sparrow had yet to be determined. What other mischief he might have orchestrated while in London remained as yet unknown.

Speaking of mischief, her phone rang en route—her secondary phone; the one only her caller knew about.

"Is this important? Only I'm heading for Downing Street."

"I remember the feeling," said Peter Judd. "But best-laid plans and all that."

"Save the lost-leader lament for your fan club. Those of us who know you well are still thanking our lucky stars."

To the country at large, Judd's tilt at Number Ten had ended in an inexplicable withdrawal from centre stage some years previously. To the better informed, the inexplicable element was Judd's continued existence.

"Now now," he said. "Let's not forget our common cause."

Diana spent several hours a day trying to forget precisely that.

Because a while back she had broken one of her own rules, stepping into a web without being certain she was the spider, and had accepted financial backing from a cabal led by Judd, thus untying herself from official, unsympathetic oversight. In her defence, the Service had needed the support. The case for the prosecution was more succinct: holy shit. Because as things stood, deep behind a Service op that had seen a Russian assassin murdered on Russian soil lay Chinese money, and most nights Diana lay awake for hours, counting how many different shitstorms might rain down if the story leaked. Her only comfort was that it was no more in Judd's interests to conjur up such an apocalypse than it was in her own. But she remained in Judd's tar-baby embrace, and judgment, she knew, was waiting down the tracks.

For the moment, though, his demands were specific to the day. "I was hoping for a little support. In the form of an endorsement."

"An endorsement," she repeated. "For your man Flint? One of us has clearly lost their mind."

"Just a few words about how the capital needs a firm hand on the tiller. That sort of thing. And you'd be backing a winner, which gives one a nice warm glow, I find."

"You seriously expect your straw man to take the mayor's job?"

"Someone has to."

"While using the fact that he didn't catch the virus as a character issue?"

"Well, his opponent did."

"It was a virus, Peter. Anyone could get it."

"And as I've just pointed out, his opponent did." His tone was the familiar one of a patient bully explaining the obvious. "I'm not saying it's a sign of moral probity. But if it was, Desmond won."

"And if it had been the other way round . . ."

"I'd be pointing out what a survivor he is. And not a pampered, scaredy, mask-wearing chicken."

"You realise some idiots believe the pandemic was caused by gay marriage? This is no better than that."

"Yes, well, once we established we've no time for experts, it's open season, isn't it?"

"Not really, no. Let me be quite clear. No way in hell am I supporting your candidate for mayor. And if he stands for anything else, I won't support him for that, either. Not for worst-dressed rabblerouser. Not for seediest looking sockpuppet. All understood?"

"I'll put you down as an undecided. Meanwhile, how's business your end? Any more special operations planned?"

"The Service currently has its hands full maintaining equilibrium. Like most other organisations. So your cabal—"

"*Our* cabal."

"—will have to content itself with the quiet life."

"I do hope you're not expecting us to fade into the background. You've opened a door that won't easily shut. You can't pretend you didn't know what you were doing."

"I don't have to pretend I wasn't aware of your dark passengers, Peter. You're the one brought them on board."

"We both know how much protection that will offer you should our arrangement become public. Which there's no need for, obviously. As things stand." The implicit threat hovered a while, underlined by Judd's leavetaking: "What was it Fu Manchu used to say? 'The world shall hear from me again.'"

She dropped her phone into her bag as the car arrived at Downing Street.

Where the small, irregularly shaped room she was shown to was a drab brown chamber, its walls bare save for various versions of the queen's portrait, ageing in ten-year jumps. These were spaced at uniform intervals, making it hard not to notice there was no room for another, unless it was to be hung on the door. In the centre of the room, two long-backed chairs sat either side of a coffee table, on which was a cafetiere, freshly made, and two cups. Diana filled one, knowing she'd be waiting a while yet, the PM being one of those who believed that punctuality shows weakness. On the mantelpiece, a carriage clock ticked, its noise curiously elongated between the not-quite parallel walls. Downing Street was more than the warren it was labelled; there was a physics-bending aspect to it. Take it apart, room by room, and there'd be no way of putting it together again: you'd have spaces left unfilled, leftover rooms too big to fill them. Though those empty spaces would be handy for sealing up unwanted occupants ... When the door opened to admit Anthony Sparrow, Diana thought, for a blurred moment, that she'd summoned the devil.

He grunted a greeting. "The PM's got something on. You can brief me on his behalf."

"'Something on'?"

"It happens. He's running a country."

"This isn't party business. Are you sure you're an appropriate stand-in?"

"A petty distinction," he said, pulling a chair back and flinging himself into it. "I'm taking this meeting, end of. Start talking."

Sparrow was a scruffy dresser, and this evening wore jeans and a red T-shirt under a sandy-brown combat jacket. He carried satchel rather than briefcase, and as with many aspects of his behaviour seemed to dare anyone to comment on it. While Diana ran through the weekly business—the threat-level checklist; budgeting issues; whispers of a hushed-up cyber-attack on a German bank; more budgeting issues—he stared at the nearest portrait of ER, the tenor of his thoughts suggested by the curl of his lip. He had, as an unkind sketch writer once commented, a face only Wayne Rooney's mother could love: faintly squashed, as if he'd spent years pressing it against a window. On the other side of the glass now, he was making up for lost time. Anyone who thought power was about anything other than settling scores hadn't been paying attention.

When she'd finished, he said, "That it?"

"As much as you're allowed to hear. The PM might delegate his duties, but I'm not about to breach confidentiality issues."

"We'll be taking a look at those guidelines." He stood. "It's a timewaste, having him fill me in after every briefing."

She said, "Since we're both here, I've a few issues."

"Make them quick." He was already reaching for his satchel.

"You're concerned about the current whereabouts of Dr. Sophie de Greer."

"That's a question?"

"I understand you asked Oliver Nash to have my predecessor look into the matter."

"The authority I wield comes from Number Ten. When I want things done, I don't ask. I issue instructions."

"That's enlightening. But you might as well hear this from me first. Whatever fantasy you've concocted, the Service has no involvement, or interest, in Dr. de Greer's whereabouts."

"I'll await Nash's report. Anything else?"

"Yes. You were in Moscow last month. Who did you talk to?"

"A lot of people. Most of them Russians. They're thick on the ground there, funnily enough."

"Any topics of interest I should be made aware of?"

"Depends how interested you are in this country's future. I was heading up a trade delegation. Keeping the beaches open."

". . . I'm sorry?"

"An observation. The real hero of *Jaws* was the mayor, because he kept the beaches open. That's what this government is doing. Keeping beaches open."

"I've heard the PM say so," said Diana. "It's no huge surprise he got it from you. But the Russian I had in mind is called Vassily Rasnokov. He's not on your appointment list, and he's not your average beach bunny. Any contact with him, I should have known about."

"You personally? What is he, your pen pal?"

"He's First Desk at the GRU. Do you need me to explain what that is?"

He laughed, half a beat later than he should have done. "No. For Christ's sake. Are you worried I've been recruited by the Russians? Don't be fucking ridiculous."

"But you're aware that any approach made by a foreign intelligence service should be reported to Regent's Park?"

"The regulations don't apply. The occasion was a social one, a meet and greet, followed by dinner. There were many people present. Rasnokov and I didn't exchange ten words."

"Which were?"

"It was weeks ago. Can you remember social chitchat from weeks ago?"

"That's the reason we require immediate debriefing after contact. And why the regulations aren't open to individual interpretation."

"Well, you've had your say, and I hope you feel better. Who told you about this so-called contact, anyway?"

"Vassily Rasnokov," said Diana.

Sparrow blinked.

"During social chitchat."

"He's in the country?"

"He is. Do you think he came all this way to drop your name? I wouldn't put it past him."

Sparrow said, "Well, he'd hardly be likely to alert you to the fact that we'd met if he'd used the occasion to recruit me, would he?"

"That depends," said Diana, "on whether or not he thought I already knew."

"Word games. My advice would be to spend your remaining time as First Desk concentrating on the more important issues facing your Service." He hoisted his satchel over one shoulder, and glanced at the cafetiere. "Is coffee always provided? I don't remember giving that instruction."

For a while after he left Diana remained seated, looking at the portraits of the queen. Perhaps, she thought, she should have let Sparrow know that Rasnokov had mentioned de Greer. His reaction would have been interesting. But there was no point second-guessing herself: she'd kept it up her sleeve, for later use. Besides, her phone was ringing.

"I was just thinking about you."

"That gives me a warm feeling right down to my nuts," Lamb said. He paused, and Diana heard a flick-and-flare. Deep inhale. "I've just been talking to your predecessor, who seems to imagine I've had a Swiss fortune-teller disappeared. Where do you suppose he got hold of that idea?"

"It's possible someone's been pulling his leg."

"I'd try pulling theirs," said Lamb, "but I'd worry it'd come clean off. Don't know my own strength, that's my trouble."

"It's one of them," Diana agreed. "Look, Claude was being a nuisance, so I threw a stick for him. Gave him something to chase."

"In my direction."

"I thought you might have fun wrestling him for it."

She could picture him breathing out smoke.

"It's not like he'd have been disturbing anything important. Slough House, for God's sake. You're already a joke. I was just adding a punchline."

"Happy to help," said Lamb. "But the thing is, it's a bit more complicated than you thought."

That didn't sound good.

"So your stand-up routine needs work. Let's talk it over. Tomorrow morning."

"I've got meetings."

"Yeah, I had a nap scheduled. We all make sacrifices."

He told her when and where, and rang off.

Diana put her phone away, took one last look at Her various Majesties, and left, mentally kicking herself for overlooking Lamb's talent for taking the straight and narrow and installing an Escher staircase. She should have considered that before she'd had Josie mess with the telephone data, adding a call to Lamb's number from de Greer's mobile—a bit of harmless fun; or at any rate, any ensuing harm would befall Claude Whelan, which amounted to the same thing. But now there was a possibility she'd loosed a cannon. And she had enough to worry about without conjuring extra problems out of nowhere.

Still, upsides: Lamb wanted to meet in the open air, which would make a change from spending her day in a series of sterile offices.

And let's face it, like everyone else, she could do with a break.

INTERMISSION

L amb bought two ice creams from the nearby van—double scoops, chocolate flakes, sprinkles—and carried them to the bench where Diana was waiting.

Still halfway through the first, he began the second as he sat down.

"Don't mind me," she said.

The remark appeared to puzzle him.

The park was barely that: a scrap of green space wedged between housing estates east of Aldersgate Street. There was a children's play area, a wooden shelter for drug dealers, and a gate onto a sidestreet where the ice cream van was parked, milking what custom it could from summer's last flourish—a strictly nine-to-five deal. The jacket you wore in the morning would leave you shivering on your way home. Though Lamb's jacket would make Diana shiver wherever she was heading: a spongy blue mess a charity shop would spurn.

As she watched, he added to the allure by allowing a dollop of ice cream to land on his lapel, leaving a spatter-trace unnervingly like birdshit. Holding both cones in one hand, he scraped at this with a finger he then licked and rubbed dry on his trousers. Then, mouth full, he yawned magnificently and said:

"We're old friends, so you won't mind me saying, but you look rough as fuck. Like you were up half the night being gang-banged and the rest writing thank-you notes."

"As always, I'm touched by your concern."

"Yeah, well, you want any other part touching you, you'll need to smarten your act up." He belched. "A man my age is coming into his prime. But a woman of yours, it's pretty much over. So a little effort, you know?"

Resisting several urges, she said, "It's been a long week."

"Yeah, I heard about the genius on the security detail."

Diana stifled a groan. The genius in question had left his gun and the PM's passport in an aeroplane toilet, where it had been found by cabin crew on a flight home from Geneva. These things were usually hushed up, but the attendant doing the finding had been French.

"I assumed he was putting out to tender," Lamb said. He pushed the remains of his first cone into his mouth, and went on: "Picture of the target, tool to do the job." He made a gun of finger and thumb, and squeezed an imaginary trigger. "I'm surprised a queue didn't form."

"You can laugh. But if he doesn't get fired, you'll be finding desk space for him."

"Up your bum. I've barely room for the moody tossers I'm saddled with now."

"What about Cartwright's desk?"

"I've converted it into a shrine."

"You're missing him."

"I've had kidney stones I miss more. And as for your latest reject, No Khan Do? If it wasn't against the rules, I'd give her back." He looked at what was left of his second cone, grimaced, tossed it over his shoulder and visibly ran a tongue round his gums. "She's trouble."

"What's she done?"

"Passive-aggressive shit mostly. But I can read the signs. It's like when pets start disappearing, and you know a serial killer's moved into the area. Or a Korean takeaway."

She shook her head. "Normally, there's nothing I like better than listening to you philosophise, but in case you hadn't noticed it's the middle of the morning, and we've both got jobs to do." She paused, reconsidered. "*I've* got jobs to do. You've got a hard day's dossing about to be getting on with. So what did you mean last night by things being complicated? And bear in mind I'm not in the mood for games."

Lamb scratched his head, and when his hand reappeared it was holding a cigarette. "Yeah, funny how that works out. Because when you *are* in the mood I've got Claude Whelan turning my staff over, looking for a Downing Street pointy-head."

"If you're after an apology, sod off. Claude was being a pest and you've got all the time in the world. If I annoyed just one of you, I call that a result."

"So it had nothing to do with your jolly at the Ivans' HQ yesterday evening?"

". . . With my what?"

"Which you left at 8:05."

"You were *watching*?"

"Well, not personally. But I like to keep an eye on my crew's work-life balance. And if it looks like life's winning, I put my thumb on the scales."

He showed her the thumb he meant. It was visibly sticky.

She shuddered, and said, "So you had them watch the embassy coverage."

"Well. I only had to get one of them do it, and the rest stuck around in case they missed anything. MOFO, they call it."

"FOMO."

He shrugged. "Either way, it'd be what they also call sad, if it wasn't so fucking hilarious."

"Jackson—"

"And how was Vassily? I met him once. Long time back. He'd just graduated to Spook Street after working as a gangster's blunt instrument. I could tell he was destined for greatness."

"How did you know he was there?"

"I didn't," said Lamb. "But I do now."

He rummaged around in his pockets and produced a plastic lighter.

"What's going on?" said Diana.

"Well, that's a long story. And it requires a flashback, a voiceover, and all sorts of technical shit."

"What on earth are you—?"

"Not to mention a gallon of coffee. There's a kiosk down the alley." He gestured with his cigarette in that direction. "Fair's fair. I bought the ice creams."

It was worth it just to have ten minutes' headspace. Diana spent it sieving through what she knew about Sophie de Greer: that she'd worked with Anthony Sparrow, been name-checked by Vassily Rasnokov, been missing for barely four days, and was evidently at the centre of some new clusterfuck, details as yet unknown. Unknown to her, anyway. Apparently Lamb had an inkling.

Which, she thought, carrying four large black coffees back to the bench, meant trouble coming down the tracks.

Upon her return Lamb grunted, accepted three of the coffees, glared at the one she kept for herself, farted leisurely, set the cups in a row, prised the lid off the first, farted again, and said, "Once upon a time—"

"Oh, please. Spare me the grace notes."

"Shut up and listen."

ACT I
MONKEY BUSINESS

It had started earlier that week: Lech Wicinski and John Bachelor meeting for a drink in the upstairs bar at The Chandos on St. Martin's Lane; Lech late, because he didn't want to come; Bachelor early, having nowhere else to be. These circumstances combined to allow Bachelor to be two drinks up, or down, by the time Lech arrived to pay for his third. The older man was drinking G&T, and had some patter prepared about how more thought went into the T than the G, but Lech wasn't listening. He was worried Bachelor was going to ask if he could move in—"just for a day or two, until I get a new place sorted." He'd been guilt-tripped before into letting Bachelor sleep on the sofa, which was how come Bachelor had ended up looking after Lech while he sweated out the virus, a circumstance pretty certain to be mentioned when the favour was asked. So Lech would have to say yes, and a few days would turn into a fortnight, and he'd end up growing old in the company of John Bachelor, spending his evenings in dismal pubs, his weekends counting loose change, his Christmases watching *The Great Escape*. Simplest thing would be to let Bachelor finish framing his request, then just leave his door keys on the table and take a header through the window. Probably why Bachelor had chosen the upstairs bar. This sort of thing must happen to him a lot.

"Fever Tree, anyway." Bachelor was winding down. "Wouldn't have thought that a selling point these days."

Lech dragged himself into the conversation, almost. "I think it's . . . Never mind."

"How are you?"

"Fine, John. Just fine."

"No, uh, relapses, nothing like that?"

"Like I said. Fine."

Though the truth was, being with Bachelor tended to bring the worst of it back; not so much the painful breathing—that sensation of being slowly vacuum-packed—as the fear that this was how it would all end: in a rented flat, furnished to nobody's liking; his companion a broken-down spook whose career made Lech's own look like a Martini advert. Would his life unfold before his eyes? The choice between death and reliving Slough House was a little close to call. And then he was past the point of deliberation, and in his fevered dreams Slough House figured largely, its rooms, its manky staircase, all swollen out of proportion, as if he were wandering through the internal organs of some giant, diseased beast. Lech had never known whether to trust the feeling of having a recurring dream, whether you actually slipped in and out of the same narrative, or whether it was one of the brain's little tricks; that hoary old contrivance déjà vu endowing never-before encountered scenes with the artificial familiarity of a shopping centre or a Vin Diesel movie. But this time, he was sure, his dream-state had been the same each time, as if every trip to a waking surface had left the gates open behind him. He'd find himself in bed, his head on a pillow, a glass tipped to his lips—*Drink this*—and for a moment he'd be here in the world. And then he'd sink back to those engorged offices with their frightening colour scheme. From overhead came thumping, as if a trapped lizard were beating its huge tail against a boulder. A summons, Lech knew, but not one he wanted to answer.

Long story short, after a while he got better.

The things that didn't kill you made you stronger, apparently, though that was a lie; truth was, too many things left you still alive but broken and disturbed, and it was better not to experience them. But he'd experienced this. And what he'd wondered since was how bad he'd have had to become before Bachelor sought medical help, or would the older man have just kept tipping water into him until he stopped swallowing, then hunkered down in the flat until bailiffs turned up? He knew, from drunken conversations, that something similar had happened before. But Lech wasn't proud of such thoughts; even less so when he recalled the look on Bachelor's face when he'd said *I think I've got it*. Instead of fear or alarm, he'd read there only concern.

So anyway. All of that, and now here they were, much later, and he was worried Bachelor was going to put the arm on him again: wanting not money but space, time, his company. Wanting to intrude on Lech's solitude, which was all Lech had left that he considered valuable. Even this small amount of it, an hour or so after the working day, he'd sooner close his fist around and keep to himself.

But Bachelor was talking. "I'm fine too. In case you were wondering."

"Oh, yeah. Glad to hear it. Sorry, John."

"You're worried I'm going to ask if I can move back in, aren't you?"

"I'm what?"

"Worried I'll ask to move in. Into your flat."

Lech said, "Look, the thing is—"

"Yeah yeah, it's okay."

"I'm sorry."

"Forget about it." He put a hand on the younger man's arm. "That's not what I wanted to talk about."

Later, leaving the pub, Lech had walked home, all four miles or whatever it was: the streets weren't fully dark, and it hardly counted as one of his insomniac rambles, but it wore him out enough that he had no trouble falling instantly asleep when he hit the pillow. But he was awake again two hours later, Bachelor's story climbing round his head. It was absurd, of course, and would lead nowhere—obviously—but at least the older man hadn't asked him the favour he'd been dreading. There was that memory, too, of Bachelor's concern when he, Lech, had been locked in Covid's monstrous offices.

He was remembering a line his father had enjoyed quoting—*everyone is more or less of Polish origin*. It seemed to fit Bachelor. Another reason for Lech not turning his back.

Which was why, the following afternoon, he'd wandered from the office he shared with Roddy Ho to talk with Louisa Guy, whose room was on the floor above, its view ever so slightly better than his. Same street, same Barbican: tarmac and brickwork and concrete. But a little higher up.

He said, "You busy?"

She was busy like a slow horse: plenty to do, none of it mattering, all of it skull-numbing dross. More specifically, she'd reached T on her library project. Library project—it sounded like something a primary school might inflict on its defenceless charges. The reality was worse. Way back when, round about the Middle Ages, Lamb had had one of his pet ideas; the kind of brainwave which doubtless struck somewhere between the fourth and fifth drink, the second and third vindaloo. Why not make Louisa's life a screaming, maddening hell? Actually that was less an idea, more a mission statement; what the actual idea was was, why didn't Louisa spend the rest of her life drowning in library-loan statistics? Because there were books out there which banged a certain kind of drum, and Lamb couldn't help wondering who, if anyone, was marching. That was how he'd put it: *I can't help wondering.* Help wondering? He could barely keep a straight fucking face. Once he'd realised every town in the UK had its own library, or used to, he'd have ordered a fifth or sixth drink, a third or fourth vindaloo. *Islam: A call to arms. The blood-dimmed tide.* He didn't even have to make these titles up. All he had to do was get Louisa to check Public Lending Right statistics for the past few decades, and match the borrower names that came up against various red-flag lists the Service collated. Thereby devising a whole new list.

"And I hate lists," he'd beamed.

"This might be a long one."

"Maybe devise a points system," he suggested. "You know. Bonus marks if they're already on the hot map. Double that if they have a . . . dodgy name."

"Dodgy name?"

"I've always thought 'Gary' a bit suspect."

So far she'd taken special notice of those who'd borrowed a supposedly inflammatory text without ever, as far as records showed, returning it. Which meant she was flagging with budding-terrorist status those who'd committed the fearsome crime of losing a library book. But it was keeping the national security candle alight, or at least keeping herself in a job. She was aware that these weren't the same thing exactly.

To Lech, she said, "Yeah, no. Same old usual. Why?"

"I heard something odd last night."

"How odd?"

He glanced around. "We have a scale?"

"Just so long as it doesn't involve library books."

"You know John Bachelor?"

She knew the name. "He's been staying with you, right?"

"He did. A while back."

"An old family friend?"

"We confused ourselves into thinking so. I met him at a wedding, so somebody's family was involved. Then we discovered we both worked for the Service."

Lech still at the Park then, and Bachelor a milkman, whose round covered the old, the infirm, the clapped-out; those who'd once fought the Cold War and now were just fighting the cold. Bachelor made sure their heating bills were paid, that there was food in their fridges, all the while growing steadily worse at managing any such thing for himself, his misfortunes reading like instructions for a midlife crisis: divorce; his working hours cut; his savings lost to bad investments. So, Lech said, he'd been adrift for a couple of years, subletting rooms when he could, sleeping in his car when he had to, sofa-surfing until he ran out of friends; all the while hanging onto his job by cracked and bleeding fingernails...The point where this was going to be more boring than the job in front of her was approaching fast. "And what's he done?" she said.

"He saw someone he recognised."

Louisa said, "I really hope there's more to this story than that. Because, you know, I could be reading lists of names."

"Before Bachelor was a milkman," Lech said, "long before, he worked on the London desk, and carried bags for David Cartwright. Once, he carried them all the way to Bonn."

"Bit of a stretch from London."

"Are you telling this or am I?"

"Sorry."

What had happened was, someone at the British consulate in Leningrad had been caught shoplifting, or buying drugs, or something, anyway, which the KGB liked catching you doing when you were working at a British consulate, especially if you were really working for the Service. And what David Cartwright went to Bonn to do was sort out a deal which would allow the poor sod in question to come home without both countries having to resort to the usual tit-for-tat fandango, firing diplomats, rolling up local networks, and generally making a musical out of one tired old song. The sort of thing the David Cartwrights of the Service were born to do, though this particular David Cartwright, Louisa knew, had been River Cartwright's grandfather. River probably hadn't even been born then, but let's not think about River right now.

The reason Bonn had been chosen was that it was neutral

territory and had good hotels, Bachelor had explained. Every meeting was conducted in at least three languages, because of course the Russians weren't going to field someone who'd admit to speaking English, and Cartwright preferred not to demonstrate how fluent he was in Russian, and as for the Germans, well, they were supplying the coffee and cakes, so why the hell shouldn't they speak their own language? Bachelor had little Russian, less German, and the whole thing would have been boring to the point of coma if it hadn't been for the woman taking notes on the other side of the table.

Louisa rolled her eyes. "So JB had the hots for the stenographer. That must have helped while away the hours."

"Yeah, except old man Cartwright put him right on that."

"She wasn't a stenographer."

"No, she was a full-fledged KGB colonel."

"Who was?"

They looked round.

Shirley Dander was in the doorway, holding an iron.

Louisa said, "Uh, private conversation?"

"Yeah, I could tell. What's it about?"

"Nothing. What's the iron for?"

"Duh, ironing? Who was the KGB chick?"

"I think Lamb was looking for you," said Lech.

"What did he want?"

"Something about a performance appraisal?"

". . . Don't believe you."

Lech and Louisa both shrugged in such perfect unison, they might have spent the morning practising.

"I fucking hate both of you," Shirley said, and went back downstairs, the iron leaking a spatter trail behind her.

"So what happened?" Louisa said.

"In Bonn? The usual stuff. A deal got made, there'll be a record somewhere. Probably in Molly Doran's archive. Bachelor was a bit hazy about it, what with everything being translated three times—"

"I really hope this is going somewhere."

"He saw her the other day."

"The KGB colonel?"

"Here, in London."

". . . Okay."

"And that's not even the odd thing. John says he's looking at her, and she hasn't aged a day, he's seeing exactly the person he remembers from Bonn. Still in her early thirties, thereabouts. Same hair, same skin. He says."

"So he thinks he's discovered Wonder Woman?"

"I'm not sure that's in his frame of reference, but you get the picture."

"Seriously? You've got a drunk telling you he's seen someone who looks like someone from his old days. I'm still waiting for a punchline."

"He sat on the opposite side of a table from her for four straight days, closer than we are now. He says he'd recognise her anywhere. And no, he's not a complete idiot, he knows it can't be the same woman. Shall I tell you what he thinks?"

"You might as well."

"He thinks it's her daughter."

". . . Okay."

"You don't think that's strange?"

"I'm still not convinced it actually happened. But even if it did, so what? KGB colonels have daughters? I'm not sure that'll light them up on the hub. It's biology, not tradecraft."

He was about to reply, but a sudden metallic crunch made both look up: Lamb's office wasn't directly overhead, but if he were hurling thunderbolts, that was roughly the direction to worry about. Only it hadn't come from above but below, a realisation they reached at precisely the same moment. "Shirley," they said in unison, though Shirley would have denied she'd been the one that made the noise—what had made the noise had been the iron. She hadn't even been holding it at the time, had she? Otherwise it wouldn't have been hitting the floor.

Cocaine logic.

She'd brought the iron into work because she was cruising Shoreditch later, and didn't want to start the evening creased. Standards. And since it was now four, which put her on her own time if you didn't count the next hour and a half, she'd decided to speed the evening up by both doing her ironing and taking a small bump to get her in the mood. It took a small bump to get her in the mood for most things these days, except those things that took a big bump, but it wasn't like she was made of money, and people didn't give the stuff away, or not round Shoreditch. Everyone had a living to make; everyone had a plan. Here was hers: hit a club or two, make enough of a score to see her through to the weekend, work off some energy on the dance floor, and—who knew?—she might decide to get lucky. Say what you like about Shirley's looks, Shirley's figure—and people had in the past—but she knew this much: deciding upfront whether you intended to get lucky pretty much put the outcome beyond doubt. She picked up the iron—which had gouged an inverted pyramid out of the threadbare carpet—and got on with the task in hand, enjoying the feeling of being productive and efficient, and trying to squash the niggling knowledge that she was being left out; that Lech and Louisa were plotting something—a KGB colonel, for fuck's sake; okay, ancient history, but still. They had some action going on, even if they were digging up old bones to find it. And weren't planning on letting Shirley join in, because if you partnered up with Shirley Dander, chances were you'd end up a blood-red mist on an office wall, or a smudge on a snowy hillside—

"What on earth are you doing?"

She nearly dropped the iron again.

". . . What's it look like?"

What it looked like was some kind of art installation,

thought Catherine Standish, though she supposed, if you clung to the details, it also looked like Shirley was trying to iron a T-shirt. It was that she was using her desk as an ironing board that was the problem, and that she hadn't cleared the desk first, making it more assault course than smooth surface. And also, the iron was either leaking or had a full-on steam setting: Shirley seemed to be having a sauna at the same time as getting her household chores done, which was in turn the point at issue. Household chores? She was in her office.

"Shirley—"

"What?"

Not a polite *What?* either; more a challenge. The best way to deal with Shirley was to tread softly, everyone knew that. Shirley had issues. Catherine, who had issues of her own, was the last person to want to make her life difficult, but on the other hand, she couldn't have Shirley making everyone else's life difficult too. It probably didn't matter much that Shirley was ironing a T-shirt in her office, but whatever she got up to in here, legitimate business or not, she shouldn't be doing it high. And Shirley was high.

Not a moment to be treading softly, then. Sometimes you had to stamp.

"What are you on?"

"On? What sort of question's that?"

"A straightforward one. You're high, you think I can't tell? What have you taken?"

"What's it to you?"

"Shirley, you're at work. You work for the Service, for God's sake. You've got a boss upstairs who'll throw you out of your job without a thought if you give him an excuse."

Job? He'd throw her out of a window.

"He won't notice. He's probably drunk. Besides, I took some cough mixture, that's all. I've a bad throat. You can't be too careful."

Shirley was saying all this holding the iron at chest height, which in her case wasn't that high, but still. With steam pouring from it, she looked like she was standing behind a special effect.

But her eyes were pinholes. If that was cough mixture, there'd be big demand for it.

Catherine said, "And why ironing, anyway? Why aren't you doing that at home?"

"Saves time."

"You're not supposed to be saving time, you're—oh, I can't stand this. Put that away. Drink some water or whatever it is you do to bring yourself down. And do not take any more . . . cough medicine."

"You should loosen up," Shirley told her. "You're too uptight. You'll give yourself a seizure."

"It's not so long ago you assaulted a fundraiser in the street. And then there's the man in the toilet at the tube station—"

"That was Lech."

"Lech was there. There's a difference."

"I get blamed for everything!"

"Not without reason. And do you really think ironing on a desk is going to work?"

"I was doing fine till you butted in."

"You're doing lots of things, Shirley. But trust me, 'fine' is not among them." Catherine realised she'd adopted a posture she was always warning herself against: arms folded, brow knitted. Damn. But she couldn't stop now: "Like I said, you've got a history of doing the wrong thing. And yet you're still with us. Which means you've been seriously lucky so far, and that won't go on happening forever."

"I've been lucky? Being in Slough House is lucky?"

"You know exactly what I mean. So put a lid on it. If I send you home, I'll have to tell Lamb why. And that'll mean you don't get to come back."

"Like this is where I fucking want to be!"

"Your choice." Catherine left, her heart beating rapidly.

When she'd heard that metallic crunch, she'd almost thought it a gunshot—a buried terror: guns had been fired in Slough House before. She was glad, mostly, that Lamb hadn't stirred, but this wasn't a source of long-term comfort. When Lamb failed to be furious now, he might be planning incandescence later. And Shirley was so far beyond last chances, her suitcase should be packed.

"What's going on?" Lech called as she passed Louisa's room.

"Shirley," Catherine said.

". . . Figures."

Louisa, irritated by the interruptions, said, "Counting down from ten now."

"What makes it interesting is where he says he saw her," Lech said. "He was watching TV. She appeared on the news."

"What's she done?"

"It wasn't about her. It was about the Home Office. About the team of ministerial aides being disbanded to ensure, what was the phrase?—a cleaner line of authority from Number Ten. All part of the ongoing power grab by Anthony Sparrow, you know?"

"The PM's enforcer."

"One way of putting it. And while they're saying this, there's footage of Sparrow coming out of Number Ten like he owns the place, with a folder under his arm and a couple of aides trotting at his heels."

He paused, except it wasn't quite a pause. He was waiting. Louisa said, "Ah . . ."

"Yeah, ah," Lech agreed. "So what John wants to know is, why is the daughter of a one-time KGB colonel carrying bags for the PM's special adviser?"

It was Louisa's turn to pause. Then she said, "That Swiss woman?"

"Sophie de Greer. *Doctor* Sophie de Greer. Sparrow's superforecaster, so-called. She's been on Sparrow's team since Christmas. There was a profile of her in one of the Sundays."

"And this didn't mention mummy being in the KGB?"

"It said little was known of her personal background. She's a mystery wrapped in an enigma, yada yada yada. Sparrow recruited her after she scored in the top two per cent in a superforecasting tournament. That's when you make accurate predictions about real-world outcomes—"

" Lech—"

"—and not just vague remarks about possibilities. What?"

"I know what a superforecaster is."

"Oh. Sorry. Anyway, yeah. That's the odd thing. Interested?"

Louisa said, "It's a hell of a stretch."

"I know."

"This de Greer woman looks like someone else. No, sorry, wait. Some old drunk *says* she looks like someone else."

"Will you not do that?"

"Do what?"

"Call him an old drunk."

Louisa thought about it, then said, "Sorry. Why doesn't he go to the Park?"

"Because, well, let's just say the last time he got involved in anything this size, it didn't end prettily."

"I'm surprised he's not here with us."

"He's an irregular, on a two-day week. They'd have to bump him up to full time if they assigned him here, wouldn't they?"

"How should I know? What's he expect you to do about this anyway?"

Lech said, "He wants me to have a look at her."

"Because you're a spook. He is aware of Slough House, isn't he? I mean, he knows we're not in the loop?"

"Yeah, sure. But I'm someone he knows. And I owe him."

"Because he looked after you when you had the virus."

"I don't know about looked after me." Lech paused for a moment. Then said, "Well, yeah, okay. He looked after me."

"Don't be so male about it. You caught a bug, it's not like you let the side down."

Lech shrugged.

"God, you're worse than River."

Outside, traffic grew heavier as the working day declined. Neither felt like they'd got through much work themselves, but that was normal in these offices, with these chores: you could spend all day shovelling sand, but if you were standing on a beach, the results weren't noticeable. The prospect of other, more fulfilling tasks was an overheard possibility, just discernible over the nudge and mutter of the traffic.

Louisa said, "She looks like she might be somebody's daughter. That's all you've got to go on."

"I know."

"And even if you're right, or Bachelor is, you think that's not going to punch you in the face? Establish a connection between Number Ten's uber-apparatchik and a former KGB colonel, even one a generation old, and it won't end happily."

"I know."

"And where would you start?"

He said, "With the Bonn meeting."

"Because you want a picture of the colonel."

"I'm guessing there'll be one in the archive. Trouble is . . ."

"The archive's at the Park."

"You know Molly Doran, don't you?"

"I know she breathes fire." Louisa stood. "On the other hand, you don't always go to the dragon. Sometimes you consult the newt."

She led the way downstairs. There was a hot damp smell on the staircase, a hint of steam in the air, as Louisa explained that Molly's archive went way back, covering all the spying the Service did before the Flood, but that, until the budget ran dry, there'd been plans to digitise everything, an all-but-neverending chore which had been dumped in the lap of—

"You're kidding."

Louisa said, "Yeah, no. Our very own Roderick Ho."

Who looked up suspiciously when they entered his office without knocking. It was Lech's office too, of course, so knocking wasn't required: still, it was always fun to see if you could catch Ho doing something quintessentially Ho-like, such as watching movie trailers, or building a spaceship out of pizza boxes. As it was, before they were both through the door he'd passed a hand over his keyboard, presumably restoring his monitors to something approaching respectable work-product. Whatever they were displaying, they were banked in front of him like a drawbridge, sealing him off from the real world.

"What do you want?"

"Do I have to want something?" Louisa said. "I was just coming to hang."

Ah, right, thought Roddy. Of course she was.

Of course she was.

Because one of the things about women—and Roddy ought to write a book—one of the things about women was, throw a little competition into the mix, and they drop the stand-off act pretty damn fast. Fact was, Louisa had had it too good for too long. If you ranked the talent in Slough House, sure, she came out top, partly because she was reasonably hot, but also because, well: Shirley and Catherine. Fifty was in Catherine's rearview mirror, so she was special-interest-only, and as for Shirley, any kind of mirror was going to offer pretty brutal feedback. Don't get him wrong, the Rodster was as feminist as the next guy, but there were ladies you shag and ladies you bag, and Shirley was definitely in the bagging area. So yeah, Louisa had had it easy, but into this three-horse race, just lately, had come Ashley Khan, and now the field was looking different. It wasn't a complete turnaround—grade inflation did no one any favours—but Ashley was a solid seven, shading to seven and a half when she didn't look like she was planning an office shooting, so Louisa was clearly starting to feel wobbly; suddenly there was competition, and what do you know? Here she was, come to hang out with the RodMeister, despite having struggled against their mutual attraction for, like, ever. It took all his self-control to withhold his trademark wry grin. You could play it too cool for too long, babe, he thought. Sure, I'm interested. But there's such a thing as market forces.

There was also such a thing as Lech Wicinski, who'd chosen this moment to return to his desk. No flair, no finesse, that was his problem. Well, that and having a face like a rained-on barbecue. You had to pity the guy, but even so: cock-blocking broke the bro code, and that was a rule, not a tongue-twister. Even a sap like Wicinski should know there were lines you don't cross.

Roddy said, "So, you wanna hang here, or go somewhere less crowded?"

With a glance at Wicinski which slid off him like a meatball from an underdone Sloppy Giuseppe.

"Nah, here's good," Louisa said.

Lech said, "Louisa says you've worked on archive material."

Ho rolled his eyes. "I've worked on all sorts, dude. Fingered every pie in the Service."

A moment's silence followed this.

"I was telling him what a fast worker you are."

"And I was telling her about this guy on the hub," said Lech, "he had the workstation next to me. And I have never seen anyone retrieve data quicker than this . . . dude. Seriously, you could ask him how many yellow cars—"

"Yellow car," murmured Louisa.

"—crossed Clifton Suspension Bridge last August, and he'd have a solid number inside ten minutes. He's a freak of nature."

"That is fast," Louisa admitted.

"Fast? It's like he's personally wired into CCTV, Google and the dark web all at once."

Roddy said, "What's his name?"

Lech paused. "We just called him . . . Mr. Lightning."

"Mr. Lightning?"

"Mr. Lightning."

"That's coo—uh, yeah, right. No, I think I've heard of him."

"You've heard of Mr. Lightning?"

"Yeah, right. If he's the dude I'm thinking of. We're kind of tight. I mean, you know. Not IRL." He nodded towards his screens. "On the dark side."

"I can picture it," said Louisa. "You and Mr. Lightning. On the dark side."

Roddy could tell she was doing just that. She had a turned-on gleam in her eyes. "So you're Team Rodster," he said. "Good to know."

"Whereas me," said Lech, "I have to say, I'm sceptical."

"Yeah, whatever."

"But then, I've seen Mr. Lightning in action."

"He's got moves," Roddy said. "Makes a good wingman. But it's like Goose and Maverick. Only one Top Gun."

"That is a good way of putting it," said Louisa. "A really good way." She touched her lips with her index finger. "Wonder how we could arrange for the pair of you to go head to head?"

"Can't do it in real time," Lech said, giving it thought. "They'd shit bricks on the hub if we roped in Mr. Lightning just to watch him trounce Roddy."

"But maybe we could devise something," Louisa said. "Come up with some insanely difficult piece of data for them both to retrieve—"

"What, and time them doing it? That's brilliant."

"Just need to work out what . . ."

Lech screwed his face up, trying to recapture a distant memory. "Here's something," he said. "Friend was telling me about a KGB colonel he saw once, a woman, in Bonn. This would have been . . . '88 or thereabouts."

"Be realistic," said Louisa. "We want difficult, not impossible."

Lech shrugged. "Sounds like you're worried you're backing Goose."

"No, I just meant—"

Roddy said, "That's it? A KGB colonel in Bonn?"

"At a meeting. David Cartwright was there. 1988."

Roddy Ho cracked his knuckles. "Ladies and gentlemen," he said. "Start your watches."

A quarter of an hour later Lech and Louisa were back upstairs with a printout, comparing the photograph of Colonel Alexa Chaikovskaya with one of Sophie de Greer they'd downloaded from the *Guardian*.

"I don't know," she said.

"Don't know? Come on. They're practically identical."

"Lots of people look practically identical."

"And de Greer's history's a blank. She could be a plant."

"You've sold yourself on this, haven't you? Yes, okay, they look alike. Mother-and-daughter alike. But what are the odds? That a KGB colonel's daughter is being used in some kind of undercover play decades after mum was on the scene?"

Lech said, "David Cartwright was a big wheel at the Park, and remind me what his grandson ended up doing?"

Louisa said nothing.

"Sometimes it's a family business."

"Okay," she said. "But you can't know for sure this de Greer woman's a blank page. Just because a newspaper comes up short on intel."

"Well I suppose I could ask Mr. Lightning to check her out."

"LOL."

"But either way, you have to admit. Not necessarily that there's something dodgy going on. But that there is a distinct possibility that there's something dodgy going on. Back on the hub—"

"Don't."

"Back on the hub, we'd follow this through. It's way over the credibility line."

"So take it to the hub."

"It may be over the credibility line, but I'm not."

"Lamb'll listen."

"Lamb can take a fucking walk. Anyway, what would he do? He'd send us out to watch her. You and me."

"You're very sure of that."

"Well he's hardly going to send Shirley and Ho."

"You've not known him as long as I have. Anyway, aren't you forgetting someone?"

"Who, Ash? She's not been here ten minutes. He had me chained to my desk the first two months."

"Which would be all the reason he needs." Louisa looked at the two photos again, side by side. Mother and daughter? Caught cold, she might even have thought them the same woman. Colonel Alexa Chaikovskaya was uniformed, her hair tied back, her expression severe; Doctor Sophie de Greer wore glasses, and had softer hair, but the eyes were the same. They might have been options on a dating site: here's me as stern librarian; me as the Red beside your bed. God, where did that come from? She should get out more. She said to Lech, "So what are you suggesting? That I give up my evening and spend it watching your supposed ringer, waiting for her handler to make contact?"

Lech said, "It's something to do, right?"

Like she'd said earlier. He was worse than River Cartwright.

He looked at his watch. "I'll leave you to think about it," he said. "Twenty minutes?"

"Not going to happen."

"See you outside."

He stopped in the kitchen on his way downstairs, put the kettle on, and was wasting moments looking for a clean mug— which went to show he was still a relative newcomer; the last clean mug in Slough House commemorated Charles and Di—when Shirley appeared in the doorway, like one of those bollards that rise up out of the tarmac when you don't expect.

"What were you and Louisa talking about?"

"We're thinking of adopting."

"No one'll let you. You'd scare a kid stupid just being in the same room."

"Always a pleasure, Shirley. But don't you have things to be getting on with? I don't know, accidents to cause or furniture to break?"

He found a mug that at least had a handle, and rinsed it under the tap.

"You're up to something."

"Shit. You got me. This whole thing about being an office worker doing boring stuff in a crappy workplace? That's just pretending. I'm actually a spy."

"I want in."

"There's nothing to be in."

"I'll tell Lamb."

"Where are we, nursery school?" The kettle boiled and he poured water onto a teabag. "Look, remember Old Street Station? Remember we decided to take out one of the newbies sent to follow us?"

". . . Yeah. So?"

"So you put a civilian in hospital. Louisa and I aren't up to anything, and if we were, you're the last person I'd want along, unless for some reason I hoped it would go tits up in the first five minutes. Clear?"

She kicked the wall hard enough to cave plaster in, and that was Shirley with trainers on. Give her a pair of boots, she'd bring down the house.

She stomped back to her office, and Lech carried his tea to his room, where Roddy Ho was still hunkered behind his screens. "Sorry, man," he said. "Mr. Lightning came in twenty seconds quicker."

"Don't believe you."

"Well, I'll do my crying in the rain." He sat, drank his tea and looked over the work product on his monitor, a list he barely remembered amassing. Was this really worth chasing down? It was made up of the names, the *noms de web*, of barely hinged individuals who'd dropped from social media after a flurry of hate-filled rants: Had they become radicalised and vanished undercover, the better to fulfil some real-world outrage? Or had they just got laid and calmed down? It was Slough House in a nutshell: a blizzard of random incidentals it might take years to sift through, leaving you with a handful of nothing, or possibly, just possibly, one solid nugget in your palm . . . Lech thought again of John Bachelor in the pub, his hangdog air dispelled as he outlined what he'd glimpsed on a news broadcast. A face from yesterday. What if it meant something? It certainly felt solider now, the photographs adding weight to the story, but all Lech was sure of was, this wasn't something to take to the Park. Not because it might turn out a waste of time, but in case it didn't. He allowed himself a moment's imagining: of presenting the hub, not with a loose thread but a tightly wound bobbin, and the reaction that would get. They'd thrown him onto the waste ground, and he'd struck gold there, and carried it back. Imagine that . . .

Oh Jesus, he thought. Just listen to me.

Wiping thoughts of glory from his mind, he opened a new browser, logged onto a Service database, traced an address for Sophie de Greer, then turned his computer off without bothering to close the other programs first. Tell me about it in the morning, he thought. Or, you know. Just burn and die.

Ho glared at him as he pulled his jacket on. "You rigged the timing so it looked like I lost."

"No, I didn't," Lech said, with absolute honesty.

"I bet Louisa knows it too."

"Louisa's got the hots for Mr. Lightning."

"Got them for me, more like."

"She should learn to hide that."

He left the office before Ho could think of a rejoinder—which gave him a ten-minute window—and took the stairs two at a time. He didn't plan to wait for Louisa in Slough House's yard, whose walls were held together with moss, so followed the alley round to Aldersgate Street, and crossed the road, and sat at the bus stop. Looking across at the glum takeaway, the suicidal newsagents, and the three storeys of dead-eyed windows stacked on top of them, he thought, not for the first time, *How did I end up here?* And felt his face, beneath its veil of scars, harden into a scowl.

An expression that wasn't clear to Louisa, looking down from her room, but even if it had been she might have failed to recognise it; might have simply noticed that she could look at Lech's scars now without thinking about what they hid: the word PAEDO, which he'd scrubbed away with a razor. Well, she was thinking about it now. But she hadn't been a moment ago. Maybe there'd come a time when she could look at Lech and simply see him, rather than the mess he'd made of his face, but she wasn't there yet. Nor was he. Everyone carries wounds, she thought. But they don't always stare back at you from every reflecting surface.

She shook her head. Maybe it would be a wasted evening, no more; maybe she'd have to terminate a pass, in which case it might as well happen tonight as any other time. And maybe—just maybe—Lech wasn't wrong, which in turn might mean they wound up in serious trouble, because whoever Sophie de Greer turned out to be, she moved in the world of chimp politics, where it was always the nastiest monkey ran the show. Anthony Sparrow, appearances notwithstanding, was currently King Kong, which made de Greer Fay Wray. If she had Kremlin connections, Sparrow either didn't know about it or did, and either way wouldn't look kindly on anyone digging into the matter. Would be likely, in fact, to bang his chest and start throwing faeces around. But that was a thing about life in Slough House: you grabbed any opportunity for excitement with both hands, and even knowing you were doing that didn't stop you doing it. Hadn't done in the past. Wouldn't now.

Louisa powered her computer down and checked she had keys and wallet. Turned the light off. The office across the landing was where Ashley Khan had been put, and Louisa looked in before heading downstairs. Ashley had been allotted the desk furthest from the door, though she'd shifted to River's desk instead. This might have been because it was better lit, or less susceptible to scrutiny from the doorway, or simply because it wasn't the desk she'd been assigned, and this was her two-fingered response. Fair enough. Louisa remembered her own early days, wrapped in a fog of misery, and she didn't have Ashley's excuse of having had her arm broken by Lamb before she'd even started. Talk about a tough interview.

Truth was, Louisa hadn't made an effort with Ashley, because you didn't. That was the rule. There was no knowing how long a slow horse would survive, even leaving aside the grim mathematics of the bigger picture. You didn't have to expect a colleague would take a bullet in the head—or a knife in the gut—or put their hand to a toxin-smeared doorknob—to know they weren't necessarily going to be around forever. Lamb's usual method of inducting a newby was to not give them anything to do for the first few months, which, if they took as an invitation to turn up late or knock off at lunchtime, would also be their last few months. So far Ashley had stood the course, but "so far" was still in single figures, if you were counting weeks. That wasn't bad going—Louisa recalled counting days; hell, hours—but it was still all uphill, and wouldn't get easier.

"Hey," she said to Ashley, who was slumped across the desk, her dark hair pooled around her.

The young woman started. "I wasn't asleep."

"Didn't think you were," Louisa lied.

"Is he still around?"

No need to ask who "he" was.

"Yes. But dormant," Louisa said, stepping inside and keeping her voice low. Sound followed peculiar waves in Slough House; syllables that couldn't be heard a social distance away might yet reach Jackson Lamb's ear. "Are you on anything yet?"

"Like her downstairs, you mean? No, not so far."

"I meant work." Not pharmaceuticals. "Has he given you an . . . assignment?"

There must be a better word than that for a slow-horse task. 'Assignment' sounded like it might have meaning somewhere down the line.

Ashley Khan said, "I'm to adjust myself to the realities of performing within attenuated parameters," and Louisa couldn't tell whether she was quoting, or had retreated behind irony.

"Yeah, that sounds about right. But, you know. It gets . . ."

"Better?"

"Not really."

"That's what I thought."

There was a plastic box on her desk containing a mixture of nuts and dried berries. Ashley reached into it without looking and collected a palmful, then sat back and regarded Louisa with unnerving frankness. "How long have you been here?"

"It's best not to think in terms of time."

"Not the most inspiring response. I was told I should just quit."

"Who by?"

"Friends. Others on the hub." Her gaze shifted from Louisa. "I mean, that was back on day one. Day two. They haven't been in touch since. None of them have."

"They're worried it's catching, being a slow horse," said Louisa. "They're shielding."

"They can screw themselves," Ashley said, her flat tone suggesting she was describing an uncanny ability rather than indicating a course of action.

Louisa didn't feel like offering an alternative point of view.

The number of people she was still in touch with at Regent's Park was zero. Less than, if you counted unanswered voicemails.

She looked round the office, which hadn't changed in any essential since Ashley's arrival. It wasn't the kind of workspace you'd try to personalise, because if you were someone who liked to personalise your workspace you'd be somewhere else, and also because it was the kind of workspace that would actively resist such attempts. Pot plants would wilt before your eyes, and photographs of loved ones fade in their frames, familiar shapes becoming ghostly presences, then absences, then blanks. A bit like your friends on the hub, on hearing the news of your exile.

What Ashley's personal space might look like, Louisa didn't know. She was young, and had barely cut her teeth at the Park before running foul of Lamb, so hadn't specialised yet; was what the Park called wet material, ready to be moulded into whatever form it chose. As things had fallen that would be down to Lamb now, so the odds were good she'd end up a shapeless mess. That aside, all Louisa knew was that Ashley had grown up in Stirling: this nugget from her personnel file, via Catherine. And, Louisa suspected, there was a little money in the background. That or some badly hammered plastic. Because Ashley dressed well, and trainee spooks enjoyed a starting salary apprentice chimney sweeps wouldn't envy.

Ashley, meanwhile, appeared to be waiting for her to justify her presence, so she said, "You've swapped desks."

"Yes, well. It's not like it's in use."

Louisa thought better of replying. Another reason for not making an effort with a newcomer was that newcomers didn't usually welcome it. This was temporary, that was their mantra. This couldn't be happening to them, so would soon stop. Wrongs would be righted, the curtain would fall. When it rose again, everything would be just the way it was.

"Anyway," Ashley said. "I'm going back to the Park."

She tipped the handful of fruit and nuts into her mouth.

"Of course you are," said Louisa. "See you tomorrow."

She headed down the stairs. Passing Ho's office, she didn't bother calling a farewell, her mild guilt at having played him—again—not being enough to warrant an apology. The way she saw it, Ho would do something offensive within the next little while, and the books would be balanced again. Having a dick for a colleague means never having to say you're sorry.

Lech Wicinski was waiting in the bus queue opposite; the only one not wearing a face mask, though from a distance he looked like he was. Louisa crossed the road to join him.

"Wimbledon," he said.

"We're doing code words now?"

"That's where she lives. You drove in, right?"

She had driven in, yes.

"So let's go."

"If you're under the impression this decisive crap comes off as macho, you're way off beam," she told him, but he shrugged.

Her car was near Fortune Park, and three minutes later they were in it and heading back towards Aldersgate Street, where both noticed, but neither commented on, Shirley Dander, entering Barbican tube station. Shirley, who saw them but pretended not to, wasn't catching a train; was heading, rather, for the footbridge leading into the Barbican itself, where she followed the painted yellow line before dropping down to Whitecross Street. The food market had packed its bags, but she found the man she was after, who worked on one of the Thai stalls, in the pub on the corner. Shirley was one of his regulars, both for the food he provided during working hours and for the cocaine he supplied on demand, and the manner in which they greeted each other and shared five minutes' gossip must have appeared, to a casual onlooker, like genuine friendship: they were good mates, these were brief times, but there were future meetings on the cards.

When Shirley left, her wallet was lighter but her pocket reassuringly held a cellophane envelope, enough to keep her from hitting the ground for a few days to come, if she practised a little restraint.

Which might involve not taking any at work.

What are you on?

What's it to you?

You're at work. You work for the Service, for God's sake...

Yeah, kind of. Not that the Service had noticed lately; as far as Regent's Park was concerned, Shirley might as well be training mice to build catapults.

You've got a boss upstairs who'll throw you out of your job without a thought if you give him an excuse.

Which showed how much Catherine Standish knew. If Lamb felt like throwing Shirley out of her job, he wouldn't need an excuse.

The hit she'd taken earlier had worn off, leaving her feeling dumpy and out of sorts. The obvious fix for this was close to hand, but she didn't feel ready to dip into that yet. *You've been seriously lucky so far, and that won't go on happening forever.* Yeah yeah yeah. Until she got Miss Bossy out of her head, there was no point relaxing. Coke had been known to make those voices louder. Last thing she needed was a travelling chorus, pointing out her misdeeds every step she took.

So she spent the next two hours on cruise control. If the City was the Square Mile, to its east was the Hipster Hectare, and Shirley kind of liked hipsters, for not being afraid to look the way they did, and not being ashamed of their stupid opinions. But they were rarer than they once were, most of their ventures—cereal restaurants, beard oils—having proved the opposite of recession-proof, and she soon tired of the safari. The original plan had been to kill time in a bar or two and then dance her mood away, but already it felt like her mood would win, regardless of the bounty in her pocket and the freshly ironed tee on her back. Catherine bloody Standish.

Not to mention Lech bloody Wicinski and Louisa bloody Guy. That pair were plotting something—a KGB colonel?— and the thought of being left out was grating on her. What had she done to be excluded? Okay, so what Lech had said about Old Street station might have been more or less true, inasmuch as, yes, she had coshed a civilian there and left him comatose in a public toilet, but that bare summary had hiphopped over that she'd done so to save Lech having his face smashed in. Which you'd think he'd show a little gratitude, even if a bit of hands-on remodelling might have improved his looks in the long run.

All she wanted was a piece of the action. It didn't matter what it was about; they could keep her in the dark if they liked. But she wanted to be there when things were happening, because otherwise what was the point of it: the endless slogging through Lamb's endless tasks? Which he only invented because he wasn't actually allowed to torture them physically, that was Shirley's take. Otherwise he'd have them all in the cellar on a daily basis.

The thought of hitting the dance floor felt hollow now, its moment past. It was time to head home instead, even if home was a cheerless apartment: its floors unswept, its sheets unlaundered, its kitchen frankly dangerous. At least it was somewhere to be. At least there was stuff to do there.

She finished her drink—her fourth, maybe, but counting was for babies—and left the bar to find herself not far from Shoreditch High. Mentally, she plotted her journey home: tube-wise she'd be better off starting from Slough House. And if she went that way she could pop into her office and collect her iron, before one of her colleagues walked off with it.

Darkness had settled on London's streets, and probably elsewhere too, but it had a particular flavour here; the shadows congregating overhead, their whispered plotting barely audible. Shirley headed back the way she'd come: up onto the Barbican walkways. Lights were on in the towers, evidence of lives lived elsewhere. She wondered what it was like, being one of the people you passed at a distance; glimpsed once, then seen no more. Crossing the footbridge, she saw that Slough House's lights were mostly off, though Roddy Ho was still in his room, doubtless pursuing some online fancy. She'd nip in, collect her iron. Catherine would be gone, and there'd be no reprise of the afternoon's lecture.

The stairs were a little unsteady, but that was Slough House for you. Always shifting underfoot.

In her room, she grabbed her iron; on the way out, she paused on the landing, hearing voices from Ho's office.

Did he have *company?*

He didn't, but only in the technical sense that there was nobody in the room with him. Taking the larger perspective, Roddy was surrounded by admirers, though that was barely worth the footnote: if the Rodster wanted crowds, crowds happened. Charisma was the word. He should link to an online dictionary, email the definition to Mr. Lightning. Not that he believed what Wicinski had said about a twenty-second victory margin, but it was as well to keep a rival in his place. Mr. Lightning might have them gasping in awe on the hub, exclaiming *fork!* and *sheet!* every time he flexed his digits, but if he thought he was a match for the Rodinator, he had brutal lessons coming. As for Wicinski, a lesser man might be tempted to seek revenge and cancel his direct debits, but the more enlightened soul would rise above the insult, and pass by on the other side.

Because, Roderick Ho reminded himself, there comes a time when you accept your maturity. Graduate from fresh-faced acolyte to wise mentor, at whose feet new generations gather, eager to collect the pearls that drop from your lips. The puppy becomes the full-grown hound; the cub becomes the lion. Which, in a nutshell, was why he was in a Zoom room now, with women digitally queued before him, each of them seeking the aid, the salvation, only Roddy could bestow.

Help me, Hobi-Wan Kenobi. You're my only hope.

How many times had he heard that?

(Six.)

But it had to be said, this latest attempt lacked what you might call feeling. Didn't do justice to herself or, especially, him.

Roddy allowed the slightest of frowns, the merest flicker of disappointment, to cross his worldly features.

"Let's try that again."

"Why, what was wrong with it?"

What was wrong with it was, he'd just told her to try it again. Had this woman never been mentored before?

He said, "It lacked . . . gravitas."

"Yeah, well, it's spelt wrong. It should be *O*bi-Wan. You've got *H*obi-Wan."

Her fellow hopefuls watched mutely from their little windows, one or two shaking their heads, as well they might. It was round one of the audition process—early days—but you had to live the part, and if you were Princess Leia, you didn't answer back to Hobi-Wan.

But then, sad truth, Roddy wasn't working with the cream of the crop. Of the eight would-be Princess Leias, six were overweight and this one downright bolshy, and even if any were capable of delivering their key line with the sincerity he was looking for, the gold-bikini round was going to see most of them hitting light-speed on their way out. They'd be in a galaxy far, far away before you could say *I have a bad feeling about this.*

He said, "If you're having difficulty with the script—"

"Didn't say I was having difficulty. I said it's got the wrong words."

Roddy's right hand gripped the hilt of his light sabre. This couldn't be seen by anyone, but it was important to have the props if you were going to project the image. Subtle, but key. Not that it was his actual light sabre, which was in a cupboard at home, in the box he'd never taken it out of, but a stand-in he'd improvised using a length of strip lighting, an adaptor cable, and duct tape for a handle. He'd plugged it in, and it actually hummed when he wielded it, but you had to be careful not to turn it on for long, on account of duct tape peeling off when it got hot. All of which was information the bolshy Princess Leia might usefully have been given—she might get the message that you gave it a hundred per cent or you took an early bath—but Roddy just sighed. Sometimes the points you wanted to make screamed like an X-Wing over the heads of the ill-informed. More in sorrow than in wrath he terminated her part in the discussion, then gazed at the remaining faces. "I'll say it again," he said. "South Bank CosPlay. One of the biggest gatherings of the Jedi community on this or any other planet. And only one of you can go as Princess Leia."

"Well, that's not true," one of the women said. "We can all go as Princess Leia if we want."

Roddy terminated her too. "Only one of you can go as Princess Leia with *me*," he told the others.

"Jesus screaming fuck!" said Shirley.

"Force-be-with-you-I'll-be-in-touch," said Roddy, killing his screens.

"I mean, shit!"

"Get out of my office!"

"Door was open."

"No, it wasn't!"

"It clearly was. Are you on Zoom? Is that a cape?" She came further into the room, whose door had indeed been open, once she'd very quietly given it a push. "Are you . . . are you dressing up?"

Roddy said, "It's not a cape."

It was in fact a cagoule draped over his shoulders, and he let it fall to the floor as he stood. If this was an attempt to reassert his dignity, it failed.

"Is that a light sabre?"

"No."

"Can I have a go?"

"No. What are you doing here?"

"Collecting my iron." She held it up in evidence. "But fuck me, this is brilliant. The others are literally going to shit themselves. I mean, literally. There is going to be shit, everywhere."

"You tell them and I'll fuck you up."

"Totally worth it. Who were those women? They were women, right?"

"Friends."

"You haven't got any friends."

"Neither have you."

"Dickhead."

"Beast."

"Asshat."

"Spreader."

". . . Spreader? What does that even mean?"

Roddy said, "You know, like, spreader. Like, you spread the virus."

"Nobody says that."

"Some people do."

They glared at each other; Shirley brandishing her iron, Roddy with one hand on the hilt of his light sabre.

If you strike me down now, I will become more powerful than you can possibly imagine.

Shirley said, "So what was that, anyway, some kind of fancy dress booty call?"

"None of your business."

"Seriously, this is everyone's business by first thing tomorrow. You might as well save us the bother and fill in the blanks."

"I don't fire blanks," Roddy said. With his free hand he waved at his laptop, nestled amidst the ranked screens. "Say hello to my leetle fren'."

"You don't scare me."

"Someone sounded their horn at me in a crosswalk once. I came right back here and sold their house."

"You'd have to buy me one first."

"I'll trash your bank account."

"Already trashed."

". . . You're gonna find you've ordered all this shit you don't even want."

"Yeah, that's normal. What planet are you on?"

Roddy looked about to reply, but thought better of it.

Shirley came further into the room, placed her iron on Lech's desk, then levered herself up, and sat swinging her legs. What had looked like a dead loss of an evening had turned around, and she was planning on getting her luck's worth. But even as she watched Roddy's face enact the seven deadly sins, it occurred to her that there was more than one way to skin a nerd.

He was waiting for her to speak, so she let him wait longer. His room was the same as hers, more or less; the same as all the offices, bar those on the top floor. But his had more kit, both on his desk and on the rackety metal shelving round the walls. Unattached keyboards and lengths of cable; boxes of floppy disks and thick-spined operating manuals. All of it junk, but if you piled up enough junk, you left your stamp on a place.

On Lech's side some attempt had been made to create a mess-free area, but not enough of one to bear fruit.

"Who'd you share with before Lech?" she asked him.

"Nobody."

"And who before that?"

"Can't remember."

"You ever had a partner?"

"A what?"

"Forget it." She gestured towards his desk. "You've got these tracing apps, right?"

Roddy rolled his eyes.

"Can you find Louisa's car?"

"Depends."

"On what?"

"On what happens if I do."

"Maybe people don't get to hear about your little *Star Wars* production."

"'Maybe'?"

"Tell me where she is, and I won't say anything."

". . . How do I know I can trust you?"

She laughed. "It's Slough House. You can't trust anyone."

Oddly, this seemed to reassure him.

He went back round his side of the desk and by the time she'd joined him had set something in motion: a little icon that looked like a silverfish trying to eat itself was toiling away on his largest screen. A blink or two later and this coloured itself in: they were looking at a skeletal street map, laid out in straight lines as if someone had tidied the city up in a burst of optimism. Pulsing dead centre was a red circle, like a pimple waiting to explode.

Shirley said, "Isn't this just Find My Friends?"

". . . So?"

"So how come you and Louisa are sharing that?"

Because Louisa didn't know was the strictly accurate answer. Some apps wormed their way into your phone as soon as you clicked on the email. Or they did if you knew what you were doing.

"Where is this, anyway?"

He zoomed out, so they could see the bigger picture. "Wimbledon."

"What's in Wimbledon?" Shirley said, but she was talking to herself.

The car was parked not far from the common, though she supposed you were never that far from the common if you were in Wimbledon to start with.

"What are they looking at?"

"'They'?" said Roddy.

"She's with Lech. They're up to something. What are they looking at?"

Roddy shrugged, and opened another browser. A quarter minute later they were looking at a street scene, broad daylight; a residential pavement. Most of it was houses, but there was an apartment block at a junction; a brick building with glass front doors showing a lobby with what looked like a cheese plant in its centre. Big green leaves, anyway. Shirley marvelled, briefly, that here they were on one side of the city looking at a building on the other, trying to recognise a pot plant in its lobby, and then reminded herself that this was film, not a live broadcast. Clues included that it was broad daylight and that Louisa wasn't in sight, though the other screen indicated that her phone remained close by.

And was, in fact, in Louisa's hand, and Louisa herself in her car. Lech was beside her, and they were across the road from the apartment block Lech had identified as Sophie de Greer's address. Without being confident she was in her flat, they knew she hadn't left it while they were watching. Louisa had suggested—several times, by this point—that the odds were she hadn't come home yet: politicos, she maintained, worked ungodly hours, and it was only just after nine. Lech had countered by pointing out that de Greer was Swiss, and as such perhaps adhered more strictly to an acceptable timetable.

"Except if you're right, she's not Swiss. She's Russian."

"Such a thing as cover."

Since this exchange Louisa had mostly been reading the news on her phone, wondering at what point she'd kick Lech out and head home. He had the air of one who wasn't going anywhere until he'd been proved right. Which was possibly just another way of pointing out that he was male.

She put her phone away. "How pissed off was Roddy?"

"Don't know."

"Hard to tell?"

"Hard to care."

"He has his uses, you know. Maybe we should be nice to him for a change."

"Yeah," said Lech. "We could scrape a few quid together and rent him a girlfriend experience."

"I'm not that sorry."

"How expensive could it be? To have someone stand him up, then laugh about it on Instagram."

"Bitter, much?"

"You don't know the half of it. Is this her now?"

It was, or seemed to be: a tracksuited figure, emerging from the apartment block and pausing on the threshold, fiddling with something on her wrist. She was blonde, but wearing goggles that obscured much of her face. Still: right approximate height, right approximate age. She bounced up and down on the spot for some seconds in a manner that had Lech nodding thoughtfully, though offered no conclusive evidence as to her identity. The tracksuit was grey, with reflective bright orange piping that matched her trainers.

"It's about mileage, not stylage," Louisa muttered.

"What?"

"I said, what do we do?"

Lech said, "Follow her?"

"Because obviously she's on her way to a secret meeting."

"Well we won't know that until she gets there."

She'd already made a start, bounding down the street with an ease which belied Louisa's suggestion that she was all kit, no grit. Louisa started the car and pulled out into the empty road. Lech kept his eyes on the running woman.

"We're going to look like an abduction attempt," he said.

"Thanks, that's constructive."

"She's probably heading for the common."

Louisa's trainers were in the boot, and under her blouse she wore a sleeveless vest that would pass for a running top in the dark. Or might do. "Eyes on her." She pulled ahead of de Greer, if that's who it was, and took the next right. A dark expanse opened up at the end of the road: that would be the common.

"She's still behind us," said Lech.

A parking space materialised: DISABLED ONLY. My boss, my colleagues, my love life, Louisa thought. More than enough handicaps to qualify for a blue badge. She pulled into it and hopped out without turning the engine off. Opened the boot, removed her blouse. Lech joined her, facing the way they'd come, as the woman drew level on the other side of the road and then sailed past.

"Ninety per cent sure it's her," he said.

Louisa had shed her shoes, was doing up the laces on her trainers. "You'd better bloody be right."

The woman had reached the road bordering the common and was jogging on the spot while waiting to cross.

"Take the car," Louisa said. "Try not to lose us." She dropped her shirt in the boot and grabbed a head torch.

"Got your phone?"

Obviously.

The woman was over the road, and bounding into the dark. Louisa pulled the torch onto her head and set off after her.

The unseasonable warmth of the day had fled. This didn't deter the dogwalkers, or other runners, but the common boasted space enough to absorb them, and it was easy to feel alone once the road and the traffic, its noise and lights, were behind her. Louisa averaged 5K a day weekdays, and hit the occasional 20 on a weekend, but had never felt part of a community, and ran mainly to purge herself of work. In her secret self, she thought of runners the way everyone else did: as roving germ circuses, scattering spit and sweat.

But Sophie de Greer, if that's who she was, looked like she didn't care. Barely had she hit the common than she was off, running not much faster than Louisa's habitual speed, but with an effortless grace that suggested she could keep it up forever. Still, she'd be visible from a distance. The orange piping on her trackie gathered what light there was and painted it in stripes across her running form: to Louisa, de Greer resembled a figure from an ancient video game.

If it was de Greer.

I'm going to stop adding that caveat, she thought. Because if it's not her, this is going to be even more of a fucking parody than usual.

Her breathing settled into a rhythm, and the path felt light beneath her feet. She could have done with her sports bra, and a warmer top, but it felt good to be in motion after a day at her desk. And if the pointlessness of the exercise nagged at her—even if this were de Greer, what good would following her do?—she wouldn't be the first slow horse to find comfort in the notion that she was at least doing something.

Breathe in, breathe out. Her muscles were finding their stroke. She'd not run more than a few hundred yards along the path before Lech lost her, Louisa fading into the insubstantial, darkening air.

He got back into her car, driver's side. He was on Windmill Road, not far short of a set of temporary lights, where passage briefly became single-lane, to accommodate roadworks. The casual way she'd left him the keys felt good. So did the way she'd headed off after de Greer: no discussion, just got on with it. Lech hadn't been Ops, though he'd watched a few from inside a van, and it always gave him a kick to see the way the guys had each others' backs—afterwards they might argue the toss, come to blows even, about how things should have gone, but at the time they just got on with it. Which was how Louisa had reacted to de Greer's appearance: it might not be de Greer, might be a random jogger, but the op was to keep her in sight, and that was what Louisa had done, no questions asked. *Take the car. Try not to lose us.* Okay, not a hundred per cent confidence, but still. When someone tossed you their car keys, it felt good. It showed trust.

Compare and contrast with Roderick Ho's response when Shirley asked to borrow his.

"No fucking way."

"It's important."

"You said that last time—"

"That wasn't my fault."

"—and it ended up in a snowdrift."

"Wasn't my fault."

"In Wales."

"It's not snowing, we're not in Wales, and if you don't lend me your car, everyone'll hear about your weird sex party."

"It wasn't a sex party."

Shirley paused. "You are so fucking straight, you know that?"

Which was more than half the problem. Get a line or two down the little prick, he'd not only lend her his car, he'd sledge on top while she took fast corners.

For a moment she toyed with the idea of doing just that, of getting some coke into him, even if it involved blowing it up his nose herself, but the thought fell apart in the face of how much it would pain her to gift Roddy Ho a line, or, indeed, see it scattered like dust across the shelves and carpet of this unlovely room.

How could anyone stand to turn their office into a graveyard for out-of-date tech?

He was glaring at her still, and seemed to be under the impression that just because he'd refused her request, that brought the matter to a close.

She plucked a keyboard from the nearest shelf. It had its cable wrapped round it, and looked no older than the one attached to her computer. In better nick if anything: its *E* was still legible.

"How come you keep all these?"

Ho said, "You never know."

"Never know what?"

"When you'll need one."

"Do you think you'll need this?" She waved the keyboard at him.

He shrugged. "Might do."

"It looks pretty standard."

"They said that about the first gen Amstrad."

"Good point," said Shirley, and slammed the keyboard against the side of Lech's desk, where it exploded in a loud scatter of plastic. When she replayed the moment in her head later, the air was filled with a confetti alphabet. In real life she was left holding a computer keyboard folded in two, its halves held together by wiring.

"Fuck!"

"I know, right?" she said.

"Don't do that!"

"I just did. And I have to say, I was not expecting it to make so much noise." She let what was left in her hands fall to the floor, and took another keyboard from the shelf. "Do you think they'll all be that loud?" She smashed it against the desk. "Certainly looking that way."

"You're a fucking maniac!"

"It's been said before." She dropped the junk and reached for a monitor: flat-screened, 18-inch. Already she was picturing the contact it would make with the wall; all those pixels whooshing everywhere, like glitter. All the crunching underfoot that would ensue.

Ho didn't dare come closer, preferring to keep his desk between them.

"You wanna make me stop?" she invited. "You're the one with the light sabre."

"Lamb'll go ape shit."

"That'll be fun. How far do you think I can throw this?"

"Put it down!"

"I'll break every piece of kit in this office," she said. "Including the stuff that's still plugged in. And while you're crying about it, I'll tell Lamb what you were using it for while it still worked. And when he's finished laughing, he'll do to you what I'm doing to your toybox."

"Put it *down!*"

Instead she raised it above her head with both hands and made a chimp-like noise. There'd be glass and plastic everywhere, and the ghost of every image the screen had ever displayed would flow into the wall it broke upon, and spend an eternity trapped in the bones of Slough House.

That was such a pleasing thought it almost came as a disappointment when Roddy screamed, "Okay! O*kay!*"

She hovered, unwilling for the moment to end. One more small explosion? Couldn't do any harm . . .

"I said okay!"

Reluctantly, she placed the screen on Lech's desk.

"You're a fucking maniac."

"You already said that."

"There's . . . *crap* everywhere now."

"There was crap everywhere before."

He came out from behind his desk and snatched up the monitor, cradling it in his arms. You'd think she'd threatened to drop his baby out of a window. Then she thought, Ho, with a baby? Jesus. Some stuff, you don't want in your head.

She held her hand out. "Keys."

"No way."

". . . You want me to start again?"

"You're not taking my car. I'm coming with you."

She hadn't been expecting that.

"You'll just get in the way," she said.

"Don't care. You're not taking my car. You'll just smash it up."

To be fair, evidence of her propensity for smashing stuff up wasn't hard to find. He looked pretty determined, and while she didn't think it would take her long to break that determination—about as long as it would take to break another keyboard—time wasn't necessarily on her side, not if she wanted to catch up with Louisa and Lech before whatever was happening happened. Besides, Ho could keep her up to speed on their position. And another besides: if she was right about being jinxed, then teaming up with Roddy Ho was a win-win.

She said, "Okay. One minute," and stalked out of the room and into her own office.

Ho thought: Christ, that was close. It was like dealing with a wild animal, one you had to talk out of its temper when you didn't even share a language. Hardly a surprise his razor-sharp recall was letting him down, not after dealing with Dander's tantrum . . . He'd come this close to bringing her down—quick jab to the throat—and was thankful he hadn't: last thing he needed was an ex-colleague on his carpet. Sure, Lamb would have seen things his way—there are times you can't keep your powers in check: ask any man—but that wouldn't have kept da Feds at bay. Imagine, the Rodster behind bars. He'd seen enough movies: it would have been a full-time job defending his sweet virtue. He'd have been unlikely to come out of it without a scar or two. He raised a hand to his face, traced an invisible line down one cheek. An eye would be partly closed, its surface gone milky. One-eyed Rod. He'd be bitter, a loner, but still devoted to the cause of justice. He was still clutching the monitor, too. He put it back on its shelf, then looked darkly down at all the broken plastic. Someone was going to have to sweep that up.

When Shirley returned she was sniffing aggressively, and wiping the back of a hand across her nose. "So where you parked then?"

He was parked where he usually was, in a residents only space the other side of Fann Street. Not that he was risking a ticket: he had an actual permit in the name of an actual resident, and if ninety-six-year-old Alice Bundle's neighbours ever wondered why she owned a D-reg electric blue Ford Kia—with cream flashing—when she'd been a lock-in since '03, well, life was full of mysteries.

"So let's go."

Shirley led the way, jigging down the stairs like they were hot; Roddy paused to grab jacket and baseball cap—when you were working the streets you had to blend in, dig? Cap on sideways, though there were fools who still wore them backwards. Then again, he philosophised, style moved faster than a bucking bronco, and not everyone could be hip to its bang and boom. Welcome to the Rod-eo. Some were thrown in the first few seconds; the brilliant few were born to ride.

"Are you fucking coming?"

Like there was an emergency waiting.

Which possibly involved laundry, Roddy noted, because she was carrying her iron. Though it was possible she hadn't noticed: never tightly wrapped, there was a more than usual bouncy agitation to Shirley's movements now, like he'd observed in clubs sometimes. People who kept dancing even when they were standing still. Poor coordination. Worse than average bladder control too, given the number of times they disappeared into the toilets: he didn't lack sympathy, but seriously, why did they even bother going out? They couldn't be enjoying themselves.

"Let me drive."

"No way."

"It'll be quicker."

Yeah, but the whole point of him being here was to not let Shirley get behind the wheel of his car.

Ignoring her, he climbed into the driver's seat, and for a moment imagined peeling away and leaving her, her stupid iron in her hand. But that pleasurable bubble burst, replaced by a vision of her returning to Slough House and continuing her destructive catalogue of the contents of his room . . . No. Safest thing was to take her to Wimbledon and deliver her into the keeping of the others. Alternatively, he could take her to Wimbledon and just abandon her there. She'd probably find her way back eventually, but it wasn't something you'd lay big money on.

Now she was tapping on the passenger window with the tip of the iron.

He leaned across and unlocked her door.

"So what are we waiting for?" she asked, climbing in.

"Seatbelt."

Shirley shook her head. "So fucking straight," she said again, then noticed she was holding the iron. She barked a strange laugh, dropped it in the footwell and clicked her belt into place. "So what are we waiting for now?"

Pulling away, Roddy glanced at his phone, still displaying Find My Friends. Louisa had moved, and appeared to be adrift from the obvious bones of the skeletal map. Well, she wouldn't be hard to find. Middle of London: it wasn't like you could disappear.

Which Louisa would have been glad to hear, even from that dubious source, because night on the common was inky deep. The lamps along the pathways were widely spaced, and somewhere round the mid-points patches of darkness puddled; every time she reached one she felt like she was stepping offstage. *Try not to lose us*, she'd told Lech, but it wasn't like he could drive along behind her. And off the lamplit paths, the puddles of darkness became seas. Anyone could be swimming there, or suddenly appear from their depths ... Up ahead, de Greer left the path and disappeared behind a cathedral. This turned out, on nearer inspection, to be a stand of trees: a brief screen, there then gone. The new route followed no path, but there was a track underfoot, the grass worn away by runners, dogwalkers, hedgehogs. Louisa turned her headtorch on, and the effect was to make her feel visible rather than to illuminate much. But she could still make out the orange piping of de Greer's tracksuit, and now, in her wake, two other shapes: a pair in dark kit, one with green fluorescent trainers; the other with the number eleven in silver on his back.

Runners ebbed and flowed—they murmurated—and you couldn't keep an eye on all of them at once. But Louisa didn't like it that these men hadn't been there, and now were; didn't like the way they'd come out of nowhere. As if they'd been waiting.

De Greer's lack of hesitation at any moment since leaving her apartment suggested that this was her regular route. If you knew about that, Louisa thought, you wouldn't have to hang around by her apartment block to pick her up. You could just wait and collect her at the darkest point available.

It was possible, of course, that she was being paranoid.

And let's not forget, it was possible that this wasn't even de Greer.

Whoever it was, if she kept on in a straight line she'd reach a road sooner or later. Possibly even the road Lech was on. Without slowing, she squeezed her phone from her jeans pocket. He answered on the first ring.

"I'm not the only one following her," she told him.

". . . Seriously?"

She didn't have words for that.

He said, "Shit. No. Sorry. Who are they?"

"Pardon me while I stop them and ask. But there are two, male, and it looks like they're watching her."

"Security detail?"

Louisa didn't think so. Who was de Greer, a political adviser? She might have high-level clearance, but not full-time bodywatchers. She wasn't royalty.

And if Lech was right, and she was some kind of plant, her handler wouldn't have a team watching her back. That would be tantamount to hoisting the Jolly Roger.

Lech said, "Maybe you'd better abort."

"I'm not leaving her."

"Louisa, if they are tailing her, and they're not a security detail, they'll be from the Park. And if we fuck up a Park surveillance—"

"Yeah, or it's two guys following a woman on a dark common."

"Shit . . . Hang on."

A padded thump, as if he'd dropped his phone on the passenger seat.

She couldn't see de Greer, and the silvery eleven was no more than a ghostly squiggle in the dark.

Lech came back. "Are you on the same path you set off on?"

"No."

". . . Any idea at all where you are?"

Yes, she thought. I'm in the fucking dark. Could you be any less helpful?

A sentiment echoed that moment by Roddy Ho, and directed at Shirley Dander, though the wording differed.

"I'm trying to drive!"

"I'm not stopping you!"

"You're fiddling about! Stay out of my glove box!"

Shirley slammed it shut. It contained nothing interesting anyway: a pair of gloves was all.

She often succumbed to déjà vu when a passenger in someone else's car. On the other hand, she often succumbed to Groundhog Day just turning up for work.

"Can you not drive faster?"

"Can you not shut up?"

She should never have let him get behind the wheel. There was a kind of purgatory in this; to feel herself rushing towards some waiting event, one crying out for her presence, while in reality she was travelling at the speed of a hobbled cow, with every traffic light in existence throwing a red glare in her direction, and every other car on the street laughing at her in its rearview mirror. The scowl she wore was like a swan's wing: it could break a man's arm if he got too close. And the way her blood was fizzing, she might burst before they reached their destination.

There was action somewhere, and she was being sidelined again. She could feel it in her bones, in the itch beneath her skin.

Shops and houses. Someone walking a dog. Streetlights and zebra crossings; the flat expressions on darkened panes of glass. London had different textures, a different grain, every postal district.

Roddy said, "How do you know what they're up to, anyway?"

"I don't," she said. "That's the point."

"Then why—"

"They were talking about a KGB colonel."

"In Bonn," said Roddy. "In 1988."

". . . You know who she is?"

"Colonel Alexa Chaikovskaya?"

"Yeah. Her. Who is she?"

"Dunno."

"So how come you know her name?"

"It was a speed test."

"Yeah?" Shirley looked through her side window, checking whether they were keeping up with pedestrians. "How'd that work out?"

Roddy's phone lay on his lap, winking up at him: he seemed able to assimilate information by glancing at a screen, as if he were one step away from being plugged into a giant motherboard. She imagined his head full of digital splinters, his tongue a slippery coil of wires. All his thoughts lined up in binary rows.

On the other hand, he didn't handle human communication well. Which reminded her:

"Those women. The ones who want to be Princess whatsername."

"Leia."

"Yeah. Was that a Tinder thing?"

"I told you. It wasn't a sex party."

"Maybe not for you. But any woman desperate enough to dress up as a cartoon character is looking to get laid."

The car might have hit a bump or something.

"Actually, Leia, laid. Clue's right there, when you think about it. Hey, is this Wimbledon?"

Roddy's gargled response wasn't audible, but Shirley could read a street sign. This was Wimbledon.

She snatched the phone before he could prevent her. "How close are they?"

"Give it back!"

"When you tell me—"

"I don't know without looking at it!"

He had a point. She tossed it back into his lap, screen down, and he fumbled it the right way up. "They're on the common. Or Louisa is. Her phone, anyway."

She'd already seen a marker for the common: they were heading in that direction.

"And Princess Leia's not a cartoon."

"She isn't?"

Roddy rolled his eyes. "Well, sometimes she is. But that's for kids."

They'd rounded a junction and a darkness opened up ahead; they took another corner, and it settled on their right. Somewhere out there, Louisa's phone was throbbing. Louisa lived miles away; even a crow in flight would have its work cut out. So what was she doing here, if not engaged on some adventure or other? With Lech? And how come other slow horses got to pair off, while Shirley was stuck with Roddy Ho? It wasn't fair.

She dipped a hand into her pocket and fastened her fist around an inch-square cellophane envelope. And then a bus rolled past, masked passengers staring out from alternating seats, and in its wake a car; the driver's face briefly visible as a grid of tattered lines.

"Was that Lech?"

It was, or had been.

He'd driven in a circle: the length of Windmill Road, then, pleasingly, left onto Sunset, which made him feel all Hollywood. He was now heading back up Parkside, whose trees hid the common from view. Louisa was out there but couldn't offer clues as to where precisely, beyond feeling she'd run in a curve since leaving the car—nobody steered by the stars anymore, or not in London, where light pollution swaddled the city like a tea cosy. And there were two men out there with her, also following de Greer, and if they weren't Park they could be anyone. It wasn't so long since a pair of Russian hoods had toured Britain, leaving mayhem in their wake . . .

But once you started a hare, you had to follow it to its den. Louisa was out in the dark because of him, which meant he had to be ready to help her if needed. All those times he'd been inside the van, admiring the way the guys watched each other's backs: here those moments were, like an immersive flashback. But he had to find her first.

He turned onto Windmill Road again. "You still with me?"

Louisa's voice was laboured. "Uh-huh."

"Are you on a path?"

"Not anymore."

"Do you know what direction you're heading?"

"I think back the way I came. But I'm not positive."

Lech rubbed a hand across his cheeks, a gesture that had changed meaning in the past year. Once, he'd have been checking whether he needed a shave. Now, he was verifying that his face remained a welter of crazy scars.

"Can you see the road? Or any road?"

"A road. Dimly."

It was a difficult distance away, difficult to estimate and difficult to keep in focus, and Louisa had other things to worry about, such as the way the ground dipped and lurched with every step. The two men in front had moved further apart, gaining ground on de Greer, and even as she watched they were putting a spurt on, as if this were their optimal moment; the darkest patch of ground between here and the world. She didn't think they knew she was there. She'd turned her headtorch off, shrouding herself in darkness, which meant she wasn't moving as quickly as them: the ghostly number eleven floating easily over the stumbly ground, the green trainers an effortless rise and fall, closing the gap between themselves and the orange piping on de Greer's tracksuit. Only Louisa felt like a whole person; a solid figure in a murky landscape.

One thing was clear, though. Whoever these comedians were, they weren't innocent souls on an evening run. They were closing in on de Greer the way dogs move in on prey, or the way Louisa imagined they might; with extra sudden speed, and joy coursing into their tastebuds.

She heard a woman gasp: de Greer realising she wasn't alone.

And then the world grabbed Louisa by an ankle.

Like most falls, this one took forever, and she was already counting its possible cost before she hit the ground: she might break a bone, or mash her face into something unforgiving. But instinct reached out a helping hand: she was halfway curled into a ball before she landed, taking the brunt of the impact on her right shoulder. *My shooting arm*, she thought. She didn't have a gun. Where did these thoughts come from? It hadn't been soundless, her brief and unexpected flight, but she hadn't cried out, and when she righted herself, and located the other figures again, they didn't appear to have heard her. Shaken but unstirred, she got to her feet. Green Trainers and Number Eleven had come to a halt. Sophie de Greer stood halfway between them. No physical contact appeared to have occurred, but it didn't look to Louisa like a meeting of friends.

She put a hand to her shoulder, gripped hard, and felt tomorrow's bruise taking shape. But only a bruise. Nothing serious.

What mattered more was—*shit*—something was missing. She'd dropped her mobile.

"She's stopped moving," Roddy said.

The pulse on his screen was stationary, as if Louisa had come to a halt out there in the dark.

They'd made a U-turn after spotting Lech, and were heading that same direction now, up the main road. To their left, hiding behind a screen of trees, lay the common. The thought of it had Shirley wriggling in her seat, as if, deep in its shadows, lay something to satisfy the restless cravings which were creeping up on her again. Which were always creeping up on her.

"How close is she?" she said.

"Dunno. But we're nearly parallel."

They reached a junction and turned, heading towards the roadworks, and keeping the common to their left. Its bordering trees thinned out, offering glimpses into the darkness: she peered, but couldn't make out anything much. Roddy followed her gaze, and unlike Shirley could make out shifting shapes in the dark—the Rodster's night vision was up there with your average cat. There were people; there was action. The scenario unfolded before him like a one-take movie: Louisa, lured onto the common by a former KGB Colonel, taking revenge for ancient defeats. There were black prisons in remote corners of the former Soviet states; Roddy knew about them—everyone did. British spies, long written off as missing in action, were among the captives; locked up with no hope of release, and treated with inhuman cruelty. It was all starting to happen right now, not far from here, in the dark. Under the pitiless eyes of ex-Colonel Alexa Chaikovskaya, Louisa was being bundled into a sack, thrown into the boot of a car, dispatched from a private airfield, and the next time she'd see daylight, it would be falling on stone-cold snow and rock. An orange jumpsuit and a bucket in the corner . . . Yeah, right. Not on Roddy's watch. His upper lip twitched, the only outer sign to betray his mental preparation for action, and something inside him hardened at the thought of the battle to come; the split-second reflexes he'd rely on—

"Red light."

". . . Wha'?"

"Red light!"

Roddy braked, and screeched to a halt in the path of the tourist coach coming the opposite way.

The noise of the coach's brakes—like a pair of pigs being sheared—startled Lech, who was close at hand, having pulled over on the far side of the roadworks, where the road became two lanes again. He was standing by the car, mobile in hand, peering into the darkness beyond the trees, and hearing nothing from Louisa's end. He'd said her name twice before the noise of the near-collision nearly made him drop his phone, though that same sound, transmitted through the ether, reached Louisa, the squawk erupting just yards from where she stood, and more audible than Lech's voice had been. She scooped her mobile up gratefully, and turned back to where the men had waylaid de Greer, if that's what they were doing. If that's who she was. She switched her headtorch back on and ran to within yards of where the trio had clustered. "Still here," she said into the phone. Then called to the group in front of her: "Hey!"

The woman had seen her approaching. The men hadn't, and didn't look welcoming.

"Hey," Louisa said again. "Are you okay?"

The one with the shirt reading Number Eleven said, "You talkin' to me?"

"I was talking to her," Louisa said.

The blonde woman pushed her goggles onto her forehead.

It was de Greer, Louisa noted with relief. One possible way of the evening ending up a fiasco was off the table. Others remained.

"Are you okay?" Louisa repeated. "Do you need help?"

It seemed to her that the woman smiled.

Green Trainers said to Louisa, "We're all friends here. We're just having a chat."

"Yeah, no, it just seems an odd place to be doing that? So I wondered."

"No need."

The accent, she thought, was Italian. The looks matched: dark features, generous stubble, probably black hair—hard to tell in this light—but product definitely involved. The guy had been running for ten minutes, and his mop looked like he'd just stepped out of a wardrobe.

Ignoring him, she spoke to de Greer. "That's right? They're friends of yours?"

De Greer said, "I've never seen them before in my life."

"She's joking," said Green Trainers.

"Then we have a problem," Louisa said, "because I don't have a sense of humour. But I do have a phone. You want me to call the police?"

"What we want," said Number Eleven, "is for you to fuck off and mind your own business."

"Hey hey hey," Green Trainers said, and spread his arms forgivingly. "Let's not get taken away. Come on. My friend and I, we'd like to invite you ladies to join us for a drink."

"The same friend who just told me to fuck off? Yeah, let me think about that." Louisa looked pointedly at de Greer. "And let's get some uniforms here, shall we?" She raised her phone, and it said, "Louisa?" Cutting Lech off, she said, "Nine nine nine," thumb poised to hit the number.

Give them a chance, she thought, to just head off of their own accord.

They didn't.

Instead, Number Eleven lunged towards her at the same time as Green Trainers said, "No, don't—"

It wasn't clear to which of them he was speaking.

Louisa, anyway, didn't get to make the call, though Eleven didn't manage to snatch her phone, either; she sidestepped him, letting her arm drop as if it held a cloak, as if he were a bull. Pity she had no sword. He snorted past, whirled abruptly, and threw a blow that wasn't a full bodied punch, more of a slap, which caught her on the shoulder. *He thinks I'm a girl*, she thought, and hit him on the nose, then danced back. He howled, more in anger than in pain she thought, and then again—more worryingly—in what sounded like delight. He bunched his fists. Seemed she wasn't a girl anymore.

Still dancing, she tucked her phone into her jeans pocket, trying to ignore the fact that it immediately started to ring. *Lech*, she thought, and threw the thought away. Concentrate on the moment. Lech, not as far away as she supposed, was left staring at his own phone in frustration: *Answer, damn it*. And then: *Where* are *you?* He walked past the line of trees; felt the grass beneath his feet. It would be the height of stupidity to just set off into the dark and hope to find her; on the other hand, there weren't any doors nearby he could kick down. This was as much as he could do.

So that's what he did, his vision gradually adjusting to the dark that stretched out in most directions. He liked the dark, Lech Wicinski; in the dark, his face was no more scarred than anyone else's. But this dark had a solid quality to it he didn't often encounter on his night-time treks; the dark feels different when not buffered by buildings. It occupies the air more completely. The world behind Lech dropped away as if a curtain had fallen, smothering the light and killing most of the sound, not all of which was mechanical. Tempers were being lost; voices raised. Roddy had stalled trying to reverse out of the coach's way, and the coach driver, an excitable type, had climbed out of his cabin to offer advice, much of which was retrospective in nature, and covered areas Roddy might usefully have attended to before venturing onto the roads or, indeed, leaving his mother's womb.

Shirley said, "Just start the fucking car."

"I'm trying!"

"Try harder?"

"He's putting me off."

This being the coach driver, who was bending down by Roddy's window, indicating with hand motions that he should roll his window down, but doing so in such a manner that nobody in their right mind would comply.

"This should have been so easy," Shirley said. "All we had to do was find Louisa. Now this guy wants to break you into pieces."

Roddy took his hands from the steering wheel and shook his open palms at the louring coachman. "You're not helping!" he shouted.

"Get out and give him a slap," Shirley suggested.

"I might just do that in a minute."

"Do you think he reads lips?"

Roddy tried the ignition again, and the car wheezed as if he'd gone for a choke-hold. The coach driver stepped away and sized the car up, estimating his chances of wrapping his arms round it and heaving it into the trees. You wouldn't have laid good money against. The car, meanwhile—electric blue, cream flashing, chronic asthma—considered its immediate prospects and shuddered, while in front of it a coachful of tourists grew restless. Behind, as the temporary lights changed to green once again, a growing queue of traffic was rehearsing a symphony; light on strings, heavy on the horn section. The rumpus was enough to penetrate the row of trees; to reach out onto the common and tap Lech on the shoulder; enough, even, to reach Louisa a further few hundred yards away, and alone now with Green Trainers and Number Eleven—de Greer had turned and fled when the first punch had been thrown. Gone for help? Louisa wondered. Or just gone?

But she was too occupied to ponder long, because Number Eleven was aiming a kick at her head, and nearly connected, too.

And now here came Green Trainers on her left, his cack-handed attempts at brokering a truce abandoned. He was hopping from one foot to the other, keeping her guessing as to his next move. It wasn't the first time this pair had tried to kick somebody's head off. But they weren't trained for it and they weren't professional, otherwise why let their target slip away like that? She could see their teeth shining: they were enjoying themselves, and weren't about to go on their merry way yet. Any time either of them made a connection, she was going to know all about it.

Her head torch was offering a target. She stripped it off and flung it over her shoulder, where it cartwheeled through the air before dropping blind to the grass. From a distance, it must have looked like a dying fairy's last flight.

Number Eleven darted in and threw a punch. Louisa stepped back, nearly stumbled, righted herself and skipped sideways to avoid another kick from Green Trainers.

They knew what they were doing. And weren't taking chances; it was as if they were used to facing down foes armed with basic weaponry—sticks and stones, perhaps; the bonebreaking standbys.

"Glad you came along, lady," Number Eleven said. His breath was coming in short pants, as if this were foreplay.

If she hit the ground they'd be on her like dogs. Everyone there knew it, and two of them liked the idea.

Be nice to have a monkey wrench round about now.

Or a partner. Someone to watch her back.

Instead what she had was Shirley, watching Louisa shrunk to a pulsing dot on Roddy's phone, which she'd swiped from his lap while his attention was elsewhere. The scale was such

that Louisa appeared motionless, making Shirley wonder if
she'd stopped for a lie down.

There was an idea—Louisa and Lech? Doing it in the dark,
out there on the common?

Hard to picture, though that might have been because of
all the racket. Roddy's attempts to start the car, increasingly
uncoordinated, had deteriorated to the point where they
largely consisted of his offering it unspecified pleasures if it
behaved itself. The coach driver, unimpressed by this
development, was standing with his hands on his hips, framed
by the windscreen. It was like being at a drive-in, thought
Shirley, right up near the screen. And watching the wrong
movie. What would he do next? What he did next was raise
both arms in gorilla fashion· *You are not gunna do that*, she
thought. But he did. He brought both fists down on the
bonnet, making the vehicle shudder, and causing Roddy to
yip—only word for it. As for Shirley, what she was feeling was
the bliss of justified outrage. He'd just assaulted Roddy's car.
That was *well* out of order.

Behind him, the tourists in his coach were gathered upfront,
staring from the wide windscreen at the unfolding spectacle.
Not a few were filming it. A lot of this was already on
Facebook, or that's what Shirley assumed, reaching into her
pocket for a face mask. The coach driver had stepped away,
looking pleased with himself: you could see the indentations
his fists had made on Roddy's bonnet. Well out of order, she
repeated to herself; maybe this time out loud. At any rate,
Roddy turned towards her. "What you doing?"

"This," she said, fastening the mask on, opening her door,
climbing out.

The coach driver nodded sarcastically. "So he sends his little
lady out, does he?"

"Little" depended on which angle you took, but Shirley was
happy to accept the compliment. Not that this diminished the
offence already caused.

"You hurt my friend's car," she said.

"Your friend's a tosser!"

"What's that got to do with it?"

The coach was two yards in front of her; the bottom of its windscreen about level with her head. She bobbed a little—once, twice—preparing her move.

". . . What's that in your hand?" the driver asked.

"We deal in lead, friend," she said—though actually it was her iron—and launched herself off the ground.

It was nearly ballet; very nearly ballet. Maybe a little less delicate. At the moment the flat of the iron hit the glass she was airborne—an echo of the clubbing she might have been doing now, had the evening taken a different turn—and in the second of contact, the windscreen went opaque; she enjoyed a frozen moment during which a huddled group of tourists stared out at her, terrified, as if their entertainment had unexpectedly turned 3D. And then she was on the ground again, having executed a damn-near perfect superhero landing—the fingers of one hand touching the ground, iron raised like a hammer in the other—and the coach behind her was blind, and its driver stunned speechless.

Roddy's car chose this moment to come back to life.

It sounded crazy loud, though had a lot of competition— horns were blaring from the traffic behind, and there was a certain amount of wailing coming from the bus. A police siren, too, had joined the chorus, though was some distance away; the noise remained a flashing blue suggestion behind a screen of trees. Only the coach driver had lost his voice, and he didn't even yelp when Roddy missed him by maybe half an inch— Roddy couldn't reverse, because the traffic behind had shunted forward, so swinging round the fat idiot who'd started all this was his only option. It would have been the work of a moment to lean across, open the door and let Shirley jump in, so Roddy really should have thought about doing that, but he was too busy avoiding the tree which had reared up, grinding against his paintwork as he passed, and suddenly all he had in front of him was nothing, a big black darkness that his headlights barely scratched, while the ground beneath his wheels was all over the place; an assault course of bumps and shallows and missing bits. He was breathing noisily—okay, maybe yelling—and the resulting sound ran up and down its own peculiar scale in time with the rockabilly motion of the car. It was all he could do to keep both hands on the wheel. *Welcome to the Rod-eo*: a lesser driver would have been thrown through the windshield by now.

Really should have given serious thought to being a stunt-man.

Because he was getting into the groove now, and it felt kind of wild. Okay, not doing the suspension any favours, but face it: a hot rod belonging to Hot Rod was going to have its suspension put through its paces sooner or later. As for the scene he was leaving behind, yeah, things had got messed up, but what could you expect with Shirley Dander providing distraction? Any job involving that mad chick was bound to go fruit-shaped. Enough to make you wonder whose side she was on. But that didn't matter right now.

What mattered right now was: on the passenger seat lay his phone, screen upwards, dumped there by Shirley when she left to kill the bus.

And what mattered was: the pulsing dot that was Louisa's phone was getting nearer. Or rather, Roddy was getting nearer the pulsing dot.

Which had been the mission all along, and he was the only one out here completing it.

The only one bar Lech, that was, though Roddy didn't know Lech was on the common. For his part, that he was on the common was about the only thing Lech did know, as far as his whereabouts went. Until the commotion following Shirley's shattering of the coach windscreen, he'd been striding in what he hoped was a straight line, this seeming a more sensible option than wandering in circles, though neither amounted to what could be called a plan. Odd sounds had drifted his way—sighs and mutterings—but it was possible, he thought, that the ground had stored away these daytime whispers; was softly releasing them, now night had fallen, like so many pockets of gas. But the noise that erupted after Shirley's party trick blew past him like hot air. He turned, and saw the distant chaos as if it were a rock concert viewed from afar: all the light and sound focused on one corner of the darkness. But even as he had that thought, something broke away from the stage; a pair of headlights had come loose, to make their bumpy way across the common. Had to be some kind of idiot, thought Lech. But given that the vehicle was heading more or less in his direction, it at least provided illumination of sorts; when its twin cones of light weren't pointing at the sky, they were throwing themselves haphazardly onto the common, and picking out movement somewhere not far ahead.

Some of this was Louisa, dodging another kick thrown by Number Eleven.

It was a favourite gambit of his, despite its lack of success so far. Perhaps he'd watched it done on screen; perhaps he thought he was doing it right. A good talking to would have put him straight, but Louisa was saving her breath for where it would do most good, this being keeping on her feet and moving about enough that neither man could land a blow. Her main problem was that there were two of them. Neither on his own would scare her much, but one mistake on her part would leave her open to being stomped on, and worse. So when Roddy's headlights made themselves known she felt her spirits lift; not enough to distract her from her current vigilance, but more than they would have done had she been aware they were Roddy's.

"Company's coming," she said.

Eleven's reply was another kick, which he signalled enough that she had no trouble dodging.

Green Trainers was more of an issue. Bald, bearded and sleeve-tattooed, he was less inclined to use his feet as weapons, but nimbler on them than his companion. And while he was enjoying himself just as much—his small, even teeth bared in a grin—there was calculation too. He was letting Eleven wear Louisa out. When she made a mistake, he'd drop on her like a raptor . . . But she had something this pair didn't, she'd walked away from *gunfights*, and that thought sparked a gallery of images: of being shot at way above London by a Russian hood; of waging a small war underground, River at her side; of decking a mercenary with a monkey wrench on a snow-covered lane in Wales. All that and more. Others, true, had died, but Louisa was still standing. And these guys were amateurs. So when Number Eleven aimed his latest kick—yawn—instead of dancing back she moved sideways, grabbed his ankle and twisted. Threw him away. She didn't break anything—she would if he tried it again—but he gave a satisfying yelp all the same.

But while Eleven was briefly airborne, Trainers made his move: nipping in, throwing a punch. It contained more energy than finesse but caught her on the shoulder all the same, and as she quick-stepped backwards, the ground disappeared beneath her foot—only a two-inch depression; the scrabbling of a fox or a dog, but enough to rob her of balance. Bad shit happened in the dark: next moment she was on her back, Green Trainers on top of her, his hands on her throat, his face too close. He snarled something, its gist clear. Those headlights weren't arriving fast enough, and she was dimly aware that Number Eleven was getting to his feet; soon they'd both be on her, and that would be that. She tried battering Trainers's head, but made no impact: his hands were squeezing, hard. Stars popped in her eyes as her left hand went scrabbling for something—anything—that would work as a weapon. A gun would be nice. An event took place out of sight, a thud followed by a sigh and a slump, and meanwhile her hand, bless it, found an object, plastic, hard, her headtorch? Her headtorch. She mashed it, bright and hot, into Green Trainers's left eye. This did the trick. He screamed, though he'd have a more macho word for it, and pulled back, allowing her to breathe once more. The night air tasted of blood. While she sucked in as much of it as she could Green Trainers slid sideways, all cohesion leaving his features. She must remember how she did that. And then a goggle-faced blonde woman was crouching beside her. "Are you all right?"

"... I think so."

Though she felt like a jellyfish must feel: all nerves on high alert, but a distinct absence of muscle-tone.

Doctor de Greer was holding a brick. Where had Dr. de Greer found a brick? Maybe she'd ordered it from somewhere, Louisa's jangled brain suggested. It was, after all, just what the doctor—

To her left, Green Trainers was struggling to his feet. She pushed herself upright, ready to kick his teeth in, but this proved unnecessary. He stumbled away into the dark. Number Eleven had already made tracks. As double dates went, you couldn't call it a big hit.

De Greer started to say something, but at precisely that moment the approaching car hit level ground, allowing its headlights to stare directly at them, and as she raised a hand against the glare, Louisa caught sight—like an image from a pinhole camera—of a stick-like character trapped in the twin beams. It had its arms raised, as if alerting the oncoming driver to its presence, an action it seemed to undertake in slow motion though in actual fact happened at the speed of reality, which in this case was about twelve miles an hour. Which felt a lot faster to Roddy, attempting to steer his bouncing bronco over the dark common, and an awful lot faster to Lech, whom Roddy clipped on his way past. For a second Lech was a blur in his own mind, his sense of self dissolving like the wisp of a dream upon waking, but shortly afterwards he was definitely corporeal once again, and every square inch hurting. Roddy wasn't aware he'd hit anything, because one bump feels much like another. Besides, he could make out two waiting figures at the far reach of his headlights, and was pretty certain one of them was Louisa. The second was also a woman, which was fine by him. There was nothing like making a good first impression, and who wouldn't want to see Roddy Ho turning up in the nick of time, dispensing whatever justice was required?

Louisa, realising it was Roddy, and who he must just have run over, said to de Greer, "Still got that brick?"

"Are you a spook?"

"What's a spook?"

"That's right," de Greer replied. "I thought you probably were."

Roddy rolled to a halt while, a hundred yards away, Lech lay on his back and swore at the moon. Even further away, Shirley was being encouraged to put the iron down by a pair of commendably unflustered police officers. All in all, just another day in and out of the office.

Louisa looked at de Greer, who seemed pretty composed for someone who'd just bopped a pair of second-division thugs on their heads with a brick.

"We'd better talk," she said.

INTERMISSION

"Piss break," said Lamb.
	He stood and stretched, releasing a dandruffy shower of ash, then shambled towards a nearby clump of bushes.

"Oh, for God's sake," Diana said, and turned away, head reeling. It hadn't been a proper flashback—Lamb hadn't even been there—but he'd evidently debriefed those involved. Sophie de Greer, a Russian plant? The daughter of a former KGB colonel, hired by Number Ten's foremost advocate of disruption? Sparrow would have a rueful little chuckle about that, once he'd beheaded everyone in sight. Assuming, that was, he'd had no prior knowledge of her actual identity.

Though it seemed likely he'd only been alerted to who she was by Vassily Rasnokov, a few weeks ago in Moscow.

And seemed certain that his unleashing Claude Whelan on Diana herself was more than the knee-jerk harassment she'd thought it.

Judging by the volcanic shaking of Lamb's shoulders, he was done with his comfort break. He was still zipping up as he headed back. "See, the thing about coffee," he was starting to say.

"Where is she now?"

"It's rude to interrupt."

"Where is she now?"

"Remember that place in Chelsea?"

"*What?* That's a Service safe house—"

"Okay, boomer. It was a gift from Judd's cabal, remember? Given how very much you're keeping that off the books, you're in no position to object." He was smoking again, or possibly still. It was hard to picture Lamb without a lit cigarette. "And I had to put her somewhere."

"How did you even get in?"

"I might have had a set of keys cut."

"Jesus . . . Who's babysitting? Louisa Guy?"

"She's not really the maternal type. I was worried she'd take her out on the pull, and maybe sell her to an Arab. So no, I've got John Bachelor there. You'll remember him. I mean, he's fucking useless, but at least . . ." Lamb gazed into space, and briefly went cross-eyed. "No. I've got nothing."

Diana was fighting an impulse to bury her face in her hands. "De Greer handed herself in?"

"For her own safety. She'd been watched for days. She thought at first it was the Park, but she said the watchers were a bit rubbish." He exhaled a series of abbreviated clouds: dots and dashes; unaddressed messages. "Which didn't rule you out, but she wasn't to know that."

She said, "Sparrow was in Moscow last month. He encountered Rasnokov at some do. I think Rasnokov told him he'd been played, that de Greer was a plant. So whoever they were, that pair on the common, they could be working for Sparrow."

"Makes sense. He's a politico, they think a cover-up's a first resort."

"But why would Rasnokov throw his own joe to the dogs?"

"It's not like we'd chew on her bones," said Lamb. "She'd get a P45 and a severance payoff. Probably do *Start the Week* and a centrefold for the *Mail*." He grimaced. "Besides, blowing her cover would be the point of the exercise. What does more damage, fiddling about inside a foreign government, or fiddling about inside a foreign government and having the whole world know? It's the difference between laughing behind someone's back and making them the joke in a Christmas cracker."

"People will write it off as fake news."

"People write everything off as fake news. Doesn't mean nothing happens. Besides, he sent Claude looking for her. And while it's tempting to say that's because he doesn't want her found, he's likely got something else in mind. Your predecessors had a protocol we don't like talking about."

"Waterproof," said Diana.

"Yeah. I seem to remember it's cropped up before."

Diana was beginning to think she'd never hear the end of it. It was Lamb himself who'd ended Ingrid Tearney's career by threatening to make public her Waterproofing of a troublesome former agent, a threat he'd had no need to make good on. Tearney hadn't realised that, whatever else he might be, Lamb was no whistleblower. On the other hand, Diana reflected, had the threat of exposure not worked, he'd doubtless have resorted to more direct measures.

He was still talking. "And if Sparrow can suggest that's what's happened here, that you had de Greer disappeared before she could stage-manage an international spook scandal, then that's the bigger story and you're the bad guy. Worst case scenario, from his point of view, it all gets wrapped inside an official inquiry, and by the time the report's made public we're too busy locking down Covid-25 to give a toss. And best case . . ."

"I've triggered an illegal abduction, possibly murder, to preserve the Service's reputation."

"And you'll be hung, drawn and quartered," said Lamb.

"But for that to hold water," Diana said slowly, "de Greer would have to disappear for real. You think he planned to kill her?"

"Only if he's an idiot. Rasnokov might burn a joe to get a job done. But kill her, and he'd tear your playhouse down."

"But does Sparrow know that?"

Lamb said, "Be interesting to find out," and ground his cigarette underfoot. "Where's Rasnokov now?"

"Halfway back to Moscow."

"He came all this way just to pull your pigtail?"

"I've been wondering about that myself." Wondering? She had half the hub working on Rasnokov's secret itinerary, without even being sure he'd had one. Maybe that was all he'd been after: London Rules, rule one, para (b). After covering your arse, light a fire under someone else's. She said, "He was here a day and a half before we knew about it."

"Face the fucking strange, no wonder you're twitchy. You've had your opposite number playing in your sand pit. And now you're worried he had a quiet dump."

"Sometimes I get sick of all the games."

"Picked the wrong career then," said Lamb. Then: "What's bugging you most?"

"I don't see why he stuck his head above the parapet. He must have known we'd clock him at the reception, but he'd already trailed his coat in the dust. He posed for a photo out shopping in Harrods."

Lamb spent a moment watching an aeroplane pass overhead. Then said, "Leaving aside the possibility he was just snooking your cock, maybe it's not you he was hiding from."

"Meaning?"

"If he'd skipped the reception, he could have come and gone without you knowing. But he had to be at the reception, because as far as Moscow's concerned, that's why he was here. So when he fills in his timesheet, he'll write, 'Took the Park for a walk down Regent's Street,' and 'Teased Taverner's prick over blinis and vodka.'" He picked up his final coffee cup. "As far as they're concerned, you're his mission. But for him, you're his alibi."

She let that settle for a moment, then said, "If you're right, the real reason for Rasnokov's visit had nothing to do with de Greer."

"Give that woman a banana." Lamb drained the cup and tossed it over his shoulder. "Rasnokov's like everybody else, he's doing his job but looking out for himself. Baiting you in the embassy, that was work. Whatever else he was up to, that's what we really want to know. What's in the bag?"

". . . Excuse me?"

He nodded at her leather tote. "You've come from the Park, you've spent all morning on this. Don't tell me you weren't reading the output on your way here."

Diana looked at him. "It's Park product. You're not cleared to see it."

"Ho do fucking-ha "

She reached into her bag and produced a block of paper, half an inch thick.

Arrival details from Heathrow, the luckless Pete Dean's surveillance reports, interviews with cab drivers and paperwork from the Grosvenor, including itemised billing, room service orders, channels viewed (Sky Sports, CNN), phone calls made (none), newspapers required (*Times*, *Telegraph*), and the contents of his bin post check-out.

"And there's video on the laptop."

"Haven't seen a good movie since *Sleeping Booty*."

Cigarette plugged into his mouth, he lowered his gaze.

It was as if he'd left the stage for the duration, becoming all function for the minutes it took him to digest the paperwork. Diana thought of the boys and girls on the hub, their faces lit by the glow of their screens as they absorbed information. Lamb's light seemed to come from within, as if it were only at such moments that he burned real fuel. She wouldn't want to disturb him. Couldn't be sure who he'd be if he were startled out of his reverie without warning.

Instead, she watched the park enjoying this last burst of summer. It wouldn't last. Autumn was bringing its weight to bear, and would have the usual effect—when autumn descends on the city, its adjectives drop away like leaves from a tree, until all that remain are the obvious: London is big, its roads are hard, its skies are grey, its noise is fierce. Months to go before that picture softened. She wondered if she'd still be in her job then. Lamb's story had handed her a weapon, but Sparrow came well protected, and it was clear he viewed her as a threat. One he intended to deal with. *My advice would be, spend your remaining time as First Desk concentrating on more important issues.*

The rasp of Lamb's lighter brought her back. He thrust the papers at her, and she pattycaked them into a neatish pile on her knees. "Well?"

"Man likes a drink."

"That's all you've got?"

"What do you want, his horoscope?" He exhaled, and his head was wreathed in smoke. "How did he look at the party?"

"Not like someone who'd been on the whisky all night, if that's what you mean."

"Despite having two bottles sent to his room within thirty minutes of his arrival. Any hookers delivered with them?"

"It's not that kind of place."

He gave her a sardonic look. "They're all that kind of place."

"We have a file on him. Obviously. Twelve-year-old Balvenie's expensive, but it's his preferred brand, and two bottles is not without precedent. I've seen you put a bottle away before heading out for a drink."

"Thanks for reminding me. It's getting on for that time."

He stood and stretched and yawned all at once. It was like watching a building collapse, backwards. When that was done, he said, "One and a half litres over a two-day stay. Yeah, okay. Not entirely unheard of, in my experience."

"Wide as that most assuredly is."

"I'm impressed he eats the bottles, though," said Lamb. "That's hardcore."

And he padded away, leaving Diana busy with the paperwork again; confirming that whatever Rasnokov had done with the two empty bottles of Balvenie, they hadn't ended up in his bin.

ACT III
APE SHIT

In the San's basement was a gym, described in the brochure as fully equipped, but lacking, Shirley noticed, a wooden horse. If they'd had one, she'd have half-inched a couple of spoons and dug a tunnel. Instead, there was a row of treadmills, on one of which an idiot was walking at a speed that indicated she needed to be somewhere in a hurry, and with an expression suggesting she was late. Most of the inmates—the brochure said "guests"—seemed similarly wrapped, tending to appear calm to the point of disconnection while at rest, but harried by demons when they thought no one was watching. Another good reason for making tracks as soon as possible. Shirley was pretty sure being a mentalist wasn't catching, but wouldn't want to bet her sanity on it.

Her morning keep-fit routine didn't take long—everyone always went on about how important cooling down exercises were, so Shirley skipped the workout and just did those instead. Some ankle touches, some glute stretches. You could hear things popping if you did them correctly, unless you only heard that if you were doing them wrong. Then several minutes of downward dog, the least dignified position Shirley had attempted without at least one other person being involved. The walls were mirrored, and it was impossible not to catch sight of herself: her head looked like a tomato this side of bursting. Time to call it a day.

Leaving, she ran into a grey-headed woman who was backing through the door carrying a yoga mat. She dropped it when they collided, and the pair mutely watched as it unrolled, releasing visible dust into the air. Then looked at each other.

"My fault."

"Uh-huh."

The woman raised an eyebrow. "Ellie Parsons," she said. "Panic attacks."

"Shirley Dander," Shirley replied. "Substance abuse," and pushed through the door.

She showered in her room. According to the computer-generated schedule pushed beneath her door there was a group session in half an hour at which her presence was "expected." Yeah, she thought, scrubbing a hole in the misted mirror. Except her presence had other ideas; she'd send her absence along as a proxy. *Hope this suits.* Judging by the mirror, it would have to: her reflection wasn't taking any crap. Her last act of freedom had been a buzz cut, which was what she generally went for when on a war footing. No way was this baby attending any session she didn't want to.

In black jeans and grey hoodie, her usual trainers, she set out for a walk round the grounds. The woman at reception gave her a smile, which was a plus, but also said something about "twenty minutes," which Shirley took to be a reminder about the group session. Everyone on bucket seats, sharing bad moments. Seriously: fuck. Shirley had no problem with people seeking help, but also had no problem, end of. The fact that she hadn't punched anyone yet proved her self-control, right?

The San nestled in a dip between hills, its tree-lined driveway a gentle slope ending in a gravelled expanse in front of the house, which was redbrick, with blue and white woodwork round windows and gables, and a big copper beech behind. It had been a farmhouse in a previous existence, the brochure explained, but those days were long gone. For

obvious reasons, there was a certain amount of security: a wall
blocked any view of the building from the road, and the gates
were controlled from within the house—there was an intercom,
and a camera, and you presumably had to have good reason
for entering, along with the right ID. There were no guards
in evidence, but she had that sense of an unseen presence
which came with surveillance, though also with habitual
cocaine use. She guessed there'd be more cameras among the
trees; maybe someone observing her on a screen right now,
admiring her buzz cut.

That said, it wasn't a fort. The outer wall ended a few
hundred yards from the main gate, melding with a row of
stables before giving way to a wooded area, separated from the
road by a ditch and coloured wire, which looked designed to
deter foxes or badgers rather than marauding humans, some
of whom would probably have the nous to step over it. And
she'd seen from her window that part of the estate's boundary
was a lake, which she doubted was croc-infested. The San
might not invite casual wanderers, but if you had a mind to
leave—or arrive—there wasn't a lot to prevent you. She could
walk out, make her way to the nearest station, steal a ride and
be in London in however long the train took: couple of days,
maximum. She'd be back in the clubs before her buzz cut lost
its edge.

And then what?

Last night, she'd tried to remember the precise details of
Monday evening, and found most of it shrouded in blurry
matter. There'd been argy-bargy with Roddy Ho—had he
thrown a computer at her?—and then they'd been in a car in
Wimbledon, she couldn't recall why, except that it had
something to do with Louisa and Lech. And then the fight
with the bus; she'd had a damn good reason for that, but
attempts to recall it broke into a welter of shattered plastic
and changing lights. Nothing stayed still long enough for
Shirley to get a fix on. But that was what happened with

memories: more memories piled on top of them, and it got so you couldn't tell one from the other.

People keep getting hurt. People keep dying. We have to look out for one another.

Catherine's words, but what did she know? She hadn't even been there for most of Shirley's deaths.

You're doing lots of things, Shirley. But trust me, "fine" is not among them.

Whatever.

But it was true things hadn't been great lately. She could remember that much: things hadn't been great.

She was in the stableyard now, if you still called it that when the horses had bolted. It felt like an empty room. Four stables either side, with those wooden half-door arrangements, all hanging open. She looked inside one. It was dark and damp. The wooden shutters on its far wall, which presumably opened onto the road, were closed. She wondered what it must have been like for the horse, stuck in here, looking out on passing cars, but didn't wonder long. It was a little too familiar.

For some unfathomable reason, she wanted to cry.

A staircase ran alongside the outer side-wall of the farthermost stable, leading to a hayloft or tack room or something—a tack room was a thing, wasn't it? Whatever it was its door was locked, but she sat on the thigh-high wall of the landing a while, gazing down the road. No traffic. A wind was scuffling about in the woods to her right. She couldn't actually see it, but she could see what it was doing.

And when that got old she descended the stairs and wandered into the wood. Tears weren't her thing: she hadn't cried when Marcus was shot. The night River took that toxic payload, she'd gone dancing. Why would stuff catch up with her now? *You're doing lots of things.* It hadn't rained lately; the ground was snappy with twigs. *But "fine" is not among them.* Maybe Catherine had a point. Maybe she had a stupid point. Maybe Shirley should stay here a while, keep her head down, wait for the bad shit to pass. It wouldn't take forever. Who knew: she might get to like it. Few weeks' R&R, and if she kept up with the exercise regime, she'd go home fit as a star's body double.

Besides, medical staff on the premises, there was bound to be someone she could score off.

"Ms. Dander?"

She turned. Speaking of staff: the woman addressing her was one of those who'd annoyed her the first afternoon. Snappy twigs or not, she'd got pretty close pretty quietly.

"What?"

"You'll be late for your session."

Happy-clappy crap, more like.

A moment hung there, during which Shirley could have gone either way. But it passed; drifted into the wood like smoke. "Yeah," she said. "Okay."

The woman knew enough not to speak as they walked out of the trees, past the stables, towards the house. Or maybe she was listening, as Shirley was, to a car on the nearby road, stretching its approach out to a long thin whine. By the time it faded, they were almost at the door.

One thing about this place, she thought. You'd know when you had visitors.

Not that you would. There was a reason they put the San in the middle of nowhere. Out-of-sight meant forgotten about.

The San was the last place on anybody's mind.

The San, thought Claude Whelan.

He used to work over the river, remember? Schemes and wheezes; devious bullshit. One side effect, he liked to think, was that he could recognise a game when someone else was playing it. Take this, for instance: one of Lamb's crew—the so-called slow horses—gets shipped off to the Service's drying-out facility *the morning after* Sophie de Greer disappears. *The morning after* de Greer makes a phone call to Jackson Lamb. It was a matter of patterns; he saw them where others noticed only random particle motion. And here was one. That incident in Wimbledon—Shirley Dander attacking a tourist coach with an iron—was too outlandish to be anything other than a cover story. And the San was too exclusive, too *Park*, for a Slough House agent's treatment.

He'd said as much to Lamb, and the crafty sod had changed the subject. *Dander's treatment is none of your business.* Schemes and wheezes; devious bullshit. He'd seen through Lamb that same moment: it wasn't Dander who'd been packed off to the San. It was Sophie de Greer.

Nor was Lamb the only one playing games. There'd been a paragraph in that morning's *Times*, tucked away on page seven: *Concern is growing as to the whereabouts of Dr. Sophie de Greer, an academic and researcher at ReThink#1, the policy discussion group headed by Number Ten's chief adviser Anthony Sparrow . . . A Downing Street spokesperson dismissed rumours that de Greer's disappearance was a result of action taken by the Security Services. "Without concrete—indeed, waterproof— evidence that any such malpractice has taken place, we can assume this is baseless gossip."*

A declaration of hostilities, thought Claude.

Because this had all the characteristics of a turf war. Sparrow had already left his mark on most Whitehall departments, the majority of whose advisory staff were now appointed by Number Ten, effectively Sparrow himself, rather than by ministers. The centralisation of authority had long been the government's aim, devolvement having been decried by the PM as his most successful recent predecessor's biggest domestic failure, a target easier to locate than the PM's least successful recent predecessors' biggest domestic triumphs. With the regions restless in the wake of economic fallout from the pandemic, there was good reason to fortify Downing Street. And it was clear that Sparrow intended

Regent's Park to become part of the fortifications, a move which would require a cooperative First Desk. De Greer's precise role in all this Whelan couldn't see, but that barely mattered. All that counted was that she was now in play, and that Sparrow had finagled the word *waterproof* into the paper of record.

What Taverner's reaction would be, Whelan couldn't know either. But he could make a reasonable guess.

It was late morning; he was drinking coffee, and staring from his back window at the summer-struck garden. Until lately the garden had been Claire's province, and Whelan a suffered guest; his presence occasionally called upon when heavy-ish lifting was required—for actual heavy lifting, a professional would be summoned—but otherwise deemed unnecessary except as a witness to her careful curation. Now the garden spoke only of neglect, and he felt unable to remedy this. The best he'd managed was the shifting of leaves and other windfalls. Claire's absence was nowhere more apparent than in the presence of unwelcome flora: the weeds that might yet strangle the roses; the harmless but unlovely dandelions. These incursions predated her departure, in fact. It was peculiar how one obsession could replace another; or if not peculiar, at least worthy of comment. Or if not that, then something else. Damn it, he was running out of thoughts. His own presence bored him. He supposed he could hire a gardener. But meanwhile, he had a phone call to make.

"The San?"

"A Service facility for the hard of drinking," explained Nash. "Also drugs, and associated behaviours. And the various other traumas that befall those who put their country's good before their own health and sanity."

Sparrow hadn't wanted a bloody lecture.

"And he's a hundred per cent certain that's where de Greer is?"

"He says eighty. But he's a cautious man."

Said like this was a virtue, rather than the tedious plaint of the ineffectual.

Nash burbled on some more, then asked Sparrow if he wanted the San's details in an email, and Sparrow asked him if he was an idiot. In this post code, emails were for when you couldn't afford a promotional video. Instead, he jotted down the necessary geography, all the while brooding at the wall, which in his mind's eye became a map in a war room. Knowing where de Greer was meant a victory flag. So did planting the word *waterproof* in this morning's *Times*. What people failed to realise was, success didn't depend on coherent strategy— coherent strategy left you nailed to one course of action, and at the mercy of events. But once you grasped that there were some problems nobody would ever solve, your options widened. Chaos became an alternative, a fertile ground out of which new possibilities arose . . . This, the bedrock of his political philosophy, had seen Sparrow through some shaky patches. He'd occasionally been knocked off balance, true. *We don't need no stinking lockdown*, he remembered telling the PM. *What are we, French?* But even this had an upside, distracting attention from a harder Brexit than the wet-legged had been expecting, and post-Covid paranoia was a flame worth fanning. Take the anti-vaxxers, or the G5 arsonists, whose celebrity-endorsed idiocy made the Home Secretary look a model of reason . . . Every national panic permitted a government to lace its boots tighter, which was why every government needed a visionary unafraid to sow chaos.

Sparrow knew this because he'd read it on a blog, or written it on his own. Or both—the distance between the two was measured in how long it took to cut and paste.

But besides all that, Sophie had been a true believer—a Brexit fluffer, giving the PM a No-Deal stiffy when it looked like one was needed—and had fervently supported Sparrow's aim of removing any latent traces of autonomy from the major

Whitehall offices. In particular, Regent's Park: history, she'd pointed out, was littered with examples of heads of secret services becoming heads of state, both the USA and the USSR figuring on that list. Never say it can't happen here. Personally, too, they'd been on a wavelength: she'd been first to nod approvingly when he'd explained to the PM that the real hero of *It's a Wonderful Life* was Old Man Potter, because he didn't allow sentiment to interfere with business. All of which, in roughly that order, had flashed through Sparrow's mind like a drowning man's last newsreel when he'd encountered Vassily Rasnokov in Moscow a month ago. *We're so pleased you've created a role for Dr. de Greer. A splendid addition to a team, I've found.*

A blank stare had been the best Sparrow could manage.

Rasnokov might have been lying, of course—he was a spook—but once home Sparrow had made discreet enquiries into de Greer's superforecasting qualifications and had learned that the tests for such abilities weren't always carried out with the rigour brought to, say, an online credit check or an internet degree. Following which he'd had an episode: glass had been shattered, and carpet chewed. Consequences contemplated. If Rasnokov had planted de Greer in Downing Street, one of two things might happen: he'd lock the information away in a Kremlin cupboard, alongside those movies of sex workers pissing on a hotel bed, and spend the rest of his career chuckling at the damage he could wreak with the turn of a key. Or he'd go ahead and bring the noise: light the story up, then warm his hands on the fire. That was the disruptor option, and Sparrow recognised a fellow expert when he saw one.

It was true that his first response had backfired: he'd reached out to Benito of the Ultras—real name, Alessandro Botigliani; who couldn't be called an ally, exactly, but they'd fought in the same woods—and let him believe that he and his confederates, who numbered about ninety strong, were on a Home Office shit-list, which Sparrow had the muscle to edit. And that long-term visas were not out of the question. More than enough to secure loyalty, though as things turned out Benito didn't have to sell him out to fuck him over, because his crew had shit the bed like the ill-trained chimps they were: instead of simply tracking her movements, his pair of goons had waylaid de Greer on her evening run and had their arses kicked from here to Sunday, sending de Greer into the arms of the Park. Which had raised the stakes higher, giving Taverner the advantage.

But some basic truths still held sway, chief among them being: lie and bluster through two news cycles, and you're home free. The headlines fed like a shark—constantly, but always on the move—and the further afield the scraps you tossed them, the more distant they became. So, the new plan was: make the de Greer narrative one about the Park being up to mischief. By planting the word "waterproof" in the *Times*, he'd cast de Greer as victim in a dirty tricks campaign, while his own role faded to that of supporting player. Sparrow never minded being way down the cast list. You got more done in the shadows.

And meanwhile, if Taverner or her lackey Jackson Lamb had de Greer stowed away in a Service facility, Sparrow would fetch her out and offer her a starrier part. One he was confident she'd be happy to accept, once the alternatives had been road-mapped for her: a nice cosy job in a lobbying outfit, or some hard yards answering questions posed by any number of hostile agencies . . .

So it was time to talk to Benito once more. His crew had been a letdown, sure, but that would put them on their mettle; besides, Sparrow had no other team handy.

Meanwhile, Nash was still talking.

He cut through the man's fawny solicitude. "What name did Whelan say they'd stashed de Greer under?" He made a jotting of the reply: Shirley D.A.N.D.E.R. "And you need to

call a Limitations meeting. Now. What do you mean, why?
I'm about to tell you why. Pay attention."

Of those lingering in the park while Diana put papers and
thoughts into order, not everyone had an evident excuse: there
were mothers with toddlers, a carer wheeling her charge's
chair, a businessman soliloquising into a phone, but also a lone
woman with her hands in her pockets, staring at the sky; a
lone man grumbling to and fro between gatepost and bin. It
occurred to her that watchers in her profession wouldn't dare
behave like ordinary people. Spooks needed reasons, props
and cover. People just did what they were doing.

So, bag looped over one shoulder, she left the park to its
late-summer sunshine. The year was turning a corner,
disregarding the havoc in its wake. One day she'd have time
to release a breath, and celebrate recovery. Just now, though,
she was wondering who to fuck up, and in what order.

Vassily Rasnokov, definitely. If Lamb's reading was right,
the embassy visit had been cover for a private game, and it
didn't require tactical genius to deduce that this involved
concocting an exit strategy. Working for a paranoid psychopath
meant walking a constant edge—you never knew what might
trigger a rage: a fly landing on a knuckle; a memory whispering
from the wings. This many years into the job, Rasnokov must
be spending half his time looking for the nearest open door,
in case his boss took it in mind to examine his innermost
thoughts, perhaps by spreading them across a carpet.

But Rasnokov was back in Moscow, and there were other
dangers nearer home. If the Russian's schemes involved sowing
chaos here in London, he'd made a good start: for all Sparrow's
studied indifference to the traditional norms of government,
inviting a foreign intelligence agent to help formulate national
policy was more than a standard cock-up even for the 2020s.
Thanks not least to Sparrow himself, lying in office was no
longer a career-threatening felony; the consequence of

misleading Parliament was nowadays a lap of honour, and you could even, as a witlessly self-revealing Home Secretary had suggested, be fucking useless and remain securely in post, provided you were no threat to the PM. But inviting a spy inside Number Ten, allotting her a coathook, that was a serious embarrassment. Which meant Sparrow would be hoping to get his defence in first.

Even as Diana was having these thoughts, she was checking her messages. Among them, an alert from the morning's *Times*. *Waterproof . . .*

The word brought her to a halt, provoking a muttered *Jesus* from the pedestrian in her wake.

She was a beat behind, and had been for days. Should have known it was a serious matter when Claude turned up at the Park: *The word waterproof has been mentioned.* Of course it bloody has . . .

But at least this answered a pressing question: who to set about fucking up first.

On the move again, she set her thoughts in order. It was clear she needed de Greer before the Limitations Committee, puncturing any claim that Waterproof had been used, and singing her heart out about Sparrow's hamheaded gullibility. The PM preferred the public to believe that his ineffectual blustering was a stage act, and he mostly got away with that. But the outing of his sidekick as a Kremlin stooge would puncture the image, and sooner than suffer that he'd bow to Diana's demands, chief among which would be hanging Sparrow out to dry.

That done, she could get on to the equally serious matter of fucking up Rasnokov, which would begin with Lamb's observation about the missing whisky bottles.

She rang Josie, who told her: "The hotel's recyclables are collected twice a week. We went through the dumpsters before the first of those. No Balvenie bottles."

Diana had the impression of events unfolding on the other

side of the connection; movement she couldn't see happening in the Park.

"And he didn't have them with him when he left?"

"He had carry-on only. They'd have shown on his X-rays."

While he could have waltzed them through diplomatic channels, what would have been the point? If he'd intended them as take-home presents, he'd not have paid hotel prices.

"Get hold of whoever cleaned his room," she said. "And find out politely, or find out the nasty way, if they walked off with a couple of abandoned half-empties. Or took actual empties for refilling with cheap stuff and selling on."

Josie took a moment to answer. "That's already been done. I think."

"Excuse me, am I boring you?"

"Sorry, ma'am, there's something going on, I don't know what."

"What do you mean, there's—"

The young woman's voice became muffled, as if she were holding a hand over her phone. Diana thought she heard her own name.

"Josie? What's going on?"

"I'm sorry—"

"Josie?"

The connection was cut.

Dead phone in hand, Diana turned a corner. She'd reached City Road. There was traffic, moving at an average speed; there was a bus at a stop fifteen yards away, its rear-end mural declaring this *her* city. There was a helicopter shuttling overhead. And her phone was ringing again.

A hoarse whisper on the other end. "Red Queen. Red Queen."

That was all.

Removing her phone's batteries, Diana dropped it in a bin attached to a lamppost, and hurried across the road, reaching the bus in time to slip on board and be carried away.

It must have rained overnight, because the mews' cobbles were shiny-wet and glistened in the morning sun, but no; whoever occupied the cottage opposite had been watering the plant-life, soaking the terracotta pots that laid siege to those premises like a Chinese army. And was cottage right, even? John Bachelor had temporarily occupied a number of properties lately—empty offices, friends' sofas, his car's back seat—but this was his first cottage, and the word sounded odd, applied in central London. On the other hand: white-washed walls, a trellis arrangement, and a small tropical forest out front. It was hardly inner city.

He turned off the radio—the PM had just shared his vision of post-Brexit Britain as a culinary powerhouse, its takeaway delivery services the envy of the world—as the kettle reached the boil. Watching such devices perform this function was his career in a nutshell. Though the role was referred to as "milkman," it mostly involved tea. But yesterday Dr. de Greer—Sophie—had praised the results, and that was the first compliment Bachelor remembered receiving this millennium.

"You're being funny."

He really wasn't.

Bachelor had babysat before, and was familiar with the mindset of the usual Service casualty: someone whose career was an open book, its index busiest under the heading

"Grudges, slights and injustices." So when Lech Wicinski had asked about his availability, he'd jumped straight over the small print to focus on more important matters. "And the per diem aspect, you'd be covering that?" he'd heard himself say, with that inward sense of shame that felt as if someone were turning his corners down. Only once that had been established had the penny dropped. The baby he'd be sitting was Sophie de Greer.

"So I was right."

"Truthfully?" Wicinski had asked. "I haven't the faintest."

But whatever was going on, de Greer had been targeted, and, thanks to Bachelor himself—who'd been the one to point Wicinski at a TV screen—it was the slow horses who'd brought her to sanctuary.

So here he was, in a Service safe house, with no current worries about food or shelter, and in his care an unfamiliar sort of client in that she was young, attractive, and in peril she hadn't brought upon herself via the familiar triathlon of alcohol, sex and disgruntlement. Also, there was something in her conduct towards him that Bachelor had to take a few stabs at before it registered. Respect. Christ, it had been a long time.

He poured water into the pot, scalding it nicely. She brought out the protector in him, a trait usually summoned by his more elderly clients. Something helpless about her; uncalculating. And they had a ready-made connection, of course.

"I knew your mother."

". . . Really?"

"Well, not *knew* knew."

He wasn't sure how much he could say about Bonn. Somewhere, there was a former spook who'd been burned by the KGB, and it had never been clear to Bachelor whether the poor fool had committed the sins he'd been accused of, or whether, rather than having put a foot out of line, he'd simply found the line redrawn beneath his foot. Standard procedure

for the time. The Cold War wasn't all muffins at Checkpoint
Charlie. Which this young woman presumably knew, her
mother having been a combatant.

"And now you're in the same line."

"I wasn't given a choice."

This made sense to Bachelor, whose own horizons, he
sometimes believed, had been crayoned in by another hand.
"Blackmail?"

"Not me," she said. "My mother. They said . . . They said
she'd be turned out onto the streets. And she's old. And . . ."

And all the things that went with being old. This, too, was
an ancient story: a lifetime's service trampled underfoot. They
wore you out, then weaponised your uselessness and aimed it
at your children. Dr. de Greer was crying, so automatically
became Sophie. He could not comfort her while addressing
her by title.

That first night he more or less ordered her to get some
sleep: it was amazing, he trotted out, how different things
looked in the morning. He'd then taken stock of the safe
house, focusing on fridge and kitchen cupboards. No alcohol.
Plenty of tinned food, though, and a freezer compartment
stuffed with ready-meals. A box of teabags, not quite stale.
Still no alcohol. But they wouldn't starve. As for sleeping
arrangements, there was only one bed; he'd settled on the
sofa, and had known worse berths. When sleep arrived it
came dreamlessly, but when he'd woken he'd lain for an hour
or more remembering Bonn, the three or four days he'd spent
staring at Sophie de Greer's unsmiling, unspeaking mother;
the most beautiful woman he'd ever laid eyes on. And here
he was sharing a house with her living image. Life brought
you in circles, if you waited long enough. It sometimes
seemed to Bachelor he'd done little with life other than wait
through it.

Now they had a routine, Bachelor keeping station by the
landing window, where he could clock strange arrivals, hear

unusual sounds, be alert for danger; Sophie perched beside
him on the top stair, as if they were engaged in a joint effort,
rather than one in which he was the knight, she the fair
maiden. He was wary of asking questions, knowing that the
professionals, when they came for her, would expect to find
her intact, but she had no such compunction.

"How long have you been a spy?"

"That's not really what I do."

"But you work for the intelligence service."

He was a milkman, he explained; a long out-of-date joke
having something to do with collecting the empties. A care-
worker, really. It was strange, he found himself saying, the
byways along which a career could take you. She seemed happy
to share this insight, and even treat it as a small joke. Which,
like his career, he supposed it was.

He made one of her own career, too: "Have you always
known you wanted to be a superforecaster?"

Seeing her laugh was a new experience. He'd spent days in
Bonn hoping to see that face smile, but Sophie's mother—
raised amidst grim state machinery—didn't have the muscles
to make that expression work.

There was a lot he wanted to know, but nothing he was
able to ask. He hoarded what clues came his way, though:

> *My mother made great sacrifices.*
> *She sent me away. I studied in Switzerland.*
> *I always knew there'd be a debt to pay.*

Fragments of a story the professionals would put together.
But Bachelor felt he knew her better than the Park's inquisitors
ever would.

When Lech visited on the second day, Bachelor asked when
they could expect company—when, in particular, Lamb would
be dropping in.

"You're asking me?" Lech said. "I'm hardly in the loop."

Afterwards, when Bachelor related this non-information to Sophie, she said, "They're deciding who gets me."

"Who do you want to get you? I mean, where do you want to be? Do you want to go home?"

"Zurich's my home. But they won't send me there. They'll send me to Moscow."

"And what's there for you?"

"Nothing."

Here, too, he understood her. There was nothing for him in London, but this was where he'd been sent, or at any rate, this was where he was.

When he assured her she wouldn't have to go anywhere she didn't want to, she gave a sad smile, and briefly rested her head on his shoulder.

It wasn't as if he were under any illusions. He was looking at sixty—could feel its breath on his eyebrows—and wasn't one of those self-deceiving Lotharios whose mirrors were twenty years out of date. His best days were behind him, an even more melancholy thought when he weighed up how feeble they'd been at the time. He'd barely hit his middle years before the mould started showing through the wallpaper, and then there was no stopping it: the capsized marriage, the punctured career, the lack of anything you could mistake for loyalty, support or money.

This, though; this could go on for as long as it wanted. He'd happily while away months coaxing life out of ageing teabags and cooking up suppers from a cupboard-load of tins; spending daylight hours on the landing, Sophie beside him, like a vision dredged out of someone else's memory. Months hoping not to hear words like:

"He's coming here, isn't he?"

It was the afternoon of the fourth day, the cobbles not yet dry from their drenching, and the pair were at their posts, looking down on the mews from the narrow window. One empty tea cup sat by Bachelor's chair; Sophie cradled the other in her hands. Without her glasses, he noticed—not for the first time—she seemed younger. He would have happily continued to study her, but forced himself to shift his attention instead to the figure she had seen through the window, pausing in the archway to the mews; a bulky mess in a shabby overcoat, lighting a cigarette before stepping into the sunshine.

"Isn't he?" she repeated.

"Yes," Bachelor said. "I'm afraid he is."

Lech said, "Let's run through that again. You brought in a homemade curry for lunch, and spiced it up with this super-powered chili—"

"A Dorset Naga."

"A Dorset Naga, right."

"Which scores, like, 923,000 on the Scoville scale."

"Okay."

"Which is the Richter scale, only for chilis."

"Okay. So you brought this in and left it in the fridge so that if—when—Lamb stole it, it'd blow his head off."

"Yes."

"And what do you usually bring in for lunch?" Louisa said.

"I usually buy it."

"Yeah, okay, and you buy . . . ?"

"A salad."

"So you usually eat a shop-bought salad until one day you make yourself a curry instead."

"Well, that's what he'd expect, isn't it? The fat bigot."

Lech and Louisa exchanged a look.

"I mean, obviously I make my own curry."

They exchanged it back again.

"What?"

"Lamb's fat," said Louisa. "And bigotry is his preferred mode of communication, yes. But he's not stupid. You might as well have labelled your lunchbox 'Bait.'"

"But he took it!"

"When a rat takes your poison, that's job done," said Lech. "When Lamb does, that's research."

"I was you," said Louisa, "I wouldn't go biting into anything you didn't prepare yourself."

And even then, not if you've turned your back on it for ten seconds, she mentally added.

"Where is he, anyway?" Lech asked, but no one knew.

They were in the kitchen, because it was that time: Louisa's need for coffee, always imminent, was at its peak early afternoon, and Lech's desire to be nowhere near his desk was at its peak most of the time. As for Ashley, neither had gauged her daily requirements yet, because this seemed an unnecessary effort until her ongoing presence had been established. Investing in a fellow slow horse was far from automatic.

Current assessment, though: attempting to kill Jackson Lamb with a turbo-charged curry showed initiative and imagination, indicating that Ashley Khan might be worth getting to know. It was just a pity the same resourceful outlook rendered her long-term prospects negligible.

Roddy Ho entered, opened the fridge, and removed a plastic bottle of radioactive-coloured drink. When he closed the door it slowly swung open again, but he didn't notice. Instead he leaned against the only length of kitchen counter not already occupied and applied himself to the task of removing the plastic screw-cap with his teeth. This took him, by Louisa's fascinated count, twenty-two seconds. Then he tilted the bottle back, took a large gulp and shook his head, as if he'd just performed some feat of athleticism out of the reach of lesser divinities. Only then did he address the other three. "'Sup?" he asked.

"You forgot to say 'dude,'" Lech pointed out.

"Yeah, well, you forgot to say . . ."

They waited.

". . . Fuck off."

"Sorry," said Lech. "Fuck off."

Louisa kicked the fridge door shut.

"He might just think I like really hot curry," Ashley said.

"Or you could rely on his famously forgiving nature," said Lech. "That might work."

Roddy said to Louisa, "That du—that guy, the one at the embassy? Who wouldn't look at the cameras?"

"What about him?"

"He left. First thing this morning."

". . . And did you catch his face this time?"

"Yeah." Roddy slurped another mouthful of bright green energy. "He sort of waved, in fact. Weird."

"So did you run him through the program?"

"Nah. Sent you the clip, though."

"You're an absolute star."

Roddy shrugged. "You can owe me one."

Ashley, who'd filled the space when she wasn't talking by looking at her phone instead, raised her head suddenly. "Oh. My. *God!*"

"What?"

"Red Queen."

All three stared. "What?"

"Red Queen!" She gestured with her phone. "It's all over the network. Like, 'This is not a drill.'"

"So it's really happening?" said Lech.

"Yes."

"Not a practice run?" said Louisa.

"No."

"Actual Red Queen. Actually happening."

"Yes! How many times?"

Lech said, "Okay, I'll bite. What's Red Queen?"

"Duh," said Roddy.

Catherine appeared in the doorway, with a suddenness which might have been alarming if it weren't a firmly established trope. "What's going on?"

"Red Queen," Roddy said importantly.

She looked at each in turn. As always, her over-neat appearance, the long-sleeved, mid-calf dress, the lace collar and cuffs, the buckled shoes, lent her the appearance of, not necessarily a governess, but of an illustration of a governess in an out-of-print children's book. Of the four looking back at her, two underestimated her for that very reason. "Red Queen," she repeated, instinctively reproducing the capitals. "I don't know what that means."

Roddy rolled his eyes. "Double-duh."

Ashley said, "It means—"

"No, really," said Lech. "I want to hear Roddy explain it."

"Me too," said Louisa.

"Yeah, no," Roddy said. "It's her story, not mine."

"That's okay," said Ashley. "You can tell them."

"Yeah. You can tell us, Roddy."

"Well, it's like—it's like *Red Queen*. You know?" He looked at Ashley, shaking his head. "Unbelievable."

"Ho, you're a waste of bandwidth," Lech said.

"Amusing as this is," said Catherine, "a little clarity would be nice."

"Red Queen's what they call the Candlestub Protocol on the hub," Ashley said. "Sort of a nickname."

And now she got the shocked silence she'd been expecting.

"Candlestub," Catherine repeated at last. "Well well."

"Ding dong," said Lech.

"Taverner's gone?" said Louisa.

"Candlestub's a suspension," said Catherine. "Not a dismissal. Or that was the original protocol. It might have been amended."

"What are the triggers?" Louisa asked.

Catherine frowned, recalling. "The usual. Conduct unbecoming. Criminal activity. Misuse of powers."

"So strike three," said Lech.

"Who's on First?" Roddy asked. Then: "What?"

"If First Desk leaves office unexpectedly, dies or is otherwise incapacitated, interim control passes into the hands of the most senior Second Desk," Catherine said, with the air of one quoting. "That's traditionally been Operations. But in the case of a suspension, the chair of Limitations takes the helm. In other words, Oliver Nash. Under close supervision of the Home Office."

"Well, this'll be a train wreck."

"Though not necessarily the Home Secretary herself."

"Small mercies."

Louisa looked down into her empty coffee cup, as if reading the future in its grounds. Diana Taverner had been around forever; had been Second Desk (Ops) when Louisa signed on, and First Desk in all but name during Claude Whelan's tenure, whose ending she'd helped engineer. Her suspension from duty would send shock waves through the Service. And Lamb had, variously, been in Taverner's coterie, confidence and crosshairs. If she went, there was no guarantee he'd survive her departure. And if Lamb went Slough House fell, and there'd be no safe harbour for any of them. And where was he, anyway?

She hadn't spoken aloud, but Catherine partially answered her. "Lamb was meeting her this morning. I've no idea what about."

Lech and Louisa glanced at each other.

"Though I daresay some of you have a better idea than I do. If Taverner's suspension is fallout from whatever you've been up to lately, I'd be seriously worried. If she goes, everyone involved is on shaky ground. And if she stays, well. I don't expect she'll be looking back fondly on this episode, do you?"

Louisa said, "Nothing we've done has anything to do with Taverner."

"In that case, you must be feeling particularly relaxed right now."

She wasn't used to Catherine being acerbic.

Roddy said, "Told you," and they all looked at him.

"Taverner," he said. "At the Russian embassy yesterday. Taking a secret meeting, like I said. Simples."

"First Desk, spying for the Russians?" said Catherine. "That's quite the merry-go-round."

Her eyes had grown dark, but no one dared ask.

Somewhat numbed, they set about returning to their rooms, Louisa first rinsing her cup out; Roddy hunting for the plastic top of his unfinished energy drink; Lech putting something in the bin. Ashley paused on the landing. "I've never asked why it gets called Red Queen," she said. "Instead of its proper name."

"Oh, I'd have thought that was obvious," said Catherine.

"'**Off with** her head,'" said Oliver Nash.

"There's a process to be undergone," said Toby Malahide. "Underwent? Either way, we're hardly hauling her off to the guillotine."

"No, I meant that's why they call it Red Queen. You know. *Alice in Wonderland*."

"Hmph."

Malahide was one of that army the Civil Service call upon when asked to put a body in harm's way: it wasn't that he was expendable, necessarily; more that his ingrained sense of entitlement rendered him impervious to damage. Early sixties by a mortal calendar, but managing to exude the impression that he'd overseen the Siege of Mafeking, he was the Home Secretary's choice of point-man for what might turn out to be a tricky undertaking, one of those shitstorms that blow up out of nowhere. The Limitation Committee's hurried assembly, its single-issue emergency meeting, its unanimous decision that Diana Taverner be relieved of her duties pending investigation of rumours that the illegal Waterproof Protocol had been instigated: all this demanded a degree of arse-covering that would require even the PM to up his game. The stake was worth playing for. If the story proved true there'd be an opportunity to overhaul the Service, the kind of power-grab that doesn't come along every Parliament. But if it wasn't true, and worse still didn't stick, Taverner would burn everyone associated with its having been suggested in the first place. Hence the need for a Toby Malahide. The Home Secretary regarded herself as the consummate politician, and if this was based on little more than the fact that she was indeed Home Secretary, it was generally agreed that she at least offered a synthesis of two main schools of political theory, inasmuch as if she ever became involved in a conspiracy, she'd find a way to cock it up. But nobody disputed her ability to put a large public schoolboy-shaped barrier between herself and impending consequences when the situation demanded.

Meanwhile, Diana Taverner, having somehow caught wind of her predicament, had disappeared into London's brilliant parade. Her last phone call put her on City Road; her last card payment had her stepping onto a bus. But she hadn't been on that same bus three stops down the road, when the first Dog on the scene boarded it. "So where is she now?"

"I'm told we're working on it," said Nash.

The Park was in a flurry, though you wouldn't have guessed with a casual glance. The boys and girls of the hub were at their workstations, and there was hush, or what passed for it in an office environment. The usual suspects had shucked their footwear, and were padding around in stockinged feet; the local hardware issued its ambient hum. But Nash, a familiar here, recognised a fractured normality. The figures by the doorways were Dogs, officers of the Service's internal security division; their presence on the hub spoke of the potential for heads to be thrust upon spikes. An edge had opened up the full length of the building, and all who worked there were balanced upon it. And Nash was acutely conscious of having wielded the shovel that broke the ground.

Malahide continued to harumph. As was common with the breed, he retained a certain bafflement that the position of First Desk had been allotted to a woman; the current complications could have been averted had anyone noticed this earlier and put a stop to it. "Because what the devil does she think she's playing at? It's admin, that's all. A temporary suspension, as laid down in Service Regs, and applied with haste—admittedly—but in absolute accordance with procedure." He spoke with the confidence of one who'd been in possession of the finer detail for five minutes, and without appearing to remember that Nash himself had supplied this. "What's called for next is a hearing, at which she'll be asked to stand down— that's what the reg demands, that she be 'asked'—while an investigation is carried out." He shook his head. "And she decides to play hide and seek. She might as well have signed a confession."

"That's jumping the gun," Nash said. They were in the office adjoining First Desk's: occupying Diana's territory would have felt an act of *lèse-majesté*, or at any rate premature. "Diana is innocent of wrongdoing until proved otherwise. Rather what our justice system is based on."

"Well, if we're talking about the justice system, old man, she might argue that one cryptic reference in the *Times* is hardly enough to base a prosecution on in the first place. Yes, yes. I know." He waved away Nash's rejoinder: that the word "waterproof," in that context, was tantamount to an air-raid siren. "Point is, this might be hush-hush"—and here he made an expansive gesture, taking in the office, the hub, the Park, the secret world—"but it's still government-issue. Which means appearances matter."

"It's not even certain she's taken flight. Her diary's clear for the next few hours. For all we know, she's taking personal time."

"Which would presume she's ignorant that Candlestub's been implemented." Malahide waggled his eyebrows. "But she dumped a perfectly good phone in a bin on City Road, which is hardly the action of an unflustered woman. No, she's aware of what's going on. Which isn't to say there's not a hokey-cokey being danced down the usual corridors. And we don't need a *little birdie* to tell us"—and here, the eyebrows saw action again—"who's calling the steps. Mark me, this is Number Ten's gnome-in-residence ploughing on with his land grab. No, if Taverner wants to fight her corner, she'd better turn up to do it. Otherwise, she'll find all that's left of her empire is a six-foot plot by a drainage ditch. Do they do table service here, by the way? Generally take a stiffener round about now."

Nash said, "We should formulate a plan of action. Clearly, an investigation into Waterproof has to begin even in Diana's absence."

"Top of the list is this de Greer woman, I suppose. There a file on her or anything?" Malahide, who'd taken the chair on the operational side of the desk, opened a drawer, glanced into it and slammed it shut again. "If she has been rendered waterproof, I don't suppose there'll be much in the way of paperwork. But there'll have been instructions. Somebody must know something." First rule of the Civil Service, his tone implied. "We need to speak to everyone Taverner's spoken to since the woman disappeared. Before then, in fact. In the days leading up to."

Nash's instructions on that score had been specific. When he'd relayed Whelan's belief that Sophie de Greer had been quietly bagged and delivered to the San, Sparrow had said, "And that's the spit we'll roast Taverner on. Meanwhile, forget about it. Because if Taverner finds out we know, she'll have de Greer disappeared again, probably for good."

Now, Nash said, "We have access to her calendar, and her staff. We can start interviewing right away." Standing by the open door, he surveyed the hub again. He wasn't sure he'd ever seen it without Diana present, and it was hard to believe he'd never do so again. But in time, if Sparrow's promises meant anything, all of this would fall under his own purview, and whoever rose to First Desk status in Diana's wake would have all the governance of a ship's figurehead: proudly leading the way, but wholly directed by other hands. Long used to the spoils and spills of political life, what surprised him most was not that it was Sparrow who'd brought Diana low—he was familiar with the Whitehall edict that it's those you have most contempt for who do the most damage—it was more that, gazing out at his kingdom-to-be, he felt, for the first time in what might have been forever, a lack of appetite.

"Right time to be woolgathering?"

"Steeling myself for what's to come."

"Just the usual day's work," said Malahide. "Seeing who'll be first to chuck their boss under a locomotive." He ran a hand over his balding head. "Ever felt this was something you'd fancy for yourself? First Desk, I mean? Head of the whole shebang?"

"Lord, no," said Nash. "I've always done my best work behind the scenes."

When Taverner's phone rang, it could only be one caller.

It had struck her, threading through the maze of alleys round Bank, that it had been years since she'd worked the streets. As First Desk, her view was usually sci-fi: the city seen via CCTV, or from satellite footage or thermal imaging; as a moving backdrop through tinted windows, from a back seat. Easy to forget the pavements sticky with gum, the air thick with street food smells; the sickly sweet aroma of burnt caramel drifting from the parks . . . London's signature perfumes, signs that the city was hauling itself upright again. Breathing them in, she felt her own spook identity reassert itself too, now she was alone and hunted. *Red Queen.* Someone was hoping to chop off her head.

Meanwhile, her phone was ringing, her secret phone; the one only her caller knew about.

"I hear you're having a little local difficulty," said Peter Judd.

The fact that he knew this already surprised her not one whit.

She'd had enough cash to buy a hat and scarf from a tourist boutique; they wouldn't withstand a second look from a Dog, but to the idle onlooker she wasn't the same woman she'd been ten minutes ago. Phone to her ear, she was on a business call. There wasn't a human soul within half a square mile who wasn't, or if there were, they were looking for her.

"Anthony Sparrow saw an opportunity," she told him. "And he jumped on it with both feet."

"You have a counter-plan?"

"I have a current intention. I'm going to use his head as an ashtray, and feed the rest to my neighbour's cat."

"Delighted to hear you have everything under control."

As she stepped out of the alley maze, her unease grew. This was how joes must feel, plying their trade on unfriendly streets. The Park would be in confusion now: Candlestub was an admin issue, suspension "without prejudice," but you didn't have to be Michael Gove to recognise an opportunity to put the knife in. Effectively, a *Sit Vac* notice hung on her office door. The hub would be crippled by speculation, Oliver Nash's committee would be staking claims, and Sparrow would be enjoying the chaos—but it was the street talent she had to worry about. With that in mind, she'd binned her phone, or the one the hub knew about; had cracked her credit cards and dropped them down a drain—only the newer reissues could be traced whether in use or not, but she was taking no chances. She needed to stay free. Once they took her to the Park, once she'd been formally stripped of status and forbidden contact with anyone with a security clearance high enough to open an Easter egg, her future looked dim.

"What's amusing," Judd went on, "is that they're after you for something you haven't done, rather than any of the things you have."

"Did you just call to gloat, Peter? Only I'm pressed for time."

"Actually, I was hoping to hear I'd been misinformed. If you end up in the Tower, it's not going to reflect well on me. It would be selfish of you to have your career go up in flames when I'm preparing for an election."

A bus was crawling lazily along Threadneedle Street, a taxi fuming in its wake. For a moment, the possibility arose of flagging it down, waving her Service card in the driver's face ... The resulting piece of street theatre would be on YouTube before the laughter died down.

"I need money," she said.

"Leave the country money, or one last bottle of Pol Roger money?"

"I'm not running. I plan to take this piece of shit off at the ankles."

"I love it when you talk violent. Makes me regret the path not taken."

The path had in fact been taken, but only a few times. And if Diana didn't look back on the episode as a mistake, exactly, she'd long since barred and chained the gate leading to it.

She needed to get to Chelsea. When it came to taking down Sparrow, his Russia-planted appointee was the smoking gun of choice.

Judd had the tone of one stroking his chin. "Some investments are best flushed, you know. As soon as the stock starts to fall."

"And some investors get caught in the blast when what they thought was a bust goes boom."

"Now, that's not an especially accurate—"

"I need some fucking money."

"There's my girl. You know Rashford's?"

"On Cheapside?"

"Talk to Nathan. He'll be behind the bar."

She felt a slight loosening of the tension that had been gathering in her chest since the words first reached her. *Red Queen.* "Thank you."

"Consider it a hedged bet. And Diana? Joking aside, if this actually happens—if you're out on your ear?"

"You'll stand by me when everyone else has fled?"

"That's sweet. No, I'll splash every last detail of our association across the national breakfast table. Without you I've no skin in the game, but I can embarrass all kinds of fuck out of the government. Their own intelligence service, funded by Chinese capital? Even the PM'll have his work cut out, lying his way past that."

"Peter—"

"I realise that means suspension will be the least of your worries, but I've never been the sentimental type. I hope you understand."

Understand? She'd have been alarmed if he'd pretended otherwise.

Judd, imagining himself dramatic, ended the call.

Keeping her phone to her ear, continuing a conversation that was now the only observable thing about her, Diana headed for Cheapside, her hat shielding her from the capital's digital voyeurs.

They'd opened the door before he'd knocked, he'd walked in scattering ash in his wake, and just like that the house was his: a little darker for his presence, less safe. Underneath the smoke, he smelled of coffee. A creamy smear on his lapel was recent. This probably counted, in Lamb's world, as box-fresh.

He revolved on the spot, taking in his surroundings, and by the time he was facing them again, a new cigarette had appeared in his mouth. It was pointing downwards when he spoke. "Fancy a walk?"

". . . Sorry?" said Bachelor.

"Oh, did I say 'fancy a walk'? I meant fuck off. Me and Mystic Meg have things to discuss."

Bachelor had known Lamb by reputation, but the reality was higher definition. Like when you've heard about a lorry ploughing through a front window, and then see it happen. He glanced at Sophie, and Lamb caught him at it.

"You need permission? Christ, it's been three days. Your cycles can't be in synch already."

"I'm supposed to be watching over her."

"Yeah, and one day this might be a musical. Meanwhile, take a turn around the block."

De Greer put a hand on Bachelor's arm. "John? It's okay. I'll be fine."

"You're sure?"

"I'm sure."

Lamb beamed. "There, we're all happy. Now get your fucking skates on."

"I won't be far away," Bachelor said.

"Don't spoil the moment."

They watched through the window as he trudged across the cobbles and under the archway, leaving the mews.

"Wrap him one more time round your finger, he's gunna burst like an overripe condom."

"I don't know what you're talking about."

"Condoms. Rubbers. The man puts one on his—"

"He's very nice. He's been taking care of me."

"He might as well be wearing an Emergency Exit sign. Soon as it's necessary, you'll go straight through him. Of course, he hasn't worked that out yet." The cigarette between Lamb's lips rose to point upwards. "Your mother. Alexa Chaikovskaya. She was old school KGB, right?"

"In the secretarial division."

"And rose to colonel. Shows an admirable dedication to sharpening pencils."

"She's in a home now. With nurses, carers. She's not in good health." De Greer bit her lip briefly. "They told me she'd be turned out on the street. If I didn't do what they asked."

"Impressive," said Lamb. "The lip chewing. You take lessons, or does it come natural?"

"Fuck you."

"That's better. Now, while Sir Galahad's off imagining all the ways you might fall on his sword, why don't we drop the crap? You work for Vassily Rasnokov. He dangled you in front of Number Ten's chief gremlin, who's just the type to be impressed by the superforecaster credentials, and next thing we know you're shaping government policy."

"Shaping?" De Greer shook her head. "I was adding my voice to a prevailing chorus, that's all. Helping steer Rethink in the direction it was already headed."

"Course you were." Lamb rummaged in a pocket and found a disposable lighter. "Sparrow already had it in for the Civil Service, didn't he, because of the cash mountains waiting for whoever replaces it with private contractors. But a little encouragement never hurts. Set a mole to writing briefs for a cabinet already a few boats short of a ferry company, you'd be entitled to think job done. But Rasnokov's more ambitious than that, don't you think?"

"What I think is, you're not like I'd pictured," she said.

"Yeah, they photoshopped a thigh-gap in my publicity stills," said Lamb. "Imagine my distress." He clicked his lighter, then did it again. When it failed to respond with more than a dry scratch, he tossed it over his shoulder. It took a nick from the wall and dropped to the carpet. "Got a light?"

"Smoking's a disgusting habit."

"Spying's pretty gross too. But I try not to be judgemental." He found another pocket to rummage in. "So where was I? Oh yeah. Your boss. He was well aware of Sparrow's general approach. The man calls himself a disruptor, right? Tossing imaginary hand grenades around, and thinking that makes him Action Man. So my first thought was, in planting you, Rasnokov was playing him at his own game. Simply causing chaos. Put you in place, then cause maximum embarrassment by burning you."

If the words startled her, it was only for a moment.

"Join in any time you like," Lamb said.

"Are you recording this?"

"Fuck, no. I'm barely paying attention. I mean, you might think you're the hottest property since Anthony Blunt was keeping Her Maj's nudes well hung, but I've better things to do than debrief entry-level spooks. My lunch won't eat itself." From a pocket he extracted a second lighter, which sparked encouragingly, but didn't hold its flame, and he was about to send it the way of its twin when de Greer relieved him of it. After shaking it vigorously she clicked once, and Lamb leaned forwards, the tip of his cigarette touching the flame.

"Don't mention it," she said.

He breathed out smoke. "But when your boss burned you, he did so to the one person guaranteed to keep it under wraps. Sparrow himself. So it's not like he was running some half-arsed honey trap. Unless you're about to tell me you've a sex-tape ready to leak."

De Greer tucked the lighter into his breast pocket and stepped back. "Sorry to disappoint you."

"Just as well. I leak a bit myself these days, tell you the truth." Lamb removed his cigarette from his mouth and studied the lit end for a moment. "Even so, your boss's little bombshell must have had Sparrow shitting himself, which sounds like a good day's work to me, and we're not even on the same side. But look what he did next. Came all the way to Blighty to whisper similar sweet nothings in Diana Taverner's ear."

"Perhaps he fancies her."

"Stranger things have happened. For instance, I got a phone call on my way back to the office just now. Want to guess what it told me?"

"You've been mis-sold PPI?"

"That someone's pulled the emergency cord at Regent's Park. Not many able to do that, but I'm guessing the PM's number one bitch-slapper is among them." Lamb took a long drag, then flicked the still burning cigarette the length of the room. It bounced off the curtain with a shower of sparks. "And that's what this is really all about. Rasnokov wasn't trying to embarrass Sparrow out of his job. No, he wanted Sparrow declaring full-on war with the Service, before the Service realised he'd invited a Kremlin pointy-head into Downing Street. And just to make sure things really kicked off, he followed that up by priming First Desk, letting her know that he'd had a private hobnob with Sparrow back in Moscow. Like lighting the blue touch paper at both ends. Because he doesn't care who wins, he just wants to see both sides taking lumps out of each other while he carries on with his own scheme."

De Greer, nodding thoughtfully, crossed the room to stamp on the sparks smouldering on the carpet.

"So congratulations seem to be in order. You were slotted into place to stoke up a little not-so-friendly rivalry." Lamb slid a hand between two buttons of his shirt, and began to scratch. "And it looks like you've managed to ease Diana Taverner out of her job."

Rashford's was open to the public, but liked to give the impression it wasn't. Occupying the third and fourth floors of a building on Cheapside, its sole entrance was sandwiched between plate-glass windows whose mannequins' blank stares were aimed at the well-heeled passerby: winter coats their current garb. The door was propped open, but the red-carpeted staircase, with its polished brass handrail, seemed less an invitation than a glimpse of forbidden pleasure. Diana, who kept herself informed of who was drinking where, knew it had enjoyed a brief vogue between lockdowns, its speakeasy vibe chiming with the panicked pleasure-seeking of the times. This afternoon, it seemed deserted. The carpet swallowed any sound her heels might have made, but the staircase seemed full of empty echoes nonetheless.

At the top of the fourth half-flight were a pair of glass

doors, and behind them a wide room, lit by dusty daylight and the one or two tassel-shaded tablelamps. A lone man sat in a red-leathered booth, absorbed in his phone. It wasn't too late to turn and run. Judd was barely trustworthy, and might have decided to play a joker. The Dogs could be heading here even now. But she pushed through the doors regardless and found herself standing by a long, curved bar. Its tender moved sleekly towards her, dropping the cloth he'd been holding onto a tap. "Good afternoon, and how can I help you?" Though the way he said it, the look he gave her, he already knew.

"I'm looking for." The name escaped her. Her memory was a series of corridors, lined with lockers; keys hung in each, with labels attached. *Nathan.* "Nathan."

"Ms. Huntress?"

That sounded right.

He'd done this before, she could tell. Had an envelope prepared, tucked under the till. She wondered, briefly, what strands tied this man, or this bar, to Peter Judd; bound them tightly enough that it only took a phone call and there was cash to hand. "Thank you."

"No problem. And let Sir know we look forward to his company again soon."

Feeling more like a joe than ever she went back through the glass doors, envelope in hand, and stopped on the landing to make a quick count: five hundred, in tens and twenties. Had she not done that, she'd have met them on their way up: three of them, by the sound of it; their tread muffled on the staircase carpet. Friends or colleagues, out-of-towners or local wetheads: any of these would be making noise. Would be laughing with each other, already picturing that first glass being passed across the polished bar.

Diana turned and headed up the next flight.

At the top of which was a second bar, shrouded in darkness, its doors locked. There was no more red carpet; a sign reading STAFF ONLY was taped to the wall beside the next flight of stairs. Someone had made a sad face out of the O. The crew of three—face it, they were Dogs—went into the lower bar; she could hear Nathan greeting them over-enthusiastically as she moved quietly upwards. There were two doors at the top. The first warned about unauthorised admittance, and was locked. The second opened, but was a cupboard. She saw brooms, a pail, a ziggurat of cleaning fluid bottles, and a plastic-wrapped palette of light bulbs, their ghostly faces Munch-like in the gloom. A metal box on the wall probably shielded fuses. If it did, and she pulled wires about, she might set off an alarm, and in the ensuing confusion grow wings, or become invisible. But it was padlocked: a flimsy piece of hardware, maybe two quids' worth. She looked in her bag, found a pen, slid it into the closed hoop of the flimsy padlock and pushed hard. The padlock broke. Dropping its parts into her bag, she opened the box to find, instead of fuses, several rows of keys, which, like those in her memory, were labelled; one read *Roof*. She took it, closed the cupboard, and paused before slipping the key into the first door's lock. Voices. Nothing of clarity, though if Nathan were cooperating, the Dogs would already be standing next to her. The *Roof* key opened the first door, and she stepped through it onto another staircase, then locked it behind her. The noise as the tumblers fell was louder than a stolen goose.

She forced herself to wait in the darkness, breathing through her mouth to make less noise. Someone was coming up the stairs. The doorknob turned and the door rattled, Diana's darkness momentarily broken by its outline, sketched in light. There was a pause. It happened again. Then the second door was tried, and its contents silently inventoried: cleaning fluids, broom, pail. Those mutely screaming lightbulbs. A metal rattle as the box was opened. She braced. Anyone on their game would join these dots: a locked door, a row of keys. A Dog discovering which key wasn't there would kick her door down in a second or two. She counted them. And then someone was heading downstairs again. She gave it another moment, then found her phone. By its light she went up eleven stairs, unbolted the next door, and stepped onto a flat stretch of roof.

Diana hadn't spent long in the dark, but London's light was still at first staggering; buildings seen from unaccustomed angles, the smell of the Thames on the sunlit wind. She thought what every joe thinks, after a close encounter with discovery: *I'm alive.* And then she regarded the burner phone in her hand, with its single contact listed, and tapped out the only number she had by heart.

Catherine had the sense of following an instruction she'd written for herself, possibly in a dream. *It's not complicated. The phone is on his desk. Sometimes it rings.* She was at her own desk, and Lamb was who knew where? *If he's out and it rings and I hear it, I'll answer it. If I get there in time.* And as she reached the receiver a strange thought occurred: How many more times would she answer a ringing landline? It almost never happened anymore.

"Where is he?"

"I have no idea." She'd heard Diana Taverner's voice often enough to recognise it. "Can I take a message?"

Silence. Or not quite: for some reason Catherine could hear an airy nowhere breathing loudly in her ear.

Candlestub had been initiated, and in all likelihood—she did not, whatever her colleagues thought, have total recall of the Service handbook—she should terminate this call, then report it. First Desk was tainted. But there were occasional advantages to being a slow horse, one of which was, it was unlikely that anyone would follow up her actions, so instead, she waited for Taverner's response.

"I need some help."

She wished she'd recorded that. Diana Taverner, seeking her help. The woman who'd done her best, some years ago, to drive a double decker bus through her sobriety: *Tell me,*

Catherine. Something I've always wondered. Did Lamb ever tell you how Charles Partner really died? Now could be the moment to discover what it felt like, pressing a heel down on someone else's throat, but even as that thought stirred she was listening to Taverner, mentally prioritising the tasks ahead. Was it habit or weakness that made her act like this? In the end, she supposed, it didn't matter. You played the part you were given, and it was never in her to be a bad actor.

The call over, she stood for a while in Lamb's musty office, trying not to picture the possible calamities Taverner's requirements might provoke.

Then she phoned Lamb, and put him in the picture.

"**Okay, you** can uncover your ears now." Lamb put his phone away. "Where were we?"

"I was easing your First Desk out of a job," said de Greer. "And you were offering congratulations."

"That right? Could have sworn you mentioned a cup of tea."

"You may have mistaken me for your housemaid."

"Nah, she's shorter, and wears a leather basque." He stood abruptly and headed into the kitchen, leaving her no choice but to follow. "Attacking the Service was your brief, wasn't it? Reminding Sparrow the Park's a little too independent, with Taverner at the wheel." He located the kettle, flicked its switch, and leaned against the counter. "So when Rasnokov let him know he was nursing a viper to his tits, he was nicely primed. Sparrow knew the Park would rip him to shreds first chance it got, so he went straight on the attack."

De Greer reached past him, turned the kettle off, and lifted it from its base. "Sparrow already hated the Park. A smoking ruin, he called it." She filled the kettle at the sink, then put it back and flicked its switch once more. "And he hates Taverner the way all weak men hate powerful women."

"Only he tried to deal with you first," said Lamb.

"He had people following me," she said, dropping teabags into a pot. "They were so bad at it, I thought they were your people at first. Slough House."

"Only they were even worse," said Lamb. "Which, fair dos, I wouldn't have seen coming either." He opened the fridge, eyeing de Greer speculatively. "You look to me like a MILF."

". . . I beg your pardon?"

"Milk in first?" He removed a carton. "Or have I got that wrong?"

She took two mugs from a cupboard and set them on the counter. Lamb divided about a twentieth of a pint equally between them and the surface, and said, "You think he was planning on having you killed?"

"No. I think he was hoping to convince me to deny I was a plant."

"How hard would that have been?"

"Maybe not as much as you might think."

"Depends on what he was offering, right? Head girl in the PM's pole-dancing troupe?" He reached for the kettle as it boiled. "And what would Rasnokov have made of that?"

"He'd have thought I was doing my job."

"But instead you jumped into our arms when Sparrow's thugs tried to snatch you."

"If that's what they were trying to do. They seemed a little . . . uncoordinated."

"Compared to my lot," said Lamb. "Who managed to get arrested and run themselves over." Steam furrowed the air as he poured water into the pot. "Still, better the dickheads you know. Bring that." He marched back into the sitting room, leaving de Greer to carry teapot and mugs.

By the time she'd done so, Lamb had kicked his shoes off and arranged himself on the sofa in what might have passed as an alluring pose in someone with inoffensive socks. "Your disappearance must have given Sparrow a fright. One thing worse than having a tarantula appear in your cornflakes is having it vanish again. I mean, where the fuck'll it show up next?"

"If you're trying to flatter me, you're not doing a very efficient job."

"I leave seduction to the professionals. Speaking of which, you planning on screwing Bachelor? Because the excitement might kill him. And you could get him to do whatever you want by just dropping 'hand-job' into the conversation."

De Greer lifted the teapot and filled both cups.

"But here's me bimbosplaining," said Lamb. "Anyway. Sparrow recovered, because next thing we know he's playing the waterproof card and sending a former First Desk out looking for you. Which puts Taverner in the hot seat. So far, so very Westminster. When you've got a guilty conscience, scream loudly and point at someone else."

"They prefer to think of it as reframing the narrative."

"Whatever they call it, it's done the trick. Because the Park's overflowing with Biro-bashers, and according to my Miss Havisham, Taverner's hiding on the roof of some wine bar off Cheapside." He slurped some tea, and scowled. "That's gunna taste better coming back up."

"The teabags are very old."

"Anyway, point is, you're in demand. Diana needs you to prove you've not been waterproofed, and Sparrow needs you so he can, yeah, reframe your narrative. Well, that or bury you somewhere. And as for me, you know what I want?" Lamb put his cup down. The hand that had held it was now wielding a cigarette. "I want to know why you made that little startled movement when I said Rasnokov burned you. Because if that was always the plan, then why the surprise?"

"I wasn't surprised."

"But you twitched."

He pulled the lighter from his breast pocket, and tossed it at her. She caught it, shook it, clicked it, and lit his cigarette. Then said, "How many of these do you get through?"

"I'm supposed to keep count? They're called disposables for a reason."

She clicked again, and as the flame burst into life held it up, so she was staring straight into it. An act of self-hypnosis, perhaps. She said, "How much do you know about Rasnokov?"

"My Top Trumps set's out of date. But I know he can plot round corners."

She laughed softly. "This was never Rasnokov's plan, Mr. Lamb. Back when he was what you'd call a joe, he had a handler. And it's her he still looks to for his brightest ideas."

"'Her?'"

"My mother."

Through the window, a figure appeared in the mews: John Bachelor. For a moment he wavered on the threshold, as if keeping balance on the cobbles were as much as he could focus on. And then he reached out and knocked on the door, and Sophie de Greer faded back into the nervous, twitchy victim he was expecting before going to let him in.

Catherine said, "And that's your mission. Should you decide to accept it."

"Leg it to Cheapside, locate Taverner, extricate her from . . . malefactors, and get her to Chelsea," said Louisa.

"That's right."

"Except she didn't say 'malefactors,'" Lech suggested.

"No," said Catherine. "She didn't say 'malefactors.'"

"And what's in it for us?" asked Louisa.

"I'm tempted to suggest Taverner's undying gratitude. But I think we all know the concept's alien to her."

"What's Lamb say?"

"He said, 'This is going to be good.'"

Louisa was at her desk; Lech by the window. Catherine had closed the door behind her, and stood regarding the pair of them. She didn't appear to be enjoying the moment, probably because she knew what their response would be.

"So what are we waiting for?"

She said, "I should remind you that it's only a few days since your last adventure. And," looking pointedly at Lech, "you're still walking like somebody stole your stretcher."

"A bit stiff, that's all. Besides, that was Ho's fault. And he's not joining us, is he?"

"No," said Catherine. "Lamb had something else in mind for Roddy."

Of all the reasons Diana had for wanting to run Sparrow's head up a pole, here was number one: that she'd been forced to enlist the slow horses for aid and succour. The only upside she could see was they'd be bound to fuck things up, and the way things stood, even that wasn't actually an upside.

She was on the roof. On the street below, a black SUV—a Service car—was illegally parked outside Rashford's door, its team, bar the driver, now in the building. Theoretically this should have been a source of gratification—her boys and girls on the hub could track a warm body through London's streets as easily as if she had a red balloon tied to her sleeve—but just once, she'd have found ineptitude welcome. Because the Dogs were here to take her back to the Park, and from that moment on she'd be officially suspended, a career limbo from which few emerged intact. And if she were relying on Slough House for rescue she'd be better off with an actual red balloon, one she could float away on.

Meanwhile, she was still carrying her secret mobile, and the last thing she needed to be found in possession of was a link to Peter Judd. Stepping back from the edge, she was removing the sim card when the mosquito buzz that had been nagging away in the background penetrated her consciousness.

Looking up, she saw the drone hovering twenty yards overhead.

This doesn't get covered in the style mags, but good-hair days bring their own problems. Running a comb through his locks, Roddy offered his reflection a steely glance, then mussed himself up again and activated the engaging, puppyish grin. Then tried a steely/tousled combo, which was a bit of a mixed message frankly, before opting for the side-parting/puppyish look.

Check. It. *Out*.

Roddy Ho is in the house.

He'd decided, after some magnificent brooding on the matter, to nix the phone call and go for Zoom. Play to your strengths, dude—he'd be an idiot not to put the goodies on the counter. Face it, he'd dazzled her during the audition; she'd seen the role, not the man, and figured him for some charismatic crumbly. Her bolshiness had been down to understandable disappointment. Only fair to let her see what lay beneath the Hobi-Wan robes. And let's not forget what you're playing for: *Any woman desperate enough to dress up as a cartoon character is looking to get laid.*

Here we go.

"Babes, I can't be the only one who felt a little friction the other night—and friction's what it's about, ya feel me? I push a little, you push back . . ."

(Miming this, so she got the picture.)

"Am I right or am I right? I mean, I could definitely be into you."

This being the chief objective, when you got down to it.

But his rehearsal was interrupted by noises on the staircase.

He waited until they'd gone—Louisa and Lech; off skiving—and decided: okay. No time like the now. It was after four so those wasters wouldn't be back, and he was unlikely to be interrupted. So: Zoom invite—"Important Follow-Up"— twenty minutes from now—despatched. Roddy leaned back and cracked his knuckles. Then thought: Hang on—was it Leia Six or Leia Seven who'd been the bolshy one? Because he'd just sent the invite to Leia Six, and—

"Roddy?"

And here was Catherine, crashing his train of thought.

"I'm busy."

"So I see. But this takes priority."

He shook his head wearily. That was the trouble with being indiroddyspensable: you were first port of call for the pea-brained.

"There's something Lamb needs you to do."

Roddy adjusted his expression to read "Born Ready," tried to crack his knuckles again, and winced.

"And if you can manage to listen without hurting yourself," Catherine continued, coming into the room, "this is what he's after."

"She's on a rooftop in Cheapside."

"And is she planning unassisted flight?"

Nash said, "I'd have thought that unlikely." Malahide's company was beginning to grate, his demeanour towards those they'd interviewed so far—the hubsters whose worksheets showed recent one-to-ones with Diana—having proved borderline hostile. When challenged, he'd raised an eyebrow. "Gone native, old boy?" A salutary reminder, Nash thought, that you always had to be on one side or another in the Whitehall Kush.

He glanced at the memo he'd been handed by Josie. "A wine bar, Rashford's?" He made it a question, though was aware of its existence, its name having made it popular with backbenchers. "She was picked up on camera, there's a crew at the premises now." He looked at his watch. "They'll have her here by five."

"And this wine bar has a rooftop terrace?"

"I think it's clear she's evading, ah, capture."

"Like I said. An admission of guilt." Malahide clasped his hands behind his head, and rocked back in his chair. "This famous window of hers, the one that frosts when you press a button. What do you suppose she got up to in her office when no one could see her?"

"We're conducting a preliminary enquiry," said Nash. "Not inventing scurrilous rumours."

"If you say so," said Malahide. "If you say so." He sat up straight. "Well, I suppose we'd better put Sparrow in the picture."

"Leave that to me," said Nash.

He left the office holding his phone to his ear, but without making a connection.

As he passed Josie's desk, unseen by Malahide, he made a follow-me gesture with his eyes, an invitation Josie accepted a few moments later.

"Remind. Me. Why. We're. Running?"

This was necessarily a conversation Lech was having in his head because, well, they were running . . .

And the answer, besides, was obvious. Cheapside was about a quarter mile from Slough House, or, by car, maybe three times that. Add roadworks, traffic lights, and you were looking at a half-hour minimum.

"She's on the roof," Catherine had said, and Lech had wondered if this were like the jolto about the cat, and she was gently breaking the news that Taverner was dead.

Louisa was way ahead, but she was a runner. Give Lech the streets after dark, he could pace ten miles and barely notice, but speed was a different story. Besides, there were people about, staring as he passed. Facial scarring made him the automatic villain. He was basically a trigger warning; a horror-meme waiting to happen.

Sod it.

A team of Dogs, Catherine had said. There for a Safe Collect—Taverner wasn't armed, and was anyway unlikely to initiate a gun battle on the streets of London. Had he imagined it, or had Catherine laid a slight stress on *unlikely*? But whatever the outcome, this had to do with Sophie de Greer, and the last time he'd left Slough House on a mission involving her, Roddy bloody Ho had ploughed him down on a dark common. What delights awaited him today?

Panting round the long curve below the Museum of London he could see Louisa at the Cheapside junction, so ignoring the pain in his thighs he increased his speed, the pavement's damp calligraphy blurring beneath his feet.

Roddy leaned back and made one of his expressions. He had several of these, and Catherine was familiar with all, but was never sure what he was attempting to convey, beyond some brand of superior weariness.

"So this Ronsakov—"

"Rasnokov," she said. "Vassily Rasnokov."

"What I said. This Ronsakov dude was at the Grosvenor two nights, only nobody knew it was him at first so he was, like, totally off radar."

". . . Yes."

"And Lamb wants to know what he got up to."

". . . Yes."

"In London."

"That's the size of it, yes. I'm sorry."

In the circumstances, she had to admit, weary superiority wasn't entirely without foundation.

Roddy reached for his energy drink.

"He might have been asleep," he said.

"Yes," Catherine agreed. "He certainly wasn't watching TV or using wifi. But he ordered two bottles of The Balvenie from room service."

Roddy looked blank.

"It's a brand of whisky."

"Yeah, I knew that."

"The empties weren't left in his room, and he didn't take them back to Moscow." Give her credit, Catherine delivered this information as if it were an important part of a soluble puzzle, and not, as it had appeared to her fifteen minutes previously, random facts plucked from an inconsequential blizzard. "So there's a chance he met with someone. Because the Balvenie might have been intended as a present."

"Balvenie?"

They turned. Ashley Khan was hovering on the threshold. She had her coat on, and her bag over her shoulder, but her departure had evidently snagged on the overheard word, so there she was, repeating it in the doorway.

"The Balvenie," she said again. "That's Vassily Rasnokov's brand."

The drone hovered insolently, and for a short while Diana saw the world from a different perspective—as one of the monitored, one of the watched—and in so doing understood the impulse the ordinary citizen has when confronted with the unceasing intrusions of daily life, "in the interests of security." So she did what every ordinary citizen does, most often internally but in this case with a kind of slow-motion deliberation: she raised her middle finger, and invited the unseen watchers to go fuck themselves. Then she turned her back on it and put the sim card in her mouth.

The drone rose higher, its buzz-saw whine diminishing, allowing her to hear more noises: a door being forcibly opened; feet coming up a dark staircase. She dropped the mobile and ground it underfoot, and was just swallowing the sim card when the rooftop access door opened, and the first of the Dogs stepped out into cold sunshine.

"One with the car. Three on the stairs."

"Stairs?" said Lech.

"There's always stairs," Louisa told him.

And there were always four Dogs, or that was how she remembered it. Though it was true that nobody kept Slough House up to date when procedures were modified.

They were on Cheapside, approaching Rashford's, outside which a black SUV was parked. A man easily identifiable as Dog leaned against it, his gaze directed at the bar's doorway. Lech was breathing hard, which was his own fault. No excuse for being out of shape.

Reading her thoughts, or perhaps her expression, Lech said, "I was run over a couple of days ago, remember?"

"At, what, ten miles an hour?"

"Still counts."

"In which case, you'd better take it easy. You can have the driver."

"In the sense of . . . ?"

"Keep him busy. So he's not watching the doorway when I come back out."

"Okay . . . So what's the plan?"

"Plan?"

"Great," said Lech. "Situation normal."

Waving two fingers Louisa left him there, a hundred yards short of their destination, and—ignoring the car parked outside—disappeared through Rashford's door.

"So your written assignment—"

"They call it a hand-in."

"Hand-in, right."

"I've no idea why."

Because you handed it in, presumably. Which didn't matter. Catherine said, "So your twenty-thousand-word hand-in was on Vassily Rasnokov."

The hand-in was part of every fledgling spook's first six-month assessment, regardless of whether their ambitions lay in field work or analysis. Most chose to critique an op from years gone by—a safe enough topic provided the career-blighting embarrassment of, say, picking an operation handled by Diana Taverner was avoided—and it had been some while since the straightforward biographical essay had been in vogue. This was largely because nothing boosted a mark like fresh information, and there was little chance of this being captured by a beginner.

Then again, there was fresh and fresh.

"I found a cross reference to a pre-digital source," Ashley said. "A case report from the late seventies."

"I didn't know Rasnokov was KGB back then. Wouldn't he have been a child?"

"A teenager," said Ashley. "And he wasn't official."

Which was a detail missing from Rasnokov's Service file: that prior to his recruitment, he'd carried a shovel on several KGB cases involving the harassment of known dissidents. The oversight was down to a misspelling—"Ronsakov" for Rasnokov—whose handwritten emendation had never been carried over to the master document. So a few small facts about his early career had been lost to history, buried in a cardboard folder deep in Molly Doran's domain, to which baby spooks were granted access while completing their hand-ins.

"Good work," Catherine said, meaning it. "That—well. It would have been noticed."

If Ashley's training wheels hadn't come off altogether, that was. If she'd finished her hand in and handed it in.

Roddy said, "Yeah, fascinating. But if this reference didn't mention what he was doing the other night, it's not much help, ya get me?"

The women shared a look.

Catherine said, "How many pieces of information did we have two minutes ago?"

He counted them in his head. "One?"

"And now we have more. How is that a hindrance?"

Something blipped: an incoming email.

"You've got a Zoom booked?" said Ashley, who was by Roddy's desk now, with a partial view of his screens.

"No."

"Because that looks like —"

"Yeah, right, it's nothing."

Catherine said, "Well in that case it won't distract you." She looked at Ashley. "I'm sure you won't mind giving Roddy a hand."

"Lamb says I'm not supposed to do anything."

"He'll make an exception for this," Catherine said.

"You think? Because—"

"*I'm* making an exception for this."

Ashley paused, then nodded.

Roddy said, "Look, I've got this thing—"

"I'll be back in half an hour," said Catherine. She moved towards the door. "Play nicely," she said, over her shoulder, and was gone.

It was all very courteous. They'd tarried on the rooftop while the more junior of the Dogs scraped the remains of Diana's shattered mobile together and put them in an evidence bag, and then they'd processed back into the building: Dog One, then Diana, then Dog Two. Dog Three—whom Diana knew by name; Nicola Kelly—was waiting on the landing.

"Sorry about this, ma'am."

Not as sorry as she would be, Diana's answering smile promised.

She took Diana's bag and rifled through it. Finding the envelope stuffed with cash, she raised an eyebrow at nobody in particular.

"I know how much is in there," Diana said.

Kelly replaced the envelope in the bag, which she didn't return.

On their way past the bar Diana looked for Nathan, but he wasn't in sight. He'd be on the phone to Peter Judd, reporting her capture. And Judd would be unsurprised. *I'll splash every last detail of our association across the national breakfast table*, he'd said, and while Judd wasn't what you'd call reliable, that was a promise he'd keep. After which, Sophie de Greer was a sideshow: Diana could have her lap dance the entire Limitations Committee for all the good it would do. Proving herself innocent of instigating Waterproof while Judd was revealing that she'd colluded with Chinese backers would be like standing up to her elbows in blood, indignantly explaining that she'd never shoplifted in her life. Meanwhile, Sparrow would be taking cover behind the hostile headlines, his role in employing de Greer reduced to an anodyne soundbite: *Clearly, there are lessons to be learned.* The ability to bury bad news was bullet-point one on the Westminster CV, practised by interns, perfected by PMs. Produce your *mea culpa* on the weekend a major royal dies. Nastier cowards than Sparrow had pulled this trick.

As for expecting aid and succour from the slow horses, that just went to show she was losing her grip. Might as well pray for divine intervention.

But as they trooped down the final staircase, Nicola Kelly bringing up the rear, the sunshine falling through the doorway was blocked for a moment by a silhouetted figure.

"**So he** was staying at the Grosvenor," Ashley said. "And ordered two bottles of The Balvenie."

She'd removed her coat and dragged a chair across so she was next to Roddy, the pair of them flanked by his screens, three of which currently displayed the Service log-in page. One of the others was downloading something; a second showed columns of figures absent any headings, and was quite possibly intended to suggest a heavy workload rather than achieve a specific result; and the third showed Ashley and Roddy, flanked by screens.

". . . Mirror mode?"

Roddy tapped a key, and the screen flipped to a gif of Yoda performing a backflip. Then he grabbed a comb from the desk and dropped it in a drawer.

"I don't like you being this side," he said.

"I'd noticed."

"And I've got this thing happening—"

"Your Zoom call."

"It's private."

"Yeah, I don't care. What have you done to trace Rasnokov?"

"Apparently you're the expert," Roddy said sulkily.

"More than you are. On the other hand, you're supposed to be good at this shit." She waved a hand at the glass and plastic world in front of them. "So impress me."

Roddy made a face.

"Are you in pain? Or was that your Tom Cruise impression? Now, let's start. Vassily Rasnokov is sixty-two years old."

Roddy rolled his eyes.

"Do you want my help or not?"

"Not."

"Too bad. We're doing this. He's sixty-two years old, and—"

Roddy trilled on his keyboard some more, and one of the Service log-in pages turned into a screenshot of Rasnokov's passport. He rolled his chair sideways, hit more keys on a separate board, and a second screen came to life, on a template familiar to Ashley. On text, indeed, that she knew by heart.

"There," said Roddy. "His Service file. Which gives me his age and his weight and his photograph. His career to date, his regular contacts, his family life, his pet dog. But guess what?" He asked a quick question, with fingers too fast for Ashley to follow, his search terms masked by asterisks. *No results found.* "None of that tells me what he was doing with two bottles of whisky on Tuesday night."

"Are you always such a dick?"

"Are you always such a . . ."

She waited.

". . . moron?"

"I'm a woman, I'm brown, I'm younger than you. Is that the best you can do?"

"Spreader," muttered Roddy.

"That's not a thing. Now. Rasnokov's file can't show us what he was up to Tuesday night, but what about stuff that's not on his file? Because like I said, some of the data I found isn't on the mainframe."

"Aren't, not isn't."

"What?"

"Data's plural."

"True," Ashley conceded. "But also, and I can't stress this enough, fuck off."

Roddy sighed.

Then the alarm on his phone went off, alerting him to his Zoom call.

The stairs were reasonably wide, but there was an etiquette, post-virus: you didn't start up them if there was someone coming down. So of the four people descending from Rashford's, three weren't expecting the newcomer to step onto the staircase, the fourth being Diana Taverner, who'd recognised Louisa Guy.

Who was weaving, as if drunk.

This wasn't going to work for long, because while she could move drunk and sound drunk Louisa didn't smell drunk. But it only had to get her up four steps, at which point she'd be level with Dog Two, who was behind Dog One: then she'd stumble, grab hold of one or the other and—well—as Lech had implied, plans weren't a strong point. But once there was a free-for-all on the stairs, then whatever plan the Dogs had clearly wasn't running to order either. And Louisa would at least have the element of surprise on her side.

Which remained true up until the moment Diana Taverner said, "Watch her. She's Slough House."

Louisa was barely out of sight before Lech approached the driver, saying, "This is Rashford's, right?"

The driver glanced at him, looked away, and then looked back, something between horror and fascination painting his face.

"I mean, you'd think they'd put a sign up. It's like they don't want you to know it's there."

"I'm busy right now."

"That's weird because you don't look it. Is this your job? Standing next to a black car?"

"I'm going to ask you to move away, sir." He'd managed to recompose himself, but it was clear Lech's appearance had touched a nerve.

Which was Lech's only advantage, so far as he could see. The man wasn't any taller than him but he was broader, and if violence broke out Lech was clearly going to get his arse kicked. Then again, Lech could have had six inches on him and it wouldn't have made a difference: Lech had been an analyst back in the day, and while his training had included a certain amount of physical activity, Dogs were coached to a higher standard. On the other hand, Louisa's instruction, *Make sure he's not watching the door*, didn't necessarily involve getting physical. He could just point in the opposite direction.

At, for instance, the traffic warden crossing the road, already snapping the SUV on her phone.

Lech said, "You know how, sometimes, there's something you need to do, and then someone else comes along and does it for you?"

"What are you on about? *Sir?*"

"Doesn't matter," said Lech.

"Is this your car?" asked the approaching warden.

The driver turned.

Lech moved away, towards Rashford's open door, so he was the only one watching when Taverner came out.

A moment after Diana had spoken Louisa was flat against the wall, her right arm halfway up her back, and while the element of surprise had certainly made an appearance, it hadn't done so in the way she'd expected. Which, come to think of it—

But Louisa didn't have time to think of it; she was busy being pinioned and shouted at.

"Are you armed?"

"Does she have a gun?"

"Check her shoes."

My *shoes?* . . .

She was still puzzling over that when Diana hooked a foot round Nicola Kelly's ankle and pushed her down the stairs.

And here was the element of surprise again. This time

Louisa embraced it, throwing herself backward and dislodging one of the pair restraining her, who promptly tripped over the tumbling Kelly, and pushing the other back against the opposite wall, where they both teetered for a moment before they too succumbed to gravity, and joined the sprawl at the foot of the staircase. A mêlée which didn't seem to inconvenience Diana, who picked her way past it untroubled, bending to retrieve sundry articles on her way.

When she stepped out onto Cheapside, in full view of Lech, she was carrying her bag, and also Kelly's gun.

All she needed was a pair of shades, as Lech put it afterwards, and she'd be Bonnie Parker.

Diana emerged into sunshine feeling like Clyde Barrow A slow horse—the one who'd been through the grinder—was waiting on the pavement, his jaw slack.

"Your colleague needs assistance," she told him. When he didn't move, she said, "Now," and he made to speak, changed his mind, and hurried into Rashford's, where he'd discover the impromptu game of Twister at the foot of the stairs.

The SUV was still double-yellow parked, an infraction being investigated by one of London's traffic enforcers, a paramilitary-uniformed Nigerian woman. She had her phone out, taking details, but froze like Elsa at the sight of a well-dressed middle-aged woman accessorised with hat and gun.

Diana, coming within three inches of her, said quietly, "Check it against your don't-even-think-about-it list, bury the paperwork, and find somewhere else to monitor. Clear?"

The woman nodded.

"Excellent." She waited another beat, and the warden scurried away.

And now the remaining Dog. It was presumably the gun, she thought—it couldn't be the tote bag, classy as it was—that was reducing everyone to marble. Instead of approaching him, she crooked a finger. He came to her with the air of one summoned by dread. She spoke.

"Your boss is in a heap at the bottom of the stairs, this Candlestub bullshit will be history by bedtime, and I'm First fucking Desk. You have two seconds to decide where your loyalties lie, and by loyalties I mean career prospects."

"Ma'am," he said.

"Good choice. Here." She handed him Kelly's gun. "Now, door."

He put the gun in his pocket and opened the back door for her.

"Quick as you like."

The others were piling out of Rashford's as the SUV took off down Cheapside, a motley looking bunch, dim and ragged, as if a trip to see the wizard hadn't paid off the way it ought. But Diana didn't look back. She was too busy instructing her driver.

"This is private," Roddy whispered furiously.

"It's not as private as all that," Ashley pointed out. "I'm here, for a start."

He'd dialled into his Zoom call because obviously— *obviously*—as soon as he'd done that she'd make herself scarce: go make a cup of tea or whatever. But she'd just pushed her chair back and settled in to watch: cramping his style. Which was a lot of style to cramp, but she was putting effort into it.

"Is there someone with you?" Leia Six asked.

Which was another problem: he'd got his Leias mixed up. Six was definitely not the Leia he'd experienced the meet-cute tension with.

"No," he told her.

"Yes," said Ashley, leaning into shot. "Hi. Are you Roddy's girlfriend?"

"No. Are you?"

Ashley made a fingers-down-the-throat gesture, and Leia laughed.

"Do not talk to her!"

"He means you," Ashley said.

"He means *you*!"

"Dick move either way."

"Out of my room," Roddy ordered.

"You're in his *room*?"

"It's an office," Ashley said. "We work together."

"What's he like?"

"You can do better."

"Now!"

"Is he always like this?"

"I've only known him, like, a week. But yeah, appaz."

Roddy seized a cable and pulled it from the monitor, to no obvious effect.

"I'd better go," Ashley said. "He's disconnecting printers now."

"We should do this again," Leia said, and vanished from Roddy's screen.

"Look what you did!"

"What?" said Ashley. "We were just chatting."

"She was supposed to be chatting to me!"

"Whatever. Anyway, she's cool. You should date her."

". . . You think?"

"Definitely."

Roddy smirked.

"I mean, she can tell you're a prat. But if we ruled prats out, we'd never get laid. Are we doing some work now? Catherine'll be down in a minute."

Roddy flexed his fingers.

"So tell me something about Vassily Ronsakov I don't already know," he said.

"Well, for a start, he's called Vassily Rasnokov."

"That's what I said."

"But his nickname as a teenager was The Fireman."

"Because he used to put fires out?" said Roddy.

"No," said Ashley. "Because he used to start them."

Lech and Louisa were walking back down Cheapside. "They wanted to check my *shoes*," Louisa was saying. "Who'd they think I was, Rosa Klebb?"

"Well, from a certain angle . . ."

"Fuck you."

"Consider me fucked," said Lech. "That was cool, by the way. Getting us out of there."

Because Kelly had wanted to arrest them.

"Good plan," Louisa had told her. They were standing in a shabby group on the pavement, the SUV a memory in distant traffic. "You can take my statement now, if you like. It involves your target driving away in your car with your gun."

There'd followed an exchange of pleasantries, after which the slow horses had made their departure.

"Do you think that counts as mission accomplished?"

"If we'd not turned up, Taverner would have been taken back to the Park by now," Lech said.

"By the malefactors," said Louisa.

"By the malefactors. Which is what she wanted to avoid."

"Yay for us, then."

"I'm sure she's suitably grateful."

"That's funny," said Louisa. Then winced and rubbed her shoulder and said, "I'll have bruises tomorrow."

"Tell me about it," said Lech.

Roddy's fingers blurred, and different sites opened up on different screens. Most of them, password pages suggested, were restricted to authorised users, the accompanying devices indicating that such users served the Crown, one way or another. These warnings didn't deter him long.

Ashley said, "Pretty slick."

"Well, *duh.*"

"And gracious with it."

Roddy shrugged modestly. "What do you think of Mr. Lightning?" he asked.

"Don't know him."

"No, I meant the name. Mr. Lightning."

"Sounds like a dick," said Ashley.

"That's what I thought."

He muttered it under his breath. *Mr. Lightning.*

None of the databases had so far yielded Rasnokov's name, nor the name he'd booked into the Grosvenor under: Gregory Ronovitch. But that had never been likely, given the undercover nature of whatever he'd been doing.

Take away the name, though, and focus on fire-related incidents, linked with the Balvenie brand-name, and—

Still nothing.

"Just put 'whisky,'" Ashley suggested.

Various hits, on various pages.

They took them one by one, the first turning out to be a brawl in a pub involving a number of off-duty fire-officers. This covered the second and third hits also.

Ashley reached for her bag and produced her Tupperware box of nuts and berries.

"Got any proper food?"

She put the box on his desk. "Your parents should have asked for a refund."

"Yeah, and your parents should have asked for a . . . Hang on."

"What?"

"That fire off the Westway." He was pointing at one of his screens: a report filed by an arson investigator the previous morning. "Look what was found in the wreckage."

Among the cremated furniture, the collapsed ceiling, the reeking, sodden remnants: two glass bottles, probably containing whisky.

"Confirmation awaited," Roddy read aloud.

"I saw that in the paper," said Ashley. "Someone died."

They looked at each other.

"You think—?"

"I think we're cooking with leaded," said Roddy, and reached for a handful of Ashley's nuts and berries. Stuffing them into his mouth, he continued, "I think we've hit the motherlode."

And then he threw back his head and screamed.

The day was losing the light when Diana reached the mews. The driver had discreetly dropped her at Marble Arch and continued on his way to the Park on her instructions: his subsequent admission that he'd lost her en route wouldn't do much for his credibility, but—she'd assured him—he'd flourish once she'd rendered the current situation null and void, a guarantee she justified to herself on the ground that if she failed to do so, he'd be the least of her worries. At Marble Arch she'd dipped underground, reappeared wearing headscarf and sunglasses bought from a street trader, and had set off on foot across Hyde Park. Late summer cast a warm glaze on everything, and there was a sweet sense of liberty in the air that the young, at least, were revelling in, but Diana felt a chasm between her own and their early evenings: they weren't being fucked over by sundry enemies, and they all had phones to play with. Still, visions of Anthony Sparrow being chewed by wild dogs amused her on the way. And now she was crossing the cobbles towards the safe house, one unknown to Park records. Opposite its front door, the tropical plants in their terracotta exile had settled into shadow.

The door swung open before she reached it. The shabby character on the threshold was one John Bachelor; an appropriate place for him, inasmuch as he was someone you just naturally wanted to wipe your feet on. Inside, Jackson Lamb squatted in an armchair like a yeti in a biscuit tin: spilling over its edges, but not seeming to care. Last time Diana had been here, the fragrance was furniture polish and fresh paint. Now the air was muddy with the remnants of what appeared to be a four-course Indian meal for seven: tinfoil trays lay everywhere, studded with plastic cutlery, and luminous spillages glistened on every surface within Lamb's reach, and also a fair distance away. Underneath all that, an expert nose might detect his trademark smog of cigarette smoke and damp wardrobes.

In the armchair facing him, legs folded beneath her like a resting fawn, was Sophie de Greer.

"Here's an interesting thing," said Lamb. "Back when he was still breaking legs for a living, our friend Vassily was known as The Fireman. Guess why."

Diana looked at Sophie de Greer, who said, "He worked as a debt collector. There were stories that it was best to pay up when he came knocking. Or you'd find your home a pile of ashes."

"Well, aren't you just spilling all your secrets."

"That would be down to my interrogative skills," Lamb said, and farted modestly. "The good doctor's poker face slipped when I told her she'd been burned. After that, well. You know me. Get the bit between my teeth, I'm like a dog with a boner."

"You certainly have similar table manners." Diana scanned the room. "Enjoy your meal?"

"Tasted better than skinny feels, I can tell you that." One of Lamb's hands disappeared down the back of his trousers, and he scratched energetically. "Speaking of dogs. You eluded them, I see."

"No thanks to your idiots. Who trained them, Laurel and Hardy?"

Lamb shrugged. "They were like that when I got them."

He raised a hand, which somehow now held a cigarette, and de Greer tossed him a lighter.

"Bring me a chair," Diana said, without turning round, and when Bachelor carried an upright through from the kitchen, she gestured towards it for de Greer's benefit.

After a moment, de Greer unwound herself and abandoned the armchair.

Sinking into it, Diana said, "A drink would be nice."

"Mi casa su casa," said Lamb, making no move towards the bottle at his elbow.

Bachelor was already fetching a glass.

Diana stared at de Greer, now perched on the kitchen chair, and looking like an applicant for a job she didn't want. "So you're who all the fuss is about."

"Sorry."

"Let me guess. You were planted to steer Sparrow in the right direction. Chip away at the democratic processes."

"It was nothing he didn't want to hear. You know what he calls backbenchers? Chimps."

"When I'm ready for your input, I'll let you know." Accepting the whisky Bachelor poured, she took a hefty swallow. "And this included curbing the Service, did it? When I nod like this, that's me letting you know."

"Rasnokov would prefer you not to be First Desk. That's a compliment, when you think about it."

"Jesus. I'm going to enjoy wrapping you up and sending you back to him."

An approaching cloud signalled that Lamb had lit up. "That's if you can find him," he said.

"I'm prepared to put her in separate parcels," Diana said. "And send one to every address we have."

Lamb looked at Bachelor, lurking in a corner. "That walk you took earlier?"

". . .Yes?"

"Take it again."

Bachelor looked like he was about to complain, but Diana's basilisk stare dissuaded him. The air in the room shifted with the opening and closing of the door.

"You're not very nice to him," de Greer said.

"On the other hand, I'm not pulling him round the room by his cock. So, you know. Swings and roundabouts."

"Why won't I find Rasnokov?" Diana said.

"Because he burned a building down the other night with someone still in it."

". . . Let's start at the beginning."

"Rasnokov slipped out of the Grosvenor first night he was here. The same night a garden flat off the Westway burned to a cinder. Two empty bottles of whisky were found in the rubble."

"The Balvenie."

"Yeah." Lamb blew a smoke ring. "Rasnokov may be a murdering thug. But he's not cheap."

"Who was the victim?"

"Don't know. But I can guess."

"So guess."

"An understudy."

"Right." Diana looked at de Greer. "Did you know about this?"

"I don't even know what an understudy is."

"Well, there's a body in a burnt-out flat without an identity," said Lamb. "Which means that somewhere there's an identity lacking a body."

"Rasnokov has a fake identity waiting for him," de Greer translated.

"More than that. A whole fake life someone's been living. Probably for years." Lamb reached for the bottle, and poured a measure bordering on obese. "Some poor bastard with a passing resemblance to our Vaseline, and with Rasnokov's own face plastered all over his ID, has been decorating a legend. And now it's ready for Rasnokov to move into. A vacant possession."

"Rasnokov's going to disappear?"

"If he's got any sense, he'll fake a death. You don't just walk away from a job like his. Not with Norman Bates for a boss."

"But he can't just step into this . . . ready-made life. If the fake Rasnokov's been creating a whole existence, then people will know him. And they'll know he's been replaced. The resemblance can't be that great."

Lamb looked at Diana. "Feel free to chip in."

Diana said, "The resemblance wouldn't need to be total. When Rasnokov steps into the dead man's shoes, he'll be about to relocate, somewhere far away. Somewhere nobody knows him."

"Couldn't he do that with a fake passport?"

"Lots of people do," said Lamb. "Trouble is, it's all surface tension. Put a little weight on it, your foot goes through." He held his glass up, and stared into its amber brilliance. "Wherever Rasnokov ends up, he'll be leaving behind an actual lived life. A quiet one, sure—our fake will have kept himself to himself, no close friends, no family—but with real roots. He'll have real jobs behind him, real debts and savings, credit history, career map, maybe the odd drink-driving escapade. All of it paper-trailed up the arse."

"And what about the dead man? What was in it for him?"

"Whatever Rasnokov promised him," Lamb said. "He must have thought his time was nearly up, that Rasnokov would arrive with money and a clean passport and cut him loose. Or maybe he knew what was coming, because he'd have had to be a fucking idiot not to." Lamb sucked hard on his cigarette, its lit end a manic glow. "Maybe that *was* the deal. Maybe Rasnokov plucked him from prison, offered him five years of life and all he could eat, after which . . . *pfft*. Might not seem so bad if the alternative's a slow death in an icy cell. But either way, the understudy came to London as arranged, and sub-let a room for cash. And what his name was these past years, and where he lives, all the things Rasnokov plans to slip into sometime soon, no one knows."

"*Battleship Potemkin*," Diana said. "He was laughing at us." She looked at Lamb. "How much of this is guesswork?"

"Most of it. But Rasnokov's nickname, and firestarting habits, come from Khan as well as Doctor Toblerone here. She might have her uses after all."

"And I assume Ho tracked down the fire and the body and the bottles."

"He's a treasure," Lamb agreed. "I plan to bury him someday. Though, point of fact, I haven't actually spoken to him. Apparently he's suffering severe mouth burns." He adopted a pious expression. "Can't think how that happened."

De Greer was looking from one to the other. "Why are you telling me all this?"

"So that when we send you back to Moscow," Diana said, "you'll be able to let them know your whole operation was a smokescreen. That should make Vassily popular. Not to mention dead for real, if the Gay Hussar has a hangnail that day."

"I don't want to go back to Moscow."

"Too bad." Diana stood. "I need to make a call." She had to call Judd, to forestall him dropping any info-bombs on the Park. "And I don't seem to have a phone."

"There's a landline upstairs," de Greer said. When Diana had left the room, said, "Will she really send me back?"

"Probably."

"They'll think I was part of it. That I knew what he was up to."

"Then I wouldn't bank on them declaring a public holiday."

"Can I have a cigarette?"

"No."

De Greer stared, then looked towards the window. There was no sign of Bachelor returning. Her gaze fixed in that direction, she said, "You forgot for a moment, back there."

"Forgot what?"

"Forgot to be yourself. You were too caught up in explaining what's going on. Being clever instead of being gross."

He sneered.

"I'd have been better off letting Sparrow's men grab me," she said. "At least he'd have tried to bribe me."

"Well, he's not gunna find you here," Lamb said. He drained his glass. "Let's face it. He thinks you're somewhere else entirely."

The day finished early—or night came too soon—so Shirley was contemplating getting into bed at a time she'd normally have been pre-loading. Midweek she rested, like any sane person—her Wednesday evenings were sacrosanct—but otherwise she'd be on the prowl, looking for something she'd recognise when she found it. A want, awaiting fulfilment. And it was in the night—in its bars and backstreets; in its clubs and on its buses—that she hunted it down, usually finding that the search itself, and the consequent adventures, placated her want for a while. But here in the San, with its well-swept floors and clean sheets, with its constant *hush*, she found herself all want, all neediness, and hated it. Stripped of camouflage, stranded like a chameleon against a neutral background, she was the centre of her own attention, and subject to its moods.

There were few other resources available. The bed on which she lay, fully clothed; the lamp, which she hadn't switched on. The moonlight falling through the window, whose curtain she hadn't yet drawn. Though she was on the third floor, the available view was of various kinds of nothing, all of them shrouded in darkness. There was no TV, no radio; they'd taken her phone "because you won't be needing to make calls, will you?" She couldn't decide whether it was the content of that clause or the way it was framed as a question that most made her want to punch the speaker in the face, though accepted that either on its own would have done the trick. It was as well she was maintaining the quiet dignity thing. There was a coffee-table book on a coffee table: *One Hundred Things to See in Dorset*. Fat chance. There was a picture of a tree. And there was almost no noise.

Which was what most bothered her. Ignore the San's various other hatefulnesses, like its institutional odours and the trademarked smile of its staff, and that picture of a tree, and what most bothered her was its hush. It felt like a religious undertow, its effect being to magnify every unintended noise. A coat hanger shifting in a wardrobe. The chink of a cup on its saucer. The people here—the "guests"—might as easily be called ghosts. They might not move through walls, but they were careful to enter rooms quietly. The loudest thing Shirley had witnessed since her arrival had been a jigsaw puzzle. It was enough to make her want to scream, and what worried her most was the fact that she hadn't. That she was as quiet as everyone else, after only a couple of days.

People keep getting hurt. People keep dying.

And maybe she was one of them. Maybe she'd die inside, if they kept her here long enough. By the time they posted her back to Slough House she'd be a drooling wreck, scared by sudden movements and startled by passing noise.

Which might have been why—lying on her bed, the clock effortfully dragging its way to 9:26—when Shirley heard sounds downstairs, she sat bolt upright.

Afterwards, Whelan was never quite sure what tipped him over the edge. All afternoon the impulse had gnawed at him; the suspicion that things were not as he had relayed to Oliver Nash. The possibility that an alternative reading existed. Back in Schemes and Wheezes, there'd sometimes come a point when you had to ask, were you the player or the game? And was the mousetrap you'd just built one you'd walk into yourself? He had helped create a character once, a role for an agent to inhabit, who was the precise and perfect fantasy partner for a target of interest, an arms dealer. The chosen agent had occupied the role so completely that that was pretty much the last anyone saw of him, though it was thought he and the target were living happily ever after somewhere south of Rio. In the inevitable handwashing that followed Whelan had been tasked with writing a paper addressing the flaws inherent in the scenario his team had developed, along with what the minutes chose to term a "structured corrective." In what was, for him, a rare display of ill-temper, Whelan's addendum read, in its entirety, *Don't use humans.*

An admonition which had been swirling round his head all evening. He had been used himself, that much was clear, and had registered no objection—the Service was called the Service for a reason, and he still felt the tug of its call to duty—but he worried nevertheless that he'd fallen into the backroom habit of forgetting that actual people were involved. In this instance, for example, what precisely was Sophie de Greer's role? Was she in hiding, or had she been snatched? Would his involvement result in her rescue, or had he helped throw her to wolves? And whose wolves: Ours or theirs?

The list of who "they" might be was a long one. But then, the question of who "we" were could be equally knotty.

There was good cause to persuade himself that, having played his part, he should put it out of mind. He remained subject, after all, to Official Secrets legislation. Besides, if the information he had relayed to Nash had been acted upon, that was an end of it: de Greer would either no longer require, or be beyond the reach of, assistance. But information was bankable, and not always spent as soon as in hand. In which case it was possible that de Greer remained where he had traced her to: the San, in Dorset. And if so, it would be straightforward enough to verify that she was safe. He might no longer be active, but he still had a name; one that rang enough bells to open a door at a remote, hardly maximum-security Service facility.

Whelan had visited the San once, on a handshaking tour. It wasn't such a long drive. Or it was, but making the effort would ease his conscience. And while it was true that, going by her photograph, Sophie de Greer was very attractive, it was almost equally true that this played no part in the decision he arrived at. Which was to put a jacket on, find his keys, and drive to Dorset.

It had been a door closing, nothing more, but it had happened without care. Someone had come in—or gone out—allowing the door to slam behind them, instead of easing it back into place.

Even during daylight, this would have been frowned upon. Would have wounded the *hush*.

Shirley hopped off the bed, wondering if she'd heard the first postcard from a rampage through the building. If someone had flipped their lid, and were even now running up the stairs, prepared to scream their excitement to the walls.

If that happened, she wanted to watch.

But when she peered down the corridor, there were no sideshows in evidence. Only the dull mumble of voices downstairs.

Dinner had been served at seven. At nine, the common room was locked. There was nowhere to go but bed. Whoever was still down there must be staff.

Except the staff knew to use doors quietly. If they knew nothing else, they knew that.

Shirley didn't spend a lot of time weighing up her next move. If the minor ruction had been caused by one of the Nurse Ratcheds having a bad-care day, and if their meltdown involved, say, a bottle of something, or a line of something else, Shirley was more than prepared to keep quiet about it. She'd be silent as a fucking aardvark. Provided whoever it was slipped her a taste of the contraband.

Trainers on, she padded to the staircase. There was a floor-to-ceiling window at its head, and she could see her reflection as she approached. If she'd been holding a candle on a gravy boat, she'd have thought herself a ghost.

Passing one of the other bedrooms, she thought she heard a whimper from inside. Night tremors.

She descended two flights silently, dropped to a crouch on the landing and peered round the banisters, like a child in a movie, eavesdropping on parents.

In the lobby below, a woman was behind the reception desk. Shirley could see the back of her head, enough to identify her as the staff member who'd fetched her from the stableyard that morning. She was capable looking, with hair nearly as short as Shirley's, and a slightly squashed nose, and was calmly explaining to a bullish looking man that he was in the wrong place, all the while with one hand out of sight. There'd be a button beneath the desk, Shirley knew. Press it and security would come.

She switched her focus to the visitor, who was broad-shouldered, and either worked out a fair bit, or spent part of his day lugging barrels from one side of the street to the other. Dark curly hair; stubbly throat and chin. Jeans and a zip-up jacket. She could make out a stain of some sort, unless it was a tattoo, on the back of his right hand: visible as he rubbed his jaw.

The woman said, "It's a private facility. We have no rooms available."

Shirley thought: Yeah, and how come he'd just wandered through the front door? The San wasn't high security, but it didn't put out a welcome mat. How come this character had got as far as the reception desk?

He'd tipped his head to one side. It was possible he thought this charming. "A friend's staying here. I'm just paying a visit, okay?"

Shirley remembered from her morning walk how you could

approach the house through the woods, if you had a mind to. Because they weren't prisoners. Even Shirley was here of her own free will, if you overlooked the fact she'd been given zero bloody option. So yeah, she could walk out, anyone could, but the other side of that coin was, if you had a pressing need to get in, it wouldn't take military genius.

"Just for a few minutes?"

The accent was familiar; so much so, it took a moment for Shirley to clock it. He was Italian. Shirley had an Italian grandfather, though she'd never met him. To be honest, she wasn't convinced her grandmother had known him all that well. Still, blood was blood: she had that accent in her genes. She knew it when she heard it.

"For the last time, sir, if you don't leave, I'll have to call security."

"There's no need. Just a quick visit."

Press the button, thought Shirley. He's a threat or he's a flake. But whatever he is, he's not a lost tourist.

And then he said, "My friend, she's called Shirley Dander. Just give me her room number, and we're all good."

Driving out of London had been easy, and traffic light. For the first half hour, Whelan listened to the news—the PM had just shared his vision of post-Brexit Britain as an imperial power-house, its weights and measures system the envy of the world —then a podcast on rising racial tension in the wake of low vaccine take-up in minority communities, before deciding silence was preferable. This carried him through the next sixty miles, and by the time he was approaching the small town nearest the San he recognised familiar territory, though one ravaged by recent events. About half the retail premises were shuttered, and a canvas banner reading "Food Bank—Tues/ Thurs" had been hoisted across a car park gantry. London, he knew, had taken a battering. But this felt like a disaster zone; a community flattened by history, and not yet back on its feet.

It was a relief to be out the other side; to leave the main road and bear left, heading uphill along a single-track lane. On his previous visit, in early summer, this landscape had been all greens and gentle browns, the British countryside at rest. Now the car was surrounded by waves of blacks and blues, shifting in the wind. On both occasions, the lane approaching the facility took its time; it bent round fields, and went some distance out of its way to admire a farmhouse. Driving slowly, nervous of curves, Whelan was starting to have doubts. It was nine thirty; late to be paying a call. On the other hand, the San was a medical institution. Not all of its guests would arrive in daylight; some would be delivered as wreckage, under cover of the small hours. And he was still a figure in the Service; his name would ring bells, open doors. Besides, if memory served, when the car crested the next hill he'd be almost there; in his headlights' beam he'd have a view of the San below; its elegant driveway behind its tall iron gates, the long wall bordering its eastern side. All of it at ease with the peaceful countryside.

But memory didn't serve. It was the next hill but one that allowed the remembered view, and when it arrived, it had altered. Whelan's car dipped, and its headlights picked out the long wall, but in place of the iron gates was a twisted mess: one still hung on a hinge, badly buckled, and the other was no longer there. The red tail lights of a large vehicle, a truck or a bus, were heading up the elegant driveway at speed. Whelan had the sense of other shadows, swarming in the darkness. All this in the half-second or so that his lights illuminated the scene. And then the lane curved again, showing him only the darkness ahead, which would in another minute reach those broken gates. Before he'd driven half that distance a bright light appeared at the side of the lane, directed straight at him, and a silhouette flagged down his car.

"Shirley Dander. Just give me her room number, and we're all good."

"I'm calling security now."

"Okay," the man said, but not to her; he was speaking into the mobile he'd produced from his pocket.

"Would you put that away?"

"Sure," he said, but instead leaned forward and hit her in the face.

The same moment the woman toppled backwards, Shirley heard a distant revving followed by an elongated crash, one which started with a metallic crunch and continued for some while as a twisted, scraping form of torture.

The woman was shrieking, and on the floor, but Shirley didn't think she'd reached that button. No alarm was sounding. Or not until Shirley jabbed her elbow into the little glass panel at the top of the staircase, triggering an electronic howl that came from everywhere at once. The man froze, then froze again as Shirley took the stairs three at a time—can you freeze twice? Don't ask me, I'm busy—sweeping a vase from its sidetable as she reached ground level and sending it hurtling at his head: it would have been nice if it hit him. But it struck a wall and shattered: water pooled on the floor, flowers rearranged themselves. Someone else was coming through the door, and he didn't look like security. The first man pointed at Shirley and shouted an instruction she couldn't hear. But she wasn't an idiot: she spun and ran back up the stairs.

. . . *He used my name.* No particular shock attached to the knowledge. There was, if anything, a sense of comfort. Here she was, miles from anywhere—exiled, even, from Slough House—and she was still the centre of events. Still pursued by bad actors.

Of whom this particular example turned on some speed, enough that he could grab her by the ankle. As she reached the top of the stairs, Shirley hit the floor face first.

"What seems to be the problem?"

Odd how he fell into deferential mode as he lowered his

window and craned his neck to address the shadow. Something to do with being English, he supposed. Or everything to do with being Claude Whelan.

It was a young man with a long face, sideburned and stubbled. Whelan could smell alcohol as he crouched to speak through the window.

"Accident."

"Is anyone hurt?"

"... Eh?"

"Is. Anyone. Hurt?"

The young man nodded vigorously.

"Many. Yes. Big accident." He put his hands together then moved them apart slowly, to indicate the violence of whatever had just occurred. "Booosssshhlilihhhh . . ."

From the direction of the San a fire alarm burst into life.

"Well, that should bring help," Whelan said, and pressed the button to raise the window.

The young man put his hand in the gap, preventing it from closing.

"What are you doing?" said Whelan.

"You have to go back."

"The road seems clear."

"No. All blocked. Go back the way you came, yes? No worries."

"I see. Yes, fine. All right, then. I'll go back the way I came."

He studied his wing mirror for traffic, then made doubly sure by looking over his shoulder, one or other of which actions satisfied his new friend that he intended to reverse to a passing place and turn the car around. The hand was removed from the window.

Whelan nodded politely, closed the window and drove forward, the car leaping a little as if eager to be on its way. In his mirror, he saw the young man prancing about: Was he shaking his fist at the car? Whelan rather thought he was. That was pleasing. His own arms were tingling in a way that might have been worrying in another context, but in this one spelt energy, coming off him like sweat.

He turned where the gates used to be, and there was the San at the end of the driveway, its ground floor lit. The truck that had ploughed through the gates had parked by its entrance; it was in fact a people carrier, now flanked by a pair of cars, their doors wide. A number of motorbikes were lined up behind, like an honour guard. And meanwhile a fire alarm pulsed steadily, beneath which Whelan could make out a different rhythm, one he had no name for, but recognised from crowd scenes: demonstrations turning edgy; railway stations when trains refused to arrive. Even inside the car he could feel the drumbeat. It was the wrong place to be—like the moment you drop a cup, before it hits the floor. Something's going to break. He stopped abruptly just short of the other vehicles, and changed gear. Then flinched as a face appeared by his window.

A fist rapped on the glass.

There was someone behind him, too, blocking his exit.

He reached for his mobile and fumbled it, dropping it into the footwell, when the fist bashed against his window once more. Words were shouted.

Open the door. Get out of the car.

Not going to happen.

He unclipped his seatbelt and bent for his phone. As he did so the fist hit the windscreen again, hard enough to make the car wobble, and causing Whelan to bang his head on the steering wheel. Sudden pain, and with it fear: What the hell had he been doing, driving into a mini-riot? And he sensed, rather than saw, other figures clustering round the car, casting shadows onto its interior.

Another thump. How much would the windscreen stand, and what if they used something other than bare fists?

He found his phone, slid back upright, and all four car doors rattled as their handles were gripped and tugged.

The San was open, light spilling onto its forecourt. And maybe these are patients, thought Whelan. Maybe this was a multiple-medication failure . . . But they were all male, and much of an age, not the diverse range of the damaged the San hosted, and how was this happening? Where was security, for god's sake? Even as he had the thought a man in a blue shirt, dark trousers, came flying through the front door to land sprawling on the gravel. He'd barely hit the ground before one of the marauders leaped out after him and kicked him in the head. Then did it again.

Whelan's innards tightened. If they pulled him out of the car, he'd be compost in minutes.

If Claire could see you now.

But she couldn't, and nor could anyone, save this bunch round his car.

But the Park must know the alarm was ringing; help must be on its way. There was no one to call, nothing to do except leave, now, quickly. Dropping the phone into his lap, he grabbed the wheel with one hand, reached for the brake with the other, and the car lurched, throwing him forward again, and then he was leaving the ground—Christ alive, he was in Chitty fucking Bang Bang—and then falling back to earth with a crunch, an impact felt in his teeth, in his eyes, in his spine. He was surrounded by mad laughter, the men howling with glee as they pounded his car with their fists.

On the gravel, yards away, the security man tried to push himself upright, and someone stamped on him.

Whelan's face was wet. Nose bleed. His glasses had disappeared. An image of Sophie de Greer careered through his mind, blonde, glasses, suit and tie, and who on earth was she really? Couldn't they just grab her and run, leave him alone? And now the bastards were lifting his car again and Christ here goes they were dropping it—

Something came loose with that second crash, something broke. He shook his head, which was wrapped in gauze. Noises we're muffled, and reached him through sound-baffling voids; vision helter-skeltered, a whirl of headlight and shadow. Figures spun, slowed, went into reverse, and then a shape rose out of fog and into focus, wielding a lump of rock. Whelan flinched, and the rock hammered down onto his windscreen. Safety glass spiderwebbed, and peeled away from the edges. Cold air swamped the car, and noise pumped back up to maximum, the fire alarm drilling into the back of his head. Hands tugged at the broken screen, peeling it away like a door on an advent calendar, revealing Whelan as the little surprise nestled inside.

The man had climbed onto the bonnet, and was reaching for him.

Whelan had only soggy thoughts left. Now they'd drag him onto that gravel, and stomp him into mush.

"Fucking copper, yes?"

This was the man crouching on his bonnet, his face inches from Whelan's own, his fists wrapped round Whelan's lapels.

"I fucking hate coppers."

And then a body dropped from the sky and flattened him.

Her head pressed against the carpet, a man bent low over her, his breath hot in her ears: give or take a gender preference, it might have been a quiet evening in.

The kidney punch, though, was bang out of whack.

The carpet's weave dissolved along with Shirley's vision, and when she gasped for breath, it was all dust and hair.

She felt his hand on her head; his weight brought to bear.

"Shirley Dander. Know where she is?"

Right that moment, Shirley couldn't have said for certain. But a voice behind her could. "I do."

The man raised his head to see who was speaking, so the book that hit him broke his nose.

His weight slipped off her and she rolled free. He was on his side, cradling his face in his hands, and the best she could manage was a two-fingered jab into his throat. Not her most powerful shot, either; not after being rabbit-punched. Still, her second go had a little more force, and the third was the charm.

"You might kill him," said the voice, but not in a discouraging way. More like: FYI.

"Ungh," Shirley said, partly in warning. The man who'd punched the woman in the lobby was coming up the stairs; not in a hurry, and apparently amused by the fate of his companion. He said something nobody heard.

The corridor was busy; all doors open, and nervous faces peeping out. Like Watership Down on fireworks night. Shirley got to her feet before Man One reached the top of the stairs.

Someone called, "Is this a drill?"

"Use the other exit," Shirley's saviour said. It was Ellie Parsons, the woman she'd met in the gym, and she was brandishing a bloodied book, *One Hundred Things to See in Dorset.* "I wondered why they left copies of this. Now we know."

"'Panic attacks'?" Shirley managed. Breathing was painful.

"Oh, I'm medicated up to the eyeballs, dear." Parsons smiled, gently. "I've called this in. But I imagine some kind of response will be automatic, don't you?"

I work in Slough House, thought Shirley. Expecting anything other than blind indifference was optimistic. But anyway, here he came, Man One, shaking his head. Man Two was prone and gagging, unless that was a death rattle. She couldn't find it in herself to give a toss.

"It's getting a little, uh, busy," Man One said. He wasn't kidding. The fire alarm, the crashing about outside, the breakage downstairs, some to-and-fro yelling. If he hadn't been using the top of his voice, they wouldn't have heard him. Given that he was, his accent was more noticeable. Uomo Uno, Shirley amended.

"Yeah, you might want to fuck off now. There'll be men with guns in a minute."

"For a care home?"

Parsons raised both eyebrows. She spoke to Shirley. "Do I look like I belong in a care home?"

"How do you think I feel?"

"We can sort this out simples," said the man. "We're looking for Shirley Dander. We find her, we leave." He spread his palms. "Nobody needs to get hurt."

"I'll be the judge of that," said Shirley.

Yet another pair were coming up the staircase; one bald and bearded, the other clean-shaven and raggy-haired, like alternates in an identikit parade. Both wore expressions bordering on glee, as if this wild rumpus were the stuff of daydreams. Without looking round, Uomo Uno held an arm out to stop them.

The corridor was bustling. The fire exit was at the far end, and dressing gowned figures were shuffling that way, though two men had approached Shirley's end and stood behind Parsons now, evidently expecting trouble. One was elderly; the other Shirley's age. He had thinning blond hair, a wispy goatee, and a nervous twitch that pulled his face to one side at irregular intervals. And he carried a bedside lamp, its shade removed, its flex wrapped round his wrist.

Uomo Uno regarded them with amusement. "If you want a fight, I can spare a few seconds. Don't think we're all as easy as him."

This with a gesture towards his broken-nosed companion, who chose that moment to groan.

The elder of the men behind Parsons said, "Naples? I'm hearing Naples."

From downstairs came the sound of shattering glass.

Uomo Uno said, "One last time. Shirley Dander?"

"I'm Shirley Dander," said Ellie Parsons.

"No, I'm Spartacus," the nervous twitcher said, in a surprisingly deep voice.

"Okay, so one of you's going to break a bone now," said Uomo Uno. "You, I think." He pointed at Spartacus.

To do them credit his back-up pair recognised their cue, but their execution lacked finesse and it all fell apart before it got going. When the first of them hard-shouldered Shirley aside she dropped to the floor, but grabbed him by the beard as she did so, pulling his head low and making it a simple target for Spartacus's lamp. This caught him square in the mouth, not hard enough to satisfy Shirley, but she was aware she could be over-critical. His companion, meanwhile, reached for Spartacus just as Parsons kicked his kneecap: not a high-scoring move, but again best judged by results, because when he stumbled the elderly linguist put both hands to his chest and pushed him back into Uomo Uno, who caught him in an embrace at the top of the stairs. For a moment they were vulnerable, one good heave away from toppling down the staircase, and Shirley released the board intent on precisely that, but someone grabbed her ankle: Man Two. She'd forgotten him. Too many people in not enough space was the problem: this needed a big finish if it wasn't to end in farce. She collapsed onto all fours again, assuming the size and rough shape of an occasional table, while Bearded Man, now upright, spat a tooth and lunged for Ellie Parsons. This brought him square into the track of Spartacus's lamp once more, which he was swinging as if creaming a full toss over the bowler's head. The resulting crunch, with liquid notes, wasn't quite drowned out by the alarm, and helped Shirley picture the impact later—at the time, she was preoccupied with stamping her heel into Man Two's face. But she felt Bearded Man all the same, as he reeled backwards and tumbled over her as neatly as if the whole thing had been choreographed, with the big window waiting to welcome him. The noise he made passing through it had an orchestral quality: one big boom accompanied by a thousand tinkling minims. And then he was gone, and a cold wind was blowing into the corridor, while the wailing alarm slipped out through the wreckage and howled away into the night.

The man who'd been scaling the car's bonnet was a bloody mess, his face mashed into the crumpled windscreen inches from Whelan's own. He remained there while whoever had just landed on top of him slid sideways onto the gravel. Glass was falling from the sky, glistening like snowflakes, turning the scene into a zombie nativity, except that, instead of gathering round like adoring shepherds, the gobsmacked crew that had surrounded the car were fleeing like frightened sheep. Whelan's hands were trembling; his whole body felt scraped to the bone. Dimly, through his now barely connected windscreen, he understood that a new noise had joined the raucous soundtrack: a bass-like *whump-whump* overhead that was possibly the wrath of God.

His soggy thoughts solidified. He was master of his car now, rattled as it was. He reached for the brake, forgetting he was in reverse, and the car shunted backwards, releasing its bloody cargo, which sprawled on the ground in the wash of his headlights. The shock caused Whelan to spasm: the car skewed slantways, and he felt the crunch of metal hitting stone. The *whump-whump* grew louder, and assorted marauders were looking skyward. Out of the San's doorway tumbled another pair, and what had looked like an unstoppable invasion appeared to be becoming a rout. But there was no sign of Sophie de Greer. She might be lying dead in a room. The invaders might be on their way because their job was done.

Whelan shook his head, then realised that his glasses, thought lost, were balanced neatly on one shoe, their arms hugging an ankle. Retrieving them, he slid them onto his nose, and the world shifted into focus: it was still a confused mess, but only because it was a confused mess, and not because he wasn't seeing it clearly. A motorbike roared to life. One of the cars flanking the people carrier was pulling away; at the same time another car was arriving: big and black, with tinted windows, and he didn't need to see its sleek, dark-garbed occupants emerging to know the professionals had arrived.

Not that order immediately fell. There was shouting everywhere. The fallen security man was still in a heap, and that, thought Whelan, was certainly something he could deal with. He climbed out of his car and was kneeling by the wounded man, the alarm still blotting out most things bar that overhead clatter, when more figures came crashing onto the gravel: one of the marauders and, in hot pursuit, what looked like a slightly wider, much less hairy, Tasmanian devil, wielding a baseball bat.

There's nothing like putting someone through a window for altering the dynamic of a situation. Uomo Uno and his bosom companion stood staring at the empty space where Bearded Man had been a moment before, and for all the attendant noise, which now included something airborne and getting nearer, seemed lost in a reverie. Shirley, meanwhile, was continuing to kick Man Two in the face, a placeholder activity while she determined her next move. His grip on her foot had long since loosened, along with any sense of enthusiasm. Spartacus was studying his table lamp, his face still twitching, but satisfaction evident there too. His companion was removing a hearing aid, which was as good a way as any of pressing Mute. And Ellie Parsons was glaring at the pair on the staircase, her crimson copy of *One Hundred Things to See in Dorset* tucked under an arm, in case she planned to add a hundred-and-first later.

Quiet evening in, Shirley remembered.

The two on the staircase reached a wordless conclusion and fled, Uomo Uno's previous nonchalance as shattered as that window. Outside, scattering gravel announced the arrival of more cars, and Shirley felt a lurch inside: it was over, would be over in the next few minutes, and she had no idea what it had all been about. Scrambling to her feet, nodding a farewell to her erstwhile comrades, she hared after them, the sound of battle still raging below.

At some point during the last five minutes, her want had stilled. The needy voice crying out for something, she didn't know what, had quietened.

Unless she just couldn't hear it for all the crap going on.

At ground level she found a scrum. Reinforcements had arrived, and two black-clad professionals in semi-riot gear—heavy vests, but no shields or helmets—were facing six of the marauder crew. The newcomers were wielding wicked-looking truncheons; the old firm relying on low-tech battery, with two lengths of lead piping and one baseball bat between them, though one hardy nutcase was attempting a headbutt as Shirley arrived, a move both ill-advised and brief. He hit the floor like a badly tossed pancake. In other circumstances, a sympathetic Shirley noted, the truncheoneer would have enjoyed the opportunity to lather his victim a while, but there was no time for such luxuries, and he was already engaged in a one-two with the baseball fan. Uomo Uno was holding back, fists bunched, eyes on the door, and Shirley padded toward him, not sure what she planned, but confident of spoiling his day. But the room shifted, or its gladiatorial epicentre did; the marauders wheeling round as the pros moved towards the reception desk, and the door became accessible. Uomo Uno seized his chance, and as Shirley followed something struck her on the ankle—she sprawled, reached out, and her hand found the baseball bat, which had come skittering across the tiles, liberated from its wielder by a truncheon. Shirley grabbed it, thanked her good-luck fairy, and was on her feet in an instant, following her prey into the night.

In the pool cast by the helicopter's searchlight, the San's forecourt had become a circus ring, in which a troupe of Service muscle was knocking seven bells out of twenty assorted hard cases. This should have been a picnic, had everyone been reading from the same script, but while the professionals knew what they were doing, and tended towards the swift and economical, the hooligans had the advantage that they viewed violent encounters as leisuretime jolly rather than occupational necessity. Those knocked down kept getting up for more, and those upright took the windmill approach: fists and feet flying; teeth ready to take a chunk from anything within reach. It was like fighting wild dogs, with the added interest of not knowing what diseases they carried.

Surveying the mayhem Whelan wondered if any of the players remembered what the evening's objective had been, or whether the whole thing was just a mad game of Chinese Whispers.

Weaving between separate clusters of violence, he helped the battered security guard to his feet, and together they crunched across broken glass to the building, where Whelan propped him against the wall. "Best stay upright," he said, having no clue as to established practice, but reasonably sure it wasn't a good moment for a lie down. Looking round, he prayed for signs of sanity, and at that precise moment the alarm shut off.

Ridiculous to pretend that what followed was silence, but for half a second it felt like it: a relief from aural torture. And then chaos poured back through the evening's open wound: the clashing of bodies and armoured sticks, the whoops and yelps of the warriors, the techno-beat of the hovering chopper, and even his own puny car alarm, which Whelan hadn't noticed until then, a limp whimper more likely to incur embarrassment than attention.

But in that oasis of imaginary quiet, he'd heard a woman's voice laying down a challenge.

"I'm Shirley Dander," she'd yelled. "Who wants to know?"

When Shirley ran through the door the helicopter was hovering twenty feet up, drowning the forecourt in light. Pitched battle was raging: a people carrier was parked slantways, frozen waves of gravel at its tyres; a small car had reversed into the front of the building; and the goon she'd helped through the upstairs window appeared to have landed on one of his comrades. *Double score!* A blood-smeared middle-aged man in glasses was an unlooked-for absurdity, crouched over a floored figure in security guard's black-and-blue livery and victim's red-and-white head wound, but she didn't pause to question the sight. The baseball bat felt good in her hands, and Uomo Uno was well within reach. He looked like he was running for the carrier, the chicken. Empty-handed, but holding the answers she sought.

Why did you come for me?

As he reached the van she hurled the bat. It bounced off his head and he sprawled against the vehicle, testing its suspension. She paused to retrieve the weapon, and by the time she'd done so he'd steadied himself, turned and thrown a punch all in the same flow, aiming for her face probably, but missing by half a mile. She had his number now. He was a thug, plain and simple. Put him in a boxing ring, he'd be canvas-patterned in a moment. But put him in a cage and he'd rattle the bars loudly enough that you wouldn't want to enter.

The good thing about snap judgements was that you could be doing something else while making them. In Shirley's case, this involved swinging the bat into his thigh, keeling him sideways like a broken tree. The fire alarm she'd triggered a hundred years ago ceased its screaming then, the same moment she chose to scream herself: "I'm Shirley Dander. Who wants to know?" He didn't reply, but more pressingly, someone was rushing her from behind: she knew this the way you'd know if a bull was approaching. Bulls have never mastered the surprise attack. If this newcomer planned to, he could start by making notes as to what happens when you give your position away early: in this case, a full-bodied swing of a baseball bat. Shirley felt the impact in her shoulders. Her attacker felt it in his ribs, and probably every other bone holding him together—not since she'd hit a bus with an iron had Shirley felt quite so fulfilled. I am fucking invincible, she decided. That was a fresh learning right there. I am fucking invincible, and I'm taking these bastards down one by one.

That was the last thought she had for a while, as the sun rose and set in the blink of an eye, all of it inside her furious, buzz-cropped head.

So that was Shirley Dander.

What interested Whelan was that she wasn't Sophie de Greer, despite what he'd told Nash; that *Lamb's got something going on*, that *he's stashed de Greer in the San, under the name of Shirley Dander*. Assertions that had made sense that afternoon. From his new perspective, sense was the other side of the county line. It was the quiet warmth of his study, where he should have stayed. *Sorry, Oliver. I'm retired.* How hard would that have been?

Someone was rushing Dander from behind, but she seemed to have matters under control: even Whelan felt the resulting blow, and he was twenty yards away. The villain hit the ground like a cartoon piano. Dander's glee outshone the helicopter's searchlight; evil and innocent at the same time, it made a pumpkin lantern of her face. And then someone blew her candle out.

It was the man she'd been chasing, the one she'd had spreadeagled against the carrier a moment before. Whelan couldn't see what he'd hit her with, but her baseball bat dropped to the ground, followed by Dander herself, and then she was scooped up and tossed inside the van: all this while fighting raged on; the Service troops heavily outnumbered, but not, on the whole, too bothered by that. Various lumps on the gravel were conquered invaders, their groans audible now the alarm had ceased. The carrier's door shut and Dander's attacker was easing into the driver's seat. The helicopter shifted overhead, and the world tilted as its spotlight slid across the ground. Whelan said, "Wait here," and let go of the wounded security man, who remained on his feet, which was a good sign. The whirring rotor blades were artificial weather, and Whelan crossed the forecourt like a mime. Someone backed into him, avoiding a truncheon; Whelan pushed and the man staggered forward, straight into the truncheon's upswing. There was a spray of blood, a destroyed face: all a blur, even with one hand holding his glasses in place, but Dander's abandoned baseball bat was there at his feet and he collected it without thinking. The people carrier lurched forward, Dander inside, the man she'd been chasing at the wheel . . .

Whelan stood, bat in hand, as the vehicle careered onto the lawn and headed off round the building.

This was what you got when you took your eye off the ball. Something landed on your head; either part of that helicopter—not an essential part; it was still airborne—or an improvised sledgehammer put together by the Italian thug who was just now learning to drive. Shirley had been flung across a row of seats, but rolled onto the floor as the carrier went into an interminable curve. A car was bleating close at hand, and ignorant armies were leathering away at each other, their repetitive clatter and thwock the motor's backbeat, but all she could see was carpet. A pain at the back of her head was coursing through her body, and when she tried to pull herself up, her hands slid from the seat covers. Whatever the bastard had hit her with, she wanted one. Any moment now she was going to make her way to the front of the vehicle and feed him whatever came into reach, but for the time being was lost in a pinball machine, rocking and rolling with every lurch of the van, which was off the gravel now, crashing over the lawn, swerving the copper beech, and scattering the residents who'd gathered behind the building after evacuating their rooms. And then they were on gravel again. Full circle. The van was back on the drive, heading for the road, and taking her with it—mission accomplished, presumably, though she'd yet to discover whose mission, and what outcome they had in mind.

It occurred to her that the evening's row of triumphs, from ushering one invader through an upstairs window to kicking another repeatedly in the head, was washed away by this end result, her having become a piece of luggage. As soon as her headache went, she'd do something about that. But meanwhile—

But meanwhile an angry metal howl ripped the night, as the van ran over something which brought it screeching to a halt. Uomo Uno swore loudly and thumped the steering wheel. Now's the time, thought Shirley, and was halfway up when the van reversed with a lurch, scraping another scream of inanimate agony from whatever lay under its wheels. She went sprawling again, and then, after a rabbit hop and another tearing sound, the van was away once more, turning right, past the stable block she'd wandered round this morning.

Its motion was lopsided, its balance punctured by its recent encounter.

A moment later she flinched, as something crashed onto the roof.

Still holding the bat, Whelan ran for his car. He might have been wearing a magic ring, rendering him invisible; on all sides, the San's defenders and attackers slugged it out, but he moved unhampered past them. The truth was, he was of no consequence; a pencil pusher, pointless in a brawl. If the marauders won, one or other would snap him in two as an encore, but while there was fighting to be done, he was surplus to requirements. Which suited him. He reached his car, but it was *hors de combat*. And the people carrier was out of sight.

He kept running, the San's geography returning to him; there was a stableyard by the gates, or where the gates had been. He remembered a staircase, a vantage point. From there he could see which direction the carrier went . . . It was less a plan than a displacement activity, but he had to do something. Besides, his body was on automatic, pursuing an agenda he hadn't known was there.

There always came a moment, didn't there, when the mild-mannered drip found his inner Tarzan?

He was down the driveway, yards from the stables, when he heard the people carrier at his heels, its headlights grabbing his shadow, hurling it in front of him. He braced for impact, expecting to lose contact with that shadow and everything else, but the moment didn't come: he felt the van's weight as it rushed past, but he was out of its path; was careering into the stableyard while it headed for the main road. There was copper in his mouth, a pounding in his chest, a sudden metal shriek as the vehicle screamed into the corpse of the wrecked gate, and then Whelan was in the stableyard, memory sending him to the far end. He hadn't run in years; was amazed to find the ability existed. Wouldn't have been surprised if it deserted him now, leaving him a puddle on the stones. But his newfound energy carried him on, and there it was; the external staircase by the furthest stable, leading up to the hayloft. Onestep, threestep, fivestep, seven. His knees trembled but held. Watery muscles were a childhood memory. At the top he leaned on the thigh-high wall. The people carrier was emerging onto the road, listing heavily—that broken gate had torn a hole in an offside tyre. A horrible idea grabbed Whelan's mind and squeezed.

It wasn't possible. He wasn't built for this. But the van had lurched across the road, was passing slowly beneath him.

And he was, or had been, on Her Majesty's Secret Service. Hadn't he?

If you could see me now, he thought, unsure whether he was addressing that same Majesty, Claire, Diana Taverner, Josie, or even Sophie de Greer, whoever she was. Then he clambered onto the wall and dropped onto the roof of the lumbering van.

Whose flip-flopping was its own funeral dirge, *da–duff da–duff*, a lament already winding down: within the minute, that burst tyre would be a roadside python. But the thump on the roof was something else and Shirley was wondering what—who—had just landed there when a baseball bat slammed into the windscreen, making a porridge of the oncoming view. Screaming his rage, Uomo Uno thumped the steering wheel, which didn't improve the situation. The baseball bat crashed down again, and the vehicle swerved from the wrong side of the road to the right, sending something banging into Shirley's knee. A three-kilo training weight. This was what the bastard had used to knock her out of gear.

Visions of clouting him round the head with it, pasting what passed for his brains across the dashboard, had to be put on hold. She couldn't stand for the rocking, not to mention the wavy motion inside her head: a dull strobing light behind her eyeballs. That taste in her throat—she didn't remember throwing up. Another outburst from Uomo Uno; another lurch from the wayward bus. These last minutes were a movie trailer; had begun with Shirley on her bed, hungry for something, she didn't know what. Then staircases and chase scenes and fights and action . . . And someone on the roof, come to rescue her. They didn't know about the Dander jinx, that teaming up with Shirley offered poor long-term prospects. Or maybe they did, but had risked it anyway; jumping onto a moving vehicle wielding a baseball bat . . . Whoever it was probably thought themselves the hero. And then that notion was swallowed, along with everything else, by blinding light, as the helicopter dropped its searchlight onto the limping van, and hovered above it for its last few moments of motion. A loudspeaker was shouting instructions, which almost certainly included the word *Stop!*, but whether that was the clinching argument, or whether the people carrier had simply run out of life, was hard to tell. With a final squealing complaint from a tyreless wheel the vehicle crunched to a halt and Uomo Uno spilled out beneath the helicopter's all-seeing eye, in full view of the approaching police cars with their angry swirling lights. As Shirley fumbled with the door, she could see the blue devils these lights released capering across pitch-dark countryside, scaling trees, hurling themselves into hollows; each followed by another and another and another . . . Uomo Uno was sinking to his knees in surrender when Shirley fell onto the road and looked up at the stars, though they were way too distant to see. Instead, she found herself focusing on a face looking down from the top of the people carrier.

"Shirley Dander, I presume," it said.

"Who the hell are you?" said Shirley, then closed her eyes and grabbed a little rest.

Night-time raids come in different shapes and sizes.

Oliver Nash was no stranger to the domestic kind: the padding on slippered feet to the kitchen; the lure of leftovers offering recompense for being alert in the small hours, dream-remnants smeared across every surface. Tonight, though, his journey involved a sudden start at the foot of the stairs, when a shadow in the living room detached itself from the furniture. With an aplomb that would have surprised those who took him at face value he recovered instantly, nodding at his uninvited guest and continuing into the kitchen, where he turned the light on. "I assume you used the spare key," he said, without looking round. "I must find a better hiding place."

"You must join the twenty-first century. This is London, Oliver. Not *The Archers*."

"But as you're here anyway, we might as well be comfortable." He reached for the thermostat and adjusted it several degrees. From upstairs came the comforting noise of organised heat awakening: a dull thunk, a whispered *whoosh*. Nash tightened his dressing gown cord. "You've caused quite the hullaballoo."

"*I* have?"

"What would you call it? You left a pack of Dogs in a heap on a staircase and used the lone survivor as an Uber. He's taking some hard knocks, by the way. When he returned Ms. Kelly's gun to her, I thought she'd use it on him."

"He knew it was a long-term investment," Diana said.

"And then you vanished like a woodland sprite. Down on the hub, they don't know whether to build you a crucifix or find you a crown. Coffee?"

"Please."

"And there's a rather good seeded sourdough. I could run us up some toast?"

"Who's been parachuted into the Park?"

"Home Office man, bit of a donkey. Name of Malahide."

Diana pursed her lips.

"Needless to say, he takes your disappearing act as a sign of guilt."

"If I'd shown up, it would have been game over. You know that."

"Indeed I do, but you know what that department's like. They've got so used to pretending they're not as smart as their boss, some of them have actually got that way." With an economy of motion belying his size, Nash dropped four slices of bread into the toaster and attended to the Nespresso machine. "And he hasn't learned from you how to think round corners."

"What did Sparrow offer?"

"What you'd expect." Nash opened a cupboard, and began excavating little tubs of jam, the size that come with hotel breakfasts. "The Park's to be, what shall we call it, streamlined? More oversight, less, ah initiative. Committee-led. With Yours Truly at the helm."

"I hadn't realised your ambitions lay in that direction."

"Upwards? Everyone's ambitions lie in that direction. Law of physics. Besides, once he'd played the waterproof card, the next step was inevitable. Either I went along, or I'd be squashed against the tiles. Though, as you'll remember, I did give you advance warning."

Red Queen, Red Queen, he'd whispered down her phone.

"Playing both ends against the middle."

"Oh, please. I'd never turn against the middle. Black, yes?" He placed a coffee cup in front of her. "Sparrow doesn't know you like I do. He thought activating Candlestub would render you harmless. Whereas I knew that putting you in a corner would get your dander up." He barked, unexpectedly. "Which, come to think of it . . ." Reaching into his dressing gown pocket, he produced his iPhone. A few taps later he passed it to her. "That came in an hour ago. Woke me, as it happens."

Diana read the activity report he'd opened. "An attack on the San? This was Sparrow?"

"He seemed to think de Greer was being held there. On your instructions."

"I approved a placement there a few days ago. For one of Lamb's misshapes."

"Shirley Dander."

"Who Sparrow thought was de Greer, right? Because Whelan steered him that way."

"Claude put two and two together and made five." He held out his hand, and she returned the phone. "Though I can't help wondering if your Lamb didn't nudge him in that direction. Bit of a disruptor, that man."

"He's been called worse. But either way, where did Sparrow find a wrecking crew?"

The toast popped up, as if it too were eager to hear this part.

Nash used wooden tongs to place the slices in a rack. "He appears to have allied himself with, I believe they call themselves Ultras? A collective of over-enthusiastic football fans."

Diana had pulled a chair out. "And where did this information come from?"

"Field work. My own, actually."

"You're a joe now?"

"I appreciate that you find that amusing. Though you might care to ask yourself which of us is seeking help."

"Help? I'm not yet holding your feet to the fire, Oliver. But the moment might come."

Nash, seated, carefully buttered his toast. "There's a restaurant called La Spezia, off Wardour Street. Sparrow has been seen—by me—visiting its premises, and it's not somewhere you'd expect to find him. So after a little, ah, surveillance, I asked the very able Josie to do some digging, and she informs me that the under-manager there, one Alessandro Botigliani, is what I believe they call a *capo* of a branch of these so-called Ultras, affiliated in his case to Lazio." Nash applied jam, and ferried the result to his mouth. The resulting expression was one frequently sought by Renaissance artists, reaching for tokens of religious ecstasy. Then: "They're of a far-right persuasion, though there's grounds for suspecting that ideology, and indeed the beautiful game, is of less concern to them than kicking many kinds of carrots out of opposing fans. A ready-made wrecking crew, as you put it."

"And Sparrow persuaded them to do his dirty work?"

"Persuaded, paid, blackmailed. Nobody ever accused Sparrow of being unable to get others to grubby their hands on his behalf."

"I'm sure ten minutes in a basement will have any number of them clarifying the situation."

"Careful. It was whispers of strongarm tactics that started all this in the first place. Besides, you're in no position to dictate events. When you failed to surrender yourself, Sparrow pulled strings at the Met. There's a warrant out for your arrest, Diana. Not to mention an emergency meeting of Limitations scheduled for ten A.M., where your suspension will be ratified and Malahide confirmed as *pro tem* First Desk. He will, of course, be taking instruction from the Home Secretary, which is to say that Sparrow himself will be effectively controlling the Park by coffee time. And I somehow doubt that an investigation into his own guilt will be top of his to-do list."

"On the other hand," Diana said, "should I arrive in person

at the Limitations meeting with Dr. de Greer in tow, where she can testify not only to the absence of anything resembling Waterproof having been instigated, but to her own status as an agent of the GRU, hired wittingly or otherwise by Anthony Sparrow in order to influence national policymaking—well. How do you think that would play?"

Nash helped himself to another slice of toast, and seemed to be addressing the array of jam jars rather than Diana when he replied.

"I imagine you could sell tickets," he said.

Even given his status as *quondam* First Desk, it had been hours before Claude Whelan had managed to extricate himself from the chaos at the San, and such release only came with the promise of a thorough debriefing once the Park had its ducks in a row. Though judging by the calls the senior agent at the scene had been getting, those ducks were currently in a flap, causing Whelan to suspect that the hostilities he'd divined between Taverner and Sparrow had ignited. Reason enough to keep his head down. He'd had cause to regret becoming involved in dirty politics before.

Driving his own car was out of the question, so after cleaning himself up as best he could in a San bathroom, he squeezed what was left from his former rank and commandeered one of the enemy vehicles, which was grubby but unscathed by combat. As he pootled up the drive towards the broken gates, manouvering round various vans into which cuffed figures were being bundled, he could see torches flickering in the woods beyond the stables as the last marauders were hunted down, and it was as much to the runners as the chasers that he sounded his horn in farewell, a thoroughly uncharacteristic action. On the other hand, everything he'd done in the last few hours had been out of character, as if, having been badly miscast, he'd thrown himself into the part regardless, and was now coming offstage expecting acclaim.

He'd received precious little so far. Some things, you had to organise for yourself.

He adjusted the rearview mirror and glanced into it. "So. How did I do?"

In reply, all he heard was the noise of the engine, and the dark road unravelling beneath the tyres.

"Did you think I was talking to myself?"

From the footwell behind the passenger seat, Shirley Dander said, "Got anything to eat?"

. . . John

John

"John?"

His name approached him as if down a long corridor, the door at the end of which was ajar, and as usual his waking feeling was one of fear: What would happen next? It would involve that door opening wide. But there was a soft hand on his shoulder, and Sophie was bending over him. The light breaking through the curtains was the now-familiar glow of the sole streetlight that graced the mews.

"Are you awake?"

It was a whisper, so he replied in kind. "Yes."

"Get dressed."

He already was.

In the dim light, he could make out the gross and sour-smelling form of a creature that might have slipped through the door in his dreams, but was actually Jackson Lamb. Since he was neither eating nor smoking he was presumably asleep. Bachelor gazed for some seconds before shaking himself free and slipping his feet inside his shoes. His mouth tasted like an abandoned nest, and his bones ached from sleeping in a chair.

Sophie, taking no chances, pointed at the door rather than spoke.

It was what, three in the morning? Bachelor had already been exiled twice tonight, sent walking the streets rather than hear ongoing discussions. On the other hand, this was Sophie inviting him. He risked a taste of his own breath in a cupped hand, and made a mental note to avert his head when speaking. She opened the door so quietly, she might have spent their captivity practising.

Outside was colder than he'd expected. Little clouds accompanied each breath; his own heavier, more pungent, than hers.

"We need to leave now."

He'd been expecting this moment.

Keep her here. No contact with anyone other than me, Louisa or Lamb.

Lech's instructions, back when his own first concern had been the per diems.

And Lech was his friend, who'd stuck by him through thin times, even though their association had cost the younger man dear. It would be the act of a rogue to betray his trust. So he averted his head to shield Sophie from his phosgene breath before replying, and to the neutral observer must have looked as if he were addressing the terracotta pots and their sleeping citizens when he whispered, "Okay."

They left the mews in a quiet hustle. Neither looked back, so neither saw the shape at the window, watching; his bulk briefly illuminated, on and off, by the repeated clicking of a lighter which seemed reluctant to burst into flame.

"I always get hungry after a ruck."

"Me too," Whelan said.

She shot him a sideways glance.

"Or so it would appear," he added.

He'd stopped the car and she'd climbed into the front, where the first thing she'd done was snap open the glovebox and peer inside. She was Shirley Dander, and had never, it transpired, been Sophie de Greer, nor even knew who de Greer was. "Does she live in Wimbledon?"

Whelan had always been good at keeping a file in his mind. "Yes."

"Figures."

"I owe you an apology," he said. "All of what just happened, the violence, everything—it was my fault."

"What did you do?"

"I jumped to a conclusion."

This, judging by her expression, was a feeble way of kicking off a riot.

I rescued you, he wanted to say. I jumped onto a moving vehicle. Remember that part? I was an action hero.

"Can we stop somewhere?"

"What, you mean . . . a bush or something?"

"Do I look like I want to eat a bush?"

"Oh. Right. No."

"I meant like a service station."

"I expect there'll be one somewhere."

"Could do with a crap too, to be honest, but mostly I need a burger or something."

". . . Yes. Fine."

"Or chocolate. Minimum."

There was little traffic about, but a light shone way behind them: a single headlight. Motorbike, he thought.

"Why were you there?" he asked abruptly. "In the San?"

Fields crawled past. In the hedgerows, tiny lifecycles churned their way through insect millennia.

At last Shirley said, "People keep dying."

He didn't know how to reply to that.

"I don't mean in general, though that too. It's just that, every time I get close to someone . . . they die."

She was staring out of the window on her side, though he guessed she wasn't seeing anything.

"So don't get paired with me. Not a good idea."

He said, "I'm sure that's . . ." but he wasn't, when it came down to it, sure of much, and whatever he was going to say

threatened to dissolve in the space between them. He hauled
it back. "I'm sure none of it's your fault."

"Keeps happening. So it doesn't really matter whose fault
it is."

This with the air of one who has reached a conclusion, and
accepted that no other was viable.

A few moments later, she added, "I suppose, sooner or later,
I'll be the one drawing the short straw."

Whelan said, "There's some kind of service station soon.
An all-night garage. They might do sandwiches."

Shirley nodded.

The fields grew wider apart as the road morphed into a
dual carriageway. Not long after he'd spoken, they passed a
sign promising a garage, toilets, food, not far ahead.

When the taxi dropped Diana off, two hundred yards from the
mews, she waited until its taillights had diminished to pixels
before heading for the safe house. The note of grim humour in
that name tolled loudly tonight—the safe house was tainted by
the funds which had provided it, and if its existence were brought
to the attention of the Limitations Committee, which would
be pondering her career in a few hours, it would go from *des
res* to *memento mori* in no time flat. But in her defence—and
there was never a time when some part of her mind wasn't
working on her defence—in her defence, her job demanded
compromise. It was her ability to function despite its constant
presence that made her an effective First Desk.

A role she planned to continue filling for the foreseeable
future, and Anthony Sparrow be damned.

The cottage was in darkness, but she sensed company even
as she turned the key. That was Lamb, flat on the sofa,
cigarette in mouth, one hand rummaging between the buttons
on his shirt. A hollow space opened inside her, one that grew
as she scanned the rest of the room, and the lightless kitchen
through its open door. "Where's de Greer?"

His gaze remained fixed on the ceiling. "What did Nash say? Apart from the obvious?"

". . . Which is?"

"That he's the one gave you the heavy-breath warning?"

She was long past showing surprise at Lamb's crystal-ball readings. "The court-martial's set for ten, the firing squad for ten past. Except I've a trump card which blows Sparrow's gunboat out of the water, or I did have. Where is she?"

"Nice to hear 'trump' in a positive context," Lamb offered. "I'd forgotten what that sounded like."

"Stop arsing about. Where is she?"

Somehow, he managed to shrug without levering himself up. The sofa shifted an inch. "Must've dropped off. Woke up and the place was empty." He removed his cigarette long enough to adopt a rueful expression for the ceiling's benefit. "I blame myself."

Approaching the sofa, she was entering the heat-fug of his body. The anger her own was generating was a match for it. "You've got to be kidding."

"I'm generally a ball of fun, yes. But this time, no. She's gone."

". . . You've been waiting for this, haven't you?"

"Been waiting for what now?"

"The chance to shaft me."

Tilting his head, he cast a critical eye. "That ship sailed." He resumed his study of the ceiling. "And all things considered, your future prospects matter less to me than whether my next dump's a floater or a stone."

"Oh, they matter. You'd do anything to fuck a First Desk over, because you think it should have been you. And that's why you've become a stinking useless wreck. It's not the dead weight of your history behind the curtain or over the wall or under the carpet or whatever metaphor your fucking mythology prefers, it's wounded pride. Because the Service used you up and shat you out." None of this seemed to be getting through. But Diana wasn't finished. "You thought you had it made back when you were Charles Partner's blue-eyed boy, you thought all you had to do was serve your time and it would be handed to you on a plate. And look at you now. Burnt out doesn't begin to cover it."

"Done yet?"

"Yes. No. You're a fucking arsehole. Now I'm done."

Lamb removed his cigarette and studied the glowing tip while it faded to grey. "Last time I saw Charles Partner, he was using the contents of his head as bubble bath. Being his blue-eyed-boy didn't look so clever then, I can tell you. As for you, I've pulled your dick out of more slamming drawers than I can count. Any time you want me to stand back and watch, just say the word."

"Where is she?"

"Like I said. Gone."

"I need her, Jackson. I need her singing before that Committee. What if she goes back to Sparrow? Because right now, he's got to be thinking about making her a better offer, and if that happens—and she takes it—what then? She'll deny being a plant, I'm a lame duck, and the PM's string-puller's still in place, with a hard-on for the Service." She was staring down at Lamb's upturned face. "And once it looks like I'm on the skids, Judd'll drop his China bomb, and that's when they'll send the carpet cleaners into Regent's Park. Every decision made for a decade, every operation I've ever had a hand in, it'll all be under a spotlight. And tell me this, how long do you think Slough House will last then? How long before questions are asked about your own career?"

Lamb was quiet for a moment. Then he squinted at his dying cigarette, and flicked it towards the nearest takeaway carton.

"Yeah, okay," he said. "If that happens, we might have a problem."

It wasn't much of a service station—a garage with a four-pump forecourt, and a car wash shrouded in darkness—but it had a

shop which, alongside its array of pasties and sandwiches, had
a mini rotisserie, and even more importantly was open. Shirley wouldn't have been averse to a spot of ramraiding had it
been otherwise, but Whelan might have objected. He'd been
through enough trauma this evening, and even her aversion
to vehicles travelling any less than slightly more than the
prevailing speed limit had to be modified in face of this.
Another triumph for her self-imposed programme of dignified
silence; she'd barely mentioned their lamentable speed more
than two or three times before they pulled up by the pumps.

"I don't have any money," she said, getting out of the car.

"I can get this."

"Yeah, you'll need to." Because she didn't have any money.
Whelan obviously needed things spelt out.

There were no customers inside, and one bored youth at
the till. While Whelan filled the tank, Shirley collected half
a dozen chocolate bars, a family bag of Doritos, a two-litre
bottle of Coke and the two least small roast chickens on the
electric spit. She waited by a window while the youth dragged
himself away from his phone to pack her catch in a cardboard
punnet, and watched a motorbike pass at about half the speed
it should have been doing. Whelan joined her as the boxed
chicken was being placed on the counter, alongside a spork
and, at Shirley's insistence, seven sachets of barbecue sauce.

"Do we need a whole chicken each?" he asked.

She made a face. "Oh. Did you want one?"

There was no eating area so they went back out, where
Whelan suggested that they eat before setting off again, or,
indeed, getting into the car. Something about the smell:
Shirley wasn't paying attention. She was literally starving.
There were children featured on charity envelopes who weren't
as hungry right now. Perched on a wall next to the car wash,
she opened a couple of sauce sachets, squirted their contents
over the first chicken, then pulled a leg free. Whelan seemed
to be trying not to watch. He'd opted for a sandwich, cheese

and pickle. Shirley gestured towards the Doritos in case he fancied a side, but he didn't seem keen.

She didn't normally open up like she'd done in the car, and had to put it down to the blow on the head. Still, getting stuff off her chest hadn't felt bad. Maybe the touchy-feely types had a point, and it was good to share—especially with someone who didn't share back. One-way therapy. Best of both worlds.

He said, "My wife left me."

Shit.

After a moment, her lack of response growing awkward even to her, Shirley said, "So, what, she found someone else?"

"In a manner of speaking."

That was annoying, when people did that: took a simple question and turned it into a fucking enigma

He said, "She found God."

Shirley couldn't help it. "Ha!"

"It's not funny."

It was a bit funny. "Yeah, that wasn't a laugh. I just thought, you know. God. Stiff competition."

"I hadn't looked at it that way."

Shirley took advantage of the pause to toss a bone over her shoulder.

"She joined an order, a closed community. Nuns. It was supposed to be for a limited time, a retreat, but she hasn't come back. And she won't speak on the phone, or answer letters. No email, obviously."

"Sounds like a cult."

"Not really. They just live an enclosed life. Grow vegetables, that sort of thing. There are bees, I think."

"Bees?"

"For honey."

"Yeah, I know what bees do. I just didn't know nuns were into that."

"These ones are."

Shirley had a vision of a nun in a beekeeper's outfit, like someone going to a fancy dress party twice.

Then the motorbike that had passed earlier returned, its headlight picking out Shirley and Whelan on their wall by the car wash before it pulled onto the forecourt, and Shirley felt a familiar lurch inside as she realised the night wasn't over yet.

Sparrow—head on his desk, laptop humming—was woken by his phone. The blogpost he'd been writing had run out of steam around the 3,000-word mark, though tendrils of it still shimmered, phrases aglow with meaning as he'd slept, but rendered incomprehensible by the interruption. *This vegetable abrogation*. He looked at his phone.

Unknown number.

He answered, and heard nothing.

"Hello?"

Still nothing.

"Timewaster." He disconnected.

It was after four.

Sparrow didn't need much sleep. He prided himself on this, as he did on other habits, traits, thoughts and words, each of which did their bit to elevate him above the herd. Phone down, he looked to his screen again, and tried typing *this vegetable abrogation*, to see if concrete shape would restore impact to the phrase. It didn't.

Blogging was a displacement activity; a way of dispelling the white noise in his head, of which there'd been plenty tonight. Word had arrived of the fiasco at the San, and the Ultras' failure to extricate Sophie de Greer. It was true that this failure didn't have Sparrow's name on it—Benito hadn't taken part himself, and he alone knew of Sparrow's involvement—so in political terms could be judged a success, but Taverner also remained at large, and if she turned up before the Limitations Committee with de Greer in tow,

Sparrow's future would become difficult indeed. Hence the displacement activity: a takedown of the government's adviser on ministerial standards, who'd recently suffered a second nervous breakdown. With luck, this blog might trigger a third. Thus melt all snowflakes, he thought, and his phone rang again. This time, his caller got through.

"Anthony?"

For a moment, he was too busy savouring her voice to reply, enjoying the way the difficulties he'd been contemplating had just whispered into silence.

A silence she broke by repeating herself. "Anthony?"

"Sophie," he said. "About time. What can you do for me?"

Shirley passed the cardboard punnet of chicken to Whelan.

"No, really, I—"

"He followed us."

At a distance. Despite the careless frenzy of the attack on the San, this character must have noticed that payback came with truncheons, so was exercising caution, making sure they were alone before doubling back to confront them. Well, that or he'd not initially noticed they'd stopped here, but Shirley was prepared to give him the benefit of the doubt. Best to treat an opponent with respect until it proved unnecessary.

Right now, the opponent-to-be was dismounting and pushing his visor up, and in the yellow forecourt light Shirley recognised one of the crew she'd faced down on the landing, the one whose comrade had gone through the window. Couldn't remember his number but he'd been there, and must have slipped away in the following chaos. And here he was, disturbing her meal, the bastard, which would be cold before this was done. Which might be counting chickens, but hell: she'd seen this joker off once already, and he'd been in company then. And Shirley had a partner now, even if only to hold her dinner.

Breakfast?

Whatever.

She rose to her feet, ignoring whatever Whelan was about to say.

In the shop, the kid was pressing his face against the window, some sixth sense for aggravation pulling his attention away from his iPhone.

Shirley said to the biker, "You lost?"

He shook his head.

"I'm making a call," Whelan said behind her.

He could do what he liked. Because there were drugs and there was dancing, sure, but what there mostly was was this, the prospect of action and the way it lit a spark inside her, which apparently was what she was supposed to be cured of. But that would be curing her of being Shirley. So Whelan could make a call, and reinforcements could arrive, but if anyone thought the interim was going to be spent shouting insults across a garage forecourt, they'd wandered into the wrong opera.

Just to make sure they were all reading from the same script, she said, "If you want to get back on your bike, I won't stop you."

The newcomer's grin widened while, to make things interesting, his hand delved into his jeans pocket and came out wielding a knife.

Shirley looked down at her fist. Just like a slow horse, she thought. Bringing a spork to a knife fight.

Then it started.

There was an all-night café off Glasshouse Street, one John Bachelor was familiar with: he hadn't been in years, but it came to mind when Sophie needed a potential meeting place at four thirty in the morning. And he was a milkman, not a handler, his experience of late-night rendezvous limited to movie images; he wasn't wearing the right coat, there was no mist creeping along the pavements. But he did his best, making

Sophie wait in the lee of a car-park wall while he performed lamplighter duty, assessing the café from the opposite pavement—just the one customer—trying to take a photograph with his eyes.

"It looks safe enough," he admitted.

"I'm going to be fine."

But what if you're not? What happens to me then?

She'd made the arrangement on the world's last payphone, and he hadn't been allowed to listen but knew who she was meeting, and wasn't happy about it. His own world had collided with the powerful in the past, one of the reasons its pillars were shaky. The last thing he needed was a similar collision now, just when he'd glimpsed a sunset ending. . .

Look at yourself, a voice in his head chided, but he knew better than to listen to that.

"What was the second call you made?" he asked.

Sophie was looking down the street. The pavements were quiet, illuminated by blocks of light spilling from uncluttered windows. She looked different from the woman he'd been cloistered with in the safe house, more confident, as if she'd shed a layer of nerves between there and here.

"Don't worry about it," she told him.

"I just want to be sure—"

"I wouldn't hand you a job like this if you weren't up to it." For a moment, the old Sophie shone through. "Just wait. Please, John?"

He nodded, and she leaned forward and kissed his cheek, the contact leaving a scorch-mark. But Bachelor forbore from touching it, and simply watched as she made her way down the road, and stepped through the door into the café.

Whelan couldn't tear his eyes away.

He'd called it in, and been assured of a swift response, but here they were, middle of the night, and Shirley Dander was engaged in hand-to-hand combat with a knife-carrying thug.

Who hadn't removed his helmet, the effect of which—a shiny black head, glinting under the lights—was science fiction, as if this newcomer were an alien killing machine, recently uncoiled from a heap of pumps and hoses. He only hoped the creature wouldn't notice that Dander's weapon was a piece of plastic cutlery.

But Dander was weaving, dancing, footloose; making quick, dainty jabs that never connected—her body language suggesting that if one did, the biker would deliquesce on contact—before whipping the spork out of sight behind her back. He'd call it bravery, if it weren't the stupidest thing he'd ever seen. And he remembered Shirley had been in the San, a sanctuary for trauma and addiction survivors, true, but also where the Service kept those of its soldiers who'd come mentally unglued.

"I've called the police."

The boy from the garage had joined him.

"They said keep right away. Keep inside."

Whelan nodded. It was the sensible thing to do.

He was hoping for blue lights, or better yet, the *whump whump* of that useful helicopter, because if help didn't turn up soon he was going to have to get involved, and he couldn't see that ending happily.

Don't get paired with me. Not a good idea.

Whelan didn't believe in jinxes.

But the fact that Shirley Dander did was keeping him on the sidelines for now.

Even without her Westminster power-suit, de Greer looked out of place. The café was the 1970s' last foothold on the capital: yellow-tiled floor, Toulouse Lautrec posters, and two-seater tables graced with vases that looked fashioned by out-patients, each boasting a plastic sprig of ferns. To blend in, she'd have had to be wearing an afghan and tinted granny-specs rather than jeans and black jacket. The man behind the counter, his ponytail presumably a job requirement, kept throwing her the odd glance, but the only other customer was buried in an almost tangible fog of misery, staring into an abyss disguised as a tea cup.

So effectively she was alone, thought Sparrow, exactly as she'd said.

A bell above the door tinkled, as if he were walking into a sit com. Ignoring the counter, he took the spare seat opposite Sophie without uttering a greeting.

"No table service, pal," said the man at the counter.

"Cup of tea," said Sparrow, not taking his eyes off Sophie.

Who wasn't wearing her glasses. Perhaps they were part of her costume: this is what a wonk looks like. His mind scanned through various discussions she'd taken part in—decisions she'd helped steer—and knew that once it became known she'd been planted by the Russian secret service, he'd become a joke. The party would survive, because it always did; the PM would remain unscathed, because he'd gaslit the electorate often enough to get away with anything, but he—Anthony Sparrow—might as well start wearing a jester's motley and bells. Or a fucking ponytail, come to that.

He hadn't mentioned this train of thought when they'd spoken on the phone.

The cup of tea was waiting, some of its contents carefully slopped over the rim. When it dawned on Sparrow that he was expected to fetch and pay for it he did so with a heavy sigh, but when he returned to the table Sophie said, "You mentioned a lobbying job."

Game over, thought Sparrow.

Once they started negotiating, it was game over.

She raised her mug to her lips, and he mirrored her action before replying. It was something you learned to do when you wanted people to think you were on the same page. By the time they realised you were holding a different book, the ink was dry on the deal.

"Why did you drop from sight?"

"I wanted to worry you."

"But now you're back."

"Like I said. You mentioned a lobbying job."

"I can fix that."

"And resident status."

"Piece of cake."

"And protection in the event that my, ah, former employers object to my new career."

"Your former employers won't want to embroil themselves in a diplomatic headbutting contest."

"Diplomatic doesn't worry me. But they have been known to adapt a more forthright approach."

"Only towards those who've been a public irritation. This will be a private arrangement. You appear before Limitations this morning and categorically deny any rumours about your affiliation to the Russian secret service. That's all I require."

She half-smiled. "To make a rumour go away?"

"It will make Diana Taverner look desperate. Desperation and First Desk don't mix. Once that's minuted, she's history. And given that it's Limitations decides her successor, and I've enough pull to determine who appears on the shortlist, yes, I can make the rumour go away. Because I'll be dictating the outcome of the inquiry."

"If you've got that much pull, why do you need me at all?"

"We both know there are processes to be gone through."

She nodded, thoughtfully. "Tell me more about this job."

And there was the deal, done and dusted.

It wasn't altogether that shaky, either, and might even work, with a following wind. But why take the risk? A car pulled up outside, and a man got out.

Sparrow said, "There are several options. We'll go through them. Meanwhile, I'd feel happier if you were somewhere secure. And to that end, I've enlisted help."

Sometimes, the timing just works.

The bell above the door jangled again, and Benito walked in.

It was a small but wicked knife. Any longer, and he'd have cut her by now.

She must have the magics tonight, or he'd have reached out and cut her anyway. But the Daft Punk look wasn't doing him any favours, limiting his peripheral vision, blurring his colour control, and as long as she kept dancing he wouldn't see that her own blade was a plastic toy. Besides, he knew what she was capable of. He was probably worried there was a window he hadn't noticed yet, that he'd be going through if she got too close.

All the same, he didn't seem to be tiring, whereas the evening's adrenalin had scorched Shirley's system, and the blow to her head—that sucker-thump with the dumbbell—had knocked some fight out of her. True, she had more fight in her to start with than the average ice hockey team, but it had been a long week. And this guy was psyched up.

It struck her again what a strangely amateur attack that mess at the San had been.

He made a lunge and she jumped back, but scored a kick to the knee before he'd regained balance. She might have had him then, but caution held her back: he had a helmet, his knife was sharp. Three inches was laughable in most situations, but on this particular date, anywhere he stuck it was going to cause grief. That thought made her snarl, which had been known to inspire consternation, but all she was getting from him, safe in his helmet, was her own reflection, and she was still looking at that when he lunged again, and she almost slipped. Recovering, she moved sideways, putting the pumps between them. And there was an idea: soak him with petrol, apply a match. Give him a movie-style ending.

Shit: the trouble she'd be in if that happened.

When he moved left, she mirrored with a shuffle to her

right. This wasn't something she wanted to play for long, because if he got the idea she was scared, that was the fight lost then and there . . . His crew at the San, they'd had no tactics. Or at best, a three-word plan: *Smash it up.* They'd not been expecting fightback, so what the fuck had they been doing, attacking a Service facility?

Unless they hadn't known it was a Service facility.

So how come they'd been looking for her?

Before she could disentangle herself from that thought, he jumped through the gap between pumps and was almost on her, an arm's reach away, and she leaped backwards, landing on her heels, ready to lunge left or right depending on which way he flickered—she could read him like a script—though he seemed focused now, staring at her hand, and the little plastic orange threat it wielded.

Idiot move.

Shirley turned and ran into the dark and silent car wash.

"On the other hand," said Lamb, and paused to scratch his chest, a sandpaper moment. When his hand re-appeared, it was, to Diana's surprise, not holding a cigarette. "De Greer, it turns out, is like you. She might be a backstabbing spider-minded vampire, but she's not stupid enough to piss on her own sausages."

"Is there a compliment in there?"

"Christ, I hope not." Still on his back, he raised both knees, like a man preparing to perform an abdominal crunch. This, it turned out, was not what he was preparing to perform. Diana took a step backwards. "De Greer knows Sparrow'll promise her anything not to go public with who she really is. But she also knows he tells the truth about as often as he gets his eyes tested, and she's not about to hand her future to a man who'd sell your medical records to a tree surgeon."

"You're up to something."

He said, "Wheel de Greer before Limitations, she'll spike

Sparrow's guns, but she'll also spill everything else she knows. Including about Rasnokov having an understudy."

"And?"

"And Limitations leaks like a Catholic condom. So you'll blow Rasnokov's game, and in a month or two we can light candles for him. But keep her quiet, let him get away with it, and you've got a former Moscow First Desk in hiding from his ex-employers, who won't bother changing the locks on their filing cabinets because they'll think he's dead. You'll own him, body and soul, and all his secrets will still be current."

"Own him? We don't even know where he'll end up."

"We've got his understudy's body. And we're supposed to be an intelligence service. How difficult can it be?"

"Do you really want me to quantify that?"

"I want you to show some balls. And instead of fighting all your battles in your own backyard, try taking on some real enemies." He'd finagled another cigarette from somewhere, and inserted it, unlit, between his lips. Having a cigarette in his mouth had never prevented Lamb from speaking. If it had, most of his lines would go unread. "And don't worry about Sparrow. He's just a Westminster chancer, and he's grown used to the people he's stabbed in the back pissing off to run a bank. Instead of rearranging his prospects with a shovel and some plastic sheeting."

Light dawned, if not through the curtained window. "The Ultras," Diana said

"My my, Nash has been earning his pastry allowance. Yes, the Ultras. Seems Sparrow gets his kicks playing soldiers in the woods with the big boys. Which makes them prime candidates for the secret army he drafted to trash the San."

"De Greer told you this?"

"She kept a black book on her erstwhile employer. Whose dubious contacts include a Soho charmer name of Benito. Have you got a light, by the way?"

"What is this, a suicide pact? I'm not striking a match in here."

"Chicken." He paddled about beneath his own bulk, and when his hands reappeared, one was holding a plastic lighter. "And Benito's the sort of ally it's best to avoid upsetting."

He punctuated this with a click of his lighter. The effect would have been more impressive if he'd produced a flame.

"You think he'll want payback for tonight's farce."

"Like I said, Sparrow's used to those he tramples on muttering darkly and exiting stage left. I don't think these boys'll go quietly." He clicked the lighter again, this time with success. Applying the flame to his cigarette, he said, "Neither does de Greer. And she's the fortune-teller."

She said, "So that's why you let her go? On condition she throws Sparrow under a hooligan bus?"

"Any objection?"

"You're assuming this Benito won't decide that sticking with Sparrow's a better bet than payback. He's virtually running the country, after all."

He said, "We're talking football fans, Diana. Not the type to change sides."

"What did you promise her?"

"That you'd let her walk away. Rasnokov's not the only one who'd like a little distance between himself and the king of the Kremlin."

"Christ. You've become an idealist in your old age, is that it? Help the joes get away, no matter whose joes they are."

"Well, exit pursued by a bear," said Lamb. "I seem to recall what that's like."

She thought for a while. "Does Bachelor know about this?"

"Too much information would only confuse him."

"But he went with her?"

"Well I wasn't keeping him here." Lamb drained his glass. "I strongly suspect the man has a drinking problem."

She thought for a while. "I haven't forgotten," she said, "that the only reason de Greer knows about Rasnokov's scheme is that you let her stay in the room while you told me about it."

His hand made a wavering motion, causing smoke to spiral and squirt towards the ceiling.

"And anyway, what happens if you're both wrong?" asked Diana. "And Sparrow's more persuasive than you give him credit for? It's both our careers you're gambling with."

"Yeah," said Lamb. "But only one of them's worth anything."

The car wash was in darkness, a low-slung chain blocking its entrance, and its three big blue brushes—two vertical; one horizontal—breathing out damp cold air. Shirley hurdled the chain and ran past a keypad at car-window height while something swiped at her back—*fuck*—and then a brush was offering protection; the pair crouched either side of it, making darting movements left and right, the biker's blade whittling the air. When Shirley hurled her futile spork at him, it bounced off his helmet into the shadows.

Which were plentiful. While the structure had no walls—just a series of struts supporting a roof that was once clear plastic—it was thick with obstacles: the rails the brushes moved on, lengths of cable and hosepipe, a metal bucket padlocked to a standpipe. What Shirley needed was a weapon, ideally an assault rifle, though she'd have settled for the bucket, or that metal bar against the nearest upright, a yard away . . . She reached it only to find it welded in place, a discovery accompanied by another scorching sensation down her back, this one lighting up her whole body, and she screamed in outrage—*chickenshit bastard!*—and span and kicked, but he was out of range. Liquid ran down her spine. *Keep moving*, she warned herself, because the biker's height and helmet were handicapping him, and the more he had to dodge and weave the more frustrated he'd get. Eyes fixed on him, she slipped round a metal box on a stand, its face a slanted panel with two spherical knobs: one red, the other green.

A Hollywood solution whispered in her ear.

Shirley dropped to a crouch and the biker moved forward, knife extended, between the two huge blue brushes. Behind his visor, she knew, he was grinning.

He'd stop grinning now.

"You're all washed up, dickhead," she said, slamming the green button with her palm.

Nothing happened.

She did it again.

Nothing happened.

Fuck.

He pushed his visor up. "Seriously?"

". . . What?"

"You think hitting that button'll make the car wash start?"

Well, yeah. That's what she'd been hoping.

"It's not even switched on."

"I thought that's what I was doing."

He was shaking his head. "There's a code." Even with his accent, she could tell he thought this ridiculous. "You buy a ticket at the counter, it's got a code stamped on it, you key it into the pad at the entrance. Then the washer starts."

"So what are these buttons for?"

"Might be a manual override," he conceded. "But it won't work when the whole thing's powered down."

"You know a lot about car washes."

"I *work* at a car wash, man." He dropped his visor. "Idiot."

"What do you mean, you work at a car wash?" Shirley said, but he was already rushing her again, with his small but wicked knife.

Just wait.

He'd spent most of his life just waiting, and here he was, doing it still.

A car had arrived and its occupant had joined Sophie and Sparrow in the café: a hulking sort, looking like he'd be comfortable whacking a cleaver into sides of meat all day long. Bachelor could picture himself, almost, deciding this was a sinister development; deciding to intervene . . . All it would take was true grit, a smidgin of star quality, and the ability to step out from the wings and act like a hero.

He shivered, and wished he had a hip flask. Wished, while he was at it, he had ten years' less bad luck behind him, or ten years' more self-belief. Or even just ten minutes' grace in which to summon up the qualities he needed, now, while the café door opened and the two men came out, Sophie sandwiched between them. She didn't so much as glance in his direction, and afterwards he convinced himself that this was the reason he remained in the shadows; nothing to do with that new arrival, whose watchfulness as the trio crossed the road suggested professionalism, or at least experience. No: Bachelor made no move because all was evidently going according to Sophie's plan. Which meant his role now was to *just wait*.

Every extra knows the show's about him.

Every stand-in knows she's the star.

But John Bachelor . . . Bachelor, watching the car ferry Sophie de Greer down Glasshouse Street, understood that his marquee moment was never going to happen. The car turned at the junction, and London's backdrop came into focus once more: its shop windows tired and garish, like a peep-show worker going off shift; its soundtrack a distant medley of overlapping noise. He was part of it, but just a small part, mostly unnoticed. His star didn't shine as brightly as it might. Though when you thought about it, that was true of everyone.

The cardboard punnet had grown cold in Whelan's hands, and, next to him, the boy from the garage was bouncing on his toes like an activated desk toy. Since Shirley and the biker had disappeared into the car wash they might as well have been transported to another planet. He'd heard the occasional crashing noise, plus a brief interlude of what sounded like dialogue—but he must have imagined that—and otherwise only the swooshing of tyres when a car passed.

The boy said, "I hope the police get here soon."

Or a Service team, thought Whelan. It couldn't be more than two minutes since this kicked off: even so his eyes kept flicking skywards, as if that helicopter might be approaching, its crew preparing to rappel earthwards, and deal with the situation. Somebody had to.

She'd been wielding a *spork* for Christ's sake.

He turned to the boy. "Don't you have a—?"

A what? A shotgun, a time machine? A cutlery set?

Then Shirley came rolling out of the car wash, her sweatshirt flapping loosely behind her, and a moment later the biker appeared too, his slow-motion swagger a statement all by itself: this fight was nearly over.

Sparrow was climbing into the back seat next to Sophie when Benito said, "What am I, an Uber?"

It took him a moment to get what was meant.

"I'd sooner be in the front anyway," Sophie said, climbing out and into the passenger seat. That was okay. It made no difference.

"Turns out she's not in Dorset after all," he'd told Benito on the phone, after Sophie had made contact.

"Where most of my crew went," Benito said. His accent wasn't that thick, considering, but he was the most Italian Italian Sparrow had come across: the five o'clock shadow, the curly hair, the hint of volatility beneath a handsome, battered surface. The shoes. Other men might have felt themselves in the shade anywhere near him, but Sparrow felt only that two-way connectivity alphas feel.

"I was fed bad information."

"The . . . opposition they ran into. This wasn't a rival team."

"No."

"They were soldiers. Armed."

"No one was killed."

"But there were injuries."

There were always injuries. Everyone knew that.

"Alessandro—"

"Benito."

"Benito, anyone who got hurt will have another set of scars to show off. Or are you telling me your crew wet their pants?"

"They've been arrested. Most of them. Some got away."

"They'll be charged with affray." He had no idea what they'd be charged with. "A night in the cells, a fine. Small price for a battleground memory."

"And deportation orders all round. That's a bigger price."

"It won't come to that."

"You sound very sure."

"I'm in a position to deliver on promises."

There was another pause before Benito said, "And that's why you rang, Mr. Sparrow? To assure me that you are able to clean up tonight's mess?"

"That and . . . something else."

Replaying the conversation in his head, Sparrow congratulated himself on how he'd explained to Benito what he needed without ever coming within shouting distance of describing how that might be achieved.

"What you're asking, it's quite . . . serious."

"Yes and no. About as serious as what happened to your predecessor, Benito. Who was also called Benito, am I right? When he wasn't being called Rico Lombardi."

And Benito was silent again.

"'Returned to Lazio,' wasn't that the story? Rico returned to Lazio. Which is marginally more convincing than 'went to live on a farm,' but amounts to the same thing. Stop me if your English isn't up to this."

Benito said, "Rico is happy and well. I spoke to him just last week."

"You must put me in touch with your network provider. Mine have trouble reaching Norwich, let alone the afterlife."

"You are a funny man, Mr. Sparrow."

"And a talkative one. Maybe, when I'm securing visa extensions for your associates, I'll ask them what they think happened to Rico. We can exchange opinions on the topic. I'm sure they'll get back to you if there's any confusion."

Benito said, "Politics, politicians. And people think we football supporters are the extremists."

"Football's your excuse for doing the things you do, Benito. And politics is mine."

Maybe, one day, there'd be occasion for a blog on that topic Sparrow thought now, as the car came within sight of the Thames, which flowed just as strongly—just as surely—in the dark as in the light. He looked at de Greer, who was also staring through the window at the water, but probably seeing something different. No one looks at the same river twice, he remembered reading somewhere. Or maybe it was drowns— no one drowns in the same river twice? Yeah. That sounded right. Any way you looked at it, you only drown once.

The paramedic shook his head.

Whelan couldn't blame him.

Even with the gore on her sweatshirt, Shirley looked at peace, and might have been sleeping. Whelan couldn't grasp the suddenness of the switch: from sixty to zero in the time it took to blow out a match. The ambulance's blue light was still strobing, its relentless throb draining colour from them all: the paramedic himself, Whelan, the boy from the garage. The biker was long gone. Only in Shirley's resting features did the looping splashes add life, probably because Shirley's face alone lacked it right then, the others being in various states of visible emotion: shock, bewilderment, and a kind of resigned irritation.

This was the paramedic. He said, "You let her eat?"

Whelan could have taken issue. Even on their relatively brief acquaintance, he was pretty certain that letting Shirley Dander do anything wasn't how those things got done. You just watched her do whatever she'd set her mind on. That or listen to her talk about it.

Besides: Eat? She'd spilled more than she'd swallowed. It was as well her sweatshirt was ruined anyway, because that barbecue sauce wasn't coming out.

Without opening her eyes, Shirley said, "I was hungry."

"You're not supposed to eat," the paramedic grumbled. "In case you need an operation."

"Stitches."

"You're still not—"

"That was good, what you did," Shirley said, this time to Whelan. "He was all washed up," she added, a wistful note to her voice for some reason.

Whelan nodded. He could have done with a lie down himself, the previous minutes having been eventful, if not entirely as planned—when he'd trained the hose on the biker, he'd had visions of a water-cannon pinning him to a wall. The actual result was a pissed off biker, sopping wet but upright, and things might have got ugly if flashing blue lights hadn't appeared down the road. As it was, the ambulance, still far enough away to be taken for police, encouraged departure: the biker, shinier now wet, had resembled a monstrous insect as he'd climbed onto his machine and gunned the motor, Whelan still hosing him, having raised his trajectory to ensure contact, which decreased the stream's effectiveness but maximised its indignity. The boy was performing a rah-rah dance beside him, shouting "Aim for the wheels!," though Whelan remained happy to mimic pissing. In its own way this was even more out of character than jumping onto a moving vehicle, but it had been a long night.

"I'd worn him out," Shirley said, opening her eyes.

"Yes."

"I'd have kicked his helmet clean off his shoulders."

"I could tell."

"With his head still in it."

The paramedic was maintaining his disappointed outlook. "You shouldn't eat chicken if you need medical treatment."

"Is that an actual law?" Shirley asked, sounding genuinely curious. "Specific to chicken?"

Speaking of actual law, there was a police car approaching, and also a black SUV, probably one of those originally dispatched to the San. Without thinking about it Whelan reached out a hand, and Shirley took it and pulled herself to her feet, leaving the punnet where it lay. The paramedic started saying something about not moving when you were injured, advice probably worth listening to, though neither were. The last hour had either contracted or expanded, whichever was the right way of indicating that it had happened in its own time zone, while other events taking place elsewhere had moved at their own pace, leaving them stranded in a moment of their own. For as long as it lasted, it seemed they were partners; and if it were already beginning to end, well, only diamonds are forever.

"Where's my chocolate?" asked Shirley.

From the back seat, Sparrow studied de Greer. She still thought she was in for a lobbying job, a whole new life, and in normal circumstances he'd enjoy bursting her bubble, but the last thing anyone needed was an hysterical woman in a moving car.

As if reading his thoughts, she looked over her shoulder. "Where are we going?"

"Like I said, somewhere safe. Until any difficulties have been smoothed away."

"And you're coming too?"

"Me? No. But Benito will take care of you, so no worries on that score."

"Where, exactly?"

Benito said, "I can't tell you that. More secure. You understand."

If she didn't, she decided not to make an issue of it.

They were heading towards Elephant and Castle. Much further, and they'd be outside Sparrow's comfort zone. He said: "Anywhere along here's fine," despite it being a barely peopled road at whatever time it was now—he checked. Four fifty. Anyone abroad would be poorly paid, if not actively indigent. London was hostile territory, depending on the hour and the post code. But he could take care of himself, as he'd actively demonstrated in both woodland and boardroom. Anyone accosting him—or demanding a meeting—would be dealt with in short order.

Benito said, "The corner after this one."

"Why not this one?"

The rolling of an Italian's shoulders can be multilingual. "Tube station."

I'm not catching a fucking tube.

"Are they even running yet?"

De Greer said, "You won't have long to wait."

No longer than it takes an Uber to show. Through his window, the shopfronts, the buildings, were decelarating. He glimpsed a sleeper in a doorway, and posters boasting happy-meals, cut-price getaways, cash prizes. Two men loitered by the locked-up station entrance, and both stopped smoking at the same moment, flicking their cigarette ends in opposite directions, as if aspiring to the condition of a firework. Benito cruised to a halt.

Sparrow leaned forward, putting his head between de Greer's and Benito's. "You're going to be comfortable," he told her.

"Thanks," she said. "Will I see you soon?"

He opened his door. ". . . No."

"Well," de Greer said. "You got that right."

Before he could climb out, one of the men climbed in, forcing Sparrow into the middle of the seat.

"What the fuck? . . ."

The other man had walked round, and was getting in the other side.

De Greer said to Benito, "Thank you." Then to Sparrow: "I was remembering something you said once. About how the true hero of *Psycho* was the psycho. Because he just carried on being a psycho."

". . . What are you on about?"

"I'll leave you to think about it. Bye."

Her door closed with a definitive *clunk*.

The men hemming Sparrow in had a familiar feel; thick legs, cable-tense arms, the kind of hard-bodied trunks you might find in a wood. Neither spoke, but sat with their big shoulders forcing him into a supplicant's cringe, staring ahead at a road that was on the move again.

"Alessandro—"

"Benito."

"Benito, am I missing something?"

"What makes you ask that, Mr. Sparrow?"

"Because I'm still in the car. And de Greer isn't."

"Right." He changed lanes, to overtake a night bus. "An interesting woman, Dr. de Greer. We had a most enjoyable conversation."

". . . When?"

"Shortly before you called me. It was strange, she knew exactly how our conversation would go. They have a name, don't they? People who can predict outcomes?"

"Benito—"

A heavy hand on his shoulder discouraged further protest.

"She knew the things you'd promise, and the threats you'd make," Benito continued. Traffic was gathering and the streetlights had grown weary, their glow a pallid offering that seemed to drop to the ground rather than reach into the dark. "And what she wanted to know was, how about if all your promises, about dropped charges and secure visas, could be fulfilled by someone else. She mentioned Regent's Park?"

"She was lying, Benito. She can't deliver on any of that. Only I can."

"I'm not sure. She was very convincing. She—"

"Of course she was convincing! That's her job!"

"She made a reasonable point. She said, why trust you, when you've already had my team run into what some people might think was a trap, when I could trust her instead? I thought that was an interesting viewpoint."

"She's nobody. She's a spy. She'll be arrested by morning, none of her promises mean anything!"

"So you know what I did? I followed her advice and asked my crew what they thought about it."

"Let me out. We'll forget this ever happened."

"Of course, not many of my crew were available, on account of last night's activities. But the Stefanos here—they're both called Stefano. I hope that's not confusing for you?"

"Stop the car!"

"Because arguably, it's simpler. Anyway, the Stefanos here didn't join in last night's fun on account of a previous engagement. Which is lucky for me and also for you, because—"

"*Stop the car!*"

"Please," said Benito.

One of the Stefanos clamped a hand round Sparrow's mouth, while the other brought a hammerlike fist down on his testicles. This combination of events occupied Sparrow for a while, but Benito was considerate enough to give him some minutes before continuing.

"As I was saying. This is lucky for both of us. For me, because I like my crew to have a part in the decision-making process."

Sparrow still couldn't speak.

"And for you because I know how much you enjoy the fun and games we have in the woods."

"Where are you taking me?" Sparrow managed to say.

"What was that expression you used? 'Going to live on a farm'?"

He couldn't be serious.

"In any case, it's nowhere you haven't been before."

Stefano tightened his grip on Sparrow's shoulder, in what might have been a gesture of reassurance and support.

But might not.

The sun was coming up before they reached the woods. It silvered the branches like a dusting of snow, or a tinkling of bells, or a promise kept.

In the days to come, news will find its way to Slough House from various corners of the wider world, one a continent away. There has been a boating accident on the Barents Sea, four friends on a fishing trip having come unstuck in wild weather, and rumours are beginning to circulate that Vassily Rasnokov, Moscow's First Desk, was involved. No body has been recovered, but that's not an uncommon outcome in such circumstances: the wind whips up the waves, and the water reveals its depths, and what happens in the gap between can remain forever an undisclosed secret. And if other possibilities exist—that, for example, Vassily has pulled off a vanishing act, the better to slip into anonymous retirement—that's a problem for his own Service to ponder, and is presumably unconnected with the recent off-the-books purchase by Regent's Park of an undistinguished flat on the Holloway Road. Here, a small but operationally experienced team has assembled; its codename Rosebud; its remit, to discover the identity of the man who burned to death in a dosshouse near the Westway, and to wait by the open door of his vacant life, to see who, if anyone, steps through it. It's a job requiring a humdrum dedication to detail, a million miles removed from high-tech movie-spookery, yet nor is it the daily trudge that the minions of Slough House endure. Because for Rosebud, a positive result to their investigation might lead them into the realms of gold, whereas for the slow horses, the end result of unvarying labour tends to be reams of dross, and no matter how much shit they shovel, they always remain in the stables.

On a more prosaic level, the Extraordinary Meeting of the Limitations Committee called to inquire into Diana Taverner's suitability as First Desk is an unexpectedly meek affair, there being no one to present a prosecution case. Mention is made of whispers on Westminster Corridors—that old chimera Waterproof has been bandied about—but since the supposed victim of the Park's machinations, one Sophie de Greer, makes a brief online appearance apologising for her failure to follow the procedure for taking sick leave, such mention is swiftly dismissed as groundless gossip. Following a short address by Taverner herself, in which she recommends that any future such sessions be preceded by the Park's own assessment of the evidence, the Committee, under the careful stewardship of Oliver Nash, bemoans the unexplained absence of the meeting's instigator, one Anthony Sparrow, before declaring the proceedings, in effect, a waste of time. The company deconvenes, the firing squad remains unassembled, and when Diana re-enters the hub that morning, it is to a standing ovation from supporters and detractors alike, who can at least find common ground in their appreciation of a skilled operator. Diana herself doesn't mind why anyone applauds, so long as they do so on their feet. Not that she is unaware of how differently things might have gone. "For a moment there, I thought we were in trouble," she murmurs in passing, but only Josie hears, and, since she isn't sure she's meant to, that young woman makes no reply. For the rest of that day, Diana fulfils promises made on her behalf by Jackson Lamb: resettlement arrangements for Sophie de Greer; the ironing out of administrative wrinkles for the multifarious friends of Alessandro Botigliani; and while this is small enough recompense for how things have turned out, finds such busywork irksome all the same.

As to Sparrow's whereabouts, these will not become clear for another day or two, but at the moment of Diana's triumph he is cowering under a hastily assembled pyramid of earth and leaves, simultaneously straining to hear every creak and whistle in the surrounding wood—the same wood in which he made first contact with Benito, an encounter he now quite seriously regrets—and striving to deny that he's hearing anything at all, a reframing of the narrative which for some reason is less effective than usual. On one level he is certain that those hunting him down, after allowing him a sporting four minutes' start, intend no more than to scare and humiliate him, while on another he is confident that they will beat him to a soup with sticks and stones. He is correct about one of these outcomes, but it will be some while before he reaches the stage of not caring which it is, so long as it happens without further delay.

Also involved in assembling piles of leaves is Claude Whelan, who is doing a little tidying in the garden—nothing complicated, nothing ambitious; a man's got to know his limitations—while he thinks back over his recall to arms, in particular dwelling on the surprising discovery that the things he'd have expected to be good at, such as ferreting out the whereabouts of Sophie de Greer, he failed to achieve, while the moments of heroism he has always quite genuinely thought beyond him proved to be his finest, well, not hour. But minutes. He spent some minutes being heroic. And when the dust has settled, he decides, and after he's been debriefed by Oliver Nash—a process whose conclusion will leave one of the two in possession of more information than when it started—he might contact Shirley Dander, who, though never having been Sophie de Greer, and indeed having no clue as to why anyone might think otherwise, proved an interesting companion: a Robin to his Batman, say. Not that he has thoughts of anything untoward—no, he currently believes that, until Claire has concluded her negotiations with God, and decided whether or not she is coming home, his own behaviour will remain irreproachable on that front; besides, Shirley has neither the shape nor appearance that he generally finds beguiling—but still, there was a moment when she took leave of him, climbing out of the car while a London sunrise struggled to be born, during which he felt they'd made a connection he'd seldom found anywhere else. He suspects she felt this too. "So long," she'd said to him, "partner." Then she was gone. He wonders if she's thinking about him now.

She isn't, and not only because Catherine has just stepped into her office, the look on her face an unwelcoming welcome. Shirley is about to be reminded that she has no business being in Slough House today; she's so certain of this that it's barely worth Catherine opening her mouth to speak.

"You're supposed to be at the San."

"Yeah, there was a thing happened? I'm surprised you didn't hear about it."

"It's still operational. And you've not been discharged."

It figures, thinks Shirley, that Catherine has already established this fact. Catherine was probably on the phone to the San before dawn, checking on Shirley's whereabouts; adding unscheduled departure to her tally of crimes and misdemeanours, and waiting to pounce as soon as Shirley reappeared.

"What did you imagine you were doing?" Catherine goes on. "Taking on what sounds like a battalion of thugs?"

At a loss for an accurate answer, Shirley says, "Yeah, it's what Thelma and Louise would have done."

"Well, I've no idea who those people are. But if Thelma and Louise drove off a cliff, would you do that too?"

Shirley doesn't know where to start.

"Don't you understand? I'm worried about you."

"I'm—"

And Shirley is about to say what she always says, *I'm fine*, but instead remembers the feelings she had on waking, could it be only yesterday? She's not fine; she just hasn't hit the ground yet. And she doesn't want to tell Catherine this, but suspects that Catherine knows; suspects, in fact, that Catherine has experienced something similar in her long-ago past.

Catherine is now standing in front of Shirley's desk. "I don't want you in danger, can you not get your head round that? We've had too much grief already. People keep getting hurt. People keep dying. We have to look out for one another."

"You've already told me that."

Catherine, who doesn't remember having done so, looks puzzled, but decides not to pursue it. "You need to go back. Today. While everything's still a confused mess, and you'll be able to get away with it."

"Why do you care?"

That one, Catherine finds easier. "What's the alternative?" she asks, and now it's Shirley's turn to be puzzled, while out in the corridor Lech Wicinski is leaving another voicemail.

It's John Bachelor whom Lech is trying to contact. Lech has only the haziest notion of what's been going on these past twenty-four hours, but he's aware that the safe house is no longer occupied: he called in on his way to work that morning—a lengthy detour, justified on the ground that he had his fingertips, at least, on a live operation—but it was deserted. Recalling the crusty array of takeaway cartons, sticky glasses, and the furry atmosphere that smoking leaves, he at least has the satisfaction of knowing who has been in occupation, but since he is also aware that Lamb's practice is to keep his horses in the dark unless he has absolute reason not to, this knowledge is accompanied by the depressing awareness that whatever happened, he is unlikely to be made privy to the details. Unless Bachelor can share these with him, but so far, all Bachelor has shared is frequent half-minutes or so of voicemail emptiness, into which Lech has poured requests for contact.

He will keep trying Bachelor, on and off, for the next few days, with the same result, but will finally receive a late-night return call, which will pull him from a rare pleasant dream. But Bachelor, aside from making no apology, will make no sense, and simply ramble about loss and beauty and similar abstracts until Lech, not without regret, will disconnect. He already knows about loss and beauty, and what little Bachelor might teach him is not worth broken sleep. But sleep won't come again, and a little later Lech will be walking London's pavements until dawn, maskless but scarred as a phantom, attempting to outwalk his thoughts. All that lies in the near future; in the immediate present Lech dawdles back to his desk, whose nearby window, awaiting a glazier, is still shrouded with cardboard, and as he sits hears a murmur of conversation from upstairs, where Louisa has joined Ashley, to clarify a detail or two:

"So Lamb sliced an atomic chili into your nuts and berries."

"Yep."

"And you didn't notice."

"Nope."

"Just as well Roddy ate some first, then."

"It was," says Ash. "Imagine. It could have been me whose mouth was vulcanised."

But she appears reasonably sanguine, as if this had never been a likely prospect.

"Yes," says Louisa, "imagine. But instead it was Roddy. Meaning he was thrashing about on the floor like a dying trout while you were on the phone to Lamb, pretending it was you who'd figured out Rasnokov's firetrap."

"Well," says Ash. "I'd have called Taverner, but it wasn't clear she was still in the picture."

"Lamb won't give you credit for delivering information."

"No. But he might give me credit for stealing Ho's work."

Louisa nods thoughtfully, remembering what she'd thought about Ash: that her anger was going to have to find an outlet, or the woman would explode. "Don't get me wrong," she says. "Roddy's a knob."

"But he's your knob?"

"Roddy is not my knob, no. In fact, let's pretend you never said that. Roddy's a knob, but you need to be careful about fucking him over. Lech's still getting calls from his service providers, asking why he's cancelled his payments."

"Yeah, but Lech didn't fix Roddy up with a date."

Because Ash has spoken to Leia Six this morning; less out of a need to placate Roddy than to test her own powers of persuasion.

"A date? He can barely talk."

"This is Roddy. Preventing him from talking is like giving him a makeover."

Still, both will be somewhat surprised when Roddy, as yet unable to speak, has a reasonably successful first date with Leia Six; and more so when, still unable to speak, he has a reasonably successful second. But by the third date his mouth will be more or less recovered, and he will turn up at Slough House the following morning with a black eye.

"So who knows?" Ash continues. "This could be the beginning of a beautiful friendship."

"You think so?"

"Nope."

"Welcome to Slough House," says Louisa, getting to her feet. "Oh, one other thing? You want to shift your stuff back where it was. River'll be needing his desk."

"He's coming back?"

"Better believe it," Louisa says.

She leaves, not pausing to look up the remaining flight towards Lamb's room, from which no noise issues. But he is there, one of his hands holding a cigarette, the other nursing a shot glass. The blind on his window is down, and the lamp by his desk, balanced on a pile of yellowing phone directories, casts the room's only light, his cigarette tip apart. And in this

self-imposed gloom, he is thinking, if he is thinking at all, of
Vassily Rasnokov, who is either floating on a cold sea or
preparing to slip into a life he's been building for years; a life
warmed up for him by a now-defunct scarecrow, whose body
lies unclaimed in a vault somewhere in Greater London. Eyes
closed, cigarette shedding its chrysalis of ash even as a smoky
butterfly rises to the ceiling, Lamb barely breathes as he
contemplates the future that awaits one who's walked away
from the spy trade: a carrel in a European library, say, or a stool
on a beach bar under a Bahamian sun. Or a life of unrelieved
ordinariness, in which the papertrails established by a now-
dead understudy—the water bills and council tax debits, the
credit cards and gym memberships, the electronic footprints,
the economic handholds; each of them locking a life into
place the way pegs hold down a tent—lead remorselessly to
their only possible destination: in the end, whatever role you
choose, you reach the end of the drama; the paperwork is
shuffled into binbags, and the tent blows away. But the
triumph lies in making the choice, rather than accepting
the part you're given. Lamb's cigarette glows like a candle,
briefly, and if his eyelids flicker, and his gaze appears fixed on
the drab painting of a bridge which is his office's sole
decoration, that's likely no more than chance; just as, if his lips
move beneath their filtered burden, and their mumble sounds
like *Rosebud*, he's assuredly thinking of that team on the
Holloway Road. But perhaps, in fact, he mumbles nothing at
all, and his exit line remains unspoken. It's possible the
trembling of his lips is a quiet belch. Well, nobody's perfect.

From the street below, a snatch of what might be music
drifts upwards, though is more likely the accidental percussion
of daily life: heel on pavement, tyre on a loose drain lid.
Whatever it is, this theme penetrates Slough House for a
moment, probably through that cardboard-patched window,
and dances round in the dust-deckled air, attempting to get a
party going. But this enterprise is doomed from the start, and

lasts no longer than it takes a sudden draught to slam a door, after which the building—its creaky stairs and broken skirting boards—its rackety furniture and stained ceilings—its peeling paper and plasterwork—its bewildered wiring, its confused pipes—its ups and downs and highs and lows and all its debts and credits—slumps into its usual stupor, as the morning's wax surrenders to the afternoon's wane. And if, outside, the day carries on with its usual background business, inside it pauses for a drawn-out beat, and then drops like a curtain.

CREDITS

Those of a mischievous mindset might seek to associate this book's title with the current Apple TV+ series of *Slow Horses*, but my regular, sober-minded readers will recognise that the phrase has been bubbling away for a while, and was always intended to take its place on a cover. As for the actual actors involved, I couldn't be more thrilled with the cast that's been assembled, more delighted with the work they're doing, or happier with the welcome Jo and I have always received on set. My thanks to all involved—cast, crew, production staff, drivers and fellow hangers-on—and especially to the writing team, whose company has long been a source of laughter and inspiration. If I named you all, these credits would roll and roll.

My thanks, too, to all at John Murray Press—and its brand new Baskerville imprint—who do so much to keep the show on the road, and all at Soho Press who got it up and running in the first place. And love and thanks, as ever, to Juliet and Micheline for all they do; to Jo, for everything she does; and to Tommy and Scout, for whatever they're up to at the moment.

A reader recently emailed to inform me that a line I'd used in *Slough House* ("Home was where, when you went there, they had to let you in") was more or less from a Robert Frost poem.

"Anyone who has read Frost," he solemnly assured me, "will pick this up right away." Damn it . . . Caught red-handed. Before sentence is passed, I'd like many dozens of similar offences to be taken into consideration. I won't list them all, but the line on page 128 that Lech Wicinski remembers his father quoting—that "everyone is more or less of Polish origin"—is from Iris Murdoch's *Nuns and Soldiers*.

This book is dedicated to my dear brother Paul, to his wife Emily, and to his children, Thomas and Matthew. But it's also for the rest of our family, with love, always. The time we spend together has never been more precious.

MH
Oxford
November 2021